PERFECTLY
REVENTABLE
DEATHS

PERFECTLY PREVENTABLE DEATHS

DEIRDRE SULLIVAN

HOT KEY BOOKS

First published in Great Britain in 2019 by
HOT KEY BOOKS
80–81 Wimpole St, London W1G 9RE
www.hotkeybooks.com

A CIP catalogue record for this book is available from the British Library.

ISBN: 978-1-4714-0823-6
also available as an ebook

2

This book is typeset using Atomik ePublisher
Printed and bound in Great Britain by Clays Ltd, Elcograf S.p.A.

Hot Key Books is an imprint of Bonnier Books UK
www.bonnierbooks.co.uk

To Sarah, Dave and Graham, with ink and love.

And so my heart rejoices, my soul is glad; even my body shall rest in safety. For you will not leave my soul among the dead. Nor let your beloved know decay.

Psalm 16

Prologue

Honeysuckle

(influenza, birth control and poison)

Our father died in flames when he was twenty-six and we were two.

We don't remember. All we have is story. Sense memory, the feeling of soft earth. His name upon a pitted slab, limestone, lichen-pocked. Orange, white and crinkled dry as paper. The smell of grave implanting in our nail beds. Our fingers scraping through to trace his name.

Tom Hayes. Dearly Beloved, you left too soon.

They found him lying in the woods, a group of children on a nature walk. In a small, round glade between the trees – the beech, the oak, the hawthorn and the elm. The leaves beneath him weren't even burnt.

'He always cared for everything around him,' Mam said once. 'Even in death, he kept the forest safe.'

1

It's not something we talk about too often.

The images I have might not be real. A voice. A lap. Helping plant the flowers in our garden. Little hands and big ones thick with earth. Memories are versions of what happened, stories that we've told ourselves enough. The fiction ivy-winding around the real, to strangle out the bad, promote the good. If you're not careful, ivy eats a house. It lets in rot.

Sometimes I remember things about plants. Little facts I don't know how I came by. And I wonder if I know because he told me when I was very small. More likely it all filtered down through Mam. We never really knew my dad to miss. But something in me turns him over, over. Stretched like a yawn, arms out and thick with char.

And, maybe that's why Catlin goes to Mass. Or why I sometimes wake up taut with terror, looking for some unknown thing to make me safe, or safer in that moment.

The world isn't predictable at the best of times. But if you're scientific about it, then all the strangest things can be explained. Maybe not right now and not by you, but always there's a reason. You can divide things into true and false, proven and unproven. Analysed, predictable, if not preventable. The more you know, the more that you can do to make things right. Knowledge is a real-life magic power, gathered up like spells to use in time.

Vinegar, a candle. Salt and sage. There's always been a comfort in the tangible. In things that you can gather round you. Hold. We all have little talismans to cherish.

Beech for wisdom. Elm for your throat.

The things you hold – they will not keep you safe though. In the end, there's not a thing that can.

2

1

Sage

(palsy, fever, life prolonged by choice)

When Dracula came to England, he arrived in a box full of earth. That's kind of what the boot of our car looks like now. We're taking half Dad's garden to Ballyfrann with us. The indoor plants mainly, but some cuttings from the garden as well. I'm excited to start growing things there. It's always soothing, helping something live.

Brian sent moving vans for all our stuff. Large, brown, unmarked things. Men from the village, loading, putting, driving. *Collinses and Shannons*, Brian told us. As if that made it clearer who they were. 'In Ballyfrann we help each other out,' he said.

And Mam said, 'That sounds nice. A real community.'

The men kept grimly lifting boxes out, and drinking thick dark tea with too much milk. Brown like earth. Like copper grass on mountains. Crisp and dead and waiting for the spring. Catlin tried to establish how many sons they had and how hot they were, based on genetics. She was not subtle. Horny never is.

The whirr of tyre on gravel. The flat mess of what used to be a cat. A mangled stain that no one seems to notice except me. It is quiet in the car. Catlin's earphones in. The radio. It will be a long drive. We got up early, loaded up the boxes in the vans. They flanked our car for the first forty minutes, then we stopped for petrol and they left us. Brian says they know exactly where to go. It's home for them. For us it will take time.

The fur, what was left of it, looked brown.

I trace a pattern on my legs, a dizzy little triskele. In my pocket is a pack of salt. The kind you get in chip shops. Candle wax. Some berries on their stalks. My clothes are always manky in the pockets. I do peculiar things to ward off threat. Detritus gathers. It isn't very scientific of me. But I am odd, and where we're going's new, and full of dangers.

I see their faces.

All the mountain girls.

The ones that died.

When Mam and Brian first told us about the place he came from, it didn't quite seem real. Still doesn't, to be honest. I wonder, when we see it for ourselves, if it will be different. It's strange, isn't it, to be moving somewhere we have never been. We haven't set foot there. Even though it isn't very far. Nowhere in Ireland is. A country the size of other people's cities. We have seen photographs, on Brian's phone. On Mam's. He took her there for weekends when they started going out.

They got engaged inside the castle walls.

We weren't there.

'My father built this castle,' Brian told us. 'He was a strange

4

man. Very big ideas. There was a ruin here before, and he bought the land with a view to rebuilding what had been, but then . . . he went a bit mad. There are places in the castle even I don't know about. He had a lot of secrets, my aul' fella.'

Going 'a bit mad' is different when you're rich apparently. Brian's father built a castle out of castles. He stole the bits he liked from where he'd been. There's some Versailles in there, a little of Kilkenny, a fair amount of that big German one the Disney castle's based on. Neuschwanstein. From the outside though, Mam says, it looks medieval. It's hard to picture, the mountains more suited to the clutch of cottages, white as eggs, where the Collins family live in their weird commune. Brian says they are the 'backbone of the village', but I feel like in a village of a hundred or so people it is not hard to be a backbone, if there are enough of you. Like, everybody's something. They'd have to be, or things would fall apart. The Collinses have been part of the village since before Brian's dad. Brian went to school with Ger Collins, Mike Collins, Pat Collins and Tim Collins, for example. And that was not a lot of Collinses, considering.

'There'll be a few Collinses at school with ye as well,' Brian tells us. 'Edward and Charlene. They're good kids.'

I stare at a patch of unshaven hair on Brian's chin, trying to be interested. The black and grey strands forcing through the pale. I wonder what he is of the village. The brain perhaps. I wouldn't say the heart.

Since she found out about the deaths, Catlin calls Brian's place 'the murder palace'. I try to shrug her off. It wasn't in the castle that they found them, after all. But something of it

5

sticks inside my gut. A heavy sort of worry. My fingers scratch at skin through layers of cloth. She pokes me in the ribs and does the eyebrows. I do them back. And it will be OK. I know it will. We pass a green sign: *Fáilte go Béal Ifreann* – Welcome to Ballyfrann, and Brian stops in the village to pick up teabags, milk. We drift into the little shop behind him, stare at the magazine racks, all the women's faces, looking out.

'These are my daughters,' Brian tells the bored-looking woman behind the counter as she waves his wallet away.

'Consider it a wedding present, Brian.' Her voice is animated but her face is slack. 'Nice to meet you, girls. I'm Jacinta.'

Catlin looks at me, as if to say, *Of course she is*.

Catlin doesn't like anyone called Jacinta. She met one before who bored her somehow, and has never forgiven the name. We pile back in the car, and Brian switches off the emergency lights. Apparently it's OK to park on double yellow lines here if you're 'just nipping in'.

I'm not so sure about that.

Rules are there for reasons.

We keep driving.

On the way, I find myself searching for something I can't really place. A clue, an omen. Catlin's hand brushes mine, and I see the same sort of thing I'm feeling, filtered through her face. Like me but not like me.

Helen Groarke was like us too, at one time. A human being, before she was a story. A girl who disappeared around four years ago, when she was our age, just a little older. On the fifteen-minute walk home from school. They found her in the mountains six months on. A recent corpse, they said. They

6

analysed the parts they could locate. An arm, the fingers painted glitter-purple. Several teeth with bits of brace attached. The remnants of a ribcage. When you are dead, your shell becomes a puzzle. Something to be looked at, piece by piece.

Without the body, or without all the body, it's hard to tell what was the cause of death. They can test and look and hazard guesses. Try to determine which parts were eaten, cut. There were bite marks, *mammalian in nature*. I remember wondering what sort of animal would eat a person. We don't have wolves in Ireland any more. We don't have bears. So maybe like a fox or massive stoat?

Catlin listed all the dead girls' names as reasons she was nervous to move here. Amanda Shale and Nora Ginn and little Bridget Hora. Fifteen years ago. Twenty. Sixty. They were all our age, or close enough. Her friends researched them, read about them, talked in that vulture way that people do. The gory details. Bits of femur, spattered blood on rocks. The mountains here are paler, leached of colour. There is a grey tone underneath the green. It's not like where we're from. Anything that grows here has to work. It isn't hard to picture death around us. There is a hungry look about this place.

We drive by the post office, the little church. The school we'll start on Monday. The petrol station, one vintage-looking pump beside a big plastic 99. The brown stuff on the flake is peeling off. It looks like the kind of place where the sell-by date of everything would be long before we were born.

Sheep litter the hills like puffs of cotton wool after you've cleansed your face, all flat and filthy. We stop to let them pass us on the road. My eyes on scenery, earbuds in and listening to music. I worry at our future like a bone.

7

Back in Cork, when we still had our home and things around us, it was easier to feel like this would be an adventure. That it would all work out, in spite of the distance and my personality. We were moving to a castle. A proper massive castle in the hills. It did occur to me that a house that looms on a hillside is rarely a good thing in books and movies, unless you want to fall for a brooding man with at least one terrible secret. Which, in fairness, sounds a bit exhausting. Hopefully it wouldn't come to that.

'It'll be fine,' I remember telling Catlin, and also myself in the mirror. And our friends. And Mam. And the plants. But all the while I found myself fingering the little paper rectangle in my pocket. The small rough grains inside.

It wasn't fine.

Catlin was, in the run-up to the move, and, to be honest, every day since birth, mainly worried about not getting enough attention. Our friends are obsessed with her, and I'm the side dish. There's something special in my sister's eyes. Her face. The way she carries herself. She draws them in. They love her right away. I'm more of an acquired taste. Like fish eggs. Catlin's truffle chips, served in a bowl with cosmic patterns on. Delightful, and probably cooler than you.

'Places pick up energy from bad stuff, Maddy,' she told me, behind the hall at school, near the skips, where people go to smoke. A week ago, when this seemed like a story we were being told, rather than a real thing about to happen. 'They drink it in, and it just lies there. Waiting . . .'

I looked at her, her uniform hanging elegantly on her in a way mine never bothered to. Her hair was piled into an elastic

8

band, and somehow even that looked right. Like hair ties were too obvious, too try-hard.

I grinned. 'Catlin, you were born to live in a castle. Relax.'

The car still moving, I remember her face, the suppressed smile, the twinkle in the eyes. The love of drama. But the mountain girls – they were people, not seasoning for stories. It feels heavy in my chest, the layers of death Catlin has pasted on this place. On Brian's home. My body warm, too warm. Bile in my gut, I'm thinking, *How much longer?*

Brian's thin shoulders hunch towards the steering wheel. He always looks a little tense. This man my mother married weeks ago. Blue dresses in the registry office. His hand on hers, his ring where Dad's once was. In our hands we held the ring to warm it as a blessing. It felt so heavy, weightier than gold.

'I want to be a father to you, girls,' he told us on the night before the move. 'A good one. Not like the kind of man my father was. He wanted my respect, but it didn't go both ways.' He closed his eyes. 'After he died . . . He had a lot of secrets. And I've spent quite a bit of time and effort sorting out his mess. Not that he'd thank me for it.'

'Your dad sounds like a douche,' said Catlin, and I elbowed her. Brian looked at us with an even gaze. His face was very smooth and very clean, except for one small gorse-dark patch he'd missed. I stared at it, distracted.

'. . . perhaps you're right. He was a lot of things, as the fella says.' He sighed. 'I want to be a better man than he was. But the more that I unravel, the more I see . . . it's complicated. Tax stuff mostly. I won't bore you with it.'

9

But I wondered.

The fields fly past our window. Getting close. There are crosses on the road. Small, hard tooth-white things poking out like artefacts. I count them.

Ten . . . Eleven.

Twelve.

Thirteen.

'Did people die here, Brian?' I ask.

He nods. 'A family from near Athlone. They were passing through, on their way to somewhere else. Most people are. The father had a seizure at the wheel, drove into a tree.' He gestures to the side. 'It's been cut down.'

Catlin looks at me, mouths, *Murder palace.* I kick her on the shin.

'Madeline's kicking me,' she whines, and Mam rolls her eyes.

'You probably deserve it. You and your *murder palace,*' she says, her hand on Brian's. His on the gear stick. She loves him. This quiet man whose father built a palace in the wild.

'It's not a palace,' Brian says. 'It's a castle.'

'What's the difference?' I ask.

'A castle's fortified,' he says. 'A palace is just fancy.'

'Fortified how?' Catlin asks.

Brian smiles at us. Mam tells him to wait. 'I want to see them see it.'

The car knots through the land, tangling us away from who we are. I feel the disconnect and swallow down. And then we're there. Here.

We thought we knew what to expect. But suddenly we find ourselves driving down a smooth, wide private road, cut through a forest, and little by little turrets, battlements and grey stone walls. A quasi-moat that's filled with shrubs and plants instead of water. Brown and green weeds poking, thick green moss. Large grey and black crows collect on the awnings. Staring dully out at everything.

This is our house. It is the place we live.

I cannot over-emphasise how much of a castle Brian's castle is. It has turrets for Christ's sake, walled gardens and a groundskeeper. It looks like it was carved from fairy tales. As we drive in, we see the other sides. It's sort of a collage. Four miniature castles, linked around a courtyard with a big kitchen garden, with a Victorian-style greenhouse. And a fountain. Because why not a fountain? This is a castle. Opulence is kind of the deal. A glass dome rises somewhere in the centre, like the hyacinth bulbs on Dad's grave. Fortification means we are protected, but why would we need that? It's just for show. No need to feel the itch my fingers feel. They trace the grains of salt through thinning paper. I've almost worried it to shredding point.

What can you do?

We put the kettle on.

2

Hawthorn

(soft belly and strong heart)

Brian gives us a tour as we finish our tea, through sitting rooms
and libraries and parlours. It's all very old-looking, battered
fancy furniture, and big, threadbare tapestries draped from floor
to ceiling. He tells us there are secret passages as well, inside the
walls. His dad designed them, but they aren't used now. There
is too much castle for one person, without adding any more
castle. I get it. There are a million rooms Brian doesn't need,
all locked and full of dust-cloth-covered furniture. Downstairs
is the granny flat. Brian's relative Mamó's basement realm.
Mamó means grandmother, but I think that Mam told us she
was his aunt. I don't know why she needs her own apartment,
when there is a whole castle, but people are strange, and I
get the sense Mamó is even stranger. She works as some sort
of naturopath (I could never trust anyone whose job ends in
-opath), which means people come to her, and she does stuff
to them, and then they think they feel better. It's not very

12

evidence-based, and as a future doctor I resent that. There are parasites like that dotted all around the country. Who'll lay their hands on you and say a little prayer for ninety quid.

There are parts of this *Mamó* littered all over the castle, earthy boot prints, feathers on the floor, a dirty trowel in the sink. A mug on the kitchen table filled with tea leaves and what looks like sediment. Mam looks a bit put out. Which is probably what the old wagon wanted. Asserting dominance, like a dog taking a slash against a wall. We're in her territory, and I don't think we're welcome. I lift the trowel and wipe dark earth away from silver blade.

Brian rolls his eyes. 'Don't worry about that, Madeline. She'll get over herself, as the fella says.'

Brian says *as the fella says* a lot. I wonder who the fella is. It might just be Brian.

I pick one of the feathers up and look at it. It's very long and very dark, the quill as wide as someone's baby finger. I imagine it bending towards me, as though it had a knuckle in the centre, and feel a small throb of repulsion mixed with the familiar need to keep it with me. I tuck it in the pocket of my cardigan. The one furthest away from my skin.

The castle tour continues. And there's a feather in every single room. The dining hall. The solar. The physic garden and the kitchen garden. The pantry and the larder and the study. Brian's office. The east wing and the west. The attic full of chests and frames and clunky, ancient things. I keep on reaching for them, until I'm jamming them inside my pockets, feeling the bend of barb, the pinch of calamus. Mam trails a finger across a steamer trunk. A little valley interrupting years and years of dust. She's yearning to get stuck in, I sense it in her. To air the whole thing out. Clean slate. Fresh start. A blank page of a life untouched by loss.

Catlin's room and mine are adjoining. They have been chosen for us, based on whatever algorithm Brian has for stepdaughter location. But we got to pick new sets of linen and little accessories and things. We messaged Brian the links to what we liked. And now they're in the rooms. As if by magic. Being rich is class. My bedroom here has crisp white sheets, dotted with embroidered little flowers. Broderie anglaise, I think it's called. A properly rich person would know these things. We are new money.

Catlin has pink throws and red and gold and black things all artfully mingled together. Mam says her room looks like 'a fancy brothel'. But in a fond way. If you were to look at both of our rooms, hers would be the one you'd pick to be a teenage girl's. Mine would be an aging aunt's. A nun's. Even though Catlin's is full of votive candles and Mary statues, all of her collection and some more. Catlin loves the Virgin Mary's look. She has a wall of Marys in her room. Mary star of the sea, Mary mourning Jesus. Mary with a shining crown, stomping snakes. I'm not that gone on Mary, as a concept. Lots of things about her feel like lies.

'Maddy,' Catlin says, 'did you hear Brian say the castle costs eleven grand to heat in winter?'

'I did, because he said it ninety times and I have ears. I think he was trying to encourage the closing of windows.'

'I felt like saying to him, "We will wear all of our jumpers to bed if you just give us the eleven grand."'

Sometimes they say twins have a psychic bond. But I don't think you have to be psychic to want eleven *thousand* euro. 'Oh my God. Me too.'

'You wouldn't appreciate eleven grand. You'd only spend it on sensible things like college and a pension.' Catlin is contemptuous.

'I would not. I'd buy drugs,' I say. And I would too. A donation to Médicins Sans Frontières totally counts as drugs.

Catlin is sceptical. 'What sort of drugs?'

'Um . . . heroin?' I offer, to shut her up.

'Cool,' she says, 'but you're not allowed to get addicted.'

'Neither are you,' I tell her. 'Now, let's put the bedclothes on your massive sex-bed.'

Our beds here can only be described as gothic sex-beds. Four-posters are the size of little fields, all carved with grapes and roses, crucifixes. Little faces peering. Small, blank eyes. I'm surprised there are no shirtless lords striding around the gardens, murmuring Catlin's name as though in prayer. Give her time, I think, stuffing a fat feather pillow inside a bright pink pillowcase and fluffing it up.

'It's not a sex-bed yet,' says Catlin. 'Not till I get my hands on a Galway boyfriend.'

Catlin is convinced that we are going to meet our soulmates in Galway. Galway boyfriends with broad shoulders and fluent Irish and possible castles of their own. She has a theory that Oliver Cromwell kicked all the properly Irish men to Connacht, and they're lurking in the mountains, brimming with testosterone and secret sensitivity. She's even started a gang: the Galway Boyfriends Gang. She is president, and I am the secretary and treasurer. There are only two members of the GBG, but we're looking to expand to four when we meet our Galway boyfriends.

'What will your Galway boyfriend be called?' I ask.

'Something pure Galway like Peadar or Ultan,' she says.

'Mine will be called Fenian,' I tell her. 'Or maybe Mountain. Mountain Boyfriend O' Galway.'

'That's *good*,' she says.

I tell her that I know. We make her bed and then we go into my room and make mine. I quite like making beds. When you're putting the duvet cover on you can pretend to be a ghost. Our rooms are almost identical, mirror images, only with different tapestries and views. Every room in Brian's castle has a view. It's a bit much really. All that landscape.

'Ultan will be able to drive a tractor,' Catlin says, as though this is an extremely desirable quality in a man.

Which it may well be. We're in the country. There are different rules.

'My one will have *road frontage*,' I tell her, 'and feed abandoned baby lambs by the hearth. With his big Galway hands.' I think I've won.

'Ah. Mountain sounds like a sweetheart,' she says. 'Ultan will have a shock of bright red curls.'

'Mountain will have straw instead of hair. Like a thatched cottage.'

'That is incredibly Galway of him,' she says, and I can tell she is impressed. 'Ultan will often walk about the fields with a calf draped around his shoulders, like a heavy rural scarf.'

16

'Mountain will only eat turnips. And he won't be able to see the English.'

'Ultan will light me fires with turf he cut himself. And then seduce me beside them.'

'Jesus.'

'I know,' she says proudly.

'Mountain will be able to fly?' It comes out like a question.

'Mountain doesn't sound real, Madeline. I don't think you're taking the GBG seriously.'

'It's a practical skill that helps him rescue puppies trapped in slurry pits. And there is *nothing* wrong with having high standards, Catlin,' I remind her. And it is true. Though sometimes I worry my standards are a little bit too high. I don't like boys the same way she does. She's almost constantly in love with people. The shape of them. Their flesh. The way they sound. The lyrics of love songs make perfect sense to Catlin. It's always high-romance. Until she gets bored.

I flop down, and feel the compassionate gaze of all those plaster eyes. I'm not sure I could sleep with all those faces there, but I suppose Catlin likes an audience.

'Madeline?' she asks, and her voice is different, more serious.

'Yeah?' I sit on the flagstones, still stuffing pillows into pillowcases. When you have a four-poster bed you need loads of pillowcases. It is a problem.

'Wouldn't it be terrible if we weren't related?' she asks.

'What?' I mean, it would; of course it would. Half of my immediate family wouldn't be there. More if she took Mam with her. Which, realistically, she would.

'Well –' she's playing with a loose thread on my blanket – 'I

17

mean, you'd miss me so much. If I was going, and you were my best friend and not my sister.'

This is true. 'You'd miss me too, you know.'

She nods. 'I would. But you're way more introverted than I am. It would be much harder for you.'

She's right. But I don't like the sound of it coming out of her mouth. A statement of fact that doubles as an insult.

'I'd get over it,' I assure her. And I would. I totally would. With all my introverting skills. Books and naps and biscuits all the way.

'No, you wouldn't.' She's confident of this. What does she think I am?

'You wouldn't either. You'd waste away from grief.'

'Ultan would mind me. We'd churn butter on the mountain side and distil our own poitín.' She smiles, half in love with her pretend man already.

'There's no such thing as Ultan,' I tell her. It comes out sharper than I had intended. Which happens to me a lot.

My sister smiles. 'Not yet.' The moment passes.

But later, in the stone walls of my room, the mountains big and silent out the window, it occurs to me that we had both assumed that I would be the one she left behind.

18

3

Milk Thistle

(spares the liver)

There are many things about this castle that are surprising. Number one: we live here. Number Two: battlements. We've been having a good explore, because that's what you do if a place has so many rooms you need two people's fingers and toes, and possibly, like, seven extra hands, to count them. Brian showed us some rooms, the 'main' ones, he called them. The library, the bedrooms, toilets, kitchen, the blue sitting room, the red sitting room, his office. His father's taste in decor was very castle, and Brian's stuck to it.

His office has a coat of arms on the wall. And, on the lintel, something even worse. A little leather fist of a thing, peering down from the door of his office. I somehow knew what it was right away. A shrunken head. It should be ghoulish, but it just seems sad, the icing on the strangest cake that I have ever eaten. The cake of our life here now. I told Catlin that it probably wasn't real. I didn't think it could be.

19

Brian says it is.

Catlin thinks it's grand. It fits the castle aesthetic. Like the swords and suits of armour we found in a small room behind the downstairs toilet. But armour's just clothes. This little thing – it was a person once, or something living anyway. And now it's just an oddment, on the thick ledge over his door, dented eyes the size of little thumb prints, hollowed out, and long hair sewn on. When we asked him, Brian told us how they used to make them. First remove the skull. Then cut the back open and scoop out all the fat. Put some special seeds under the eyelids. Sew them shut and pin the lips together. Then boil it. Afterwards dry it out with rocks, mould the features with your hands while the flesh is still moist. You make it into anything you want. A boy. A girl. A thing.

And when you're done, you sprinkle it with ash.

'Where did you get it, Brian?' we asked our head-collecting stepdad.

'My father picked it up. On his travels.' He smiled. 'It's supposed to be protection from your enemies. You kill them, and you shrink their heads, and for as long as you keep that head, their ghost must serve you.' He waggled his fingers, making light of it. But I felt strange.

'It's a little sad,' I told him, thinking of a tired ghostly slave.

'It is,' he said, a little smile on his face, 'but people don't do that stuff now. Most heads are made from hides, to sell to tourists.'

'Who was this?' asked Catlin, still staring at it, like it was a friend whose name she was trying to place.

'A girl,' he said. 'I don't know any more about her though.'

There was a pause, and then he said, almost to himself, 'I don't know if I'd want to. There's such a thing as knowing too much.'

He smiled at me, like I knew what he meant. And I thought of all the times I have known too much. They've mainly involved things Catlin has told me. Secrets people wouldn't want me knowing about their lives. The messy stuff. Not much actual mess here though – it is immaculate. Too immaculate for one Brian to do all by himself.

'How does he keep this place, like, clean? Do we have servants now? It feels like this level of clean would take at least one servant,' I ask my sister, ratting at the small white flecks of skin around my nail, as frayed as afterfeather, but not as soft.

'Stop being weird, Maddy,' says Catlin. 'The servants will talk.'

'We don't have servants. They would have greeted our arrival on the stairs,' I tell her, picturing the awkwardness of that. I'm really glad we don't have, like, a staff. Imagine all the extra interaction, having to thank people all day long. Ugh.

'But I'm invested now. I would like to fool around with an attractive butler. Named Higgins. He would school me in the ways of love, and I would use those skills to marry well.'

'Take me, Higgins!' I gasp, caressing a trowel, as though it were an ab. 'Meh. It doesn't work. And don't exploit the servants, dear. It isn't classy.'

'I don't have to be classy, Mad. We're new money . . . I will say it's not the sexiest name I could have chosen,' she says. 'But I stick by it. And by my beloved Higgins, who gives me fresh bedclothes and screaming orgasms.'

'Catlin, what of Ultan? Don't break his rural heart.'

'Don't slut-shame me,' she says.

'I amn't *shaming* you. You have no shame for me to shame you with. But can we keep the orgasms more gaspy than screamy, please? We have adjoining rooms. And I sleep light.'

My sister thinks about it, and she nods. 'You have yourself a sexy, sexy deal.'

Catlin and me decide to do some re-potting and planting in the greenhouse, smoky glass in a green-tinged frame. It looks like a massive jewellery box from the outside. Spanish moss trails from the roof like lace.

I keep finding little grey-brown woodlice in the corners, some whole and others worn to almost dust. Mam calls them 'pigs', those little tank-like insects. You see them teeming underneath dead wood. There is something tomb-like about this place. It's too big for one man, and for four people it is still too big. And all the little deaths inside the corners, heaped up neatly, like they died polite.

My two hands are flat on the ground, feeling for the best place to put this little sapling. It's a baby sycamore. I grew it in a yoghurt pot at first, from a helicopter. Mam says I have green fingers, like my dad. It's not that hard – you read up what they need and just do that. I am quite good at knowing when plants are a little unhappy though. Takes one to know one. Probably I just like healing things. Plants are my version of mindfulness or yoga, all that other stuff they demand you do at school to reduce your stress, as though they haven't stressed you with that stress, at least in part. It's soothing to help a green life out. And a lot of stuff is just like us. They need to eat, they need the space to grow, the air to breathe. To not be hurt.

22

Catlin's sorting peace lilies. They take over when they're in the pots, like mint. She rips them apart, a vulture at a carcass. I put my hand on her arm.

'Let me do it.'

'You'll take ages,' she says. 'I want to unpack more and go exploring.'

'I know, but Catlin . . .'

'Hmmm?' She quirks a lip that way she has, like when a cat shows you one of its teeth, just so you know they're there and don't get notions. My fingers rummage softly through the soil and gently tease the networked roots apart. Catlin's face is focused on her phone, the shine of the screen. I can see it reflected in the whites of her eyes, as the light dims in the garden. She almost looks like an alien. Not of this world. A beautiful anomaly. She smiles, and her teeth glint soft. Like little pearls. Our big teeth look like baby teeth. Everything about us is tiny. When you complain about it, people tell you to shut up. To eat a sandwich. Which is fair enough, but I would like to need less help with shelves.

The greenhouse is lit with strings of LED lights. It's adorable. Like somewhere you'd get married. If Mam and Brian hadn't had their small 'big day' already.

'I bet this place would be *amazing* for parties,' Catlin says. 'We could get all our friends from Cork. Invite them down. Not right away – I know Brian doesn't like guests he doesn't know. But, in a while, I think we could convince him.'

Catlin says *we* when she means *I*, and sometimes when she means *you*. I sigh. I hate parties. They always end with people puking in bins. I hold their hair, and tell them that it wasn't the tequila. That they'll be fine. That I won't tell their mum/dad/sister/cousin Joan. I don't really mind though, looking after drunk people. Calmly helping them puke different colours. Offering pints of water. Doctor practice. Better than hanging round in corners not being as good as Catlin.

I see a face, staring from the garden. Mamó approaches, like a mean shark. I mean, I assume it must be her. Her salt-and-pepper hair is in a long, tight braid down her back. She's wearing the sort of brown smock that screams, 'I am your new herbalist step-relative.' I like brown, but I don't like the way she wears it. Or her in general. Reminding us that our home was her home first with her walk and smock. I roll my eyes. Catlin sees her too.

'Mamó,' she says, like she has just crossed something off on the official Ballyfrann scavenger-hunt card. She waves enthusiastically. I groan. Mamó's eyes are dark grey-blue, and she doesn't look friendly. She might bite us. Or worse, make *loads* of small talk.

'Don't wave at her. She might want chats.'

'She won't,' my sister says. 'She clearly hates people – look at that glare.'

'Why take the chance?' I ask, confident in my rightness. 'She's a creep. The face on her.'

The old woman stomps into the greenhouse. Not an annoyed stomp but the confident stomp of someone whose house this is. Her stomp tells us it's her land and we're trespassing. And she's allowing it, but just for now. She has a very eloquent stomp, I think. Most people's legs are just like, 'Hey! I'm walking from this place to this place and not threatening anyone while I do it.'

24

I miss the sound legs of our old home.

Meanwhile, a massive raven swoops down and perches on the edge of the greenhouse roof. It looks like she paid it to follow her. To amplify the creepery. Its dark beak is open as it stares at us.

As they both do.

'Hello, Mamó,' says Catlin. 'Love the smock.'

I try to kick her in the shins but she dodges me.

'Twins,' she says. As though that was our name. She's such a douchebag. Outdated and unnecessary. Vaginas are self-cleaning. I know this because Catlin once yelled it at me across the room at a house party. For *no reason*. It's not a memory I treasure much.

Mamó gathers several tools inside a thick black bucket. Looks at one trowel, growls and puts it down. She's lucky trowels don't have feelings or she would have made a very blunt enemy. The raven walks overhead, along the greenhouse frame. I can almost feel the scrape of claw on wood. The two of us stay silent as the grave while she goes about her business. It feels like Mass, like speaking would be rude. It's quite oppressive. I pull a leaf from off a nearby bay tree. A little one. A bay-be. I crush it till it cracks and put it to my nostrils, close my eyes.

When I open them, she's staring at me.

I hold her gaze until she turns to leave. Before she reaches the door, her hand darts very quickly to the corner, and when she brings it back, she's holding something. I see the flicker of a string – a tail? – before she strides away.

'That was awkward,' I say to my sister, hoping she can sense

25

the confusion and dislike behind the words. 'I hope she's not around all the time.'

'Madeline,' my sister says, tearing leaves off, folding them, 'we're here for at least two years. We'll need lifts into the village. Give her a chance. Have you seen how good she is at holding mice and striding?'

'Was that what she was doing?' I ask, but she doesn't answer, too busy staring after our new relative. The raven spreads his (or her – I'm not sure how to tell when nothing dangles) wings and takes off across the garden after Mamó, the dark wings darker than the dimming sky.

Catlin's impressed lips shape the word *fierce*.

Was that what it was? I snort, and press my hands into the chocolatey, rich compost. Place the plants inside. It's winter, but I think they will survive here. I think that I can make that happen, with care. If you have the right tools, the right information, then the outlook improves. At least in general.

Catlin holds up a fat leaf folded over. 'It's a swan,' she says. 'Like *meeeeeeee*.' She stretches her neck and tosses her hair. My sister's always known that she was lovely. At least one of us is. She's going to have, like, eleven friends in Ballyfrann from tomorrow, probably. So, basically the entire population of the place. Perhaps she will be elected mayor.

The light has dimmed away to almost nothing. We work in the greenhouse, surrounded by carnivorous plants and succulents, labelled neatly in a cramped black hand. It must be Mamó's writing; it's not Brian's. She's sneaking around at the edges of our lives, I think. Or maybe it's the other way around.

The mountains rising dark to touch the stars. It looks as

though the world's been ripped in two. Dip-dyed darkness. Smoothing down the earth, I hold my tongue. Plants can go into shock after repotting. They need water, warmth. Indirect sunlight. Kindness. Care.

I look at Catlin. All confidence and bluster. And I want her to be happy here. Even if I don't think that I will be. I don't know if I can be happy anywhere. We both know that I'm not that sort of fish. That sort of plant.

'Mad?' my sister asks, her bright eyes kind and lined with perfect kohl. I close my eyes. There's no point in comparison. Not really.

My hands scrape at my fingernails again. Soil and blood and everything is strange.

4

Broom

(dropsy, taming dogs)

Catlin is fishtail-braiding her hair at the kitchen table. She did our nails last night. Hers shiny purple, mine grey. We're starting school today. My fingers flutter, picking at the oilcloth. I taste something sour in my stomach. The panic builds. I put down my cup of tea, and begin to tidy. Scrub the tea stains out of china cups. I can see Mamó curled over something small in the garden. It's soft and dark. I cannot tell if it's a clump of earth or a young bird. Her fingers clasped around it and her expression vacant. She rises, meets my eye before she turns away. I start, as fingers trail across my shoulder.

'I'll get those,' Mam tells me.

'No,' I say, shaking off adrenaline. 'It's fine.'

'I've time,' she says. 'I'm a lady of leisure now.' She smiles. We both know she'll be busy all day long. It's who she is. Mam is a primary-school teacher, and she's taken a career break, so her job in Cork will be waiting if she needs it. Mam and me are alike that way, I think. Plan for the worst. Except she also hopes for the best. I scrape my toast into the bin, half eaten. Catlin smiles at me, stuffs her second slice into her mouth.

'We'll be late!' she says. 'We're meeting Layla at the end of the driveway. In ten.'

The driveway's very long. We have to run.

Layla Shannon is a tall, blonde wisp of a girl. She looks like she would appear out of a mist. In moonlight. By a lake. Doing ballet. For a prince. A fairy prince. I can't be dealing with her. She's our groundskeeper's daughter, and lives in a lodge on the grounds of our fabulous castle because what has our life become?

Layla waves at us, her long, pale fingers curled together like the wing of a bird. 'Hey,' she says. Her voice is low.

'Hey,' we both say back. Catlin looks her up and down. Me too, but only because she looks like the sort of person who doles out swords and prophecies in books. Her hair is tied into a high, messy ponytail with what looks like twine. She has a stain on her school skirt.

'Your lace is untied,' Catlin points out. When Layla kneels down to tie it, she's basically still taller than us. It isn't fair. Catlin rises to her full height. Asks Layla about the school, the village. Her brothers. Where people go to drink. I lean back against the cold stone, my hands stuffed in the pockets of my duffel coat. I think about the bed I left behind. All cosy and warm and not full of people. A space where I could snooze and be alone. I look down at my battered record bag. It has a book and a spare book in it. One is about the Spanish flu epidemic. The other is about the missing girls.

29

Layla laughs, as though she and Catlin were plotting a hilarious crime. 'You're funny,' she tells my sister. 'I like that.'

Catlin looks at her with squinty eyes. The sunlight is bright this morning. The mountains bleached, the trees warped like wrought bone. I notice something at Layla's feet. A soft, small thing. I crouch down, look at it. A little pygmy shrew. Its dead face thin, eyes wide. Little mouth all opened, little blackhead teeth nesting inside. Like ants.

'What are you doing, Maddy?' Catlin asks. Her face is horrified.

'Sorry,' I say to Layla and Catlin, standing up. 'I don't normally examine little corpses.'

'It was a pygmy shrew,' says Layla. 'I had a look at it before ye came. Poor little thing.'

I smile at her. 'They have the weirdest little noses, don't they?'

'They always look so disappointed in life.'

'Whyfor am I a shrewwwww?' My shrew-voice comes out squeaky and aggressive, but Layla seems to get what I'm going for.

'The world is big and it frightens me.'

'Send help.'

'Send *so much* help.'

We giggle. Catlin shrugs, brushes down her skirt. Crouches to the little corpse, takes out her phone and snaps it.

'Another body found in Ballyfrann.' She quirks her mouth.

And then the laughter stops. Catlin's face is all, *Why did I say that?*

It is an expression I recognise from me.

30

The bus pulls up.

Layla doesn't sit near us. Grey roads snake like rivers through the landscape. We roll clunkily through the mountain pass. They were found here, I think. Stare out the window.

Helen Groarke, most recent of the girls.

Amanda Shale. They found her cold and broken on her birthday.

Nora Ginn looked older than fourteen. They think that someone held her for a while.

Bridget Hora, small like us, but older than the others. Not by much though.

I leave my book inside my bag. Remind myself that it's the sort of thing that people don't like to talk about. Which is weird. It was so long ago for some of them. Twenty, thirty years. No one that people here would have known, apart from Helen. It isn't that the deaths of strangers matter less; it's just they're not our deaths. We don't have a responsibility to mourn them.

No one knows who hurt the mountain girls. But in books on unsolved Irish murders, they always get a chapter. At least one chapter.

I look at Catlin, on her phone, scrolling through the news from her friends back home, until her pale face clicks back into repose. Until she has remembered that she matters. I roll my shoulders back until they click.

We pass the green sign, chipped and rusted over. Flakes of paint peel off. Rough brown pokes through. I look back as it shrinks away behind us.

Fáilte go Béal Ifreann
Welcome to Ballyfrann

31

I crook my mouth at Catlin. It isn't a smile. And neither is what she gives back to me. She butts her shoulder gently against mine, as the bus rattles through the mountain. It sounds as though the engine is a metal box full of loose bolts. Too loud to put on headphones to block it out.

'It looks so lonely here,' my sister says. She says lonely like it could apply to her somehow. Like it is not my word.

'We won't be lonely, Catlin. You are *magic*. And we have each other. We will surely make our own fun. Out of turf.' I tell my sister things that might be lies.

She nods. 'I normally don't worry about stuff, Mad. I don't put my foot in it. And yet. Here it is. My foot.' She curls her toes. I hear the crack of bone.

The bus pulls up outside some spiked black gates. Chain ropes around them, like a snake around its dinner. Three separate padlocks are attached. The railings around the school are painted black, but are bright brown with rust.

'Who'd want to break in here?' she asks. I shrug. It's basically a series of abandoned prefabs, clustered around a plump white cottage with curranty little windows. Some of them are boarded up with wood or wavy shed-roof iron. Corrugated.

'At least it's safe?' I venture.

'Nothing's ever safe in Ballyfrann,' Layla mutters as she passes by. 'Have ye had your tetanus injections?'

I pull my black polyester jumper down over my grey polyester skirt. Button up my duffel coat again, as wind bites skin.

And it begins.

This school is very different to our Cork one, way less sanitary. Lots of greys and browns and terracottas, holes worried

32

in paint, where you can see the colours from before poking through time. Like the rings on a stump. The prefabs must be older than they seem. Brian went here, we know that. When it was just the cottage. The culture shock is strong. I almost cry with relief when I see a plastic chair with a penis drawn on it. I look at Catlin. See she's happy too.

'Just like home,' she says to me. 'Do you see the detail on the balls?'

I nod. It does look old. 'Maybe it's Brian's,' I say, instantly realising my mistake when she makes retching noises. 'I meant his *work*, Catlin. Jesus. His *work*. Argh.'

Over the course of the long, cold day, Our Lady of the Mountain Village School starts to grow on me. Like a fungus, or an oddly comforting series of warts. The bathrooms, in a separate sort of shed-yoke, smell of cigarettes and wee. Someone has taken the batteries out of the smoke alarm. It beeps unsafely every now and then. Punctuating the silence all around.

I kind of like it here. It isn't bothered with unimportant things like appearances or adequacy and that's fine. There are only about thirty of us in the entire building. Like, one per cent of the population of our old school. It's ridiculous. We basically met everyone today. It took five seconds.

Layla has two brothers, Fiachra and Cathal. They mountain-bike to school, 'too active for the bus'. Catlin pokes my ribcage when she hears this. Twice. One for each physically fit possible Galway boyfriend. I don't know. I suppose I can see it a little. If you like your David Bowies young, and with acne.

There are six people from the village in our year, apart from us. Charley Collins, a broad-shouldered girl with the fiercest

33

eyebrows I have ever seen, her brother Eddie, Layla, Fiachra, Cathal and another new girl who's starting sometime soon. Some kids bus in from the towns near Ballyfrann, but not too many. The nearest town is an hour away, and lots of kids from there just go to Galway city for their lessons. The kids from Carraig stick out, with their normalness and polo shirts. They look like regular country kids. Who knows what side of a GAA pitch their bread is buttered on.

There's, like, a glow of health and muscle off the kids from closer to the castle. Does everyone here exercise? What's wrong with them? Have they no Netflix? I don't like it and I don't trust it. I glare down at my hands like I'm Mamó. Mamó, who, by the way, refused to leave the village to come to Mam and Brian's wedding despite her actual name being the Irish word for grandmother. *We* should be glaring at *her*.

'What are the teachers like?' asks Catlin, not really caring, but wanting to fill up space. She's eating salad with a travel fork she uses to stab her question into the air. It has pomegranate seeds in it, and feta. Mam is over-compensating. It won't last.

'OK. I mean, we don't really get to know them or anything. The teachers don't stay long, maybe for like a year,' Charley says. 'It's too far out. There's nothing to do, if you're not from here. They fill up their CVs, move somewhere else.' She says somewhere else like other people say Paris or New York. I remember her father from the wedding, and the move. A wide, red-faced man, surrounded by wide, red-faced brothers. Hairy fists.

'The Collinses,' Brian had told us. 'I'm related to them, distantly. Everyone in Ballyfrann has Collins blood. In their

34

veins – or on their hands, they say.' And then he laughed. 'It works out well. They take care of their own.'

The wedding was a deeply awkward day.

'What do people who are from here do?' asks Catlin hopefully.

Charley shrugs.

I look out the window, the teacher's voice becoming background noise. The mountains dark and angry, blurred by clouds. The trees blade-sharp. I shiver. So does everyone, in fairness. The heating in the building doesn't work.

Miss Feehlihy, the principal, is a creep. She shakes our hands and tells us several times how great Brian is, offering no helpful information before retreating off into her little office. Her bottle-blonde hair looks fire-hazard dry.

'What's the deal with her loving the hole off Brian?' I ask my sister, who raises a perfectly shaped eyebrow.

'Your eyebrow has some innuendo on it,' I tell her.

'Jesus, sorry. How embarrassing.' She wipes it off with a hand that she then uses to give me the finger. Her nail polish is flawless. Mine's already in bits. This place is full of splinters, and other things that bang and catch and snag.

'She definitely has the horn for him,' Catlin says. 'Mam probably cock-blocked her.'

I shake my head and point to the poster on her door. Puppies and kittens. It is the crappest thing either of us has ever, ever seen.

'She cock-blocked *herself*, Catlin,' I tell her.

Our faces sombre. Recognising tragedy.

The Ballyfrann kids are friendly but distant. Like we were

35

their aunts or nerdy cousins. We eat together at break and try to make our way into a group at lunch by asking about where things are and following them.

Here is a sample exchange:

'So, what's Miss Edwards like?'

'Like a teacher.' Thank you Cathal or Fiachra, one of Layla's brothers. The way he says it isn't like a dig. More a why-are-you-asking-me-things.

'Do you know the castle?' asks Catlin. Looking at her face, I can see the physical effort all this trying-to-make-bored-people-interested is taking. She isn't used to this.

'Yeah.' It was more syllable than word. *My sister needs this, Eddie,* I think. *Please try to care.*

Eddie has a babyish, open face and wouldn't have gotten the time of day off Catlin in our old school. I look at Catlin's face and notice an almost imperceptible twitch. She was tallying. Eddie runs his big, thick fingers through his tufty, red hair and doesn't notice.

'We live there now,' she offers.

He says, 'OK.' As though castles were caravans.

We eat in silence.

Sometime later, a terrible thing happens. Catlin says to Charley, 'I like your pixie cut.'

And Charley says, 'Thanks,' and bites into her sandwich, like she doesn't know that when a girl says a nice thing to you, you have to say one back. I can sense the hairs on the back of Catlin's neck pricking up. Her brain scrolling through all the things about her you could compliment. Her hair, her skin, her eyeliner, her brogues. The little cameo she's wearing with the

36

Infant of Prague on it. She looks at me in semi-desperation. What is wrong with these people?

I look at Catlin.

'Smoke?' I say.

She smiles.

I haven't started smoking or anything, but escape from social situations is a beautiful thing. When you are a pretend smoker, you can take off for ten to sixty minutes and no one will ever know. We sit at the back of the overgrown school garden, behind a bush, beside a wrought-iron gate. Our fingers move along beside each other, turning flaking brown to something skeletal.

'Don't let them get to you,' I tell my sister.

'I won't,' she assures me, sucking her cancer stick to ash in twenty seconds flat and lighting another.

'A woman after my own heart,' says a smooth, deep voice. It's a lanky yoke of a man. Staring at us through the railings. He's wearing a leather jacket, jeans. A white T-shirt. His hair is slicked back. All that's missing is the motorcycle and he'd be a 1950s bad boy from the wrong side of the tracks. He puts a large, pale hand on the gate and hops it easily. Dusts off his trousers.

Smiles and waits for us to be impressed.

Only one of us is. Catlin raises her eyes to his, shoulders back, boobs out.

'You're Brian's new children, right?'

'Stepdaughters,' I tell him. I want to say 'step-women', but that might sound even creepier than children, to be fair. Who says the word *children* in a flirty manner? Predators, I think. I glare at him.

He holds out his hand.

'My name is Lon Delacroix. Short for Laurent Delacroix.' His voice is warm. He raises both his eyebrows plaintively as if to say, *Don't leave my hand alone*.

Catlin nods, and takes the strange boy's hand. Her eyes light up a bit. She's found a snack. I look at the poor fecker. He doesn't know what he's in for.

He chats to us as though we were people until the bell rings, and I can feel it nourishing my twin. An older man, but not like creepy old. Like, college-age. Lon seems grand, maybe a bit up himself though. What's he doing sneaking around the schoolyard, like? It's odd.

On the way back into class, Catlin pokes me in the ribs again. She gets the same place almost every time. It's sore. I can feel a little bruise beginning to form. A little purple welt of boy-potential. The day passes as days do, and by the end of it I'm exhausted. Meeting new people is hard. I feel like I'm doing a series of job interviews and if I don't get the job I'll end up lonely for the next two years, doing my homework and watching Catlin flirt with inappropriate older men. It wouldn't be the worst thing in the world, but it wouldn't be ideal.

We're quiet for most of the bus ride home. Listening to the Ballyfrann kids interact. I feel like they have cast us as observers. It's weird and things, but also a little bit refreshing. Why should they be our friends, like? They don't know us, and we don't know them.

Travelling back, the sky already dimming, I listen to the rattle of the bus. The bright of the cat's eyes in the headlights. The hedgerow alongside the road is patchy, bare. I count seven white crosses on the roadside. A cluster and another and another. A little pattern in this unkempt place. The whirr of tyre on road grates loud, louder. Nails on chalkboard, scraping danger deep into my brain. Anything with wheels can be a weapon. I need to leave. I'm stuck. I'm stuck. I'm stuck.

I look at Catlin, on her phone again. Her face is focused, glowing with intent. The other students talk. I can't hear what they say, not exactly. More the hum of it. Mixing with the harsh metallic clicks. We're trapped inside a metal shell together. Counting crosses passing on the road.

Eight.

Nine.

Ten.

Eleven . . .

Mamó slices past us in a blood-red tin can. I only catch a flash of hemp and hair, but I know it's her. A wave of recognition laced with anger. No wonder there are crosses on the road if that's the way the locals drive.

Twelve . . .

Thirteen . . .

I think of the small shrew we saw this morning. Its little paws. The moisture on its nose. We're so close to nature here. Lots of hidden life. And hidden death.

5

Juniper

(contraceptive, also good for teeth)

When Mam was pregnant with the two of us, we were nestled so close together in her womb that for a while the doctor thought that we might be conjoined. I'm glad we weren't. Catlin would probably make me do all the hard jobs. Tweezing eyebrows. Hoovering and such. And I'd have to sit around closing my eyes while she kissed all the boys. All of them. Including Lon. The only item on her Ballyfrann to-do list.

That would be more punishment than fun. I would not like to be so close to that side of her life. The messiness of lust and indecision. In fairness, though, Lon might be in for a world of hurt. She's made more than one boy cry. Once through an entire hurling match, during which he scored several times. Which only made him sob harder. 'Because I knew I'd never score Catlin again.' I imagine Lon's perfect face crumpled up with sorrow. I don't know what that would even look like. When I picture Lon in my head, his face is expressionless.

Our first week in school has passed without any major incidents. We haven't set anything on fire, or made any enemies. Or friends. The Ballyfrann kids are grand, but it's hard to spend time with them when Catlin keeps taking increasingly long smoke breaks to flirt with Lon.

'He's easier than they are, Mad,' she tells me, as I awkwardly hang out beside her.

'I get it, Catlin,' I say, leaning against a sycamore tree, feeling the mulch of leaf under my boots. 'But it's not easier for me.'

'I'm not stopping you from hanging out with them.'

Only we both know that she kind of is. I'm fairly independent in a lot of ways, but new groups of people isn't one of them. And it's hard to say it out loud, because it shouldn't have to be said, but as I open my mouth to try, there he is.

Lon fecking Delacroix.

'Catalina!' he exclaims. 'Fancy meeting you here.'

Catlin exhales a long thin curl of smoke.

'Lon,' she says, with a smile.

It's not her real smile. It is her smile for boys.

'Maddy,' Lon says, with more warmth than he should be allowed to feel for me. He should not be the person who is soundest to us here. I know it's for Catlin, so it's something like a lie, but it's annoying.

'Hi, Lon,' I say, taking out my phone and scrolling through pictures of our old life in Cork while playing a mournful power ballad in my head.

'That's a nice phone, Madeline,' Lon says, completely ignoring my ignoring. 'Mind if I take a look at it?'

I look at Catlin.

Catlin looks at me.

I look at my phone.

Sadly, like a child relinquishing the last Haribo in the pack to a mean auntie, I pass it over.

'What's the PIN?' he asks.

And Catlin tells him.

Urrgh.

He scrolls around for a bit, in silence. The screen glares at him like it was me.

'Ha!' he says, and hands it back to me with a flourish. 'I took the liberty of sending myself your numbers, ladies.' He grins. 'I hope you don't mind.'

'Actually . . .' I begin, but Catlin stops me.

'Bit desperate of you, to be honest,' she says. 'Come on, Maddy, we better get back to class.'

'See you tomorrow?' Lon asks.

'No school tomorrow, Lon,' I remind him.

We walk away and don't look back.

As we turn into the building, Catlin squeaks at me, 'I can't believe he took our numbers!!' Her tone of voice has changed to something like glee.

'I know,' I say. 'It's a bit much.'

'No, it isn't. It was suave.'

'Suave is such a disgusting word. *Suave*.' I make a face like I've vomited a bit in my mouth.

'There's nothing wrong with the word *suave*. And there's nothing wrong with a boy being interested in us.'

'In you,' I correct her.

'Well, in fairness, I'm the one who talks back, Maddy.'

'I'm not jealous. Like, I don't talk to him because I don't like him that much.'

'Then stay with Charley and them at lunch.'

I make the vomit-in-my-mouth face again. But this time it is sad pretend vomit. The vomit of my own limitations. The vomit that holds me back when all I want is to be a normal human who can hold conversations and make friends.

When we go back into class, the first thing my twin does is check her phone.

I pay attention, take notes and try not to worry about things that mightn't happen. Focus on the things I understand.

6

Calendula

(for harmony and scars)

It's a pale autumn day, bright skies and sharp winds that sliced through the green wool of my jumper earlier, as I gathered mint for the water jug. I was almost grateful to the chill. I needed a distraction from Catlin, who woke me up this morning with an enthusiastic, 'Morning, Maddy. Would you like a coffee? Let me tell you about the sexy dream I had featuring Lon. In detail.'

And then she did.

She is the worst person I have ever met, and I would sleep for a hundred years rather than re-hear that. I don't like the idea of her meeting someone right away. She shouldn't get a safety blanket when she's supposed to be my one. I need help interacting with the tiny group of people who live here. It's weird there are so few. Aren't villages supposed to be, like, communities, where everyone knows everyone's business and things? I suppose they probably know all our business already. We just haven't learned theirs.

People are always going in and out to Mamó, sometimes with mysterious boxes and eyes full of tears. That's probably half of what they pay her for. To keep their dirty small-town secrets like a crap priest. I legitimately saw someone handing her a brown envelope yesterday. It looked like it was full of old dry leaves. She glared at me as she stuffed it in her pocket. I was peering from a turret window so she couldn't have known I was there. And it's not like she has resting glare face. She was just glaring *in case* someone was watching. For fear they'd feel un-small for even a second.

Catlin brought up Lon eighteen times today. I started counting after number five. Now, in fairness, they have been messaging on the regular. I did not reply to the single message he sent me.

Hello Maddy. This is Lon. Now u have my number. And three smiley-face emojis.

I don't trust people who smile too much. They're either too happy, or lying. I'm glad he had the good sense not to show up in my dreams, rescuing me from things. But that's kind of not on him, that's on my lovely sensible subconscious that doesn't go wild over people within seconds of meeting them. I don't really get the whole fancying-people thing. I mean, there are people I prefer seeing to other people. And people who smell better than other people. But I'd generally prefer to read a book, or complain about something. Which is fine, like sexuality is different for different people. And for me it is mysterious and intimidating and possibly another way to fail. When you're attracted to a person, your brain releases chemicals. You lose your appetite, you might not sleep. Your heart rate increases

45

and you feel what sounds a lot like panic. Catlin doesn't mind that sort of thing – she wants to be swept up, to fall and burn. But burning is a horrible sensation. And falling's not much better. Some people die of fright on the way down.

I have spent a good part of the day watching Catlin prance about in an old smoking jacket she found in the attic. She is always finding things in the attics here. Brian's dad bought up a lot of estate sales, so the castle is full of boxes of old things; Brian says he doesn't know the half of it, in that voice he gets when he talks about his dad. The deeper one. Our stepdad clearly has daddy issues. He is lucky to have ended up with someone like Mam. And we're probably lucky to have ended up with him, even if it's only so Catlin gets to live in a flea market where everything is hers for the taking.

Catlin is grumpy that nobody from school has messaged her or added her on anything. 'Not even Layla,' she moaned, as if it is a truth universally acknowledged that Layla is terrible. 'And she's *staff*.'

'Layla's all right,' I tell her. 'And she doesn't work for us. Her dad works for Brian. That's a different thing.'

Catlin might need to check her brand-new privilege. We've only been living in a castle for about fifteen seconds. What is she at with her 'staff'? I don't like the idea of people having to be nice to us because our stepdad is rich. People should be nice to us because Catlin is charismatic and I'm also there. It is the way of things. At least it was.

Instead of scavenging cool things from our stepdad's house, I have been spotting old women. One very particular old woman. Every time I visit my plants, it seems Mamó is in the garden, looming. And then I have to say an awkward, 'Hi,' and she might nod at me if she feels like it, maybe. My skin gets all crawly around her. Like I'm slightly allergic. And who knows? Maybe I am. It wouldn't be the weirdest thing to have happened. I'm pretty sure I heard her call the raven 'Bob' earlier. While feeding it a piece of raw meat. It's finger-tongue reached out from the beak to stroke the meat before it gobbled it and croaked its thanks. I'm not sure why I got the urge to spy on her a little. It's like when you have a big spot, and you hate it, but throughout the day your fingers keep coming back to it. Pressing against it, feeling the little ache. The new disgust. Mamó is a big spot on the face of my life here. And I need to stop picking at her. Or find a good concealer.

At least we have a library, where Catlin flops down on the fainting couch with a deep sigh of existential dread. 'Ballyfrann is a ridiculous place and I want to go home. Where is my butler?'

Brian doesn't have servants. Just Layla's dad, a lot of dust-cloths and a cleaner we never see, who comes for two hours a day. Catlin is very disappointed.

'Higgins would have ruined both his career and your chances with the beautiful Ultan,' I tell her. 'It is hard right now, but you're better off this way.' I nod my head as though I am an expert on juggling imaginary boyfriends. Which in fairness I could well be. They are imaginary.

She's draped despairingly along the couch, like an old-timey woman in crisis. I run my fingers through her hair, untangling snares like roots, like an old-timey maid who isn't sure what to do in said crisis, but knows the importance of good hair. I do what I can.

'Everybody hates me. Except Lon.'

Fecking Lon and his constant messaging.

I grit my teeth. 'I think you mean that they don't love you yet. Except Lon,' I say. 'They will though. It's a given.'

'No, it's not, and Lon doesn't love me – he's just being, like, welcoming or something.' She waggles her eyebrows and flashes of sexy fireman Lon reappear in my subconscious.

I shudder. Pointedly.

'Stop,' she says. 'He's nice, and kind of hot, and he works in Donoghue's so he's probably our best chance for alcohol and shenanigans.'

'Who says *shenanigans*?'

'I do. I say *shenanigans* now.' Her voice is full of the certainty that comes from not second-guessing every word that leaves your mouth, or regretting that you haven't.

Donoghue's is the local pub, and it does not look like a shenanigans sort of place unless you enjoy yelling at GAA players and singing Republican ballads. Which I, as a rule, do not.

'He's fifty-seven,' I tell her.

'He is not! He's probably, like, nineteen? Maybe twenty.'

'He's eighty-three,' I say. 'He showed me his ID. It was sepia. And the date-of-birth part just said "yore".'

'Stop it. He's four years older, five tops.' There is a pause. My sister smiles. 'He's . . . mysterious. Intriguing.'

I snort. Lon is as mysterious as a man who offers to show you the puppies he has in the back of his beat-up van. Everything cool about him is suspicious. Leather jackets, old paperback books by important men. Cigarettes that smell like long-dead grandfathers. All things that can be bought. A bit considered. I like my crushes artless. And with pens.

'He's kind of desperate,' I say. 'You could have that anytime you wanted, then send it back like a bad sandwich.'

'Ah now,' she says, but I can see her smiling. It's nice to be desired. Or so I've heard.

We go downstairs for dinner. We are pretending that we are fitting in more than we are. It is very easy. Mam and Brian are all about each other. Cooking together. Going for mountain walks. Watching television curled like kittens on the sofa. It is extremely unimpressive and I hope it will eventually stop.

I'm happy for them though. It's weird to think of this being a house for only Brian. All the space; you'd get lost in your thoughts. So isolated. I don't think that it would be good for me. If I were him. Which clearly I am not.

And he is fine. Enjoying his roast potatoes, and the lamb, drizzled with a glaze they made from scratch. His voice is high for a man's, and quiet. But when he speaks my mother listens, her face intent. She's made a new best friend. And it is lovely. But it used to be the three of us, and now it feels like we are two and two. On different teams.

I bite into the lamb. It's tender. I can almost taste the jumping little muscles. I love meat. But I know where it came from. Me and the lamb, we're made of the same stuff. I clean my plate.

Raven tongue on raw meat. Dew on grass.

Mam wipes a little sauce from Brian's chin.

'We're thrilled you girls are getting on so well,' she tells us. 'We're proud of you.'

'We are,' he says. He smiles. I grin right back. I mean, it's

49

weird, the new dynamic. But he's good for her, even if he's a little nondescript. You'd meet him and you mightn't remember exactly what he looked like, until you'd met him once more. Maybe twice. It's nice to have another boring person in the family. They'd only been going out six months when he proposed. He asked us first, all awkward in the kitchen. 'I'd never want to take your father's place,' he said, as we eyed the massive diamond he'd picked out, 'but I love Sheila, and I want us to be family. In a way you're comfortable with.'

It was probably the most we'd ever heard him say at once. We hugged him and gave him our blessing. He does things by the book. He gets it right. Mam needs that in her life. Romantic drama is kind of better when you're our age. I can see how Brian would be appealing to my mam. I think she feels that we are safe with him. His house is the most interesting thing about him.

'If I were to get with Lon . . .' Catlin says, as we clear up the dishes.

I make a face at her.

'What?' she asks. 'He's hot. He is objectively hot. And I'm not saying I'll fall in love with him or anything. But, like, it's something to do. Just as, like, an experiment. To see if having a boyfriend would make things easier.'

'It wouldn't make things easier for me,' I point out.

'It might,' she says. 'You wouldn't have to talk to Lon as much. Because I would be kissing him. On the face.'

'On the *stupid* face,' I tell her.

'Yes,' she says. 'The stupid, handsome face.'

'Don't leave me alone though, here. With all the people?' I say. It comes out whinier than I intended.

'I won't,' she says. 'You know I have your back.'

It's true. She always does.

Later, in bed, I count leaves and faces on the hard, dark wood, trying to sleep. It takes a while.

A woman's face – asleep or maybe dead.

A man with a very small mouth.

Ivy choking round, through hair and hollows.

I think of Brian and Lon. And our dad, Tom. I think about this book we had at home. I think it had been Dad's. It was full of lore and superstition. One of the things that stuck with me was about how certain people believed that getting remarried was a sin, once you'd been widowed. Because, in the afterlife, both husbands would be there, and they'd both want you. They described a woman screaming, sawn in half by demons. Caught between two worlds inside a hell.

I venture to the window and open it a crack. There's an old nest in the corner of it. Feathers woven soft through twigs and dirt. I put my hand on it. It feels solid. The breeze is cold, although the floor is warm. Almost too warm. It doesn't feel like winter in this house. The lavender plant I brought with me sits on my desk. I feel for it in the murky dark.

Sometimes it dies in winter. I keep it in a clay pot and only water it a very little.

So far, so good.

It likes the warmth, this soothing little life.

I break a piece off and murmur, 'Thank you.'

Fall asleep while focused on the scent.

51

7

Bird Cherry/Hackberry

(fruit astringent, bark for plague)

Last night, Catlin woke up with a fever. I heard her coughing, groaning through the walls. She is a terrible patient. Even a mild chill turns her into a Victorian heroine, wasting away in bed while her husband is off fighting in the war. Only with more demands for toast and sympathy. The walk up the driveway on my own was OK. I saw Bob eating what was either a dead cat or a stray binbag. I am becoming increasingly suspicious of the birds here.

I narrow my eyes at a scrawny robin watching from the wall, as Layla and I wait. Our breath misting through the air so white it's almost solid.

'Corpse of the day,' she says, and gestures down. I see another robin, lying there. There is a deep wound in the centre of his fat red breast. His claws in the air are twisted like the little branch that's left when you have eaten all the grapes. I trace the downy underside of his wings with my finger. It's delicate as lace. A little frosty. A thing that small would not be hard to kill.

'When we were younger, Mam used to tell us he got the red chest from bringing water down to souls in hell,' I say.

'That's dark,' Layla says. 'Your mam sounds metal. No wonder Brian married her.' I look at her, trying to gauge whether or not she's joking. With her voice, sarcasm can be hard to detect. It always seems to be there. Lurking like a hidden predator.

'Brian is the least metal person I know, Layla. He wears socks and sandals,' I point out.

'Appearances can be deceiving,' she says, narrowing her eyes at the robin, like a cat about to pounce. 'Our mam used tell us that they were spies for Santa.'

'We got that too,' I say. 'Little feathered narcs.'

'Maybe that's why the other lad killed him,' Layla says, her aristocratic face serious. 'Because he was a grass.'

'That tiny little brain knew far too much,' I say. 'Do you really think the other robin, like, murdered him?'

'It's what they do,' she says. 'They're vicious things, birds.' She sighs. I notice something pulsing underneath the robin's feathers. I kick it with my toe. One lonely maggot dribbles out. A fat, white, hungry thing.

'Nature is cruel,' I say to Layla. 'Cruel and disgusting.'

'As a teenage girl, I endorse that statement,' she says back, rubbing her stomach ruefully. 'And bleurgh.'

We move away. Closer to the clear grey road. I watch our breath cloud misty. No matter how early or late we are for the bus, we always end up waiting. It is like it's playing hard to get.

'What's wrong with Catlin?' Layla asks me. I can tell from her tone she's just being polite. It's weird that little deaths are easier to speak about than families here. I shrug my shoulders.

'Temperature and things.' I'm really boring. I can feel how boring I am welling up in me, waterlogging my brain . . . I'm one question away from comparing things to badgers, I can feel it.

'So, you're a triplet?' I ask. 'Sorry if that's a really boring thing to say. I hate when people say it to us.'

'No, it's OK.' Layla smiles, her eyes are really brown, like almost black. 'Actually, I'm a quad. It's just that Fiachra ate our brother in the womb.'

'Wait – what?' I look at her. I can't tell if she's joking.

'I'm joking,' she says. Which helps a bit. And then there is a pause. 'Well, kind of joking. Actually, there's no knowing which of us ate Aodh. He would have been called Aodh. If he'd lived.' She swallows.

'Fair enough.' We stand together quietly for a while, the cold wind biting through our hats and scarves. I see a bright red dot move across a mountain. A drip of blood. It could be Mamó's car. It's not my business. There are more important things than creepy old women trying to be friends with me or something. I shake my head.

'It's freezing,' I say.

'Yup. The wind is horrible.'

The bus arrives, like a beautiful metal angel.

Layla smiles at me and she says, 'Bye,' before she sits with Charley. Are we friends now? Is that what that was?

We weave around, gathering people from different places. I think of Catlin, cosy in her bed and I feel jealous. She was good last night. She's always minded me. Even when we were little. She includes me, and whatever I'm worried about, in her nightly prayers. Which is a very granny thing to do. I don't believe in Mary, God and Jesus, but it's nice to be a priority. It's nice that I am loved like that. Religiously. And it seems to work a bit as well. Like, when Catlin asks for things, they tend to happen. She cares an awful lot about her friends; they take up space inside her heart. I want friends too, but moving here has taken something out of me. I need to calm myself. I need to gather. I wonder if I can leave it for a week this time. I normally last about three days before I give in. I work at that. The trying not to do it.

We're halfway up the mountain when the bus stops. Past the old quarry. Centuries ago, there was gold and silver in these mountains, Brian told us. Over time, humans came along to leach it out. Maybe that's why the hills have such a pallor, though they're massive. They stretch towards the sun, all sickly stark.

'Hello.' A girl, her smile brighter than it should be on Tuesday morning riding in a death-coach, sits down beside me. Her eyes are bright and her hair shines with drops of what looks like rain. It isn't raining though. So cold and dry the earth looks like its thirsty.

I realise I'm staring. Say hello. Her smile broadens. It looks a little like a crescent moon. Familiar-strange.

'I am Oona Noone.' Her voice is warm. So warm.

I look at her.

'You are new here? I am new as well. I come from France.' She's still smiling. Her voice is low and clear, with a smoothness to it. A voice that could convince you to do anything. I work the muscles in my face a bit. I show my teeth. It'll have to do. How did she know I was new? Do I look new? And what does new look like? I look down at my shoes. They're nicely scuffed.

Oona from France has wide, chocolatey eyes and soft-looking brown skin. She's even smaller than we are, and we're barely five foot tall. Oona looks up at me through her lashes when she speaks. She has thick, wavy hair. She's curvy – but her neck is slender, snappable. Something about her makes me feel protective. I want to mind her, put secret jars of stuff under her bed. To tell her to turn back. This place is harsh. Full of little corpses. Empty nests.

Oona tells me about France, about the move and how she finds Ballyfrann. She likes the landscape. They have a freshwater pond behind their house; her father fishes in it and she swims. The water's warm compared to the wind apparently. I raise an eyebrow at her, from inside two jumpers and a duffel coat. Warmer than the wind does not mean warm.

'It is,' she tells me, putting a hand on the crook of my arm. 'You'll have to try it sometime.'

'That sounds cool,' I say, and almost mean it. Oona is convincing. She's so friendly. She doesn't belong here in this school full of Ballyfrann sullenness and rejection. I don't want her to bat her eyelashes at cold shoulders. Somehow, Oona's presence makes me more confident about things. I have a small, perfectly formed, French girl to support now. I am going to be sociable. I am going to say, 'Hi!' to people and follow it up with other things as well.

I will not mention badgers. Even once.

'Oona isn't a French name,' I say, presumably like many other idiots before me.

'I am half-Irish,' she says. 'My mother's French; my father,

56

he's from here.' She pronounces father 'fazzer', like a cartoon French lady. It shouldn't be as adorable as it is. I wonder if she has a spare pen.

'We came here to have more space. To be free. In France it can be . . . difficult.' I don't know what she means. Is she an olden-days Huguenot? Or, like, a naturist? She could just mean racism, I realise. I don't know what it's like to be brown in France. Or in Ireland either, for that matter.

'Difficult how?' I ask. Her hand is still on my arm. It's soft and warm. A lovely kind of heavy. I look at it. On me. I swallow down.

She stares at me for a moment, and then says something about people not understanding Irish culture, and her mother being an artist and needing to be somewhere wild, with landscape. Something about the way she phrases things niggles. It feels less real than what she said before. In her almost perfect second language. It's not the words themselves, but something underneath them. A sort of effort.

Chocolate eyes on mine. There are little flecks of blue inside them.

She says 'artiste', not artist, for her mother.

She smiles at me.

I want to be her friend.

'We just moved here as well,' I tell her. 'Mam married Brian, who's from here, like your dad.'

'I have heard of Brian,' she says. Of course she has. Because he is apparently Ballyfrann-famous and possibly metal. 'You live in the . . .'

'Castle,' I finish her sentence awkwardly. There is no way

to tell someone you live in a castle without seeming like an entitled brat. I wish that I could run away and hide somewhere with my salt boxes and pride remnants. But there's nowhere to run to. Even my enormous castle is a bus ride away. I wish I also had a private jet. Or a Higgins to call in case of emergency.

It's almost a relief when classes start. But also not. Because there are so few of us, so there's pressure to interact more. Answer questions. If people talk or pass notes, everyone notices. The Ballyfrann kids are friendlier to Oona than they were to me and Catlin, and I can see why. She's basically a human ray of sunshine. At lunch, they include her almost right away. What is the secret? Maybe being lovely, and not trying. They're nicer to me than they were last week as well. Fiachra even compliments me on a well-made sandwich, bless his greedy heart. I give him half. He eats it in two bites. I think about the fourth quad, and shudder.

I wish Catlin were here. I wish I had an oak leaf or some rowan berries in my pocket. I need to stop all that. It isn't real. I can't let what I am when I'm all by myself bleed into school. It's hard enough. I need to do my best. I need to try.

Maybe if Oona likes me, and my sandwiches are on point, I could weasel my way in here. I listen to them talk about people in the village, on TV. About the youth club. They're all in this youth club and they're super into it in a very real way. They almost ordered hoodies, but Lon, who apparently facilitates the youth club, said no. Lon detests hoodies, and I am becoming increasingly convinced he is the worst. He is head of a one-man campaign to change the youth club's name from 'The Youth Club' to 'The Hellfire Club'.

'Makes sense,' I tell them, 'seeing as he isn't really a youth. What age is he anyway?'

'I'm not sure,' Fiachra says. 'Old enough to boss people around. Maybe, like, twenty?'

'Twenty seems fair,' says Layla, popping a toffee into her mouth. 'Like, any older and it would be seriously creepy for him to be in youth club.'

'Because ye are, like, youths.'

Fiachra snorts, and Charley nods, as though I have said something incredibly wise. I smile at them.

Waiting for the bus, Lon approaches, gangly legs and neck. He's really tall. Even for normal-sized people. He smiles at me. 'How ya, Maddy?'

'Hi, Lon.'

'Tell your sister I'm sorry she's not feeling the best. Could you give her this for me?' He hands me an envelope. He looks at me like I am knock-off her. Inexpensive. Just a little . . . less. He pauses, leaning on the bus stop with one leg making a triangle on the pole, like a rockabilly flamingo. His arms akimbo. Lon likes to take up space. I blink at him. He's saying things to Charley now, about the club. His hair is something else. I bet that takes him time. Time and product.

'. . . the old Hellfire Clubs of the eighteenth century . . .'

His cheekbones are threatening to burst out from his skin. Lon is exactly the kind of boy who would secretly contour his own face for maximum rock-god impact. And lie about it. He's spindling himself towards the gang of schoolkids, gesticulating like he's holding court. He told Oona he liked her name, and grinned like he deserved a gold star for being kind. His grin's

59

the same way that it is with Catlin. If she weren't beautiful, he wouldn't care.

'. . . in homage to their reckless, rebel souls . . .'

His voice is a low, quiet purr of a thing. Making fun of me, all latent sleaze. He releases a wisp of cigarette smoke, and I can't help but inhale it and stifle a cough.

'Lon loves history,' Eddie tells me. His voice is unobjectionable. The sort of voice you could take anywhere. When it's not wobbling, it's actually quite manly. He would make a good Galway boyfriend for Catlin, I think. Solid. Dependable.

Oona sees through Lon a little bit as well, I suspect. She looks at him as though he were an interesting sculpture. Of a prick.

'I too like history,' she says, smiling. He smiles back at her. Not getting that she hates him. That we both hate him. I smile at Oona, then I smile at Lon. Everyone's smiling, but only some of us know why.

'I like history as well.' This is not my finest conversational offering, but I run with it. 'Especially the famine times. They're fascinating. I kind of like reading about the struggles of the normal, underprivileged people. Like we would have been back in the day. Not aristocrats,' I finish.

Oona smiles at me and I smile back. Look at me, saying things and getting smiled at like a proper human being.

'Don't you live in a castle though?' asks Cathal.

He has me there, the sibling-eating bastard.

'We only just moved in,' I offer lamely.

'Madeline and Catalina are the stepchildren of a local man called Brian,' Lon explains, in case anyone would think I was a person in my own right.

'Her name is Catlin, Lon. But, yeah. We are.' I'm trying to make an effort, but I can feel the surly building under my skin, honing my usual sense of danger into something more immediate. My fingers twitch. I want to run away. Or slap him. Maybe both.

'Brian's great,' Lon tells me. 'Very involved in the local community.' He says it like he's complimenting me. On my breasts. At a bus stop. Outside a prison.

'Brian is great,' says Charley. 'He offered to pay for our hoodies and everything.'

'Would you ever shut up about them hoodies?' snaps Lon.

'Don't tell my sister what to do,' says Eddie, his voice an octave lower, thrumming. Very definite. I remember what Brian said at the wedding about the Collinses. And clearly so does Lon, who shuts right up.

'He gave us the money anyway,' says Fiachra. 'We spent it all on beer and trampolines.'

'Nice,' I tell him, and he nods at me. It does sound nice. I wonder how many of them ended up in A & E that summer.

'Brian is cool,' says Layla quietly. 'He lets people be who they are.'

I have never had a conversation this long about the merits of any adult with more than one person at a time. If I didn't know Brian, I would be decidedly creeped out by him now.

'He does,' I say. 'Mam loves him, like. They're happy.'

Oona sits with me on the bus home. We chat a bit (not about Brian, thank God) but mostly kind of lull together. Looking out the windows. When I'm with a stranger, I normally feel like I should be saying things. Like if I don't, they'll find out what I'm like and then dismiss me. But this feels grand. Easier. Like I have made a friend. And one is enough for the time being.

I think of Oona's expression when our eyes met. There was something there. A little pool of warmth. Something rare.

I walk with Layla up the driveway, smiling. I look for the robin, but something must have taken it away. There is no trace. Another day. Another body lost.

The mountains loom.

8

Bay Leaf

(cancer, skin and hair)

The castle is grave quiet, statue still. I call for Catlin or Mam, but no one answers. It's a little bit of a relief. Reporting back about the day at school is exhausting. I take off my shoes so they don't leave wet footprints on the flagstones and traipse to the kitchen, to make a cup of tea and start my homework. I need to wrap my head around some stuff – our maths teacher is of the 'it makes sense to me so it will clearly make sense to you' variety, and I don't want to end up sobbing into my maths paper. Catlin says I shouldn't worry about college till final year, but Catlin would say that. The only medicine she wants to practise is drinking too much cough syrup 'to see what will happen'. (She threw up sugar-vomit is what happened.)

Too much trigonometry later, I raise my head. Mamó is at the kitchen table, drinking from a brown ceramic mug filled with what looks like dishwater and twigs.

I cannot tell how long she has been there, watching me work.

Annoying me silently. Like a spy. Her face is disinterested and her skin remarkably smooth for a woman who is, in Catlin's words, 'as old as balls'.

I rise and begin putting my things back in my schoolbag.

'You'll have a cup of tea with me,' she states. It is in no way an invitation. I incline my head and sit opposite her. She busies herself with mugs and spoons and teabags. She knows where everything is.

The urge to rearrange things just to mess with her is strong. I swallow down. I am calm. I am mature. I am impermeable.

Like granite.

'Any visitors today?' I ask. My voice is smug. I cannot help myself. I'm wasting all my energy not raising an eyebrow.

'A few clients, yes.' She tilts her head. The way owls do. Her eyes are very large and very bright. Her hair is grey. Her face is buttered leather, only paler. Her sleeves rolled up. She has a farmer tan.

'And what did you do to them?' My voice comes out meaner than I intend. Something about her makes me want to kick things.

'Helped them, mostly. Except for this one woman, who wanted me to –' Mamó swallows – '. . . *cleanse* her aura, with the help of some healing crystals she had purchased on the Internet. And so it fell to me, to explain to her, the things I will and things I will not do.'

Her face is implacable.

I look at her.

And Mamó looks at me.

'What won't you do?' I ask.

'I don't engage with things that are not useful,' she tells me, her bright eyes taking in my face. I feel as if she is counting every pore.

'I thought you'd be into all that New Age stuff,' I offer.

'People often assume as much, until they know me.' She takes a long sip of the brew. It's tea but thicker, blacker. More treacly.

'Brian tells us you're a homeopath.'

'Does he now? I'm something of a herbalist. My mother handed down her skills to me, from a young age. And if you have a skill, and stay in one place long enough, people come to you. Sometimes I will help them. Sometimes not.'

I look at the cup in front of me, thick with milk. She didn't ask me how I took my tea. And when she plonked it down I didn't thank her.

'Catlin has some crystals,' I tell her. Thinking of the little quartzes, polished lapis, unakite and moonstone she litters through the Marys in her room. Only for the look of them though, really.

'Catlin would,' Mamó says. 'But you've a bit more sense.'

I take another sip and tell her that I hate homeopathy.

'Don't waste your energy,' she tells me, 'hating useless things.'

'But it kills people,' I start to tell her. 'I read that –'

'Life kills people, Madeline,' she tells me. 'Sometimes people help their life along though. It can be . . . frustrating.'

'I want to be a doctor when I'm older,' I tell her, and she nods.

'You're not afraid of work, so. That makes sense. I've seen you with the plants. You like to heal things.' She pauses. 'That little tree of yours needs far more water though. Don't be afraid to drench it. It won't hurt.'

'They all have different needs, the different plants. I mean, it makes sense. But it's hard to know.' I shrug. 'I do my best. And thank you.'

She moves her head. It isn't quite a nod. Her hair is in a bun at the back of her head, not like the kind that ballet dancers have, lower but somehow neater. She wouldn't look out of place with a headscarf. Her blouse is buttoned up to the very top. Her fingernails are several different colours, not painted, like with varnish. Maybe stained from leaf and clay and root.

'What do you make of the village?' she asks.

'It's OK, I suppose,' I tell her.

She says, 'Hmmm,' in a way that makes me feel like I should say more things. Like at a job interview where they ask you your strengths and you say, 'I work hard,' and then they look at you and you get stressed and offer, '. . . like a badger?' and you know you aren't going to get the job so you look at your feet until they speak again.

I have only done, like, three job interviews, for summer jobs, but I'm fairly confident that they went very badly.

I could tell.

'There aren't very many people our age. Which is hard on Catlin. She always has a lot of friends and things.'

'And you?'

'That doesn't bother me,' I say, and realise it's true. 'I was nervous going to school, but it's OK. I kind of like my space.'

She makes a noise and then stands up. Her cup is empty. Work to do. I feel like I should shake her hand as she leaves.

Did I get the job, Mamó? I wonder.

66

I still don't like her, but now the feeling's mixed with something else.

I look down at my small clean hands and wonder what the future's going to bring. Will Catlin make all the friends and leave me awkwardly chatting to old women? Is that what life will become?

The thick tea is pooling in my stomach like a hot meal. I wash the cups and look out the window, at the gardens. Mamó is walking past a hawthorn tree. Through the dim, I see the flicker of a wing, the flash of an eye. Her snatching hand towards a branch. Was that a bird? She stuffs it in her pocket. I can't be sure. She moved so quickly, slinking through the dark. A predator. A weasel. I scrub the brown stains from the white ceramic. I rest the cups upon the draining board. Stare out the window till it's too dark to see anything at all.

When I mount the wooden staircase, Catlin is in her bed, sipping from a very familiar-looking brown ceramic mug.

'What is that?' I ask, pointing at it like it has offended me. Which, in fairness, it has.

'I don't know. Mamó gave it to me. Here, smell it.' She thrusts it out. I hold it up to my face, inhale the scent. It smells a little like sage and a little like seawater, but something about it feels right. Like it's the opposite of poison.

'Weird,' I say. 'And you just took it? Is it at least working?'

'I don't know . . . I still feel rotten,' she moans. 'My stomach and my head.'

'You poor thing,' I murmur, feeling a bit smug that Mamó's stupid tea hasn't helped much.

'Stop smirking at me, Maddy. She basically thrust it into

my hand like a grenade and stared at me till I started drinking. Then grunted and left. I'm too sick to be dealing with rude strangers.'

'I'm not smirking. She gave me tea as well. And plant advice.'

'I've been sick one day and you've made a new best friend.' Catlin's mock-offended.

'She's not my friend,' I say. 'I get the feeling she is up to something.'

'You think everyone is up to something.'

'They usually are. *You're* always up to something.'

'Not today,' she says, and leans back on the pillow with a sigh. 'I'm too tired and disgusting. This stupid place will be the *death* of me.'

'You're roasting hot,' I say, pressing my hand to her forehead. 'Do you want me to get Mam?'

'No,' she says. 'I just want you. Will you sleep here tonight?'

'Of course,' I say. 'Try hard to be contagious. I'd like a day off school.'

'You don't want this,' she tells me. 'It's just . . . uurgh.' Her eyes close and she curls in on herself.

'But you know what isn't uurgh?' I ask, like a salesman from the 1950s, with a bright smile and raised eyebrows.

'Stop,' says Catlin. 'I'm not in the mood.'

'Not in the mood . . . for a love letter from Lon?' I ask, waving the envelope in front of her face like a paper fan on a hot day.

'What?' She sits up straight. 'Give me that.'

Her face intent, she reads it twice. I try to look over her shoulder, but she hides it.

'What did he say?' I ask.

'Private sexy things.' She waggles her eyebrows.

'He did not.'

'Of course not. He's not a creep.'

I let that comment slide, and she shows me the letter. It's more of a note, really.

Catalina –
I missed your beautiful face today. Return to me soon.
– L

'Wonderful how he made you being sick all about him,' I tell her.

'Maddy, stop. It's lovely.' She smiles, and gives the note a little kiss. I leave her there, rereading the note.

I brush my teeth, cleanse my face and lay out tights and knickers for the morning, and then return to clamber in beside her.

'Don't billow me,' she grumps. She's hot as stoves.

I tell her about school, and tea with Mamó, but she mainly wants to ask me about Lon. How he looked, and what he said exactly. I try to be helpful, but it's hard because he's so boring and terrible. Catalina. Who changes someone's name to please themselves? It's not a nickname even. When she drifts off, I lie there for ages, trying to get comfortable and failing. There's a feeling of definite un-safety. Not exactly danger. Just un-safety. Something's here, clicking through the pipes. It's lurking in my temples, in my fingers. I can feel my shoulders start to tense, my joints engage. I'm used to this, I know just what it means. Like stomach cramps the day before my period. I'm

69

going to need to gather something soon. I hate this feeling and I hate myself.

Mam taking me aside before we left, to go through all the remnants in my room.

'You understand that this isn't normal behaviour, Madeline.'

I nodded.

And I did. I do.

I curl into a little ball and close my eyes and dig my nails into the soft pad below my thumbs and count and count until my breaths ease. Catlin moans and rolls towards me, waking up. I can sense the sick off her. Her hands are clammy, sweating. She rubs my back and tells me things, small gossips about people we both know, imaginary clothes she'd like to wear. The unimportant, fascinating things cover up my worry like a snowdrift. She keeps it up until I fall asleep.

I dream of forests where teeth litter the ground like fallen leaves. When I reach to touch them, the texture is all wrong. They melt against my skin. Mamó is there.

The world is big and soft. And very cruel.

9

Wormwood

(lulling spasms)

This morning, before school, I have a bit of a rant at Mam about Mamó.

'Is she, like, just allowed to be in our kitchen all the time? She has her own house and things. It's weird.' I jam a croissant into my mouth. It is fresh, still warm. 'Wait, did you bake this?'

'No,' she says. 'There's a French family after moving up the mountain, apparently. Brian went to say hello, and came home with these. The father bakes. He's Irish, but he learned.'

'That must be Oona's dad,' I say, without thinking.

'Who's Oona?'

'Just this new girl,' I say. 'She seems nice.'

'Look at you,' Mam says. 'Making friends.'

'One twin falls, the other rises,' I say, pouring coffee into a KeepCup for the bus.

'Your poor sister,' she says. 'Struck down with the Black Death the moment she had to do something hard.'

'That's so mean,' I say. 'She's really sick.'

'I know,' Mam says. 'She's also really milking it. She sent me this yesterday.' She takes out her phone, shows me the screen.

I think I could eat something. If you made me toast this exact shade.

And then there is a picture.

'Jesus Christ.' My sister is a monster.

'I didn't get it right the first time,' Mam tells me, 'so she found the strength to get up from her sickbed and return her order to the kitchen.'

I look at her and open my mouth like a surprised Internet cat.

'I know,' she says, 'that we live in a castle now, but that does not mean she gets to be a princess.'

'I think Catlin was always a princess,' I tell Mam. 'I'll miss my bus.'

'I'll have a word with Brian,' Mam tells me on my way out the door. 'About yer wan.'

I'm not sure if she means Mamó or Catlin.

The day passes kind of boringly. I eat with the Ballyfrann kids, and mainly listen to them sharing in-jokes. Oona looks at me a few times with new-girl solidarity. I awkwardly try to weave a French 'thank you for croissants' into the conversation, but end up saying something like, *I ate your daddy's delicious present*, and she doesn't understand what I mean because he didn't tell her he gave Brian croissants and I want the floor to swallow me up. I should have let Catlin breathe on me more, I think. No health is worth this shame.

But she sits beside me on the bus, so maybe she got that I didn't mean to be a creep. Or maybe she likes creeps. We chat easily, and it's kind of amazing to not be racking my brains for the next question to ask, the next thing to say. I just listen, and speak. Like a normal human being making a friend. Oona is a gift, and I am grateful. I feel her warmth filling me up, making me feel valid on my own. I hope that she feels the same way too. She might. When she gets out, she waves goodbye at me before she turns and walks towards her house. It means the world.

At our stop, Brian is waiting for me, with a mug of tea. He has one for Layla too. She thanks him like it was made of gold, before heading away home.

'I thought I'd walk you to the door,' Brian says.

I tell him thanks.

There is an awkward pause and I take a sip of the tea. It's perfect. Warm and strong with the right amount of milk. No need to send Brian a series of images depicting my order, I think.

Brian smiles. 'Your mother said you were wondering about Mamó, and I thought it best to walk and talk together. You never know when she's around the corner. Like a cat.'

I smile at him. 'She does show up everywhere.'

'She always has. But the castle is her home too, as the fella says. She's been through a lot.'

'How are you related?'

'She's a distant cousin of my father's. She left the village when she was a young woman, but then she lost all belonging to her and came back. We gave her a place to live, because she's family.'

'That's sad,' I say, and it is. Poor Mamó.

'It is,' Brian agrees. 'She has done a lot for people in the

73

village, over the years. And she was very good to me when my father died. I had a difficult few years.' He swallows, and I see his Adam's apple bob up and down. A half a smile.

'There was another reason I wanted to walk and talk. Sometimes, when there's other things to focus on, it becomes easier to share hard truths.'

I reach a hand out, rub his elbow awkwardly. Now would be a good time for a hug, but I think both of us would also hate that.

'My father was, what you would call, domineering, I suppose. I've been very isolated for a lot of my life, Madeline,' he tells me. 'And it's a blessing to have met Sheila, and yourselves as well. But older people are set in their ways. They fear change. And between me getting married and fewer people in the village coming to see her, Mamó feels . . . well, it's very hard to know how that woman feels. But I want us to be kind to her. And to each other.'

'Yeah,' I say, nodding slowly.

'You're a compassionate young woman, Madeline,' Brian says, 'but I don't want you to feel uncomfortable in your own home. So, if anything . . . unusual were to happen with Mamó, if she were to make you feel uneasy in any way, I would hope that you would come to me, and tell me.'

Brian's accent is strange, a little sing-songy. We thought it would be the way everyone in the village spoke, but they don't. It's only him.

I think about Mamó, about losing everything. My skin feels too warm underneath my coat. I want to go inside, to sit in the kitchen and drink tea. Brian is telling me things I need to know, but my head is swimming a little or something.

74

I feel his hand on my arm.

'You look flushed, Madeline. Are you all right?'

'I feel . . .'

'You must be coming down with whatever Catlin has. And there's me, walking you around in the cold. Apologies.'

'No, Brian, it's OK. I'm glad we talked.'

He grins at me. 'Me too. And if I'm ever getting ahead of myself with this stepdad business, let me know. I'm new to it. I'm learning.'

'You're doing fine.' I hold up my tea. 'Gold star.'

'Thank you, Madeline.'

I think of the lonely child Brian was, and the lost woman returning to the village she grew up in. I finger the little packet of salt I keep in my pocket. We all need comfort. Things to keep us safe. The more you get to know people, the more broken it seems we all are. Is that what growing up is? The world hurting you over and over and over again.

Brian goes up to his office to finish some paperwork. I sit at the kitchen table. Mam is starting dinner, sliding the knife across bright red bell peppers until they're thin. She puts them in a bowl and dices onions.

'Do you have homework to do, or are you going to help me?' she asks.

I tell her yes to both. It feels more normal than I've felt today.

At dinner, I shake a little salt into my hand. Look at it. My finger still feels warm. I could be coming down with something maybe – my fever feeling hasn't gone away. My heartbeat slows as I hold the white grains in my fist.

Mam takes my hand. 'Put that in the bin, love. There's no need.'

I do what she tells me, feeling like a freak. Mamó is in the garden, burying something. The body of one of her many enemies, I suppose. I think of what Brian said. I should be kinder.

Mamó finishes what it was that she was doing, and strides away. Her back is very straight and very proud. I feel the absence of the salt in my hand, and go back to the table.

I barely taste the dinner going down.

10

Aspen

(bedding, heat)

Salt. I wake up in a dark room needing salt. The posts of my bed pierce the night like the trunks of skinny trees. I cannot see the branches. Empty nest outside my window waits. I need to look at it. I need to touch it. The shock of the warm floor under my bare feet. Underfloor heating, I tell myself, feeling the faint growls beneath the surface. It's warm enough to feel as if it's alive.

I crack the window open and reach my hand out, feel for the small nest. Inside it is a small, fat egg. Round as a raindrop, cold as a stone. It is heavy to the touch. It's winter. The mountain wind bites into my skin. I hold the egg in my hand. Pull it to me, close the window. The night can stay outside.

I look at it. It's creamy-coloured, splashed with reddish brown. Smeared old bloodstains. I close my eyes. The wind whips against the window. How lonely to be dead here. All alone. You are a person, then you're just a body. Evidence.

Something to be scooped up and examined. The egg is small inside my palm. I reach my index finger out to touch it.

And it crumbles into dust, like the powdery wings of a childhood butterfly. Before I knew the things you shouldn't touch. Little particles, small and soft as ash, litter the floor. No clue to what it once was. Life to death.

The need for salt begins to heighten.

I can normally hold it in until I wake up in the morning, but there can be an urgency as well. It's a little like needing the toilet with your whole being. Ignoring it is not always an option. And there's a danger there that's very real. Or feels that way to me . . . if I need the thing and cannot get it. Sometimes bad things happen. Little ones or big. I cut my finger with a sharp knife, peeling vegetables. Lose my footing and fall down a stairs. Or Catlin does. Or Mam. Coincidence, is what I tell myself. Until the feeling wells in me again, reminding me what I already know on some deep level.

I want to be a doctor, for God's sake. It makes no sense. The logical part of my brain knows that. But there's another part. A reptile part, something old and hard and deep inside me. I shake it off. Salt will make me feel much better now. Will soothe me back to sleep.

I throw a towelling dressing gown on and pad downstairs, and downstairs again, and down another stairs and through the kitchen. When our house was left behind, gutted of the things that made it ours, it looked too big. This castle's layered with stuff, ours and other people's, and it's still so empty, still so full of space. Feelings aren't facts, I tell myself. I'm safe here. The egg was just an egg. An empty egg inside an empty nest outside my window. The small ghost of a bird that might have been. Beady eye and flap of feather dark. I close my eyes. I open them again. I walk along.

It probably would be better if there were fewer things with eyes here. Portraits and animal trophies and statues of people twisting up like they're in agony but smiling with it. I think of Nora Ginn, who liked to dance. Her face was like a person that you'd know. Brown hair, blue eyes and freckles. Something ate that girl and spat her out. My fingers brush an elbow as I pass. It's cool and smooth. Marble starts as limestone, then it changes. We steal it from the earth and carve it into waxy human shapes.

The moon a slice of something through the window. I keep on moving, weaving through the halls. It takes a while, particularly because I'm being stealthy. Mam would kill me if she knew what I was at. She hates this part of me that isn't normal. But I can't help the way I am. I can't. I'm almost there. The knowledge calms me down.

Brian's kitchen is adjacent to the herb garden, which is probably why Mamó was able to ferret her way in so stealthily. Like so much of the castle, it's a weird hybrid of things that Brian's dad liked. If a Victorian stately home's kitchen had a baby with the kitchen in a medieval convent, and that baby were also a kitchen, then it would be exactly how our kitchen is. A pot-bellied stove, a wide fireplace, a massive oaken table. Flagstones and a cauldron. Pots of herbs on the windowsills and burnished copper saucepans hanging up.

I quietly turn the handle of the larder. It creaks a little as it opens wide.

Dried haunches of meat and strands of garlic trailing from the ceiling. Smooth white tiles and rows of wooden shelves with little pots. There's so much food here. Was it always like this? Who did Brian even have to feed before we got here? There are six kinds of jam.

'That's too much jam,' I mutter as I poke around for salt. I find it, next to pepper. Brian's as organised as Mam, I think. No wonder they got married.

There are several boxes, cardboard ones, red and white and blue, with little metal spouts that slot out of the side for pouring. I take one down and hold it in my hand. Feel the weight of it. The smooth sides and the sharp corners. The feeling doesn't go. I take a second. And a third. I want all of the salt. Stacks of it. Enough to satisfy my stupid impulse and then some more and then some more again.

Something smooths inside me as I hold the three boxes in my hands. One for me and two for Mam and Catlin. And not too big a gap left on the shelf. I put them in the centre of the table. I start the kettle boiling for some tea. Tear mint and sage from small ceramic pots and crush them with a spoon into a mug. My body hums with nervous energy. Too keyed up for caffeinated things. When I get collecty, I feel like all of me's about to shiver, twitch with it or something. There's energy inside, and not the kind you can exercise away. It's like your stomach just before a fight. That kind of weight.

Science. Science. Nothing's going to get me.

The glass looks black, the brightness in the kitchen cancels out the night-time. Something moves beyond the windowpane. I turn the light off, look outside, for ages. It could have been a person or a fox. A ghost that I imagined. The stars are bright. The moon's a little sliver. Everything in me is stretching taut. The kettle clicks and I turn the light back on. The garden fades away into a smudge.

I draw the blinds, pour the boiling water on the leaves and blow on it to cool, which never works. My brain is chanting: 'Salt, salt, salt, salt, salt.'

I blow again.

Which is more important – sleep before school or not being a crazy person?

The second is probably not an option though. A spoon of solid honey in the tea. I crush the leaves some more and stir them round.

Clockwise?

Counter-clockwise.

Counter-clockwise, thrice or seven times.

Salt in hand, I pad my way upstairs. Across the floor and reaching under the bed in Catlin's room. I slide the salt in. And then I go across the wing to Mam. The corridors are dark, the cornicing is twisted. I feel the hum of spiders spinning webs. Everything is sharper, more in focus.

I'm not sure if it's panic or relief.

Mam is sleeping soundly, Brian beside her. It feels like more of an intrusion now. That she is not alone. That he is here. The blanket's half off Brian's torso, and in the moonlight it looks as if something's written on his body. He snuffles, and he snuggles into Mam. I crouch down low and shove the salt beneath the bed.

When I rise, things look like they're supposed to. A trick of

81

the light. I make my way down the corridor, feeling exhaustion leach the tension from me. I could sleep for a week. I have three hours, and that will have to do. I climb into my bed and pull the covers over me.

I hear the night-time sounds of Ballyfrann. The rustle of leaves, the clanking of pipes, the screams of cats or foxes having sex. Catlin thinks it's funny, but I hate it. I always wonder *What if it's a child?* A child outside in pain and somewhere, lost.

When we were little, we had a book of stories from our dad. It had been his when he was very small. And some of them were cool, but some were frightening. There was this witch, her house had chicken legs. Her face melts to Mamó's while I curl up in bed.

She used to lure young girls inside her house. And sometimes she would help you. And sometimes she would eat you. It was up to her. She had the power.

Until you ventured in, you couldn't know.

Baba Yaga, Aoife from the children of Lir, Mr Fox, even the Virgin Mary. Scary folk, the kind you should appease. They all had secrets. Like here. It feels that way. Like everyone's a door.

We should be careful.

11

Alder

(diagnosis)

Catlin isn't in her bed when I get up. I've slept through my alarm. I'm so late. I throw my horrid polyester on and run downstairs. Catlin and Mam are sipping coffee at the kitchen table, like two women in an ad for espresso. Their hair is sleek, their faces are made up. A shaft of sunlight caresses their beautiful heads. I have a hole in my tights, I realise. Visible leg hair furzing through it.

'What took you?' asks Mam. Her tone is off. There's something forced about it. Over-happy. Catlin's face is casual. They have been talking about me, I realise. My mouth is open. I need to say something.

'I didn't sleep,' I tell her, and leave it at that. Mam butters me a slice of toast. I stuff it in my mouth, and grab my bag. 'Maybe I'm coming down with whatever Catlin had.' My voice comes out more bitchy than I mean.

'I feel much better,' Catlin says to me. She's dressed for

school as well. Her uniform looks tailored on her body. Mine has an actual leaf sticking to it. I don't know where it came from. Mam peels it off and puts it in the bin.

'The state of you.' I amn't in the mood. Her face is softer though. 'Maybe you aren't well. We might have to give you some of Mamó's special tea.'

I snort and shove my lunch into my bag.

On the walk to the bus stop, I ask Catlin what Mam and her were saying.

'Nothing,' she tells me, but she has a mask on, so I ask again.

'Look,' she says, 'I think you know. She found it and she's angry. But we have school, so you can't get upset right now, OK?'

'I can't control when I get upset,' I tell her. 'That's not a thing.'

'I know,' she says. 'But it's the usual nonsense about making a mess and being weird and do you need to see a counsellor and stuff. We've heard it all before.'

'We have.' I sigh, and Catlin's eyes meet mine. The same shape and colour, but very different souls that live behind them. I can see her worry about me. Not the salt stuff – she doesn't really judge me for that – but the conflict.

I hate the knowledge that a difficult conversation is coming. It's like a handful of copper coins shoved down my throat. The weight inside my stomach, the tang of something awful coming soon. I swallow hard. I need to change the subject. Happy things, before I start to cry. I tell Catlin about Oona. How pretty and sound she is, and how she swims.

'She sounds painful,' Catlin tells me blithely.

84

'Well, she's not,' I say. 'I actually spoke to people around her. And they listened!' It is sad that I say this so triumphantly. But here we are.

My twin glints at this.

'Progress! I'm proud of you. Anything strange?'

'Apparently Lon runs a youth club. With trampolines and drink?' I screw my mouth into a very, very small mouth indeed, trying to communicate how excited I am not about the youth club.

Catlin is checking her phone. All her friends in Cork are fighting now that she is gone. Catlin was the cool glue that stopped everyone getting with each other and/or becoming enemies, apparently. Factions have emerged, and they're all trying to get her onside. It's like her Christmas. I watch as her fingers swipe and tap and press. She takes a picture of her outraged face. There is a pause.

'Drink?' she asks. My sister is predictable.

'Drink, Catlin,' I confirm. 'Look at you. All gagging for the sauce.'

'The hot, hot sauce,' she says. And does a little dance. We have a hot-sauce dance. It is very graceful.

'We need to join this . . . What's it called?' She looks at me.

'The youth club.'

'Urgh,' she says. 'It needs a better name. Like, something edgy.'

Oh, Catlin, I think. *Please do not be the worst.*

'Yes,' I tell her, 'because Mam will love us going to the Doom Doom Hell Orgy Association.'

'That's not a very good name. Too many words.'

'We could call it the Doom Doom Room for short,' I snap at her.

'That's almost good.' She grins. 'We definitely have to join though. Unless there are, like, matching hoodies. Because those are terrible.'

Charley won't like that, I think. It's weird what a difference a few days make.

'What have you got against hoodies?' I ask her. 'You have, like, four of them.'

'I like the zippy ones,' she says, making a zip with her hands, as if I don't know what a zip can do. 'But we wouldn't get to pick the colour. Plus I hate being like everybody else.'

'You really do,' I tell her. 'I like a hoody, me. It makes me feel all warm and safe like a fleecy tortoise. Ballyfrann could do with being cosier.'

'I hate this stupid frost. Look at these, like, ice-trees. What even are they? WHAT ARE YOU, TREES?' She gives a tree a kick. It's pretty rude.

She looks at me. And in that moment I know that we are going to join the youth club. And that I will probably hate it.

I sigh. 'The trees are fine, Catlin. They're just being trees. Don't mind her, noble oak.' I rub its trunk. We're almost at the end of the driveway.

'I know they are,' she says. 'We kind of have to join, Maddy. We can't just languish in the castle. Like ghost brides.' She tosses her hair. 'I don't have the right nightdress to be a ghost bride. You can't phone that shit in.'

'You have a point.' I shove my hands deeper into my pockets. 'It just seems like so much work. All this, with people.' I gesture at Layla's back. 'Like, look at this. LOOK AT IT.'

Layla turns. 'What?'

Catlin distracts her with Cork drama. Layla listens politely to tales of people she doesn't know making each other very unhappy but pretending to each other's faces that they're OK. In case they offend anyone.

When Oona gets on the bus, I am sitting beside Catlin, so she sits in front of us, leaning over the back of her chair until the driver growls at her to put on her seat belt. She rolls her eyes and obeys.

Catlin mouths the word *painful* at me and I mouth the words *shut* and *up* back at her. I wonder how she missed how great Oona is, like did she not see her face and hair and hear her voice and words? Oona's hair is damp, and I see her running her fingers through it, and then wiping them off on her school skirt. It doesn't really matter what Catlin thinks of her. I don't like everyone Catlin likes.

A lanky case in point is lurking like a spider at our stop as the bus pulls in. Catlin smiles and nudges past everyone to get to him, like he's made of concert tickets and chocolate cake. The way they look at each other makes me feel uncomfortable. It's very *hungry* or something. And, no more than my morning-time anxiety, surely that kind of thing is private. She doesn't even notice me filing past her with the rest of them. I sigh, and save her the seat beside me anyway. It's fine.

The kind of fine that's pronounced *fiiiiiiiiiiiiiiiiiiiiiiiiine*.

Classes pass without much drama, and when lunchtime comes, Catlin runs out the door to Lon, who is waiting at the school gates for her *like an actual paedophile*. I am not party to their chats, but they must be good because she comes back looking all flushed and grinny. He's there again when school lets out, and he gives her a big, long, lingering hug before she gets on the bus. They maintain eye contact as the bus pulls away and it's oddly sexual and thoroughly off-putting. I sacrifice a seat beside lovely Oona to sit beside Catlin, and she messages Lon all the way home and barely says two words to me. I take out my book, and try to focus on the words thorough a cloud of grumpy. Oona catches my eye between the seats, like, *You OK?*

I nod and roll my eyes like, *she always does this*.

And it's true. I have been ignored at house parties, in parks and once on her friend John's cousin's boat while Catlin was off being Catlin. This is partly why I always bring a book and a spare book, but . . . I don't know . . . I had my own friends too and my own life, and there was never anyone at the end of the day who mattered to her more than me, I knew. And I feel like Lon is beginning to matter to her in that strong way, that important-person way. And it's not anything I can put into words, but there's a feeling of being left behind. And it's really stupid, because nothing has happened between them that I can put my finger on. But she's never had an every day boy before. A boy who was more interesting to talk *to* than *about*. And that's what worries me. Because without her here? I'll be alone.

But I can't say any of this because it would be moaning, and I need her on my side for the inevitable conversation about how flawed I am with Mam. And I am flawed. But nature is imperfect. The bus pulls in, and myself, Catlin and Layla get off.

'Would you like to come up to the castle for a cup of tea or something?' I ask, surprising myself.

Layla looks at me, with clear, dark eyes. 'No,' she says. 'Sorry, I have plans.'

'Another time,' I say.

'Yeah.' She grins at me and turns down the pathway to her house. She walks so quickly with her long legs that it seems unnatural. Fiachra and Cathal are still biking in and out, though it must be dangerous with the frost filming the mountain roads. I wouldn't like it, I think, pressing on.

Catlin is still staring at her phone. I don't think she even registered the conversation.

'Catlin?' I say.

'Mmm?' she murmurs back. And, 'Just a second.'

She types away as we move down the path beside each other but not with each other. I look at a sycamore leaf, desiccated, hanging by a fibre from a tree. It's hunched like it's in pain. Like it is hanging. I reach up to the branch and pluck it off.

It's too weak to resist.

12

Elder

(rheumatism, flu, traumatic injury)

When we get back from school, we eat with Mam. She's made chops. Mine has a little circle of bone inside the middle, full of marrow. I lift it to my mouth and suck it out. It tastes like blood and fat. Mam's teeth tear at a little cube she's chopped up on her fork. The meat is tender, brown to almost pink. I think about the life that we have taken. Maybe more than one. The sheep on the mountains, fleece and dirt and little sunken faces. I swallow something like them down my throat.

Mam has been trawling through the attic, finding things. She wants to redecorate the castle, make it a little bit quirky and a lot cosier. She has her work cut out for her there, I think. Battlements and cosy don't really gel.

'I'm just a little bored,' says Mam. 'I don't miss work, but I miss working. I think I need a project.'

'It's good to have a thing,' Catlin says. 'Maybe Brian would let you use the good Internet in his office to google pretty castles.'

'I don't know,' says Mam. 'He's pretty protective of that office. I brought him up a cup of tea the other day, and he nearly jumped out of his skin.' She smiles and rolls her eyes.

Catlin gets up. 'Off to change my tampon,' she announces. 'Before the castle is bathed in blood. It's kind of nice not having Brian around too much. I can talk about periods and things. I mean, not that I'm censoring myself, but we'll ease him slowly in to my menstrual cycle.'

'One awkward moment at a time,' I say. It's weird that I'm not having my period too. Like, we're normally creepily in sync. We got our periods on the same day, and everything. I feel a worry in me. Brewing like a tea until it's strong. Something's wrong with us. We don't belong here.

Mam interrupts my internal worrying with some lovely external worrying. It's that mixture of annoyance and concern. Don't be weird and why are you so weird, both at once.

'Madeline?'

I swallow. I know exactly what this is about.

'I've cleaned it up. I don't want to have this conversation again.'

I hate how odd she gets about this. I'm not doing drugs or having sex. I barely even drink. I study hard and I'm nice to her and Catlin most of the time. Mam needs to recognise how privileged she is if salt is all she's worrying about.

Catlin bounces back into the room. 'I'm all plugged up like a beautiful sink.'

'Catlin.' Mam sighs.

'Don't make me ashamed of my body. I'm a moon-blood miracle and I will not be silenced by the likes of you.'

91

'Yeah, Mam,' I say. 'You need to be more respectful of Catlin's flow.'

We decide to head upstairs to roam around and scavenge fancy items from the many crates of stuff. The only clothes shop in Ballyfrann sells the kind of things that people Mam's age wear to weddings. Fussy, structured dresses, fascinators. Support garments.

I give out a bit to Catlin about Mam and the salt.

'What's her problem, Catlin? Does she not want me to be crazy in front of her fancy new husband?'

Catlin wraps a blue silk piano shawl around her shoulders. 'She took the salt out from under my bed too, as if it's any of her business what my sister does in my bedroom in the middle of the night while I'm fast asleep.'

'You're not making me feel like less of a freak, Catlin,' I say miserably.

'Fuck them, Mad,' she says. 'We're here for two more years. Just enough time for me to get Lon pregnant and feck off to college while he cries into his pint.'

I prise open a box, which turns out to be full of old swords. Catlin takes some out and rubs them. Grumbles that they're blunt.

'What were you going to do if they were sharp?' I ask her.

'Wreak havoc . . . Ooh! Some skulls!' She has found a steamer trunk of skulls. They're mostly sheep, but also several birds, a deer and some dogs. One of them is human though. I touch it. It is small. A woman's head. I think of Nora Ginn. Of Helen Groarke.

We all end up as old, forgotten bones. It just takes time.

'I can't believe he has a human skull,' I say to Catlin.

'I know,' she squeals. 'It's amazing! Would it be weird to spray-paint it a colour?'

'Maybe,' I say. 'It used to be a person. A girl, I think. The shape of it. The size.'

Bridget Hora, Nora Ginn, Helen Groarke. Whose head was it? The one they didn't find? Catlin touches my elbow.

'Catlin, we should tell Brian about the skull, I think. It isn't normal. Having human bones inside a house.'

'You're right,' my sister tells me. 'I love this place. It's fully, fully haunted.'

'Have you seen anything?' I ask her.

'Sometimes when I'm praying before bed . . . Don't roll your eyes at me, salt-girl.'

'Oi. But go on.'

'I hear what Brian says are "the pipes". But it doesn't sound like pipes at all. It sounds like . . . something else – little shrieky breaths and sometimes footsteps.'

'Why have I heard none of this?'

'I assumed you had. Because salt. Anyway, you know the way I am.'

I do. Catlin has a vivid imagination – when we were little she used to see people that weren't there, like all the time. They'd be in her nightmares, and then bleed out into the daytime too. Praying helped. And maybe that's why I started doing what I do, with the gathering. To protect her.

I wonder . . .

'Did you put back the salt Mam took out of your room?' I ask her, concerned.

'No. But if you do, I won't say a word.' She looks at me. 'The sounds don't frighten me, Madeline. They're not . . . They're not the thing we need to be scared of.'

'What do we need to be scared of?' I ask her.

Her face is very serious. 'That Brian will take all of my cool skulls away when you tell him about the human one. Murder palace problems.'

'In fairness, Catlin, you want to decorate with someone's head.'

'*Brian* decorates with heads. He has that shrunken one in his office. Oh! Maybe that's where the skull is from. The two might go together, like a set.'

'I don't know what to do with you. You're scarier than ghosts sometimes.'

'Skulls!' exclaims Catlin happily again. It doesn't take that much to please her, really. 'They're going to look fantastic on my altar. I wonder if he has any Marys?'

Catlin's Marys have graduated, and now she basically just has a massive altar in her room. It's getting bigger as she gathers stuff. It has her pictures, icons, Mass cards, miraculous medals, nazars and Hands of Fatima. And now, apparently, the skulls as well. This altar is fine with Mam, apparently. It counts as decoration, not a symptom. It does look cool. But so does everything she fecking does.

I wonder what Mamó would think of all of Catlin's talismans. I think I'd like to show her. See her face. Catlin has been getting more and more into religious iconography over the past while. She always liked the pictures. Pretty ladies in white and blue, stars around their heads, snakes at their feet. She has all these old Mass cards in a shoebox. The

94

only person that she really knew in there's our dad. The rest are Mam's friends, and some strangers. I saw her steal one from a friend's house once.

'She won't need it,' she told me, grinning. 'She didn't even like her Auntie Méabhdh.'

Catlin's morals are like those optical illusion pictures people share. Sometimes you have to tilt your head to spot them. I help her with the skulls, because I am a good sister.

'This is the closest we have ever come to disposing of a body. *Bonding*,' I tell her.

'Sisterly bonding. We're skull-pals now. Bone twins.' She's carrying, like, seven skulls in her two teeny hands.

'Bone twins sounds like a porno.'

'It does at that.' She pauses. 'Do . . . Do . . . you girls do *everything* together?'

This is a question we've actually been asked, and more than once. I make bass-line sounds, and then pretend to vomit.

Sometimes, when Catlin gets stuck in an evil laugh, it keeps on going. And I join in. We cackle until we have to sit down because our ribs hurt too much. It's the kind of laughing I really only do when she's around.

I love my sister. Skulls and bones and all. But still, there are some troubling facts emerging. Like the fact that she had another sex dream. About Lon. This time he was interviewing her for a job, and it turned into another sort of job altogether and I stopped her there because NO.

A world of NO.

'No.'

'But it was –'

'NO.'

Catlin hates when I don't let her finish. It is one of her pet peeves. She squints at me.

'You really don't like him?'

'No. I really don't.'

She smiles at me. 'I'm going to kiss him anyway.'

My stomach twists. My eyes on the dark hollows of the skulls.

13

Wild Cherry

(prepare the stalks of drupes to soothe or bind)

I wake up, sweating like I have been running. Rain beats on the windows. Dreams of foxes interspersed with screams. We're high up, but the mountains here cast shadows, day and night.

When we told Brian about the skull we found, he laughed at us. Gently, but he laughed. 'Typical Dad,' he said. 'He didn't ever open half the trunks he bought at the estate sales.' His hand outstretched. 'I'll give it to the guards though, just in case.'

He tucked the pitted bone into his satchel. The light caught grooves upon it. Carved by time, or maybe something else.

The moon is waxing, fatter slices building.

Skulls in Catlin's room of things long dead.

I blink, and try to think of salt and safety.

My ears strain for the breathy creak of pipes.

What can my sister hear that I can't hear?

Girls go missing all the time in Ireland. You hear about

97

the right ones on the news, the ones with parents, girls who come from money, pale-skinned, pretty. Missed. I've shared the photos, seen the posters peeling on the lamp posts, bins and walls. Sellotaped or glued. The pictures bleeding into text with rainfall. Printed out by families or friends. Loving, hopeless hands that clutch at nothing.

And, in time, they might be found, in isolated places. The mountains that we drive through on the bus – I picture them, the faint trodden paths from years of feet that line the slopes like slender threads a foot's breadth wide, through bush and grass, like veins upon a leaf. You have to know, or really look, to notice. It would be the same, I think, with bodies. You'd have to look, but mightn't think to look.

I comb my fingers through my damp-lank hair. So many missing girls, lines and lines of them, like beads on string. Why do they haunt me when they're not my business? Why is it so warm here at night? Everything outside is icy, freezing. The pelt of rain against the windowpanes. I must ask Brian to turn the heating off. I end up kicking blankets, tossing, turning. And thinking of the other girl I know once lived near here. Helen Groarke. Catlin told me at the time that people only cared because she was hot, and was she even hot, like, Maddy, really? Anyone can look that way in one photo, from the right angle, with the right filter.

A girl can turn into an ellipsis so easily.

I reach out for my phone.

And there she is. And there she is. And her.

Their faces when you google Ballyfrann.

A tiny village somewhere in the mountains.

They never found Bridget Hora's skull. Just bones and hair and little scraps of fabric. I look at her. Zoom in on her eyes. There is no way to tell with people, is there? She's small. The skull was small. We're small. Our skulls would look like that. If something happened.

The bodies were spaced out. Bridget died the year that Mam was born. They think that they were killed in different places. Different ways. Four girls is not a lot. In the scheme of things. Even in the scheme of missing girls.

Myself.

Catlin.

Oona, Layla.

When you put a face on death, it hurts.

Helen Groarke had long, dark, pretty hair. She wore it poker straight. And she was pale, with freckles on her cheeks. She's wearing orange nail polish in the photo they all used. It really suits her. She was wearing a little purple dress when she went missing. Brown boots, black tights. A fluffy yellow coat.

Salt under the bed to keep the ghosts at bay. I breathe away the stories.

Helen Groarke. Whose friends held vigils here, but something's missing. There's a chunk of something I can't find. I get up. I need air. I need fresh air.

Amanda Shale. I'm running down the stairs like there's a fire.

I dig, but not for treasure, in the night.

Nora Ginn. I get a bunch of keys from in the larder. They hang on an iron loop. Cold to touch. I press them to my face.

Bridget Hora. The moon is brighter now that I'm outdoors, and it is colder. I can think. My brain is getting sharp. There's something in my room that makes me warm and tired. The window's open, but it doesn't work.

Every brutal death becoming story. Girls that turn to bones that turn to ghosts. Someone dumped them here like they were rubbish. I think of Catlin, Oona, me.

Hot feet on freezing grass. I run my hands through plants and something's easing. Something's better now that I am here.

Help me, I ask the earth.

What's wrong with me? Too many things to count, like salty grains.

Basil. Bay. Calendula or camomile.

Bay might be alive out here. It's cold. I fumble in the dark. I should have brought my phone, I think. Their faces though. I didn't want to carry them. I couldn't.

A light approaches.

Bodies in the hills, skulls in the attic. I crouch down closer to the ground, hands pressed on frost.

'Madeline,' a voice says. It is Mamó.

'Um. Hi,' I say. She looks at me. She's wearing one of those headbands with the torch on, like miners have on their hats, only without the helmet, but apart from that, she's dressed like a normal person. No pyjamas with rabbits on them for Mamó. I blink a little in the light. It's hard to focus on her face. The halo all around it is too bright. She looks like she's the patron saint of wagons.

'Tea?' she asks. And then, and not unkindly, 'Do you need help?'

'I'm fine,' I say. I'm breathing.

100

'OK then.' She turns to go. 'Goodnight, Madeline.'

I watch her fade back into the garden. There isn't any tentativeness at all. And what would it be like to have that surety, to be a person, firm inside a place? I cover my face with my hands. The cold seeps through.

I feel the cramps begin.

The blood is coming.

14

Chicory

(eliminating parasites)

Catlin and I are walking through the forest. The evening is burning into night. The trees are sad and skinny. Needle pale. We see the white tail of a rabbit running. It bobs beneath the furze and disappears.

We're meeting Layla. She messaged us to ask. She goes fell-running here, moving quickly through the dangerous slopes. She ends up here most evenings, apparently. Ballyfrann is full of the bizarre.

I'm sleeping a little better, at the moment. Water beside salt and six old nails. It keeps on taking more to keep me calm though. More objects gathered. More of me to hide away from Mam. I need for them to work. I want to focus hard in school, even if it means drinking the tea Mamó gave Mam for me, after the night she found me in the garden. Anything that cools me down at night. It's fever-warm inside my bedroom, weirdly. And when I open windows, there are sounds my brain turns into ghosts. Sharp mountains and dark valleys. Hollowed out like the eyes of a skull.

Oona has insomnia as well. We talk about it, sometimes, on the bus. I sit beside her now, on the way home. Today she wore a little lacy vest beneath her blouse and I could see her collarbones above it. She's so beautiful. Not in an I-want-to-look-like-that way, but in an I-want-to-look-at-her way. I kind of can't believe she's friends with me. Or getting to be friends, anyway.

The tea came in a small brown bag, with a message scrawled in crow-black script.

For Copping On.

'She's kind of a magnificent bastard,' is Catlin's take on Mamó.

I'm not so sure, but I'm still drinking the passive-aggressive tea before I go to bed. Anything that helps me not have freak-outs. To be more like a normal human being.

'I wonder,' Catlin muses, 'if Mamó has a Lon-attracting tea.'

'You wouldn't need it,' I tell her.

'I know.' She smirks. 'He *loooooooves* me.'

It is true. He does loooooove her. They have become a sort of little gang. The last day, when I tried to join her for a smoke break, Lon told me, 'You don't smoke, you're not allowed.'

Catlin laughed, and then I was genuinely made to go back in. Which was some nonsense.

On her phone, she has a special beep that's just for him. A wolf-whistle. It is, apparently, hilarious. One of their little in-jokes. And if she doesn't reply, he rings, to make sure she's safe. It's a little creepy, but she likes it.

'Why hasn't he kissed me yet, Mad?' she asks me.

'Because sneaking into school to kiss a student is a level of creepy even he's uncomfortable with?' I ask. 'Like, maybe he wants to kiss you on a burning Viking boat, or a rocket that's going to the moon.'

Catlin looks sceptical. And she's right to. I don't know much about the business of kissing. I've only kissed, like, five or six guys. The 'or six' is because he didn't use tongue even though his mouth was open. I'm not sure what we did together, House-Party-Paul and I, but I wouldn't call it kissing. Not exactly.

'I'm not a Disney princess though,' Catlin tells me. 'I am a proper girl. With proper lusts.'

'Maybe it's not about you though,' I tell her. 'It could be about him.' This feels wise. I have the idea that a lot of things Lon does are mostly about Lon.

'Working up the courage,' Catlin says, and I restrain my side-eye. Hold my tongue.

We reach the crossroads, both paths up the mountain. One up left, another to the right. We take the right one. It curls around the rocks and comes out at this jutting, flat sort of ledge. If you want to go beyond that lip, there is no path, you have to climb it properly, like a mountaineer. We sit and wait for Layla. Catlin has a little bottle of whiskey and Coke. She took it from Brian's press. The whiskey, not the Coke. It's probably expensive. It tastes heavy. We sit and drink and look back at the castle, the hanging bits of trees and lichen, moss. The sheep have gone inside now for the winter. The only creatures we see are crows. There are always crows around the castle. It's like they know they're being picturesque.

Catlin deftly rolls a cigarette and then another. Her nails are longer, filed into a curve. The way Lon likes. It's pretty, I suppose, but unhygienic. I rest my head on her shoulder and look at all the landscape. Dead things wait in stasis till the spring.

'I feel like I'm in rehab here,' she says. 'Or on a reality show or something. Being watched.'

I nod. Catlin is exactly the kind of person who would have done a stint in rehab. Not boring, real-person rehab. The fancy celebrity-filled ones where you fall in love with expensive men who buy you things like islands.

'We should ask Mam to drive us into Galway to get supplies,' I suggest. Catlin nods. She is not thinking about the same supplies that I am thinking of. (Jelly beans and Tipp-Ex.)

'Good plan.' She pulls out her phone. 'I hate living in a village. Even if I were friends with everyone I'd met here, I'd still only have, like, nine friends. Including you. It's not enough.' She sighs.

'I know,' I tell her, counting all my friends, including Mam. Four. Five if I had more self-esteem. Three and a half, realistically. I'm still not sure about Oona.

Layla bounds towards us, looking flushed. She twists sweat out of her long ponytail, and winds it in a knot on top of her head. Her face is lightly feathered with sweat. She's wearing shorts, in spite of the cold.

'I had the best run,' she says, plonking herself down and staring at the mountain. 'Do either of you run?'

'I do a bit,' I say. She smiles at me.

Catlin looks at Layla. 'I'm not big into exercise,' she tells her. 'Maybe if there was something to run from . . .'

'Like Lon,' Layla says, and Catlin laughs.

'I wouldn't run from Lon. Not yet at least. I kind of really like him.' Her face is happy, but she's almost shy. She's giving Layla a piece of something real, something important.

But Layla's face is grim. 'And he likes you,' she tells her. Her face is strange, expressionless. A mask. There is a pause.

'Do you want some whiskey and Coke?' asks Catlin.

'I'm good, thanks,' Layla says. 'My life is weird enough without the drink.'

She waggles her eyebrows as if we know what she means. We do not know what she means at all.

'Weird, how?' says Catlin.

'Ballyfrann is . . . Actually I will have a drop. Thanks, Catlin.' Layla takes a gulp and passes the bottle back.

'Ballyfrann is what?' I ask her.

'Ballyfrann is very . . . Ballyfrann. It's not like the real world, is it?' she says. 'I mean, not that I have much experience of the real world, but I have seen it on TV, and I feel that we get a pretty raw deal here.'

'The Internet is terrible,' I tell her. 'Oona sent me a gif last night and it did not load for fifteen minutes. That's too long to wait for any gif.'

'I don't know though,' Catlin says. 'Like, there's loads of nature and stuff. And we get to live in a castle.'

A wolf-whistle emerges from Catlin's bag.

'Lon?' Layla asks.

I nod at her.

'It would be. Jesus Christ.'

106

Catlin moves a little bit away, angling her phone to get reception.

Layla turns to me. 'Does Brian know?' she asks.

'About what?'

'Herself and Lon.' She gestures to Catlin's back.

'No,' I say. 'It's none of his business who she's seeing.'

'Might be worth telling him,' she tells me. 'Just a thought.'

I take a swig from the bottle of whiskey and Coke. It's sweet and sharp and earthy. I'm not sure if I like it, but I find I want more.

'So,' Layla says, her smile a shepherd's crook, 'Oona, eh?'

'What do you mean by that?'

'Nothing,' she says, her grin widening. 'Yet.'

She's very full of questions, I think. But I suppose that's how you make friends. And I would be curious as well, if I'd grown up with a small bank of people and suddenly someone made a lodgement of more people in the bank of people.

When Catlin comes back, Layla takes us up the mountains to a little ledge where people meet up in summer.

'When I say "people", I mainly mean me and my brothers and possibly a Collins or two,' she says.

'It's cool,' I say, looking out at the darkening trees below us. 'It almost looks like the top of them's an ocean.'

'Careful where you swim,' she says, and laughs.

'How was Lon?' I ask Catlin.

'Fine,' she says. 'He just wanted to check I got home safe. I told him I was back at the castle, in case he got worried.'

'Good,' Layla says. Catlin looks at her. 'You wouldn't want to worry Lon too much.'

'No.' Catlin's voice is slower, careful. 'It's early days yet.'

'Early days,' says Layla. Crooks her mouth.

I wonder if she has a thing for Lon.

We talk about that later, walking home in the approaching darkness.

'I wouldn't be surprised at all,' says Catlin. 'There's a very small pool of tappable men in Ballyfrann.'

'This is true. And she's related to two of them. Like, it's Eddie or Lon, basically. Unless she's bi. I hope it doesn't make things weird for ye.'

'Do you know what? I actually don't care. Because he likes me.' Catlin's smile is bright and full of hope.

'Of course he does,' I say to her. 'You're magic.'

'I kind of am,' she says, high-fiving a tree. 'But that doesn't mean everybody fancies me. There's free will and things. It's a sort of sex lottery.'

'Can I point out that I don't find Lon attractive at all?' I say. I could go on, but I don't want to ruin this. She's just so happy, thinking about him.

And then we turn a corner and we stop.

A dead thing in the road, splayed valley wide, red on grey and green, and blue and purple.

I had never seen a fox in real life before, only in books. In photographs. On screens. It is bright orange. Sunset. Autumn leaves. The feet are black, the tip of the tail white. Its fur is only soaked in blood in patches. No flies buzz. The ribcage has been forced apart, the insides scooped and tangled. It looks fresh.

Catlin's frozen. I crouch low beside it, sniffing, looking. Running torchlight up and down, across, for details.

I don't know what compels me to do that. I need to find out more. There is something off about the fox, and not just that it has been tortured, killed.

Our father, charred to flakes upon the earth.

'Madeline,' Catlin says. She says my name again. 'Maddy?'

I kneel down and put my ear beside the fox's mouth. I feel the heat emanating from it. This is recent. It will leach out soon. It will be cold, as dead things always are.

A matter of minutes, I think. While Layla told us gossip about Lon, somebody was tearing this apart.

'There's something wrong,' I say. 'About this fox.'

I can feel her eyes on me, as mine scan the forest floor, the leaves, the trees for clues. The blood paint-bright and all the woods a canvas. I look at her.

I feel the wrongness pouring from the earth.

Catlin's lips are moving and her hands are clasped. I realise she's praying. I look hard at her, not with normal eyes. It isn't helping.

Our breath pools over the little corpse together. She peers at the delicate ribcage, white bone through the red. The clean lines of an incision, with a scalpel or those fancy cooking knives Brian bought in Asia. There were jagged edges too though. Like something had been tearing it, or eating. Some bits were stuck with pins into the earth, splayed wide apart. Like a butterfly in a box.

Catlin strokes its paw. 'The poor dead thing. I hope it's found its peace.'

I eye the branches, thinking of the person that did this. They could be close. They could be very close. They could be here. I pull at her and tell her we should go.

109

My sister nods.

We walk back through the woods in dark and silence. She links my arm like we're kids again.

The fox rests on the soft floor of the forest.

A mockery of something lovely once.

15

Cowslips

(St Peter's herb, for helping things along)

The forest is harsh on the way home, the crossroads almost flickering in the moonlight. I keep an eye behind us in the night, and so does Catlin. The path is oil-slick dark, a black snake's tongue. I feel as though we should have been dropping breadcrumbs on our way to meet Layla. To guide us home, like children in a story. Catlin's hands are cold and she is shaking.

I rub my sister's back.

'Madeline, it reminds me of something . . .' she tells me. 'I can't think what. But looking at that fox, it didn't feel like it was a dead animal. It felt like it was someone that we knew. Like, gut-punch hard.'

I swallow. 'I felt it too,' I say. 'And I kind of . . .'

'Do you want to throw salt at it?' she asks, her mouth a little crooked. Catlin knows me well. Salt for danger. Metal objects buried in the ground and wrapped in cloth.

'Oh, *so much* salt,' I tell her. 'Like, ocean-level salt. Poor little dude.' I'm trying to keep my voice light, but it isn't working.

'It feels as though the forest's not for humans,' Catlin tells me. 'It's like it's uncharted. Off the map.' She's murmuring again, she's saying the Hail Mary. I know it calms her down, but it's making me so anxious here right now. My breath comes fast. She quiets then. She knows me.

'I want to know . . .' she begins, and then trails off. 'Do you remember? Something about the fox . . .'

'Catlin, you're not making sense.'

'You know,' she says, 'when you've had, like, this really detailed dream and then you wake up and all you can remember is, like, images? The general sense of it. The how-it-made-you-feel. And, like, you're turning bits inside your mind, and waiting for other bits that will never come. And then you see, like a bowl of cereal or the colour blue and get a little flash?'

'If you've been getting a little flash, Catlin, you should report it.'

'Stop, Madeline. I'm trying to explain.' Her hand is ratting through her hair, as though it were more tangled than it is. As though this were a thing that she could fix, if her ponytail were smooth enough.

'You know that book that Dad had when we were small?'

I nod, and then I realise it's dark, so I also say, 'The stories, yeah?'

'Was there one about a fox or something? Something like the thing we saw? A fox?'

'There was that Mr Fox guy, I remember. The murderer.'

'I remember him. *Be bold, be bold, but not too bold*,' she chants. 'No, no, it wasn't that. I've . . . I've lost it.'

Her voice is sad, frustrated. We're almost halfway down the castle driveway. It's wrong that it's so normal. Everything's the same shape that it was. Except our brains, and small bits of our hearts.

The castle, when we get to it, is empty. We call and call and run through rooms and halls, sheet-covered furniture like odd-shaped ghosts. Sometimes, when you leave a scary thing, the normal stuff around you makes you almost forget that it has happened. With this, though, the strange of it keeps bleeding through. Statues look as if they're about to move. Shadows are dangerous. My breath sounds harsh, like it's someone else's breath. We can't find Mam or Brian. We try their phones, but they don't even ring. My body hums with action.

Catlin looks at me. 'We have to do something, Maddy.'

'I don't know if there's anything we can do. It won't bring it back, like.' It sounds lame and lying, coming out of my mouth. Not that I think we'll resurrect the fox, but there has to be a thing. A concrete thing. To mark the little murder that we found.

Catlin's mouth keeps moving, and her hands. Her head tilts up.

'You need to see Mamó,' she says, and her face is very sure. I'm glad that someone's sure. I feel too young to deal with this myself. It's too much death.

And that is why we knock on Mamó's door. The smooth dark wood of it. The iron knocker, shaped like leaf and moon. I swallow down. I can't hear any movement, but Catlin's leaning in. She nods.

'Someone's inside.'

I knock again. The door cracks open. Mamó is wearing men's flannel pyjamas. Her hair is in a braid all down her back. She looks quite put-upon and strangely normal. I never thought about her asleep before. She doesn't seem the type. Unless it was with one eye open, watching.

'What is it now?' she barks, as though this were something we often do.

'There was a thing,' I say to her, so helpful. We step inside. Catlin looks at everything. I can see her big eyes drinking in the jam jars full of things, the many plants. Mamó sees it too, turns to her as though she were an unexpected mouse. An inconvenience.

'A thing?' she repeats, her face impassive. 'Be more specific.'

'We found a slaughtered fox in the woods. It isn't safe.'

She makes a disdainful sound, but goes to pull on her boots and a long brown duster. She grabs her car keys from the kitchen counter.

'Go home, Catlin,' she says. Catlin looks at me. I look at her. She doesn't move.

Mamó glares at her, and in a tone of *I shouldn't have to explain this to you but it seems I do*, she adds, 'Wait for Brian and your mam. They'll worry if neither of ye are there.'

Catlin quietly nods. Mamó nods back.

She turns to me. 'Take some jars with you. You'll know which ones,' she says, offering me a black canvas shopper. It has a strawberry embroidered on it. It is the least Mamó bag I've ever seen.

I scan the shelves, and pluck and choose a few things. I do not need many. I close my eyes and let my fingers find them. My breathing slows, as this clicks into place. I find my calm.

114

Mamó decidedly picks up a little brown doctor's bag from beneath the coat rack. And a massive shovel. Why does she have shovels in her house, the way that normal people have umbrellas? She lashes it over her shoulder, and we stride towards the car. She doesn't lock her door. I notice that.

The trip consists of Mamó, hands grimly on the steering wheel, firing question after question at me, about what we were doing in the forest. About the things we saw. The temperature. The placement of the organs. How decomposed or otherwise it had been. The gender.

'It was male, I think,' I offer. 'But it was hard to tell. The pieces were all . . . moved around and things.'

'What things?' she barks.

'Like bitten off or cut. And there were pins.'

And she says, 'Hmmm.' And glares. Mamó loves glaring. It's probably her favourite thing to do. Except for glowering.

'There's something in the fox,' I say, and amn't sure exactly why I'm saying, 'a kind of . . . something . . . It's warm there. Much too warm.'

I can hear the fear whining through my voice. Annoying me. I want to be more calm. I should be calm. It's only a dead animal. I see them at the bus stop, on the road. A normal part of living in the country. Nothing to be frightened of at all.

Mamó tilts her head at me, like an owl would, looking at a mouse.

'Plenty of things that you can do with blood,' she says, 'and some of them leave things behind you after.'

'Is that what the fox was? A . . .' I try my best to find the proper word. '. . . *sacrifice* or something? Did a person do it, like?'

115

'We'll say no more of it,' she tells me, 'until we're finished. We don't know what is listening.'

'Ha,' I say. I think she might be joking. She did a thing with her eyebrows that was definitely either a joke or a threat. She pulls in at a sort of moonlight glade and grabs a lamp and the shovel from the boot.

'Let's walk,' she says, holding the light aloft like an old-timey night watchman.

We move, walking for what seems like forever. It's hard to gauge the distance in the dark. Everything looks wild and unfamiliar. I can feel the give of leaves under my feet.

When we stop, she gestures to the shovel. 'Dig.'

'How deep?' I ask.

'I know people say six feet under, but I prefer a healthy ten,' she says.

I raise an eyebrow, but I get to work.

She looks through the canvas bag and makes some sounds that aren't quite disapproval, but come close.

'You forgot the Hart's tongue,' she points out.

'How was I supposed to know what to bring?' I ask.

She doesn't answer.

Digging a grave in silence takes forever. The slice of shovel into earth, the lifting. My biceps hurt. The last time I dug a hole was on the beach, when we were small. This is nothing like that. Forcing the blade in, scooping out the velvet black, the rocks. The discordant sound of metal hitting stones.

I'm standing in it when she tells me, 'Stop.'

She pulls me out. She has really strong arms for an old woman, rippling muscles. She should have dug the hole herself,

116

I think. It would have been faster.

'Let's find this fox,' she says. We set off to the crossroads, at a pace. The woods are darker now, I use my torch to light the way. It makes the things it touches ashen grey. Devoid of colour. Mamó strides ahead. She doesn't seem to need or want the light. She leads. I follow. Everything is still. A photograph of something I once knew. I can feel a warmth beginning to build within me like a fever.

I remove my coat. She looks at me, and nods. We do not speak. The fox is still there when we reach the crossroads. I step on something soft. It doesn't give. A kidney? Mamó bends down to smell the fox, to look.

'It's fresh,' she says.

'How fresh?'

'A couple of hours.'

'So we might have disturbed whoever . . . ?' I let the question hang unfinished, in the air. And there it stays.

Mamó calmly opens her doctor's bag and takes out some binocular-looking things. She peers through them. Up and down and around. It should look more ridiculous than it does.

'There's something heavy here,' she says. 'Some wrong.'

I nod. The sweat is beading on my face. I want to curl into a ball and sleep. I want to run.

'The wounds are strange,' I tell her. 'And the fur . . . is roasting hot.'

'It senses you,' she says. 'You need to push through that. Can you feel the weight of it as well? The nudge?'

I nod. She's right. Something is pulling at me, straining like a peculiar aftertaste at the edges of my brain. Something heavy and bilious. Something like a threat, or like a plea. But the kind of plea a bully makes for your pocket money. Something that needs fixing, rearranging. My gathering squirms and fattens in the pit of my belly.

'I can feel something.'

'That's the Ask,' she says. 'You won't like the Answer. I need three orange leaves, as orange as the fox, and three red leaves, as red as freshest blood. And holly berries.'

'What's the Ask?' I ask.

'Did I misspeak?' she snaps. 'Bring me the things I need to make this right.'

'Fine.'

And it is fine, even though my muscles are aching. I want to collect the leaves. My urges are in tune with what Mamó wants and it truly is the weirdest thing, but it is right as well. I feel validated. I turn the worry off and click into a sort of focused calm. Turn the torch on my phone to the brightest setting. I have this. It is winter, but leaves litter the forest floor. I crawl along on hands and knees, feeling for the textures that I want. When I find one I like, I raise it to the phone and check the colour. It can't be mottled. I need it to be smooth and bright and whole.

I get them, and run back towards the crossroads. Mamó is bent over the fox, holding a beeswax candle. Her brow is furrowed.

'Now, rub the leaves over him while I say the words.'

I look at her in disbelief. 'Seriously?'

'I'm sorry if I gave you the impression that I was a *jokester*.'

I shrink a little and do what she says.

118

As I rub the leaves along the fur and nose and blood and bone she mutters in a tongue that isn't English or Irish but kind of like a mixture of the two that's maybe spliced with German. I feel a hum within the fox's body begin to shift. It isn't unpleasant exactly. Pins and needles, deadening the flesh.

It ebbs into the leaves. My body cools.

We put the leaves inside an old marmalade jar 'to contain it'. Then it's time to bury the fox.

'We'll use your coat,' Mamó says.

'What?'

'You have it taken off. It's dirty anyway,' she tells me. And she's right, but scooping all the parts of fox into it isn't the best use of my coat or my time, I think. The fox is cooler now, slimy and disgusting on my hands. I feel the give of flesh as I grasp at it.

That could be me, I think. We're all so delicate.

We burn the leaves over the fox's grave. She wipes the jar on the last clean part of my coat and puts it back in her bag. I think of Dad again. How easily we're hurt. It only takes a minute for the leaves to smoulder into nothing. They were already dead. They weren't in pain.

I feel a ripple suck out of the leaves and down into the ground.

'That'll shut it up,' declares Mamó, brushing grave soil off her big flat hands.

'Shut what up?' I ask. I shiver, and she hands me my coat. It's damp and reeks of fox. I glare at her and do not put it on.

She sighs, her face impassive.

119

'I have to know,' I say, my voice quiet. She looks at me, and even though it's dark I think she sees.

She sighs again. As if I were an inconvenient guest. I can sense her brain, working out how to phrase it best to such an idiot.

'Somebody invited something in. They left the door unlocked, to make it easy. Could you feel a signal off the fox?'

'Like heat?' I ask.

'It's different things to different people. But what got called, it could decide to come.'

'Does it have a name?' I wonder, as though it matters. As though a name would put my finger on exactly what it was, and what it did.

'Names are for ordering things,' she tells me, 'and this yoke is disordered, cruel and angry. And when you call a thing like that, it bashes through quite strongly. Leaves a hole behind it in its wake. And other weaker things can use that hole to get into the forest. And even though they're weaker, they aren't weak at all. Compared to us. There are people in the world who want things, Madeline. And they don't much care how they get them.'

'I see.' I do not see, but I want her to go on, at least a little.

She pauses, and I can see her trying to twist her words into the sort of language that I will understand.

'When you call someone on the telephone for the first time, because you have not called the number before, you can't be sure, precisely sure, it's theirs. There may have been some error. Someone else may pick up. And they may not be who you want at all.'

She says the word *telephone* like the way Mam says *app*, I realise. How old is Mamó?

'And even if you think you're hearing the right voice, in the end it's just a voice. There's no blood or bone to it. It's nothing you can lay your hands on, touch. I like my help to come from things that I can get a handle on. The other sort of help's too close to hurt.'

Listening to her, I'm distracted by how crazy this all sounds. It's like a story, not like something real. And I don't like it. I don't like the way that I believe her. I don't want this world to be the world. I want the one I know. The one that's safe. Or safer, anyway.

'Was someone trying to summon something, Mamó?' I ask.

She barks a *ha* at me. As though what I've said were thoroughly ridiculous. I shrink a little and she takes a breath.

'The Ask is an invitation, not an order. You wouldn't last long out here, trying to boss the big fellas around.'

The trees are very tall, and I am very tired. This is too much, I think. I want my mam.

'Mamó?' I ask. My voice sounds whiney, thin. 'Can we go home now?'

'Yes. I think we can.' I follow her tall back through taller trees. The castle is dark and quiet when we get back.

121

16

Hart's Tongue

(spleen and fire)

I follow Mamó back inside her lair and sit on a plump armchair drinking tea. It feels strange that she lives in a place with armchairs and a kettle. A granite countertop, a little stove. It feels as if she should live in the sort of house a hobbit lives in. And always have at least one cauldron on the go. I lean towards her, formulating questions in my brain.

Before the words come out, she blinks at me, and speaks.

'You did OK tonight. You needed Hart's tongue, bog butter, basic soil. Those were the ones you missed. You got the rest.'

She's speaking like I know what she is talking about. Like I've gotten a C+ on a test. I always get at least a B.

I inhale slowly, push my shoulders back.

'What did we do?' I ask. 'I mean, what did it mean?'

'You mean, what did it mean?' She says this slowly. As though she is being incredibly patient with me.

'Yes.'

'It meant,' she says, 'that we were being careful. When you leave the house, you lock the door behind you.'

'You didn't. Lock the door.'

She looks at me. 'My door is always locked. But not with keys.'

'What does that even mean?' I ask.

'I don't believe in taking stupid risks.' She takes a long drink from her yellow earthenware mug. It has a star on it.

I take a breath, and ask a stupid question.

'Was it . . . magic?'

Mamó leans back in her seat. 'I wouldn't call it that. T'was more *insurance*. Nothing like the good stuff.'

'So. You can do. Like. Spells and things,' I say. She inclines her head a little. 'Are you a witch, Mamó?' I feel the blood rushing to my cheeks. There's no way for that question to sound anything but strange, coming out of my mouth. Mamó doesn't react, her voice is calm. She just continues on.

'I told Brian, when he married that . . . your mother, that he'd have to be explaining to ye the way things are in the village.'

'And what way is that?' I ask, ignoring the fact that my lovely, gentle stepfather apparently believes in magic.

'I promised him I wouldn't say too much. And I am of my word. But, I will say this, be careful. This village is a sort of –' she scans the room, and settles on the fridge – 'fridge. And some of us are fridge magnets. And some of us are food.'

This is not a very informative analogy, but I get the sense that explaining things is not Mamó's strongest point. She yawns pointedly.

'Do you not have a home to go to, young one?'

'This is my home,' I point out, wanting more. I want to understand.

'This is *my* home. It's just attached to yours, now up the stairs. We'll speak sometime again.'

I obey. I don't know what to think. Dawn is breaking as I venture in. The rooms are dim. I go into the kitchen, grab the salt, and carry it up to my bed beside me.

Catlin's waiting for me in my room. Her face is stained, as if she has been crying.

'Madeline!' she says. As though I had been gone for seven years.

'Catlin?' I ask. 'What's wrong? Are you OK?'

'Ugh. Fine,' she tells me, wiping at her face. 'I just got really weird. I felt like you weren't coming back or something. Like you were being dragged away from me. And then, after you left, I kept thinking about that story in Dad's book. The one I almost thought of. You know the one I mean.' She's looking at me, and I can see the sheen of sweat on her forehead. She absently bites her right index fingernail, peels off a little crescent moon-flake.

'What story, Catlin?' I ask her, climbing under the covers, wrecked.

'The one I was thinking of before – the forest-devil one. I remember it now.'

And I remember the stained grey cover and the yellowed pages of Dad's book, the illustrations black and white and intricate. Mam's voice stumbling as she read the words.

'I think it was the first thing I ever heard that really frightened me,' she says, and her voice is low. I close my eyes and picture

124

it, one of us on either side of Mam, listening transfixed. Wanting it to stop, and not to stop.

Catlin pulls the covers tight around us both.

'Where the woman's child was sick, and she took a calf and brought it to the middle of the woods and called the devil . . . ?'

'It's coming back a little . . .'

'And she killed the calf. And prayed and called the devil again. And when he came, she offered him her soul to save her child.'

'Oh, Catlin,' I say, remembering. 'You hated that. The way the child recovered but it didn't love her any more. It couldn't. The devil had taken her soul. And so, she wasted. Wasted, and when she died, the devil came for her, and took her straight to hell.'

'It's a horrible story to have in a book for children.'

'I'm not so sure it was meant for children,' I say. 'I mean, it has so many deaths.'

'I remember being so scared.' Catlin's voice is quiet. 'That people could stop loving people. That people could go to hell like that. I think that's when I started praying, really. As insurance.'

There's that word again. Two different places, and two different mouths. Does that mean something?

'Madeline?' Catlin nudges me.

'You're not that weird,' I tell her. 'Have you seen my massive piles of salt?'

'Did you fix the feeling at the crossroads?' she asks. I squeeze my eyelids. Don't know what to tell her.

'I hope we did,' I say. 'I hope we did.'

I stay awake, thinking of the fox's dead mouth, pink tongue lolling limply. The bright stare of Lon's eyes upon my sister, the smile of him, the way it feels, a promise and a threat. I picture him smiling and smiling wider and wider, his mouth too big to be a human mouth. There are no wolves, but people can be wolves. I feel afraid of something I don't yet know.

Being in the world comes at a price.

17

Camomile

(insomnia)

I'm sitting beside Oona on the bus, feeling the bump of road under the wheels. This bus is so old and rickety that you can feel the texture of the tarmac, when the road changes from old to new. Oona is fiddling with her hair, twisting the little sticky-out bits at the nape of her neck. It used to be longer, rippling like a river down her back; she cut it off before she moved.

'I needed change,' she says, and shows me pictures, her looking like a mermaid that grew legs, smiling with some friends from her old school. One of the girls is in all the pictures. She's tall and blonde and healthy-looking. With thick eyebrows. She looks like she could shoot an ad campaign for a perfume called 'Better than Madeline'.

'Who is that?' I ask, keeping my voice bright and casual, like a slogan T-shirt.

Oona's face is just a little sad. 'My girlfriend, Claudine. I really miss her.'

She touches her finger to the screen and leaves a little trickle of moisture along it, rainbowing their faces with a streak. I wonder if she means girlfriend the way the Americans say it, or the real way.

It's not the sort of thing I want to ask out loud. Better to play it down. To not use labels. Not to make it a big deal – I mean it isn't one. There were some kids at our old school who were LGBTQ. No As, as far as I knew. Although sometimes I wondered about myself. The way I felt, when I was kissing guys. It wasn't special. I don't know.

I look at the photo of Claudine again.

My stomach twists.

'She's really pretty, Oona,' I say.

And Oona smiles. 'She is.' And then she sighs the cutest, Frenchest sigh.

I look at her, and she looks out the window. Oona likes girls, I think. There's a mixture of relief and fear and something else. Claudine looks like a tool.

Lon is leaning on the bus stop today, reading an old Penguin paperback of *On the Road* and rolling a cigarette simultaneously. For effect. He has two cups of takeaway coffee by his feet, to help Catlin stay awake after her 'rough night'. She thinks it's sweet. I stomp into the yard, with very malicious eyebrows, leaving Catlin curled into his stupid chest, all whispery. Her head almost against his skinny ribcage. He reads her out a section, and she makes an appreciative noise, as though she hadn't read the book already, found it boring. Bunch of pricks that prick about in a car.

We lie to people that we want to like us, so they think that

128

we are more like them. It is a thing. But I don't have to like it. There's nothing worth pretending for in Lon. I mean, he is handsome. If you like that sort of gawky, athletic thing. A male model who also plays guitar and won't stop going on about it. That vibe. Whiff of desperation to be cool off him. Everything about him reeks of prick.

In fairness though, I would rather see Catlin happy than lonely, and she shines around Lon recently. Like a pregnant woman or a bride. Just glowing. His hand on the small of her back, helping her off the bus, as though she were a princess or a child. I'm trying to be happy for my sister. She likes to be adored. I have no frame of reference for that.

At five to nine she's still out at the bus stop. I stomp out, to bring her in before the start of class. I hate to be the sex police, but I don't want her to get in trouble either. Not so early into our time here.

'You OK, Mad?' she asks.

I nod my head. 'Just wrecked. Come on.'

'It was a long, weird night,' she says, ignoring my hurry-up eyebrows.

Lon reaches out and actually ruffles my hair. 'Cheer up, Madeline. It might never happen.'

'What, finding a tortured fox corpse in the woods and not getting any sleep?'

Lon's face falls a little, then rises again. Like a villain in a computer game who just. Won't. Die.

'Welcome to the country, girls. It's dog-eat-fox.'

Catlin laughs. I glare. He smiles again. 'You need to learn to take a joke, Madeline. It's fine.'

It isn't fine, but I make the corners of my mouth turn up at him. Oona comes up behind me, links my arm. Her hair is still a little wet from her morning swim. I can see droplets suspended in the strands, as small and perfect as beads of rain on spider webs, shimmering in the ice-white winter sunshine. I wonder what she uses in her hair.

'The driver really bombed it today,' I tell her. 'I could hear every part of the bus clinking.'

'We survived,' she says, 'and that's the main thing.' I feel the warmth of her arm on mine, right through my coat and jumper. 'Do not worry, Madeline.' She says my name as though it were a pastry. *Ma-deh-len*. She makes it sound so soft.

'How was your swim this morning?' I ask her, and she looks up at me, and she says: 'Beautiful.'

A thud inside my insides at the word.

Swimming is like breathing for Oona. It isn't exercise. She really needs it. She's always coming in with soaking hair and she never catches cold.

Some of us are fridge magnets and some of us are food.

What does that mean?

It doesn't make any sense.

We catch up with the others. Oona grins at them widely. She has this kind of smile that's down and sideways but really, really big. Like a fat half-moon is climbing up her face. Like it could crack in two from all the happy. It shouldn't be attractive but it is. I wonder if she wanted to catch up with them. If I was being boring. I scroll down through my brain for something interesting. There is the fox, but I don't want to talk about the fox. It's weird and creepy. I don't want to be corpse-girl.

130

Know a witch. In the dark it seemed so utterly possible, but now, in the daytime, reality feels far more firm and solid. I need to have a good chat with Mamó, I think. Gather data, establish all the facts.

School passes quickly, and lunchtime isn't half as dragged-out awkward. Catlin doesn't mention the fox either. Which is weird, because she's normally the one to make small things more dramatic than they are. Maybe she's too busy being happy with Lon. She hops the fence and goes off with him for almost all of break, and when they come back her hair's a little mussed and she widens her eyes at me in a way that screams 'NEWS'.

She pulls down the collar of her school shirt a little, and there's a bright red mark on her neck, about the size of a leech. Of course. Of course he would, like, *brand* her. She looks all proud. My stomach dips a little. I don't know why I feel so weird about this thing. It's not like I am jealous. Or that he's done anything I can put my finger on. I just have a sense of . . . I don't know what. Like doom, but not quite doom. So maybe douche? The niggle lives in the same part of me that needs to put salt under people's beds. The stupid part. The part I'd like to quash.

'We went to the stock room in Donoghue's and . . . he *kissed* me. Also hand stuff. It was just like my dream, only he wasn't a fireman or a rock star or a corrupt policeman . . .' (Wait, what?!!) Catlin murmurs to me. I look to see if anybody heard. I swallow down bile. I can see it though, through a vintage filter in her head. A sepia romance. Catlin really likes the look of things. The sound of them. The story. The details and the trappings matter a lot.

When school is over Catlin stays behind. 'I'm going to hang out with Lon for a bit,' she says. 'I'll tell you everything later.'

'Does Mam know?' I ask.

'She'll be grand. She wants us to make friends.' This much is true.

I tell her to have fun and tell me everything.

I'm not so sure I want to hear it though.

Beside Oona, I watch my twin's body curl into Lon's. He crooks a smile of ownership at her. The two of them get smaller. Her body melts to his and fades from sight.

132

18

Creeping Savory

(for lust, digestion)

Mamó's been away a lot since that long night. We've had some people come, and knock and wait, and sigh and leave. Their faces resigned. I still don't know what sort of help she offers. But I want to. I walked back to the crossroads one evening last week, just to look at it. It felt like there had not been anything there. No menace at all. Just calm.

Catlin and I are heading into the village – Catlin's meeting Lon (of *course* she is) and Oona messaged me to go for a walk. Mam drops us halfway there, and, as soon as she's gone, Catlin turns to me, eyes wide.

'There's going to be a youth-club lock-in soon,' she says. 'Lon lets them drink in his pub, and nobody says anything because it's probably safer than the alternative.'

'What, not drinking?'

'No, like going up to the mountains where they found all those dead women and drinking there.'

'Jesus,' I say slowly. 'You're not wrong.'

'Yup,' she says. 'Even murder clouds have silver linings.'

We traipse past the butchers and the shop that has a post office inside it. The squat, dark church is there, behind black wrought-iron railings.

Catlin turns in. 'I want to light a candle.' She's halfway to the door by the time I roll my eyes and follow.

'Whyyyyyyyyyyyyyyy?' I moan at her. I am not gone on churches – they're too close to weapons for my liking.

This church is small and fat. It has thick dark walls with stripes of bright white marble. I think they're fossils. Things that lived before there was a church. I head in after her. It smells of Mr Sheen and fresh-cut flowers. The pews are honey dark and shining. The stained-glass windows filter out the light so it's really dim. I trail my hand along them as I look for Catlin. She's huddled to the left of the altar, crouched towards a table covered in dripping candles, red and white and trailing wax like tears.

Above the candles, in a little alcove, is a squat white thing. A motto is mosaiced over its head.

'*Our Lady of Ballyfrann*,' I read.

'They say that she'll protect you if you need it.' Catlin's face is grave. Her eyes are focused on the lump of wood. I can make out the curve of face and head.

'Who says that?'

'The priest. Father Byrne.'

I nod my head. Our Lady of Ballyfrann looks like a maggot with a human head. There's something strange about her, but a power too. I breathe in the waxy air, thick with frankincense, and wonder what my twin is thinking. Why

134

would she need protection, and from what?

'She didn't do a great job with all those other girls that got murdered,' I comment, shrugging.

'Maybe they didn't ask,' my sister says. Her eyes are staring up, shining with reflected candle flame. Suddenly I shiver.

'Madeline,' she says, 'this place. Do you feel . . . scared here ever?'

'All the time.'

She reaches out to hold my hand. 'Me too. I don't know why . . . I have so many reasons to be happy . . .'

'It could be the mutilated fox?' I suggest.

'It totally could be that.' She smiles her Catlin smile at me. 'I'll just say one quick Hail Mary and we can get out of here.' I see her lips trace the familiar words. The wood of the statue is dappled with shadows moving in the candlelight.

Something here is wrong.

I feel it too.

The daylight, when it comes, is a relief.

'It was really dark in there. Even for a church,' I say to Catlin.

'Yup. It's beautiful though, isn't it?'

'It is,' I say. It's what she wants to hear.

Catlin checks her phone.

'Shit. Eight messages from Lon. He'll be raging I'm late.'

'You're, like, five seconds late. He'll get over it,' I tell her.

'I don't know. I don't want him to think I'm rude,' she says. 'He treats me like such a laaaaaaaady.'

'You are a laaaaaaaady,' I tell her, as she runs towards the pub, almost knocking over a bin. This is the good thing about Ballyfrann. Everywhere is runnable. Except the castle.

135

Oona waves. She's wearing a navy pea coat, standing beside the old petrol station. Her face looks fresh. A sort of glisten-blush. She asks me where my sister is. I tell her that Catlin's off to see Lon. She makes a little motion with her mouth.

'What?' I ask.

'I don't like Lon,' she tells me. 'I've heard some things. Your sister should be careful. I feel he is a . . . how to put it . . . prick.' She pronounces it *preek*. It sounds so classy.

'He *is* a preek,' I tell her. We have so much in common, me and Oona. It's kind of amazing. 'He is probably the worst man who even lived. Bar none. Why do you hate him? Is it because of his smug face? What have you heard?'

'No. Not exactly. Just things about him being, uh, obnoxious. And things.'

'What things?' I ask, remembering what Layla said before, up in the mountains. About not wanting to worry him. The grim twist of her mouth. I wish that there was something concrete. A reason I could put my finger on. She told me to tell Brian about the two of them. Maybe I should. I need to talk to him when I get a chance.

'I'm not sure. I don't know.'

I try to meet her eye, to press her further, but she looks away, eyes up to the white sky. Neither of us wants to go to Donoghue's in case we'd run into Lon and Catlin. I don't think he's working, but his flat is right above it. Catlin's never been there, but she thinks that today might be the day. Which creeps me out a little and I don't want front-row seats. Oona takes me to a little bakery with tables in the back. It's called

'Collinses' and is, unsurprisingly, run by the Collinses. There are about a hundred of them living here, apparently. Five generations.

'Wow!' I say, thinking of how little we know about my dad's family. Once he died, they left us to ourselves. 'That must be something.'

'It is hard to make friends with a Collins, I think,' Oona tells me. 'They value family so much. We are outsiders. I went to Charley's house the other day, and even though she invited me and everything, I didn't feel like I was welcome there. They glared at me, you know?'

'That's terrible,' I tell her. Then say, 'Mamó glares at me all the time.'

'That's different,' she says. 'She glares at everyone. It's fairer.'

'What do you think she . . . ?' I start to ask, but I don't know what I'm asking, how to put it. The woman plonks the teapot and mugs down, and we go quiet. Wait for her to go.

Oona takes her tea black with a little spoon of honey stirred into it. She makes a happy sound at the first sip. I smile at her, and she smiles back.

There is a pause.

'We went inside the church,' I say, for something to say. 'Myself and Catlin. She wanted to light a candle.'

'To Our Lady of Ballyfrann?'

'Yes. What's the story with that thing? It's so strange-looking.'

'My dad grew up here, and he said to me that it was older than the town. The story is that there was a farmer with a withered hand who lived here and he went out cutting turf and found that thing, and when he touched it, his hand healed up, so he took it to the priest and he decided it must be the Virgin Mary. Apparently there were a few more miracles as well.'

'Why haven't I heard of it so? You'd think it's be all over the Internet, or at least on postcards and things, like Knock or Ballinspittle.'

'My father says people here like their secrets kept,' Oona says.

Do you have secrets, Oona? I wonder. I flinch a little as she reaches out to pick a bit of something off my shoulder. It's unexpected. Why would her lovely hands want to touch me?

We leave the shop and walk out past the pub, over the roads towards the mountains, and talk and talk. After a while, she links her arm through mine and rests her head a little on my shoulder. I can feel her soft hair against my cheek. It's still a little damp. But she is warm. A pleasant sort of moisture. She smells like lavender, fresh water. So easy to breathe deep. I'm hyper-aware of her, the movement of her body. Her warmth beside my own. Her little face. Underneath my skin is almost humming. Like I'm about to start collecting things, but not so worried-nervous. Leaves crunch and shine beneath our feet as we walk on. It must have rained while we were drinking tea.

I look down at my hands. The cuticles are rough, the nails are chipped. Nothing about me is good enough for anyone. When Oona sits, she crosses her legs twice, around and around again, curling in on herself like an ampersand. She's different to every other person that I've met. There's just . . . this thing about her. This warmth, this depth. I want more and more.

We walk until the stars are in the sky. Until Mam rings to ask me where I am.

19

Ragged Robin

(muscle strain and love spells)

Oona's mother drops me home. She looks like an older version of Oona, but taller, more angular. She asks how I am settling in to the village. I ask her the same. We both say grand. She has some paint on her jeans, and I remember she's an artist, ask her about painting. She loves the landscape here, the colours, she says. So stark. Oona has less to say to me when her mother is there. They speak in English to each other though, for my benefit, I assume.

When I get off at the driveway, Elodie Noone tells me to 'be careful'.

I laugh and thank her, but her face is still. Oona is in the passenger seat, so I can't tell if she waves goodbye to me as the car pulls off. I hope she did. I waved to her. Awkwardly, like everything I do.

Catlin and Mam are already at the kitchen table. I feel the heat against my night-cold cheeks. We must have walked for miles and miles. I try to keep the smile off my face. The warmth in my heart is just for me right now. I'm not ready to voice it.

'I think she met a boy, but she won't tell me anything,' Mam says. Her voice is high. Mam gets all excited when she suspects there's gossip. It's annoying and adorable.

'Did she now?' I put the kettle on and get some biscuits.

Mam rests her hands on her chin and looks between the two of us. Catlin tells her little bits of what happened. She doesn't say Lon's name. Or that he's older. Just that they met, he showed her places in the village he likes and then he bought her tea. They held hands walking all day long, she says. He didn't once let go.

Her voice is low and strangely sweet. The top button of her blouse is undone now, and she's rolled up her sleeves. Just a bit of artful disarray. She laughs a bit, when she is telling the story. Looks out the window. Says, 'I feel all special.'

As if she wasn't special all along. I never think of Catlin doubting that about herself. But maybe lately, with all of this change, she needed this. If I didn't know who he was, if I hadn't met him yet, I think I'd like the idea of Lon. The way she sees him. Quiet and sound and tall and dark and kind. A proper human being, and not a creep who's mostly made of things that look cool from the outside.

'He held me so tightly, Maddy. Like he was never going to let me go. It felt like in my dreams,' she says to us. 'It's so romantic. Like, he is literally the man of my dreams.'

I roll my eyes. Mam tells me to 'lighten up', that 'my turn will come soon'. As if love were a turn on one of those little rides for kids outside a supermarket. She doesn't understand me, not at all.

140

I think about the fox between two roads. Someone asked for something. And could that something be my lovely sister? I don't like the weight of secrets on me. I haven't been able to articulate what happened between me and Mamó that night. Not properly. Not even to myself.

But it was something. The law of conservation of energy states that it can be neither created nor destroyed. The charge I felt – it had to come from somewhere. And was that heat the little fox's life?

Nora Ginn.

Helen Groarke.

Bridget Hora.

Amanda Shale.

I think of Lon. His dull, copper-penny eyes. His wide, white smile. The smattering of stubble he contrives. He looks so bland, so normal. I don't get it. Though Catlin doesn't either. Me and Oona. Our 'friendship' – it isn't just a friendship. I think that we both know that, but it is up to me to say the words, and I can't. No more than magic. Some things are too big to let be true.

Mam and Catlin, with me joining in, of course talk about Lon until bedtime. Catlin goes through every interaction since we moved to Ballyfrann, framing them so differently to me that it's hard to know who's telling the truth. It's all one picture; we're probably just using very different filters. Or something.

He texts her goodnight kisses before bed. She kisses her phone, and I call her a fool and she laughs at me.

'I feel like a fool,' she says. 'I feel like I'm losing brain cells

141

every time I'm near him. It's like he's kicking out the stuff that normally lives inside my head and replacing it with all of this new happy.'

'That doesn't sound so bad,' I say to her.

'Madeline?' she asks me, her voice lower. 'Will you come with me to the pub thing?'

'Really, Catlin?' I was kind of resigned to going anyway.

'Yeah. I need you there. In case none of the others want to talk to me.'

'You'll have Lon though.'

'I know. But I want both of you. He might think I'm weird if I'm only talking to him all the time. Please?' She holds out her little finger for a promise. I think of the jut of rib outside the fox, the harsh white flash of it against the red.

I sigh. I grasp her pinkie.

It is done.

'There's something drawing him and me together, Maddy,' she says to me, eyes widening. 'I think it might be fate. I've never felt so attracted to anyone before. I mean, I think about him all the time. Like, *all* the time. Like, even when I'm praying. Or plucking my eyebrows. When he kisses me, I feel he's marking me. That now I'm his. With other boys, it was always mostly about me and them. The me was first. My happiness. My needs. But with Lon, it feels like he's the most important thing.'

'He's not,' I tell her. 'You are. You're my sister.'

'I know,' she says. 'I know it's not feminist and it's not right, but I just want to please him. I want him to look at me and feel the way I feel, and when he does it feels like it's a present from the Gods.'

I throw a facecloth at her.

'Don't be weird. What's pushing you together is your genitals. Your genitals fancy each other. Well, yours do him. It's hard to say. With genitals.'

I am aware I should stop saying genitals. Thankfully, Catlin looks at me as though what I've just said makes a kind of sense. 'His genitals totally fancy my genitals, Madeline. I know for a fact they do. I have evidence.' She grins. 'Hard evidence.'

I cover my face with my hands, and glare at her through the gaps between my fingers.

'I cannot believe you just said that.'

'Me neither,' she says in a small voice.

'Are you ashamed of yourself?' I look at her, furrowing my brow like an angry teacher.

She swallows once and then decides she's not.

'No. I regret nothing. Which is also what I will say to Lon when I lose it to him the night of the lock-in.'

'Argh. Too much information. And also, no.'

'I didn't ask your permission,' Catlin snaps.

'I know you didn't. But . . . first of all, too soon, and secondly, do you want to have an audience?' Lon probably wouldn't mind an audience at all, I think.

'Look, it's my body and I get to do what I want with it. And I want you to support me.'

'What, to stand at the side of the bed waving pompoms and cheering?'

'Lon would probably love that.'

'Eww.'

'You just hate feelings and the people who have them.'

'Maybe I just hate Lon?'

'You can't hate Lon. Because then I would hate you.'

God help us both, I think. And I say goodnight. I think we'd end up having a proper screaming row if this kept going. And I don't want that. I don't want us to move further apart than we already are.

I get a glass of water with fresh mint in, and make sure the window's open wide. I'm going to bed later and later these days, avoiding sleep and all the fear it brings. Outside the window something howls, probably a rogue husky. I open up my book, turn on the bedside lamp and settle in. My phone vibrates. It is a picture of Oona. She says, 'Bonne nuit.' She's wearing an oversized T-shirt to bed, and her hair's all sticking up. I send her back a picture of my toes poking out from the bed. A little kiss.

The world's not bad or good. It is both, and kind of all at once.

20

Oregano

(throats and insects)

Mamó is home. Not that I've been stalking her. Well – maybe just a little. I want answers. It's more of a stake-out than a creepy stare-fest. Though obviously there is some overlap between the two. I've been keeping an eye out for a pair of binoculars in the attic.

I lurk outside her door, a little afraid to approach or knock.

'Stop gawping and get in.' Her voice is sharp, so no change there. I think she's being friendly. Almost friendly. It's hard to tell. She generally glares. I venture down the little cobbled steps. It's surprisingly bright here, for a basement. There are big windows, slanted to trap sun. Lace curtains let in light but hide what's going on inside from people outside.

She has an awful lot of plants in pots. So many growing things. I pick one up and stroke the leaves and sniff it.

'What's this?' I ask. It's leafy like a plant, but growing on some rocks.

'Lungwort,' she says. There is a pause. 'It is a lichen.'

She puts the kettle on the little stove and replaces several jars on their shelves. She has floor to ceiling jam jars, vials and little roundy bottles. I take it in, all organised and filled with mulch and bones and different-coloured liquids. Some of them look quite a bit like blood.

'What's lungwort for?' I say, and then realise the clue is in the name. 'Apart from lung stuff?'

'Wounds. Ulcers. It's not for any one thing really. None of these are for any one thing. It depends on the person that needs them, and the person that's working with them. And other factors.' Satisfied her shelves are set to rights, she takes two china mugs and plonks them on the counter. I search the ceiling for a thing to talk about. A thing that isn't: 'Magic. Tell me. Now.'

'Are you all right?' I ask. Her face is pale, and the shadows under her eyes are dark.

'I've had a lot of extra jobs to do. Since the fox. And clients keep on coming.' She closes her eyes, but only for an instant. 'Every one of them takes something from me.'

She rubs another lichen with her hands.

'This one is called ruffled freckled pelt. It grows on oak, maple and birch. It was hard to convince it to grow here. Wasn't it, pet?' She's speaking to the plant and she is smiling. I don't think that I've ever seen her smile before. Not properly. Not fondly. She turns to me.

'Your sister. Where does she spend her time?' Her face is grim again. It makes more sense.

'That's her own business. Ask her,' I say, a little bit offended.

146

'Fair enough,' she says. 'But there are things you should be wary of in Ballyfrann.'

'Such as . . . ?'

I wonder who she means. Whoever killed the fox perhaps. Layla and Oona already seem to be wary of Lon, but I can't imagine Mamó being wary of a pretentious teenage boy. Could she mean magic people? Other witches . . . Is she, like, a witch? What does she call herself? It's label worries all over again. I have so many questions in my throat, but they won't seem to hop out of my mouth. It's brighter in the basement than it was in the garden. The light in here is strange. I'd love to have a proper poke around her flat. There's a solidity to it, a safety. All the jars, the herbs, the plants, the leaves and bones and shells. They all make sense.

'You've got a head on your shoulders.' She eyes me for a moment. 'More or less. You'll figure it out.'

'I need more information,' I press on. 'Who should I not trust? And why?'

'I always think it best,' Mamó says, 'to start with everyone. And as you gather knowledge, you can amend. The world is sharper here than other places.'

'Sharper how?' I ask her. 'You need to speak more plainly.'

'What I need,' she says, 'is for you to open your eyes and look at what's around you. I don't owe you my effort or my time.'

She takes another sip, and when she speaks again, her tone is more conversational. 'You want to study medicine?'

The dire-warnings portion of the evening appears to be over. Now, awkward chitchat. I roll my eyes. I liked the danger more.

'Yes,' I say. 'I told you that before.'

'So did your mother.' She stirs her tea. 'She *popped in for a chat*. Her words, not mine.'

'And did ye chat?' I ask.

'I do not chat. I speak. And I listen.' She sighs. 'She's a nice woman, your mother. Soft, but not too soft. I didn't encourage her however. I'm not here to make friends.'

'What are you here to do?' I ask.

'I'm here to work. Drink up your tea. I'm only on a break.'

I drain to the end of the mug and put it in the sink. I can feel the curiosity welling up in me.

'Mamó,' I say. 'I want . . .'

'I know what you want to know,' she says. 'But are you ready?'

I look at her. I don't think that I am. But I have to know.

'I am,' I say.

I swallow. I can hear the helpless glug of sound breaking the silence. Mamó starts brewing more tea, silently. The clang of spoon on teapot. It's hard to wait. Catlin would be charming her and grumbling. But I'm not my sister. I fix my eyes on her and settle in.

Mamó's eyes are darkly tarnished grey. The barrel of a gun. She is a weapon. When I first moved here, I thought that they were blue. I can see the knuckles bulging through the rough skin of her hands, her rainbow-stained nails. This is the closest to awkward I've ever seen her.

She swallows. 'I know you don't have much truck with pseudo-science. And I don't either. But people come to me for things – things that doctors, lawyers, counsellors can't help with. And I try my best for them. If there is something I can do to help, I do it.'

148

'Like the mafia?' I ask.

'Hmm.' She inclines her head. It's not a nod. But it is also, troublingly, not not a nod. 'In ways. I suppose *witch* would be a better way to say it. A wise woman.'

'OK.' I had kind of guessed this part already, what with all the witchcraft I had seen her doing. But that doesn't mean it doesn't sound pure weird coming out of someone's mouth like that, so blunt and practical.

'My mother was one. And hers before her. They always had a child that they trained up. To be the next wise woman. It takes at least a lifetime to learn the skills to do an all-right job.'

'What skills are those?' I ask, sitting up straighter. I want to be as tall as her. To look her in the eye.

'Various ones.' Her mouth is a straight line. 'I couldn't bear a girl to train. And then you moved here and I thought you might be a suitable candidate. You have the nature for it. And the talent.'

'How do you know?' I ask. I don't feel natural or talented. I don't feel very much of anything.

'I took the time to notice. 'Twasn't hard. The way you are with plants. The things you gather. They're another tell. Ingredients.' She spits into a handkerchief. It's nasty green. Maybe she has the flu, I think. She rasps her throat clear and continues quickly. 'Dreams can be signs as well. You've spent yourself on keeping something out and now you're tired. There are things that you can do to ease that, but it'll never be fully safe.'

'Tell me about magic,' I say, trying to keep my voice calm.

149

To remove myself from the ridiculousness of the situation, and the pulse of excitement throbbing in me at the thought of it. I need to be objective, to gather information to store in the fat jar of my brain for later use. But also, witches! Do I get a broomstick?

'I can do that,' she says, 'if you agree to . . . intern . . . with me. That's what ye call it, isn't it, these days?'

'What, unpaid labour?' I ask, but I'm slightly goading her.

'An apprenticeship. I'll teach you skills. Of course, you'd have to leave school to pursue this. It's not a part-time thing, this life of mine.'

I gawp at her. That's ridiculous. I want to find out more about this thing that I have inside me, not, like, immediately become the single member of a weird basement woman cult. No. Just no.

'That's not going to happen. For one thing, Mam would in no way let me leave school. Not that I would. For what?' I say, and my voice comes out exactly as contemptuous as I feel.

'If you were amenable, we could discuss a . . . *compromise* of sorts.' I can tell from the shape of her mouth that it costs her to even suggest this, to have to stoop to hearing what I need. 'Brian would support you.'

'I still haven't gotten the chance to chat to Brian.'

'I thought as much. He can be quite . . . elusive . . . when it suits him.'

'Why don't you just tell me what he knows and save him the trouble?' I ask, in case it's worth a shot.

'Brian will tell you what he knows, in his own time,' she says. 'Openness doesn't come easy to some people – and I don't want to overstep the mark. You're his family; not mine.'

'But –'

She exhales at me. The glare is back. 'Look, I won't go into it – the ins and outs and things – till you agree. It's mainly helping people, problem-solving, healing. Staving off a range of ills.'

I think of Mam's face, sad, sitting on the edge of my bed. Worrying about my stupid brain. About the salt. About the both of us. I don't know what to do. I don't know who or what I want to be. Or what I am.

'What if I turn out not to be like you?'

'Oh, don't mistake me, girl. You have a talent, but we are not the same. You're far, far weaker.'

Her face quirks into a little smile. I think that that was humour. I look at rows of jars that line the walls blend to one sharp shadow.

'I need to think,' I tell her. I don't want my world carved up and altered. I want to be the same as other people. I want to be the normal kind of special. Where people ask you what shampoo you use, not to be their magical apprentice. Where stepdads take you to McDonald's, and give you the odd tenner if you're lucky.

Jesus, Brian, I think. *Why can't you just be quiet and sound and boring and that's it?*

'Get back to me quickly,' she tells me. 'It's straightforward enough, my offer, and we should be starting soon.'

'It's a big commitment . . .' I begin.

She glowers at me. 'I'm not asking you to do me a *favour*, Madeline.' She says my name as though it were a threat. 'We'll speak of this again. Now go away.' She blinks at me. I feel my feet and quadriceps tensing. I rise without meaning to, without thinking.

I obey, head out into the dark of the night-time garden. But I can't go to bed. Not right away. I head into the greenhouse, check on the plants. Stroke leaves and run my fingers over soil. I ground myself in things that I can touch. That grow, and live, and never make me wonder if I'm crazy. That don't ask more from me than I can give.

Everything feels different. Something strong is coursing through my veins, and maybe she put something in my tea or maybe something was waking up. I wonder why it's easy to believe her. Surely the rational explanation would be that she is mentally ill and lying to me. But the impossible seems somehow more likely than the possible. And I don't like that, fogging up my clarity, my life.

Two more years, I think. And then there's college. In the clearing, when there was the fox, Mamó said to me that I wouldn't like the Answer. I don't know if I'll like the other answers any better. I mean, I want them. But there are sacrifices I won't make. I won't give up my normal for her danger.

I walk back through the garden. The grass is wet against my feet, soaking through my socks. The daisies all closed up and bright as stars. The moon . . .

The moon is *hungry*.

21

Jacob's Ladder

(drying up of tissues)

The lock-in tonight is, apparently, a youth-club event. Which shouldn't surprise me. This is what you get when Lon runs your youth club. Urrgh. I'm not sure what other youth clubs do, but I feel like it's crafting or organised sports activities. Maybe a camping trip. Like, things that aren't actively illegal. I wish I didn't have to go. My head is racing and my heart is pounding. I can't tell Catlin the whole story until I find a way to make it sound not crazy. She wouldn't listen anyway. Unless I said *Lon* every other word.

'*I* Lon *might* Lon *be* Lon *a* Lon *witch* Lon.'

I Lon *don't* Lon *know* Lon *if* Lon *I* Lon *want* Lon *to* Lon *be*. Lon.

'I can't believe you had tea with Mamó,' she says. 'Lon is terrified of her.'

'He is?' I ask, pleased.

'And Mam as well – she went down for a chat one afternoon

and made some joke about natural medicine and Mamó ran her. The old wagon.' Catlin is impressed.

'Ran her?' It sounds much meaner, out of my twin's mouth. *Poor Mam*, I think.

'Maybe she doesn't want a new friend?' I say. 'She is from the village, after all. Maybe she has enough people.' It sounds lame. And implausible. I can't imagine Mamó having friends, the way Mam did back home, with wine and book clubs and occasionally exercise. I mean, you never know, though.

She did, however, literally say, 'I'm not here to make friends,' last night. Which I'm keeping to myself so far, because if I tell Catlin any more of it, the magical stuff will come out and I can't face sharing that. Not yet. Not till I've gathered more information. Claims like that, you need evidence to back them up. It sounds impossible to me, and I *believe* it. I don't know how to put it into words for other people. And I'm fairly sure she would tell Lon. And it's none of his business how much of a witch I am.

'Why is she having tea with you? Maybe she's *grooming* you.' Catlin widens her eyes in a horrified manner. Mam was always worried about us being groomed when we were little. I used to wear hats all the time, for fear a stranger'd brush my hair and steal me.

'Mamó is not *grooming* me, Catlin,' I say, a bit offended, even though I still don't know what she *is* doing. She is probably grooming me. Just not for sex. For witchcraft. The worry in my stomach swells and grows. But I can't say that I'm not excited too. I mean, it's magic. The things inside me that I thought were wrong. Maybe they're power.

154

'Well, if she is grooming you, which I still fully think she is, she'd want to make more of an effort about it. Take a shower, like.' Catlin wrinkles her nose. 'She smells of turf. Who wants to smell like turf?'

'Why is Lon scared of her?' I ask her, interested.

'I don't know,' she says. 'Because she's disapproving?'

Her story does check out, but I wonder if there's more to it than that. Knowing what I know now, I'm curious about who else here knows about magic. I mean, they seem really fond of Brian. Does everyone? I think of Oona, Layla. I wonder who I should be wary of. Lon, clearly, but probably for douche reasons as opposed to danger ones, I reckon. I reckon or I hope? And Brian. I remember our conversation about Mamó. About what I should do. If she made me uncomfortable. Maybe I should talk to him about it, ask for help. Advice.

If I were more extrovert, I could interrogate people subtly at Donoghue's, making lifelong friendships as I went. If I were more extrovert I'd be getting with Oona right now instead of staring at pictures of her on my phone more than is socially appropriate.

'What are we going to wear?' I ask my twin. 'What do people even wear to lock-ins?' Catlin's much better at things to wear than I am. And this is new. Like, do we go dressed up like for a disco, or the sort of casual that takes more time than normal, like for a house party?

'Like yourself, but better hair and make-up . . .' Catlin says. 'Actually, I was wondering if I could borrow something of yours. The pink and white dress?'

'I thought you hated that,' I say. 'You told me it was only fit for 1950s cowgirls.'

'Hate is such a strong word. People change.' There is a pause. I look at her suspiciously.

She sighs.

'OK. I want to wear it to please Lon. He likes me to wear dresses and my hair down. Like a proper lady. In a film.' She plays with the edge of the blanket. I bite back a rant about Lon and his opinions and the patriarchy and everything that's wrong with the world in one skinny bastard, and find the dress in my wardrobe and give it to her. I'd rather have her happy than be right. She stands, and holds the dress against her body.

'He'll love this.' Her eyes are shining. She looks like she is feverish. Puts it on her bed and takes a picture. Sends it off, and waits for his approval.

I don't know how to react. The room is quiet, can't even hear her breathing. Little grains and leaves inside my boots and pockets give me strength.

'Are you OK, Catlin?' I ask.

'Yeah,' she says. 'I am. I just . . . I really want to make him happy, Madeline. I want him to love me back.' Her eyes are wet. She's blinking back the crying.

I give her the tightest hug. Has she lost weight? It feels like there is less of her to hold.

'Catlin. You are amazing. If he doesn't love you back, then he's an idiot. And besides, he does. He totally does. He's always looking at you. Staring. Sending messages to say goodnight. He waits at the bus stop every day just so he can see you. It's either love or stalking.'

Catlin laughs. 'He doesn't want me putting up photos of

156

the two of us,' she says. 'We kind of had a little row about it. It's fine he's not on *social media* or whatever.' She does a little voice for social media. Her Lon impression is a lot kinder than mine, I muse, but then again, it would be.

'. . . but, like, if we're a couple, I want everyone to know,' she says. 'Otherwise, it isn't fully real.'

'Did he give you a reason?' I ask.

'He has some crazy exes,' she tells me. 'And he says that he's a private person. But he isn't. Have you seen the way he dresses?'

'People can be private in some ways and not in others,' I point out, deciding not to add, 'like me, with my sexuality and witchcraft,' because we both have enough to deal with without unpacking another trunkful of skulls.

'True. I just . . .' Her face is grim. 'I don't like the thought of other girls before me. When he talks about them, and he doesn't do it often, I feel all helpless and small. Not good enough.'

How dare he use the ghosts of other girls to shrink my sister! I swallow down retorts. It's not the time.

'You are you, and who you are is amazing. I don't want to say, "You're better than those girls," but I can one thousand per cent guarantee that you probably are. Plus, they're in the past, and you are in Lon's present and his future.'

She smiles. I keep on going. Catlin needs this.

'Who kissed four guys in one night after we got our exam results?'

'Me,' she says. I see a little smile.

'Who got asked to the debs nine times before she was even in second year?'

157

'Me,' she shudders. 'Creeps. I was a baby.'

'Remember when Kevin O' Neill asked you out and you said no and he . . .'

Her face is brighter now. '. . . Started to cry and beg in front of everyone?'

'Yeah.' I smile. 'That was just cruel, Catlin. You're the one who breaks people's hearts. Not him. You are my sister. And you're magic.'

'I love you, Mad,' she says. 'I feel a bit better now.'

She wipes her eyes. I look at her.

'I know you said not to say anything bad about Lon, and I won't, but if he makes you feel like you aren't good enough, that's bullshit. You might doubt him loving you, but I will always love you. No matter what. We're blood. And if he ever, ever, makes you feel like there were better girls before you, then he is wrong. Remember. You're Catlin Hayes. And he is just a boy from Ballyfrann.'

She grins at me. 'Not even from Cork, like. What the hell was I thinking? I am *class*.'

'You are,' I say. 'You really, really are.'

'OK.' She rubs her eyes and shakes her head a little. Shakes it off. 'What are you going to wear? Because I already have my Galway boyfriend. Whereas you, my love, have only got potential.'

I wish the world could always be this way. The two of us, together, laughing.

Safe.

158

22

Primrose

(tea for frenzy, leaves for wounds)

Mamó is giving us a lift to the pub in her cherry-red Toyota. She has to go to Ballyfrann anyway, for 'various reasons'. I'm almost annoyed that Catlin's here. I want to know exactly what Mamó's doing. How her work fits in to the world of the village. Who is dangerous here, and who is not.

'She probably means the bank or something, Mad. Let her have her little mysteries,' is Catlin's take on it, which doesn't work because banks aren't open that late, so she is clearly doing something witchy. Possibly with wands. I have much fear of missing out. I could be finding out information about an elderly woman right now instead of going to the stupid pub. The actual dream, like.

We messaged back and forth inside the car. It's cleverer than whispering where Mamó's concerned. I have a sense her hearing's awful keen. Every now and then she meets my eyes in the rear-view mirror. Her gaze is very steady, and knowing.

She told me to be wary, and I am.

My eyes are heavy and there is a weight on me this evening. Last night I borrowed back the dress I gave to Catlin, sewed salt and flakes of rowan bark in the hems. I feel as if there is something to be guilty about. Ashamed. I have been warned. I have not passed it on. Perhaps I should.

'Who'll be there tonight?' asks Mamó, glaring at the road, as though it were a thing she could defeat. The traffic lights turn green almost immediately. Probably out of fright. I wonder what it would be like to glare at everything and everyone. To never wear a face you didn't mean.

'Everyone. People,' says Catlin.

'Oona, Charley, Layla, Fiachra, Cathal. Lon,' I say, trying to be open with her. And not to follow it up with, 'TELL ME MAGICS!!'

'Hmm,' she says. 'Lon.' It is the most contempt I have ever heard pumped through one syllable. Her eyes still on the road.

I suppress a smile. That is the correct amount of contempt for Lon, I feel. Catlin disagrees and is having a rage-gasm in the back seat, fingers flying off a rant to me. It has nine swears in, some of them surprising.

I see her swallow, gather and collect.

'Why the tone, Mamó?' she asks. Mamó doesn't dignify her with an answer. I wish she dignified more people with answers. And also gave better answers. We're driving up a small, steep mountain road. Catlin kicks the seat in front of her, softly but with venom.

'Mamó?' she asks. And I can tell she's going to begin stirring.

'Yes?' Mamó's voice is curt. For not a change.

160

'What about Oona?'

What about Oona? How is Oona any of Catlin's business?

'Oona Noone? The mother's a bit odd. Artistic, like. The father's got a temper. I don't know much about the young one yet. Well able to go, I'd say. The Noones always were.'

She nods. And that's as much as she says until we're halfway up the mountain.

'What a bitch,' exclaims Catlin, once we're free of the car.

'You're not wrong,' I say. 'But why did you have to bring Oona into it?'

'Well, she talked shit about Lon, and you didn't look annoyed enough about it.' She turns to me. 'And Oona is your new *best friend*.'

'Oona is not my new *best friend*.'

'She is. Look at the grinning head on you. You think she's class. You want to lesbian-marry her.'

'Shut up,' I say. It's true though. I'd wear pale grey and she'd wear white with the faintest tinge of blue to match the little flecks around her pupils. We'd honeymoon by the ocean. But that is all beside the bloody point. The cheek of her.

'Don't be a homophobic prick, Catlin.'

'You can't be homophobic to straight people, Maddy.'

'You totally can. You don't, like, need a gay person to be around for it to be homophobic. That's not a thing.' I can feel my face flushing. If she knew how I felt, maybe she'd be nicer about it all, but how even do I put it into words? I feel like Ballyfrann is jumbling up my headspace. Making everything a little warped.

Catlin's looking at me with her mouth wide open, like a sentient gif.

161

'You're properly annoyed at me,' she says, as if she really can't believe it.

I glare at her, taking it all in, from head to toe. She looks like a young lady. It could be fifty, sixty years ago. In that dress, with her hair down, make-up simple. She could be Bridget Hora, Nora Ginn. Another girl they find upon the mountain.

I try to shove the stubborn thought away.

'I'm not annoyed,' I tell her.

'You so are.' She smiles at me. 'You think you'd know by now, the way I am.'

We venture up the road towards Donoghue's. It's your typical old-man pub, wooden seats with maroon upholstery, whitewashed walls with different things stuck on. Some of them are weird. A bracelet made from braided hair. A cat's skull. Others are just jugs or glass spheres half draped with netting. I wonder where pubs get all the random stuff they put on walls. Is it bit by bit or in a job lot?

The pub smells of spilled beer and turf. Some old guys sit in the corner, sipping their pints. There's an open fire in the corner, with colourful bean bags around it. They seem really out of place. A surly-looking man is wiping down the counter. Lon is in a small room at the back, and, BUT OF COURSE, he is DJing. There's an elaborate sound system hooked up. The music pulses through the lino of the floor. It's hard to tell what colour it is, what with the combination of dim light and stains.

Layla greets us, flushed with drink and energy. She points out where the toilets are, the people that we know, and those we don't. She's moving differently tonight, weirdly buoyant, bopping her shoulders along to the music. Lock-in Layla's fun, I think. I like her.

'Hi. We're allowed to drink soft drinks and beer or cider, but not what my dad calls *hard* liquor, or they won't let us do this again. And we have to pay for everything, obviously. If you don't recognise someone, they're probably a Collins,' she tells us.

Catlin's eyes are fixed on Lon, as though he were the most important thing. She used to be her own most important thing, I think. I hope that I've reminded her of that. At least a little.

'Whose is the guitar?' Catlin asks, nodding to one propped up in the corner. 'It's not Lon's. Lon's is black.'

'Shocker,' I snort, and then do a little smile to try to soften my contempt. I don't want to get into a row.

'Fiachra brought it along – he was trying to impress Charley, but she wasn't super into it.'

'Why?' asks Catlin. 'Fiachra's cute enough.'

Layla looks at us. 'No, he isn't. Ugh.' She says it fondly. 'My brothers are both idiots. Most of his songs are about his mountain bike. He uses girls' names, but a sister knows. Charley deserves better. Plus, she needs to be careful around boys and things.'

'Why?' I ask. 'Is she OK? . . . I mean, did something happen?'

'No,' says Layla. 'Nothing like that. It's just. She's a Collins.'

'What difference does that make?' Catlin's voice is high. She doesn't get it.

Layla lowers her voice. 'They marry each other.' We look at her, aghast. She flaps her hands. 'Oh, not in an incest way. In an arranged-marriage-to-distant-cousins way. It's what they've always done.'

'That still sounds a bit . . .' Catlin looks at me.

I close my mouth. Reserve my judgement.

Layla starts to say more things but is immediately interrupted by Lon, because no one speaking could ever be as important as what Lon has to say. I tense my eye muscles.

'Did I hear *twincest*?' He smiles.

'No, Lon,' I say, with what I hope is a neutral expression on my face that hates him very much. 'Just plain old-fashioned incest.'

He grins a toothy grin, pleased at having made me feel uncomfortable. The kind of grin a weasel would grin. If it had perfectly straight human-sized teeth. And if I hated weasels.

I look at Lon. I wonder. I reach into the compartment, slowly. Take out some of the feeling in my bones. Push it through my eyes. Just a little hint. To not mess with us. A Mamó glare.

I would rather ingest a maggot than kiss you on the mouth.

His smile freezes.

I change my expression, bat my eyes, like an innocent forest creature. Catlin looks at me.

'What's going on, you two?'

We both say, 'Nothing,' at the selfsame time.

Her voice is high, and loud across the room. 'So, Charley, Layla was telling us you're going to get arranged married. How do you feel about that?'

I close my eyes. I hate it when she does this.

Charley walks across the room. Says, 'Yup.'

'Does it ever bother you?' asks Catlin. 'That it could be an old guy, or a creep?'

Charley starts to speak, 'Look who's bloody . . .' but Lon murmurs, 'Catalina, be nicer.'

She mutters a sorry and she shuts her mouth.

I look at Lon. He smiles at me. Does that thing where he uses

164

the small of Catlin's back as though it were a steering wheel. He ushers her up the stairs, so they can 'talk', in his apartment.

I look at Charley.

Charley glares at Layla.

Layla shuffles.

'I'd rather be arranged married than go out with Lon,' I offer. It only breaks the tension just a little.

Charley snorts. 'True.'

'He'd call you Madelina?' Layla offers, and I laugh.

'Urrgh. He would and all.'

Layla turns to Charley. 'I'm sorry I'm a gabby drunk. I didn't mean to tell people your stuff. I just think it and all of a sudden I say it, and sometimes I think, *Don't say this thing, Layla*, but it's already out. Like a greyhound, or a pony. My mam loves gambling. I'm worried about her. There I go again.'

She sinks into a chair, still looking like a graceful ballerina but one who is utterly, utterly ashamed of herself.

Charley cuddles in beside her. 'It's fine. I mean, it's the truth. It's just my truth. And I don't always like it. The idea. I'd like to, like, "play the field", and stuff.'

They curl together, having a best-friend moment. I sit on a stool, wondering how much they know about this place, and what it would take for them to tell me. This makes me feel like a crap spy, so I head up to the bar and order a lemonade. Awkwardly. I might build up to cider later on. Like, I have no issue with underage drinking, it's just it feels weird being in a pub and that being OK. Like, it's all a bit *sanctioned*. When I get back to the table, Eddie has joined the girls, looking scandalised.

'I only went up there to get my coat,' he says, 'and I saw a lot more of your sister than I wanted to see.'

I gasp. 'Is she all right?'

'Yeah, she's grand. Laughed at me.' He turns bright red at the thought of it. 'I felt really creepy and awkward though. Like, what they do is none of my business . . . But the way Lon smiled – I think he *liked* me seeing them like that.'

Ugh. That is the worst thing I ever heard. I resist the urge to storm up there and pull him off my sister. She'd never speak to me again.

'Why are ye even friends with him?' I ask, typing a quick 'u ok?' into my phone.

'He has a pub?' he offers.

'Fair enough.'

Catlin sends me back a lot of aubergines. She is the worst, but definitely grand. We spend the next few hours chatting and drinking, while Lon and Catlin stay in his apartment. It's not like Catlin to miss this much of a thing. I drink a pint of cider, and feel the sugar harsh on the top of my stomach. I need to pace myself, seeing as she's left me here alone.

'C'mere,' I say to Layla. 'What's the story with his crazy ex-girlfriends?'

She shrugs at me. 'Dunno.'

Fiachra cracks open a can, his face dark. 'Who – Helen?'

'Like Helen Groarke?'

'*Exactly* like Helen Groarke.' He opens his mouth, and starts to speak again, but Charley shushes him, and clears her throat.

'I don't really like that word. *Crazy*. It usually means girls who ask boys questions.'

166

'Or message them twenty-five times in an evening.'

'Shut up, Fiachra.'

The conversation shifts. I'm still no wiser. I listen to the hum and dip of talk, and think, I know so little about these people. Their motivation, history. It's new to me, but it is far from new.

And there are secrets, big and small, they're keeping.

Her name was Helen.

What did Fiachra mean with his *exactly*? They might have known her, Helen Groarke. Who moved away and came back as a corpse. I suddenly feel cold. Lon is only nineteen. He would have been fifteen. When she was found. A little younger than she was. But still . . . it's the same age difference between him and Catlin, pretty much. It could be, could have been. I try to slow my heart and parse my thoughts.

There are things you should be wary of . . .

I think of the first time we met Layla, when Catlin brought up the corpses in the hills. I look at the bodies of my classmates, hearts beating, eyes blinking, muscles tensing and relaxing, and scroll through my phone and start to type a message. How to put it . . . ?

'Did u know . . .'

'Lon's ex-girlf . . .'

'We need . . .'

But nothing that I want to say is right. I feel a sickness creeping up my throat. A dull sick ache that's creeping like a vine through me. There is ivy on the walls of the castle and it ferrets through the rock and brick, it curls in everywhere, invading space and causing problems, cracks. Brian says it shouldn't have been planted there, not in the first place. Once it's introduced, it's hard to kill.

I close my eyes.

I blink.

The room is loud.

The voices, rising, falling. I feel like I am watching on a screen. I amn't one of them. I don't belong here. I wish that I could leave. I cannot go.

I take a breath. My hands inside my pockets, fingering at lavender and bark.

'Where's Oona?' Charley asks. 'I thought that she was coming?'

'She will.' Eddie blushes. 'She'll be a little late. Her dad was being grumpy about lifts.'

I look at him. His face is red, and smiling. I don't like it.

'I ... er ... messaged her to ask.' A little grin. I've never noticed before how much his face needs smacking. Those cheeks and eyes.

I bite down on my lip and check my phone. Three messages. I smile.

And something crystallises here, inside this room, looking at the boy who likes the girl that I might be in love with.

As close as I have come to love, at least.

Eddie is still saying things. I take a break, and venture down the stairs to the grimy little bathroom. The walls are old and once white, and covered with writing. Scraps of poems, and people's names entwined in marker hearts. I scan the wall for names I recognise. I don't see Lon, but Helen's there. The second name scraped out, gouged through the paint.

I put my hand over the writing, close my eyes and try to do the thing I did with Lon. The hard stare. It doesn't work. I'm just a girl, leaning on a wall.

A useless creature.

When I go back up, Cathal is talking about a dirt-jumping competition he won this summer. I've just worked out it's mountain bikes when she arrives. Dressed in jeans, a little black T-shirt. A necklace made of copper wire and smooth green sea glass. Her hair is scraped into a tiny little ponytail. It's really cute. I smile at her, she says hello and comes in for a hug. She kisses my cheek on one side and then the other. I freeze.

Every part of me is waiting for more.

'Excuse,' she says. 'I forgot and did the *bises*. In France, when we say hello, we do a kiss.'

I nod. I've heard of this. It is a thing. I smile at her. Her eyes meet mine. I see the little flecks of palest blue. For a second they seem to move around, silver fish inside a deep brown pool. I'm conscious that I'm staring. I lower my gaze.

But when I look back up, she meets my eyes.

'Come outside with me,' she says. 'I want to show you something.'

'I need to get my coat,' I say.

'I'll wait.'

On the way to get it, I grab Layla. 'I'm going out for a bit,' I say.

'With Oona? Say no more.' She grins.

'Yeah . . . Would you mind, keeping an eye on Catlin?'

'Madeline,' she says, 'we're all below. She will be grand. Go. Chat.' She takes a sip from her pint glass. 'I mean, we hate him. But she's safe. Go on.' She nudges me, as though I were a domino. 'You can worry tomorrow.'

And I will. But, as I reach the door, I feel something like hope. I put away the things I should be scared of.

And venture out with Oona, in the night.

23

Deer's Tongue

(to draw a woman to a woman)

We walk through the village, past the lit-up places, into darkness, and it doesn't feel dangerous, but quickens my breath. Oona's moving at a faster pace than normal. Even with my slightly longer legs, I have to trot to keep up with her.

'Come,' she says. I follow her through trees and over rocks.

We walk for ages till we reach the lakeside, water flat and dark. The water's moving. I can barely see it but I hear it, see the little tilt of moon on flow.

'Here,' she says, 'is where I swim each morning. It is like my church, a sacred place.'

I smile at her and see it's not a joke. She places the flat of her hands against the water.

'I wanted to come back to it with you.'

My heart is beating so quickly.

'Today,' she says to me, 'has been so hard. I need a friend.'

I ask her what is wrong. And so she tells me. I hear it but

there's something else as well, a kind of panic rising and then dulling.

Oona is worried Claudine might be losing interest. She hasn't been replying to her messages. She's worried that she's met someone else. I can feel my heart beat in my chest, can feel my ribcage opening. Widening to let in loss and hope.

'I was always the one who was more in love,' she says. 'I knew this.'

Her tilted chin. I know it too, I think. I tell her that it's hard and that I'm sorry and that I'm here. She smiles at me, and tells me that she knew I'd understand. She turns out towards the dark and shining water, as though it were a friend who could explain. I try to think of something else to say or do. A helpful thing.

She pulls her top off, over her head, and smiles that half-moon smile. So soft and bright. I want to tell her that she's mad, it's freezing, but it's like I've been put on pause. I want to be her friend. I want to kiss her.

I don't know what to do. Or how to move.

She is wearing a little lacy bralet. It is green. Her panties are brown. Her skin is brightly dappled in the moonlight, like the water in a swimming pool.

'Come on,' she says, and runs into the lake. She doesn't look to see. She knows I'll come.

I take a breath, remove my coat, and pull my dress over my head. It is exactly as cold as I thought it would be, but I try not to show it. I've never really liked the sensation of being surrounded by water. Swimming is an awful lot of work. I'm wearing a sports bra and black boy shorts. It looks like a bikini,

171

I tell myself. I always worried when we went swimming. That people would look at me, compare. And find me wanting.

I am wanting now.

Catlin didn't mind as much as me. She's very unselfconscious. Oona's pretty unselfconscious too. And that makes sense. She's perfect. She looks like the title character in a film about beautiful people. I look like the title character in a film about a girl who has a spot the size of a hillock on the corner of her chin.

I peel my tights off.

Where has Oona gone?

And suddenly I see her head rise like a tiny Loch Ness monster in the middle of the pond. She moves so quickly, flicking and twisting like a beautiful eel. I put a toe in.

'It's freezing,' I say into the silence. I don't think I'm expecting a reply. I swallow. *Nothing worth doing in life is easy*, is a thing that Mam says sometimes. And it isn't always true. And I don't think that she meant it for right now. But I say it and it makes me braver. I take a step. I take another step.

Be bold, be bold, but not too bold.

And I'm submerged. I can feel my skin goose and pucker. I can feel my teeth begin to shake. I kick my legs and close my eyes so tight and power through it.

And suddenly her body's next to mine. She grabs my hands and loops them round her neck. She's stronger than I thought. And she is swimming, pulling me along. My breasts and ribcage pressed against her back. I can feel the strong flick of her legs. The sureness of her body, in the water.

I sense her smile. I hope she senses mine.

She pulls me under.

172

24

Yarrow

(for the wounded)

Catlin is furious with me for going off. Of course she is. Everything in the world is all about Catlin. Before anyone makes a decision, she must be consulted or everything will crumble into dust. It is the way of things. It was foolish to rock the boat by making choices. I understand this, but she's also wrong.

'You weren't even around most of the night,' I say. 'You were hooking up with Lon the whole time.'

'Not the *whole* time. Not while you were gone,' she says, all pale and tense and doing that thing where she over-enunciates words to show how calm she is. How reasonable she's being.

'So it's OK for you to go off with Lon and leave me alone, but it's not OK for me to go for a walk with Oona?' I ask, although it's not a question. Not really.

Catlin glares at me, and wipes down the surface of a battered steamer trunk with a J-cloth. It looked pale grey, but it was really black. We're cleaning out the unused rooms for Mam. To 'surprise Brian', when he comes back from yet another work trip. As if we need more secrets in this place. How much will Brian tell me, if we get the chance to speak before he's off again? I wonder what he's told Mam about it all. I spray some glass cleaner on an old foxed mirror. The veins and stains of ancient rotting glass. I peer at Catlin's reflection. She's sitting on a dusty ottoman, waiting, but I'm waiting too. For something.

I can't explain myself. I am voiceless. Full of wanting things I cannot have. I don't know what, but some of it is Oona.

The moon was fat on our way back to Donoghue's. We didn't speak. Outside of the water. But we held hands and everything was charged, and I could feel the distance between my body and her body, as though it were another part of me. A phantom limb.

As we walked in, she let go of my hand.

Catlin was bright with anger as we arrived, the others talking quietly among themselves. Clearing up. Fiachra and Cathal drained the cans before they binned them. Charley washed the glasses, Layla swept. They're all so good, I thought. Even when they're drunk, they tidy up. The grumpy man behind the bar was gone.

'I rang and rang,' Catlin yelled at me, performing her rage for an audience of everyone in the pub but mainly Lon. 'Mamó is looking for you on the road. I thought you were missing, like those girls.'

I met her eyes.

Helen Groarke.

Amanda Shale.

Nora Ginn.

Bridget Hora.

Ghosts passed between us. And I could sense her almost

174

move to hug me, but Lon put his arms tight around her. He met my eyes and smiled behind her back. I felt a hint of something dark in him. A little scare that ran right up my spine.

Her name was Helen.

'You were wrong to scare your sister like that, Madeline,' Lon scolded.

Because, apparently, he is my dad.

'I'm sorry, Lon?' I said, doing my best to pronounce his name the same way Mamó did.

I see you, Lon, I thought. *For what you are.*

I looked over at Oona. She was helping Charley tidy up the cans into a bin bag.

'Where were you?' Catlin asked.

I didn't say. I think that I was waiting for Oona to say something. *She was with me. It wasn't all her fault.*

That kind of thing.

And then a beep.

Our lift was waiting.

Mamó's little red car carved our way home through the forest. The beams of light the only bright thing in the deep and dark. I played what had happened over and over in my brain. What it meant, and all that it could mean. And all it didn't.

'Aren't you going to ask her where she was?' Catlin spluttered.

'No. I'm not her keeper,' Mamó told her.

Our eyes met in the mirror, grey and green.

She wants to be.

We parted ways, and Catlin stalked in silence to her bedroom. I knew she felt betrayed.

And I did too.

By my own stupid feelings.

When we left, Oona didn't look at me.

I don't like this. This feeling in my gut like she might want me, but she might not want me. The lurch of that.

If I told Catlin about Oona, she'd forgive me. It would be bigger than the grudge she holds. I know this, but the silence stretches longer.

A cavern yawning wide between us both.

A crush seems like such a reductive word, but it is one. What I have.

And I am crushed.

Why would she ignore me like that? I feel my eyes well up. A tear drips on the hard pine attic floor.

I think of Mamó, her jars and bottles. The people piling in to ask for help. I wish there were a treatment for this sort of thing. A lure, so I could bring Oona near to me and keep her close. I want her head to nestle in the crook of my arm. I want her on my stomach, on my hips. I want her skin on mine. I want to fall asleep beside her, wake up smiling. I want, I want, I want.

I'm sick of wanting things I'll never have. I'm sick of almost everything about me. I wish I were a ghost and not a girl. Then looking never acting would be fine. I spend so much time stopping my arms from reaching for the things I want and know I'll never get.

I wish that I were good enough for Oona.

I wish that I were better than I am.

Catlin wraps her arms around my back. She presses her face between my shoulder blades.

'It's OK, Mad,' she says. 'It's just you scared me. I amn't used to being the sensible one.'

She smiles at me. I smile a little back.

'You look so sad.' She passes me a clean duster. It's yellow and it's soft. I wipe my face.

And I could tell her now, if I wanted to.

If I was feeling brave.

But I can't, not yet. It's like a stone I'm holding in my mouth and I want to spit it out but if I did it wouldn't be my stone.

And so I say, 'I'm sorry.'

'It's fine, Mad, really,' she says. 'It's just this place. It gives me the creeps. All this murder underneath the surface. The mountain where you were last night is where they found a lot of them, you know.'

I do know. But last night I didn't think. My heart too full.

'I dream about the girls sometimes,' she tells me. 'I've been reading about them, lighting candles, saying little prayers. It's not that I'm being morbid. It's just . . .'

She sits down on the floor beside me. Her fingers scratch a stubborn floorboard stain.

'It's the history of this place, I mean. It's fascinating. But it's also real. The fox we found. Those girls – they have stories, but they're not a story. And I've been acting almost like they are, and then last night you were gone. And part of me knows that you were off with Oona, for whatever reason . . .'

She looks at me pointedly. I stare at my toes.

'. . . and you being gone made everything feel real. And I was there with Lon – Laurent, I mean – but I didn't want him near me. I thought of the fox. The body like that. I just

177

wanted to run outside and find you and make everything OK. Whatever it was . . .'

I tell her that I get it and I say I'm sorry and I mean it this time. It must have been weird for Catlin, waiting for me. She's normally the one who has adventures. The one who's fun enough for both of us. But we won't be living in each other's pockets forever. We'll go to places and we'll build our lives. And that's what I want, but I am worried about it too, that when it happens I will be bereft, missing the part of me that has friends. But I'm realising that's not true.

'Maybe that's why I don't like Lon,' I tell her. 'Because he's taking you away. I mean, I see you all the time, but not as much.'

'Laurent thinks that too,' she says, and smiles at me.

Of course he does. The sly prick.

'Did you tell him that you loved him?' I ask.

'I tried to,' she says. Her hands gesture in the air, reaching for something I can't see. 'But the words just wouldn't come. I looked at him and I thought *iloveyouiloveyouiloveyou* but I didn't want to say it too soon, or have him see me as needy or anything.' She looks towards the wall, twisting the red and yellow duster in her hands, wringing it as though it were heavy with fluid. 'I want to make it easy for him to love me, Mad.'

'It is easy to love you,' I tell her. 'You don't have to say it to feel it. Maybe wait a while. Until he says it, or until there's a perfect time. Maybe at the party, with other people there, it was too much pressure.'

She seems to take that on-board.

'Catlin?' I venture. 'You know Lon's ex? Helen.'

'What?' Her voice is sharp. 'Where did you hear that name?'

178

'Just at the pub,' I say. 'And . . . do you not think it's a bit weird that she had the same name as the dead girl?'

'Not really,' she says. 'It's not an unusual name, I mean. Helen.'

'Yes, but Ballyfrann is tiny.'

'It is,' she says.

I feel my guts tangle and stiffen, heavy like wrought iron.

'Was the Helen his Helen, Catlin?' I ask.

She looks at me. 'How do you compete with someone who isn't there any more?' she asks. 'I mean . . .' She sounds wistful, sad, but I'm jarred into horror, and my voice is sharp.

'You DON'T!' I say. 'If someone's ex is dead because of murder, that's what they call a *red flag*.'

'She moved away, Madeline. Jesus Christ –' she starts, but I keep going.

'Catlin. She moved away, and then they found. Her. Body. You remember. You reminded me. And I left you alone with him last night. Jesus Christ.'

'It wasn't the same Helen, Maddy,' she said. 'He would have said. We spoke and spoke for ages. He really opened up to me.'

'Yes, opened up his bag of *murder* tools.' My voice is brittle, panicked.

'STOP,' she says. 'This isn't a thing to snark about, or make fun of. This is my life. I love him.'

'What did he say to you, exactly?' I ask her. 'About Helen.'

Her face is very serious. 'He told me she was kind, and she was beautiful, like me. And that he really fell for her, but she broke his heart, and soon after they broke up, she moved away. And it took him a long time to get over it. And he wasn't sure he ever would, entirely. Until he met me.'

179

'Catlin, that is terrifying,' I tell her.

'Madeline. I am telling you. It wasn't the same girl. He would have said.'

'Would he?'

'*Yes*. He absolutely would have. I know not everyone likes him, I'm not blind. He knows that too. A lot of the people he went to school with moved away for college, and it's lonely for him. He tries his best. Like, that's why he runs the youth club. To try to fit in. And no one gives a shit. Like, he did so much work last night, organising the venue and the sound equipment and everything. And at the end of it, no one so much as thanked him . . .'

'Does even a small part of you think . . .'

'. . . that he had anything to do with it?' Catlin finishes. 'No. Absolutely not. I believe him and I love him,' she says. 'I wish you could talk to me about this like a normal person, without jumping to conclusions.' She sighs, letting her hands flop down into her lap. 'It's very frustrating.'

'Umm.'

'Madeline,' she says. 'You can't be stirring Mam up about this. Twisting things. She'd worry, and she's got enough.'

'Maybe she *should* be worried.' I barely get the words out, before she cuts me off, her voice incredulous.

'What?' Her *what* has more syllables than normal, to fit in all the contempt. I shrink a little. I have a point. A sharp and shiny point. 'Are you even listening to yourself?'

'I mean, you were angry with me for going up to the mountains with Oona last night. And she's, like, half the size of Lon . . . Can't I just –'

'NO. Lon wouldn't hurt a fly, Madeline,' Catlin says.

180

'That's LITERALLY what the man in *Psycho* says at the end of the movie *Psycho*. Did he actually say to you, in words, that it was a different Helen?'

'He didn't have to,' she says. 'I can't do this. You don't know what you're talking about, Maddy,' she snaps at me, and her voice is filled with spite all over again. 'I'm going for a smoke.'

She turns on her heel and flounces out of the room, as haughty as a lady in one of the portraits Brian's father bought to put up on the walls as pretend ancestors.

I sit cross-legged on the dusty floor, unpacking what just happened. Deep down in the shame-pit of my stomach, I'm conscious she's right. I don't know what I'm talking about. I've never loved before, or been loved back. But, all the same, I know enough to know where danger lurks. Not to blindly follow where your person leads you.

Unless . . .

I think of Oona, nose and eyes and face. Her collarbones, the way she says my name. If I were to find out . . . what would I do with that? But Oona's not even a bit like Lon is. She scares me in a different kind of way. A safer way.

Telling her the way I feel.

There's not enough salt in the world.

She let go of my hand. She moved away. Of course she moved away.

There is another heart inside her heart.

I sit on the floor, scared for Catlin, worried for myself, draw stars into the dust and wipe the cloth over them, dark night sky.

I'm not the girl that people fall in love with. I'm the girl you use to forget that girl.

25

Agrimony

(cure-all, slumber, calm)

I was in a cavern. I wasn't sure exactly how I'd gotten there. Implausible things were happening all over the shop in Ballyfrann, I mused, deciding to go along with it. Maybe the cave would be full of self-esteem and biscuits. I peered around hopefully. In a world where teleportation was possible, biscuits could definitely happen. I mean, biscuits are not an impossible dream, defying God and science. My stomach growled.

This place was wide, and large, and dimly lit. Filled with stalagmites and stalactites, the points of them a-drip. Everything was velvety and moist. I didn't feel drunk. Not exactly. But I certainly felt something. Not myself.

Through the dim, I could make out the tall figure of a man. I moved towards him, dispersing mist. I knew the way it smelled, this fog. It belonged to somewhere, or someone maybe. I couldn't place it though.

It wasn't real.

I looked down at my hands and they were still mine. My feet too, though they were bare. The ground should have been cold, but it was warm and soft. More like a rug than gritty cavern floor. Where was I, really?

He smiled at me. I couldn't see him smile but I could sense it, trickling through my body like relief. He beckoned with one hand and I approached. There was music playing. Something like a theremin, or a synth. Hard, high sounds through soft moist air. I felt the doughy ground part beneath my feet and I was falling. I was falling down. He caught me.

Strong arms tight around me, pressing against the white cotton of an unfamiliar nightgown. Lifting me up. Carrying me somewhere. To a bed. A big soft bed, with silky black sheets. I could see the cavern around me. Something written on the walls. The letters chipped. I couldn't make out what they were exactly, like I had forgotten how to read. Or like English was Cyrillic. I knew the shapes meant words, but not which ones. I tried to focus on them, but the more I worked at it, the fuzzier they grew before my eyes.

A needle on a record player. The music changed, to something older. Throbbing. I tried to get up but it felt like all the blood had left my body. Like I was light and heavy all at once. Black and grey and spattered red on white. I closed my eyes. The world was spinning. The mist, when I tried to part it, was thicker. There are things I'm not supposed to see.

The man was there beside me. And his face . . . I knew that face. I knew him.

It was Lon.

He was wearing black, a T-shirt and waxed denim jeans. He

183

smiled at me. His hair was slicked right back like he had recently climbed out of some sort of sexy swimming pool or hot tub.

'Hello,' he said. 'My dove.'

In one swift motion he removed his shirt. His chest was hairless, lithe. He wore a little chain around his neck. I glanced awkwardly at the rock formations, pointing up and down. Dripping on me. There wasn't really anywhere to hide. Nowhere to look. The awkwardness was clearing out my head though. That was something. I wished I were a dove to fly away. A fox to bite him.

'You are not normally so reticent.' He smiled. 'I kind of like it. Playing hard to get. And I will get you. In the end.' He lay beside me, running bony fingers through my hair. I could feel his breath. It smelt of spearmint. Tin. I looked down at my bare arms. They were very pale, and I could see the fat blue veins weaving through them like green ones on a leaf. It's weird how plants and animals have veins. And rocks as well. There were ribbons of limestone, granite, quartz running through the walls. Not lots of them, small neat lines, like seams.

'I –'

He put a finger to my lips. His skin was very warm and very dry.

'Shhh . . . my doe. Don't be afraid of me. I'll protect you.' I looked at him. It felt so nice and warm. Like I was safe here. Like I could believe him. But he was Lon, and this place wasn't real. I couldn't move my arms. I tried to blink.

'I'm not your doe,' I muttered.

He swallowed.

'. . . Maddy?'

'Lon ...' I said, and noticed that my voice was different here, all soft and purring. I sounded like a kitten. Like a dream. He leaned towards me, his eyes darkening.

'Have I been here before?' I asked him. Something in the smell, the look. This place. I knew it. He leaned in to me. I felt the urge to run my fingers all across his skin. It was difficult to remember that I hated him, that Oona is the one I want that way. That he was my sister's and not mine.

I tried to think of solid things again. Of salt. Of water. Metal, blood and earth. Tea. Of cups of tea. The sitting room in our old house in Cork. Of comfort things. I sucked them in like breath.

He bent to kiss me. Everything was slow and fast at once. I could see his lips, parting like the entrance to a cave. The glimmer of his teeth. I took it in.

Not mine. I blinked as if my eyes could hurt the air.

Could impact.

I blinked again, as though I had an angry eye infection. Outraged, repeated blinking.

The veil around his face became less gauzy. He was clearer now, and so was I. What was I – what were *we* – doing?

'You'll need to leave, if you are going to be like that,' he snapped at me. 'If you can't be a good girl, then get out.'

His voice sounded deeper, harsher, older as he said that. I saw him wave his fingers over my face.

Then nothing till I wake. The morning pouring bright through the windows. The green of garden and the black of furze. The grass rust-coloured towards the mountains. I wonder if I could find that lake again. I think I could. It wouldn't be the same though.

I walk the seven hundred or so miles to the kitchen and check the shelves. The box of salt I left under my bed has been replaced.

It's Mam. I know it is. Always tidying. She's hidden it away from prying eyes. The evidence. The oddness of her daughter. And it is odd.

I am odd.

Do I, deep down, so deep down I shudder at the thought of it, somehow fancy Lon? Is that what that dream was? An explanation for why I don't like him, that I'm jealous?

I drum my fingers on the hard oak table. I'm not going back to sleep, I know. I put the radio on and make fancy coffee in Mam's French press. I'm worrying about the salt again, thinking of a secret place to hide it, when Brian comes in.

'Hi, Madeline,' he says, in his sing-song voice, as if it were perfectly normal to have a stressed-out teenager sitting in the kitchen all alone so early in the morning.

'Welcome back,' I mumble, hoping he will go away and leave me to my stress.

'Thanks. I only got in late last night. A few hours ago, really. Tried to sleep but –' he shrugs his shoulders – 'nothing doing, as the fella says. Can I have some coffee, please?' he asks. In his own house. He's always so polite.

'Help yourself,' I say, gesturing towards it.

He does, and sits beside me. He's wearing flannel pyjamas and a navy blue towelling dressing gown. He looks like a dad in a television show.

'What has you out of bed?' he asks.

'I had a bad dream,' I tell him. 'You?'

'I'm sorry to hear that, Madeline. I wanted to get up rather than continue to disturb Sheila with my tossing and turning. And there's a phone call I'm expecting in –' he checks his watch – 'half an hour or so. But coffee first.' He takes a sip and smacks his lips. 'This is very helpful. Thank you.'

'You're welcome,' I say, and I smile at him. Then, 'Brian?'

'Yes,' he says, his face is open, honest.

'You know the way you told me to come to you . . . if Mamó was . . . strange or something?'

His shoulders straighten, and I see him put a new self on, like a suit. Something authoritative. He sips his coffee, waits for me to speak. He knows I will.

'We found this dead fox. Me and Catlin did,' I begin, feeling stupid articulating it. 'And there was something *wrong* about it. It wasn't like badgers on the road, rabbits in the field. A person did it. Sliced it open, in the middle of the crossroads.'

He nods stiffly, and says, 'Go on.' I notice the sing-song tone underneath his words again, and something else, flitting over his features. Only for a second. Barely for a second. But still. There. I don't want to say too much, I realise. But what exactly is the right amount?

'And Mamó – she told Catlin to wait, and ye would come home. And I . . . we went back there, and cleaned it up. And she told me to be wary of Ballyfrann, but that it wasn't her place to tell me why. Brian, why should I be wary? Should I be afraid for Catlin or for Mam?'

He lets out a long, distracted sigh. I can see him composing the answer in his head. Not lying, but deciding what to tell me. I get the sense it won't be all he knows.

187

'I'll answer the second question first. No, Madeline. You don't need to be afraid for Sheila or your sister. This can be a complicated place, and its secrets aren't mine to tell, and some of them are . . . difficult to put into words for people who haven't grown up here. But one thing is certain: everyone in Ballyfrann was terrified of my father. Self included. And, because I am his son, there is a certain level of respect accorded to me and mine.'

'OK,' I say. 'This all sounds a bit criminal.'

'I'll be honest with you, he wasn't far off it . . . There's too much to go into this early in the morning, but he was not a good man, Madeline. And I am trying my best to be one.'

'We never knew our father, not properly.' It comes unbidden.

'And, sometimes, I'm not saying that it's so in your case, that can be a good thing.' He closes his eyes. 'I find this stuff excruciating to talk about, and I've done a lot of therapy . . . which, if he were still alive, would be enough to get me written out of his will, most likely.'

I smile politely. I don't know how we got from me asking questions about Ballyfrann to unpacking Brian's childhood issues, but I don't feel qualified to have this conversation, and it's very warm in the kitchen. I sip my coffee, to give me time to think. To clear my head.

'What was the fox?'

Brian swallows. 'From your description, Madeline, I'd say it may have been a sort of prayer. Something similar to what Mamó does with her . . . workings, and to what you do yourself – the salt Sheila found under the beds.'

I look at him again. His eyes are fixed on a point above

188

my head, his face is stoic. He looks like he is wearing a mask. Maybe Brian just doesn't like talking about his feelings. A lot of people don't. I don't. His tartan slippers drum against the flagstones. I look down at my toes. One of them has dirt under the nail. A little grey. When I lift my feet, there are little sweat marks in their wake. His voice still going, weaving up and down.

'. . . I know I probably haven't given you everything you need to know, but this is an old place. A lot of history. And, it will take time.' He swallows again. 'I don't want to ask you to keep anything from your mother, but I will say that I was hoping to share with her gently, and in my own time, the more unusual aspects of the village. And it would feel odd, to have you as my confidant and not her.'

'I get that, Brian,' I say. 'But I still have a lot of questions.'

'I know.' He reaches his hand to my arm and squeezes it gently. His voice is higher now, and quieter, and I feel a sense of calm. He understands. He will take care of us. It will be fine.

'And thank you for your patience, and your honesty,' he continues. 'You're coping well, with all this change. Much better than I would, in your place, I think. Madeline, I really want this to be successful. It's important. The two of ye are important. When I married your mother, I kind of married both of ye as well . . .' He exhales heavily. '. . . That sounds creepy, doesn't it?'

I crack a smile. 'Yeah. I kind of know what you mean though, Brian. And I appreciate it.'

He looks at me. 'I told Sheila if you need to put salt under our bed to feel like you're at home here, that's fine by me. But she'll do what she thinks is best. She's a good mother.'

'She is,' I say. 'And you're a good stepfather.'

'I'm not sure that that's true. But I am trying.' He looks calmer now that he's said his piece. He pours another cup.

'I'll take this with me. Fecking Tokyo.' He shuffles off upstairs. I didn't hear the phone ring. Maybe he just wanted the conversation to be over. The kitchen's cooler now that he is gone, I realise.

The stars are out, but technically it's morning. How desperate would a person have to be to kill a fox, I wonder. What were they after? I wish there was a way to just make people tell me straight out what I want to know. It will be hard for Brian, to tell Mam whatever else there is. She hates my salt, and my salt isn't a weird pagan murder village or a terrifying dead father.

I drain my cup and switch on the immersion for a shower.

I need to clear my head, still muggy from the dream and kitchen heat.

It's all too much, and somehow not enough.

26

Ginger

(jealousy and balance)

Catlin sits in the kitchen with a mug of tea. She isn't drinking, just staring blankly into it. Her eyes are empty, the shadows underneath bruise-dark. They look like someone's gouged them on her face with clumsy thumbs. My heart hurts looking.

'Catlin?' I ask.

'What?' she says.

'Are you OK?'

Her face is confused. 'No.' She grabs her cup and holds it to her chest. She leaves the room, and I am all alone. I look up at the shining copper pots, the heavy rafters. You could hang a thing from one of those. Strings of onions or garlic, or a body. I shake my head. It's filling up with something I don't like.

I think of Catlin's face, before we moved here. It was the same as mine, but brighter. Better. And now, she's weak as well. When you move plants, sometimes they fail to thrive in their new soil. They wilt and flop, leaves dry out. Bits fall off, no fresh growth. It's hard to watch.

I put my hands hard against my eyes and press them deep towards my brain, my skull. There is a tension welling in my head. I feel it humming like a coming swarm.

The entrance to Mamó's house in front of me. The hard door cold on my knuckles. Three harsh times I knock. The door clicks open.

'Madeline. Hello.'

'I've come about your offer . . .' I tell her. 'I want to . . .'

She looks at me. I'm not wearing a jacket. It is cold.

'Come and help me in the garden,' she says. 'First we'll work and then we'll have a talk.'

She goes out the back door to the physic garden. It's bigger than the courtyard one. None of the herbs are labelled.

'What's this?' she asks.

'Sage?' I venture.

'And what's sage for?'

I scan my brain.

'Look at it,' she snaps. 'Touch it. Smell it.'

I take the sprig, give a sniff and try my best to remember what I know.

'Um . . . For guidance?' Maybe I should have said for when you're worried your sister is in love with the wrong man. Brought it up organically, like a smooth detective.

'Depends on the kind of sage. This one here is green. And this –' she gestures to another plant – 'is marshmallow. Wild garlic. Lady's finger. Honeysuckle. Mint.'

'We're here for mint,' I tell her.

192

'Why do you say that?'

'I feel it.'

She says nothing, but she steps aside. I pluck eighteen separate mint leaves. Stack them one on top of the other. Roll them into a cylinder. The moon is bright. She hands me a little jar. Her dress is neat and brown and she is wearing Birkenstocks with socks. Her hair is loose. Normally she wears it braided back. It hangs down to her shoulders and it suits her. She glares at me. I twist the jar tight shut and hand it back.

She's after me. She wants to be my boss. It is a weird dynamic, being headhunted for witchcraft by an in-law.

'Caw,' I hear, and turn. The raven on a branch beside her. Mamó takes a slab of juicy-looking meat out of her pocket, feeds it to him. He eats it and she murmurs things along. He's very big. His beak is thick and cruel. This is too much witch for me. I snort. He flaps. She glares.

'Wait in there.' She gestures to her house.

'What, so you can discuss things with a blackbird?' Nervousness is making me prickly, I can feel resentment building up. Why am I here? Why do I have to do this? Why the raven?

'Baaaaaaab is no blackbird.'

'It's pronounced Bob. Ugh,' I snap.

She glares at me, I stomp towards the flat. A raven always wants to eat a carcass, and they'll eat any carcass. Owl or fox or goat. Even human. I think of his stern beak. The downturned opening. They eat our dead.

The eyes from little lambs.

This is her pet?

Or her familiar.

The creaking rasp behind me meets Mamó's voice. There is a music to it. I push the door. It opens slowly, like there is a force that's pushing back. Is that a spell as well? I wonder. It's cold inside. I poke the fire.

Beaks on carrion. Claws that grasp until the flesh gives way. The beak was black and pink inside. A little tongue. It had a little tongue. I cannot handle this. I want my life right back the way it was. I want my sister safe. My world arranged.

Mamó's voice breaks the silence. 'So. You've thought about my offer?'

'Yes. At length.' I swallow.

'And what have you decided?' Her voice is even.

God, I hate this. I'm terrified that whatever I say will be the wrong thing. That I'll regret deciding either way. I think of her finger, pointing me back to the house. I think of Brian and his little chat. I think of Mam, quietly removing salt from floors. Knowing what I did and saying nothing. She hates the bit of me that Mamó wants.

She wants an answer. I don't have an answer.

This place is like a tick upon a dog. It's sucking all the certainty from me.

'I want to know some more about Lon,' I say.

'What does that little rip have to do with this?' she asks me, her voice harsh.

A little rip, I think. A tear in something. The writing I saw before, on the wall.

'Is he dangerous?' I ask. 'I had this dream . . .'

'What did it feel like?' Her face is very sharp, her eyes pierce through me.

'Warm and muggy, kind of like . . .'

'Like what?'

Like I would do anything that he asked of me. That I would have to, unless I fought myself.

'I don't know. Strange. It wasn't like a normal dream. I had a feeling, just like with the fox?'

'*Just* like?'

'A little different.'

She sighs, as though I am a toddler who will not eat her dinner. I feel like one; I'm getting cranky now. All these questions about my instinct. Can she not use her own?

She looks at me, and tuts. She literally tuts. I want to kick something. Her hands reach into cupboards, grabbing jars and mixing things together. She puts a little kettle on the range and turns back to me.

'You need to tell me if that boy is dangerous. Catlin is –'

'I do not *need* to do anything. I choose to ask you here. To share the things I know. In my own time.'

'But –'

'You have instincts, Madeline. Use them. Draw upon them.'

'I can't live life on instinct.'

'No. *You* can't.'

I sigh.

'Mamó. I don't know what I want.'

'Your eyes are opening, Madeline,' she tells me.

'I always wanted things, and I still want them. To go to college. Learn. To have a *life*.'

'This will be better.' Her mouth twists. Is she smiling? 'Not in terms of fun or anything, but if you want to help. To work

195

and help. That's what you'll learn to do. It's what I'll teach you.'

'I have enough,' I say. 'Without giving up everything, I want to hear what you have to say. To work and help at whatever it is you do for people. You're talking about leaving behind the parts of myself that nourish me, and nourishing the ones that make me sad.'

She looks at me, and superimposed on her eyes I see Mam's ones, the disappointment there. If she knew where I was, what I was thinking. Brian's voice inside my head along with hers. And Catlin – if I'm off learning witchcraft, she'll be alone more often, more and more. And Lon will leach in everywhere, around her. I want my twin to know she has a person. I want her to know that she is loved. And not the kind of love that wants to own her. The blood-thick love. The kind that doesn't stop.

My thoughts are racing and her eyes still scan my face. I think she can see me deciding that this is all too much right now.

'I think –'

'But it's a waste of talent not to –' she begins, and I interrupt her, which is probably a stupid move, but she interrupted me first.

There are so many things I feel like I've been keeping in, it's almost cleansing to just let it rip. A sort of power, in this place where everyone is constantly reminding me how little I know, how little I can do. How little what I want even matters.

'Everyone has talents they don't develop. I could be really good at playing ukulele, but I'll never know. Because I could give a shit about the ukulele.'

'What we do . . . isn't the ukulele,' she almost spits at me. I glare at her, riding the wave of my anger towards the door.

196

'It is in this analogy. I am trying to explain,' I say. 'This. Decision. It's twisting all the things I knew around, and that is not a sudden process. I need time. And if I don't have that, then it's a no. It has to be a no.'

'Time can be a curse,' she says. 'I have heard you, Madeline. Now, sit. I'll give you tea to ward off dreams.'

'And Catlin?' I ask.

'I've been doing my best for your sister,' Mamó tells me. 'The tea I gave her was similar to this.' She opens several jars and begins mixing.

'What should I do,' I ask, 'to keep her safe?'

'I don't know that you can, Madeline,' Mamó says me. 'There are things in life we have to lose.'

'What does that mean?' I ask.

She sighs and stirs. 'Madeline. You've turned down my offer, but here you are, still asking questions. There are journeys we take. And ones we don't. If you won't do the work, it's not my job to educate you. Ask your stepfather about that boy. If he's any sort of human, he'll do something. And in the meantime, get that down your throat.' She thrusts it at me, in a thick earthenware mug. I take a sip, and gag.

Seawater, and nettle and rose and . . . fennel? And little white stones, small and shaped like teeth in the bottom, underneath the sludge.

'Drink it all down,' she tells me. 'It'll sort you.'

I do. And maybe it does. I do feel calmer. Colder. Or maybe it's the thing crossed off my list. Next step is to do something for Catlin, I reckon. Telling Oona how I feel is scarier than Lon, so I reckon I'll save that for last.

197

'Goodbye, Mamó,' I say to her.

I try the door, but it won't open. She calmly reaches over, turns the latch the other way, inclines her head.

'Off with you. You know where I am, Madeline. When you need me. And you will need me.' She says it like it is a certainty, perhaps a threat.

'We'll see,' I say, and as the door clicks behind me, I hear her voice saying, 'We will,' behind me. She might be a wise woman, but she is also a petty one.

The raven caws, perched on a windowsill above my head. It's holding something small inside its mouth. A shiny pebble, round and solid. I feel hairs rising on my skin. I crush the urge to reach my hand right out, and keep on walking.

27

Mustard Seed

(to warm the body up)

I haven't heard from Oona since that night. She hasn't been at school. I'm trying not to send her any more messages. I don't want to pressure her. Scare her off me. I want to make it easy for her to be with me.

Like at the lake.

I traipse up the stairs, smelling dinner, ignoring it. I cannot cope with people wanting things from me right now. I thought that I would get a straight answer from Mamó, about Lon. I thought that maybe she would try a little harder to convince me.

I want to be wanted, and I want to be left alone.

Things that are impossible together. Witchcraft and a normal, happy life.

I spoke in anger, but my words were true, I think. I need to kill that part of me. I remember when Mam started going to church every Sunday. It was when we were about seven or eight. We all went, until I was thirteen, and then she let me make the choice myself.

I think of the driftwood woman, on the altar, surrounded by candles. The shadows dancing on her wooden flesh. That's the sort of strange that people tolerate. Charms and spells to keep God on your side. It could be magic too, but not for me. It makes me feel uneasy. Helpless. Small.

I don't want Mam to light candles for my mental health and worry as I drift away from her. I don't want her to lose another person that she loves to something strange. I think of my father, burnt inside a glade. I close my eyes and almost smell the tang of something in the air. Leaves on the forest floor. Charred body, verdant trees. There is a puzzle there, if I could solve it.

So many things around me feel so . . . paused. On hold, until my life is normal life again.

I've still been keeping things inside, not telling anyone. I'm not ashamed of how I feel or anything. Or only a little. It's not that I have fallen for a girl, but that I've fallen so hard for someone who doesn't care about me. I don't want Mam and Catlin to know I've been rejected.

And I don't want to be her second best.

I think of the story of the forest devil. You take a living thing to certain crossroads. Something full of innocence is best. You bring a sharp knife and a steel resolve and you take the thing and plunge the dagger in. And you can play with it, if that's your thing. It makes the call you're sending ring a little louder.

The devil listens to the sharpest hurts. The little death is like a signal flare. A statement of your need. But something else as well.

Permission.

And if he comes, you have more work to do. Lay out a bargain. Offer him your soul. He can say yes or no. Or even maybe. But if he listens, you can do big things.

Before you die.

I think of what myself and Mamó silenced. The Ask, she called it. A sort of prayer, Brian said.

What did whoever hurt that little creature intend?

I wonder what I'd sacrifice for Oona. I couldn't kill a thing to get me her. But it wouldn't be real then. It mightn't work. I wonder, when the fox was sliced apart, was it for love, or health, or power? Or if it's just a story in a book, upon a tongue. Putting sense upon things with no reason. I think of all the stories in Dad's book. They ended well, more or less. You can thwart almost anything, as long as you know the rules. It's just I'm not familiar with them yet.

And there are rules. And there are rules for everything. No one tells you what they even are – you pick them up by getting things all wrong, and then when you've made sense of them, they break, and turn to something new.

It makes no sense.

At night I dream of my father, his face above me, mouth shaped into something like a prayer. The tang of lemongrass. The hum of bay.

Small white stones pitted in the bottom of a mug.

Small white crosses rising from the ground.

My heart is racing.

Everything is still.

I gasp awake.

28

Mullein

(influenza, gout, aches of the head)

This morning in the bathroom, there was a bruise on the nape of Catlin's neck. She whacked it on the edge of the sink, she said. When she was doing something with her hair. It was the size of a two-euro coin. The shape of an egg. An angry purple-blue.

I noticed others, clustering her arms. Green, yellow, brown. The size and shape of little pebbles. Fingerprints. I opened up my mouth to start to ask. Before I drew a breath she started speaking.

'It's nothing. I'm clumsier than usual here. Maybe because my brain is taken up with all this love. It can't be good for me, being so adored.' She did a swishy arm movement, like she's a goddess in the middle of a fountain, a bride on top of a cake. More like herself again, the marks aside.

I smiled at her and nodded. But.

Bruising's when you bleed beneath the skin. Dappled skin, like algal bloom on water. Underneath the surface, she's been hurt.

Helen Groarke.

I can't ignore the past. Not any more.

I look at Mam across the kitchen table, wondering how best to bring it up. A time when I could get her on her own.

The three of us are by ourselves here now. Brian is away on business again.

'What exactly is his business?' Catlin asks, biting into a slice of toast. 'You think he'd be able to stick around more, seeing as he's rich and things.'

'Rich people have to stay rich,' I tell her. 'This castle is a pricey place to live.'

'I think he could afford to cut back on the heating a little. It's almost too warm. I keep kicking the blanket off me during the night.'

'Me too,' I say.

Mam looks at us. 'What are ye talking about, girls? It's freezing here. If I didn't have three hot water bottles and Brian in the bed, I'd get frostbite.'

'You should take my bed tonight, Mam,' I say. 'Like, I can hop in with Catlin. She won't mind.'

'I could mind,' says Catlin. 'I don't. But I could.'

'You could do anything you want to do,' I tell her. 'I believe in you. God Bless America.'

She snorts. 'Why does no one ever say God Bless Ireland?'

'Because America sounds more dramatic. And also, God has spent too much time here already, getting nuns to sell babies and whatnot.'

'The church is not God's fault, Madeline.'

'Then whose fault is it?'

'Yours.' Catlin glares at me. 'And I think we're all overdue an apology.'

'I'm so, so, so, so, so, so, so, so, so, so, so, so, so sorry,' I tell her, holding my hand to my heart and crying pretend tears. 'I didn't know that I was the secret pope.'

'Well, you do now. So start wearing impressive hats.'

Mam looks at the two of us, her face confused. 'What are ye on about?'

'Were you not listening to our interesting and important conversation, Mam?'

'No, Mad. I was somewhere else. Thinking about Brian. There's something . . .' Her face gets a strange look, like she's trying to do a quadratic equation without any paper to write it down on.

'Wife in the attic,' says Catlin, very matter-of-factly. 'It's always a wife in the attic when lads have castles.'

'I wish he did have a wife in the attic,' Mam says. 'She might tell me what was going on.' She pauses, taking a long slug of tea. 'I get the sense he doesn't want to worry me. But if there's a reason to be worried, I'd rather worry about what it is than about all the potential things it could be, you know? I mean, the castle costs a lot to run. There's huge pressure on him, and I'm not earning now.'

I feel my throat clamming up. I know more than either of them does. But if I told them . . . what would I say exactly? Brian knows things. Mamó is a witch, and there are sacrifices in the forest. I don't think it would comfort anyone to hear that stuff. He did say that he'd tell her, in the kitchen. And he will. He'll have to. I swallow.

She trails off.

'That's probably it. The money thing. I'm just being silly. Every relationship is different. And your father did have secrets too.'

I think of my father's hands enveloping my small ones – his nails stained with yellow, green and blue. Strange colours for a man or for a garden. Any maybe it's just flashes in my brain. Something in me filling in the gaps. Colouring in the spaces that he left with bits of people.

Why would I give my father Mamó's nails?

'He did?' Catlin is intrigued. 'What kind?'

'I can't think of any off the top of my head,' Mam says. 'But he definitely had at least four.'

'Maybe Brian is keeping a good secret,' Catlin says to Mam. 'Like a surprise holiday. Or a new pony!'

'You hate ponies, Catlin,' Mam reminds her. It's true, she does. One stole her thunder at a birthday party once and she never forgave the species.

'I know. But the idea of a surprise pony is still kind of good. A sturdy little dude to cart my schoolbooks around. And I'd give him hay and maybe make him a sunbonnet with holes for his ears like in a book or something. Lon would befriend him.'

I think of the grey dapple of a smooth coat, marble mottled. I look at my sister. There are things I want to say and can't. We fall silent once we've left the house, walking up the driveway, past the bare and sweeping ash, the skinny little rowan trees, the hawthorns crumpled up like whipping boys. Yew trees line the journey to the gate. They like to have those sorts of trees in graveyards. And no one's ever sure how old they are. A hundred years. A thousand. They hollow out with age. A space inside.

At the bus stop, I look at Catlin, twisting around Lon like

205

tangleweed. Her hair all messed. Her happy, perfect face. His mouth. Her neck. I'm so far away from her today.

I think of Oona. Beautiful and strange. *Where have you been?* I think. *Is something wrong? Is it to do with magic? Are you like me? Is everybody something?* My brain fills up with question marks and clouds. The bus passes her stop. She isn't there. I feel it like an ache.

Twigs and plants through the smudged window. Some of them are white as broken bone. Recently, I have been drafting a coming-out speech in my head. The best I can come up with is: 'Not that my sexuality is any of your business. But I like girls. End of discussion.' It's short and to the point, but it would probably end up way more emotional and teary. I get a nervous flutter even considering it. Like if I do, there'll be no going back. It will be out there.

And the thing is, if I can have such a huge revelation about who I am in such a comparatively short period of time, who is to say I won't have another one that moves me to a different place again? Maybe I should just say, 'I am currently identifying as extremely gay, but in the future I may be open to other suggestions. End of discussion. P.S. Magic is real, so the salt stays under your beds.'

I look at Lon's face at lunchtime, searching for danger. Knowing Catlin doesn't want me there. I need to tell Brian about this, like Mamó said. And as soon as possible. His reaction will tell me what to do. I think of his conviction that we're safe here. Because of who his father was, or what. It feels like I am planning to betray her. Because, whatever happens, it will hurt. Lon loves that Catlin loves him. His copper-coloured eyes above her head. When people died in olden times, they used to put coins on their eyelids. To keep them closed. Helen Groarke. Her pale face wasting till she's earth and bone.

I let myself be ignored for twenty minutes, then I stomp inside.

'The two of them,' I say to Charley, and I roll my eyes.

'I know.' She smiles. I wonder if she means it, and I squint.

'Are you OK? You look like you've a pain,' she asks.

I think of Lon, and gesture towards the pub.

'I might do actually.'

She snorts at this.

'So, Charley. You never told me the full story about his ex.'

She shrugs. 'I don't know it to tell, to be honest . . .'

'You must know something about Helen,' I say, threading some of Mamó's steel through my voice.

She pales at the mention of her name, crosses herself. 'I don't want to talk about it.'

'Why?' I glare at her.

She squares her shoulders at me. 'Don't try that stuff on me. It doesn't work.'

'I don't know what you mean,' I say, filing this away for future reference. 'Have you ever kissed Lon?' I ask.

'Ugh,' she says. 'I'd rather eat a knife.' Her tone gives me a shiver in my gut.

After school, his eyes on her seem kind, although he scares me. Catlin laughs at something that he says, and pucks him in the stomach. 'You're as bad.'

Her face alight with love. I see her happy and I hold my tongue.

One of us should get to be OK.

A normal girl.

29

Dog's Tooth Violet

(divination, healing)

The morning light is bleaching through the garden, making green things grey and red things bright. I'm swollen up with worry about Catlin. I can't stop scrolling through the things I've seen, making them turn sinister in my mind. Lon's eyes on me, expressionless before they flicker back to Catlin's form. His large hand snaking all around her hands. The tips of her fingers barely meet the first bend of his knuckle.

I stare too much at Lon, I realise. Taking him in. Do I read menace into innocence? Maybe she did fall over. She's never lied to me before, not about important things like that. She knows I love her and will protect her. Something in this place has hurt my sister. No matter how much I want her to be fine, she isn't fine.

I slip on my black boots, a jumper over my pyjama top, and pad down the stairs, trying to keep as silent as possible. Channelling a fox. Or something that doesn't get noticed right away. A hedgehog maybe. Or a little badger.

I think of roadkill, swallow down the dread. I have been getting up earlier in the mornings to go out to the greenhouse and look at the plants. There is a sort of tension in the air that won't relent. I pick off one of the thorny yokes that stuck to me on the walk through the garden. I crush it in my fist until it hurts and then I blink and blink and blink again. Squeeze my eyelids tight and harsh together. Scan for something. Writing on a wall. Familiar smell.

There's something lost here, that I need to find.

When Catlin loses something, she prays to Saint Anthony. I don't believe in saints, but there is something to this panic in my stomach. Back in Cork, Mam had a friend who died. It was cancer, but she always wondered if gaps the husband tore had let it in. Life doesn't work that way, I told her then. I do not know that now. My certainty is gone. There's magic in the world. And it's more dangerous than I could have known.

I think of Catlin, trying to please Lon. I think of his arm around her. His mouth on hers in front of other boys. The egg-shaped bruise. Holding her back from hugging me that night, his knuckles white with tension on her shoulder. I think of his big hands clutching the back of her head when they kiss. I think of skulls. Of Bridget, Helen, Nora and Amanda. A girl can so easily turn into a ghost.

If something were to happen to Catlin . . . If he were to hurt her . . . I would never forgive myself.

On my way back to the castle, I catch sight of Mamó. She's with the raven, digging up what looks like delph and meat, placing chunks and chips in a little jam jar full of water.

I stare at her until she turns to me.

'Mamó,' I say.

'Madeline,' she says.

'Caw,' says the raven.

Of course it does.

I glare at her.

She glares back.

Hers is better.

We both have work to do. Just different work. Time to get to it.

Brian's car is in the driveway – he must have come back late last night. I find him in his office, sending emails. He looks tired; there are bags under his eyes. His hair is grey in parts and thin up top.

'Madeline.' His voice is glad to see me. I plonk two cups of tea down on his desk. He passes me two coasters.

'Thank you, love. You're up early.'

'I was out in the garden.'

He sighs. 'Trouble sleeping?

'I wanted . . .' I start but then get worried. I don't want to put more on anyone than they can take. And he looks really stressed. 'I didn't want to bother you, but . . .'

His face turns serious. 'Madeline Hayes, I'm here for you. Spit it out. I'll see what I can do.'

I exhale slowly, then breathe in again.

'Oh, Brian. It's Catlin.'

'All right.' His voice is neutral. 'Tell me more.'

'She's been seeing this older boy, and I don't like him and I've heard some things.'

He doesn't even pause. 'Lon Delacroix,' he says.

'That's the one.'

A long, long sigh from Brian. 'OK,' he says. 'We'll nip that in the bud.'

'What's wrong with Lon?' I ask.

'Nothing you could put your finger on.' Brian looks beyond me, over my shoulder at the door frame. 'There was something with a girl before. Helen. Allegations were made, and then the whole thing escalated. I don't want him next nor near you girls.'

'Helen Groarke,' I say.

'Yes,' Brian says. My stomach jolts. Either he lied to her, or she to me.

'Do you think he had anything to do with it? What happened.' I cannot keep the shiver from my voice.

'No one could prove anything,' Brian tells me, with another heavy sigh. 'But there was a suspicion. And that's enough, more than enough, to nip whatever this is in the bud.'

'He hangs around the school,' I say, trying to keep my voice as close to neutral as I can. The words feel like a betrayal in my mouth. I can picture Catlin hearing us, her features twisting into anger, hate.

'Does he now? He might want to rethink that.' Brian's face is grim. His voice is lower, different. I do not know this man, I think. Who is he?

'I'll have a chat with your mam,' he says. 'When she gets up. Don't worry, Maddy. You did the right thing there, confiding in me. I'll take care of it.' His voice is sure, confident. This must be the kind of Brian he is at work, why people fly him all around the world.

'Thank you, Brian,' I say, and really mean it.

'You look tired, Madeline.' He reaches an arm out to take my cup. 'The tea's gone cold. I'll put the coffee on.'

I do feel tired, I realise, all of a sudden. Exhausted even. Brian rises to go. 'See you downstairs,' he says, and walks out purposefully, like the business-dad he is.

His office is really warm. The underfloor heating must be turned way up, I think. The shrunken head is lolling just a little to one side, balanced on the dark wood of the lintel, all wizened and remoulded. Soft grey bread with nostrils, cheeks and eyes. Those features lie, the truth of them forgotten.

Corpses in the mountains, in the house.

I stagger up. I'm feeling very drained, for some strange reason. I press my hand to the wallpaper, feeling the soft relief of shapes. I haven't been in here for more than a few minutes before. And never by myself. I haven't had the time to take it in. I should move, I should head downstairs. Brian will be waiting. The wallpaper in his office is off-white – darker than cream, with patterns carved in. Can you say carved with paper? I don't know. They look like they're carved. There's something natural about them. To the touch, it feels like the pelt of something. A solid, organic texture. I shake my head, trying to shed my mind-fog. Outside, I see the curl of the blue path to the courtyard, spot a little creature hurrying down the trail. I close my eyes. It could be a rabbit or a rat. A little dog. It's hard to tell from here. It feels like I'm inside a computer screen, in a story or a film, and looking out but I can't break the barrier between me and the world. I can't get through. There's something I'm not doing, and if I could just . . .

212

But, as my eyes swim, something like a pattern is developing. A sort of shape that's underneath the shapes. There's something wrong about it, like one section is slightly paler than the others. But not in colour. In another way. In something else. I touch my hand to that part of the wall, to the left of Brian's desk, and it is warmer. There is something here. The wild roses and birds, linking intricately together. The cruel downturn of beak. The sharp of thorn and claw. I sigh, and press my hand harder against the wall.

It gives beneath my hand. It starts to open.

30

Chickweed

(itches and the lungs)

Little receptacles line the walls. Jam jars, bell jars, vials and old glass bottles full of dried-up little things. Feet. Eyes. Skin, leaves, powder. Shards of bone. There is only a very little light. The door clicks shut behind me and I start.

When we first moved here, Brian told us there were places that he didn't know about, things his father built inside these walls. But this is some next-level wizardly nonsense. I'm not sure how to feel. Secrets are unnerving, but secret passages are kind of . . . magical. The proper kind of magical. That real good scary Christmas-morning feeling.

My excitement wanes a bit as I realise that the dark has enveloped me entirely. I cannot see my feet or hands. They say when you are sensory-deprived, your other senses start to compensate. I wish they would. I wish I had my phone, some sort of light. The stone is rough and jutting – unpredictable – and I am very glad of my thick boots.

My mind keeps replaying the conversation with Brian. Fluttering between two kinds of guilt. Does it count as betrayal when you're worried about someone's safety?

It will to her.

She's going to be so mad. Maybe I should stay here in this musty, cobwebby passageway, and forge a new life among these cool jars. I could work my way up through the ranks of the jar-folk, carrying small and large items alike and being respected because of my pockets.

I inch my feet gingerly along the path. Baby steps. There could be a drop here, easily. Eroded steps. A surprise torture dungeon. Brian's decent, but his house is weird as hell, pieced together by his father's wants. Castle upon castle. Halls in walls. I wonder if it is a murder castle. How long have I been walking step by step? It seems to take me ages, tightrope-walking foot in front of foot. My mind is clear. I do not have to worry about the fallout from Catlin, or the story with Oona. I only have to get back to the light. I breathe the air in, dusty and thick with unfamiliar stuff. It's coating my oesophagus with paste. Coughing doesn't help. I need to keep on moving. Through the dark.

The walls feel rough and dry beneath my fingers. Brick meets brick until I reach an edge. I feel the sharpened slant of wall beside me. Two paths diverge. And I don't know what's right. I close my eyes, breathe in a layer of scum and try to think. Place my two hands flat upon the ground. It isn't earth. It's concrete, and it's harsh. There is an unfinishedness about this place. I get the sense that there is something here I will not like. Or that there has been, maybe, in the past. I'm not sure if it's intuition, fear.

I choose to venture on and see what happens. It feels strange to be eaten by Brian's house. I keep on searching, hoping in the dark. My hand finds a door, thick and smooth with varnish. I grasp the handle, turn and it doesn't give. I kick and bang. Scrape at it until hard flecks are caught beneath my nails. It doesn't help. I might be here forever. Like the bones inside the steamer trunks.

I leave the door and carry on, piece by piece. There are some letters carved into the wall. I can't make out the words. A zigzag, a circle, then some random scratches. Someone else was here before me, I think. And for long enough to do this. Pass the time with chipping glyphs into stone. I shudder.

I keep on walking, feet upon the path. The cement turns to flagstones, to pebbles, then to something soft. A fleecy damp. I put my hand down, pull at it, and smell it. It's moss, or something that's a lot like moss. I hope that's a good sign. I still can't see, the walls are close and it is getting colder. I wish I had something to keep me warm.

I move until I meet a metal door. I feel for, find, the latch. It's fastened with a padlock that has rusted. I can feel it flake beneath my touch. There's dust on it too. I don't think it's been used for quite a long time. My fingers search the ground for anything at all to bash it open. I find a stone; it's small and thin and sharp. I saw and saw at the little lock. I have to hold it steady with one hand for this to work. It takes a while. I feel it start to give. My hand slips and the sharp edge slices deeply down into my palm. Blood drips. I use the stone again, my left hand stinging. Warm blood on the smooth surface. The shackle gives.

I push it open. Stumble into brightness. There are steps overgrown with ivy, brambles, nettles and herb robert. I see some bottles poking underground. Glass and stings are nothing. I am free.

The fresh air feels so healing in my lungs. I cough out dust and make my way down the steps and down and down again until I hit a road. My clothes are thick with dirt. I turn and walk until I hit the main street of the village. I make my way towards the long road home. My muscles ache. The sky is grey. I wonder how long it has been. Since I pushed in that door.

The bright red car pulls up beside me. 'State of you,' she tells me. 'Hop in.'

'How did you know I'd be here?' I ask.

'Brian called me – said you'd gone wandering in the walls. There's only a few places that you'd come out in one piece.'

'Wait – what?' It's hard to tell if she's joking or not and then I remember she is Mamó.

'Did you break the padlock?'

I nod. She says, 'You'll be replacing that for me.'

'For you?' I ask. 'Is it your secret passage to Brian's office then?'

'It was in his father's time. I mainly use it for storage now.'

'What was it for before?'

She grunts at me. That's all I'm going to get. I nod at her. It's easier than speaking. My throat is dry. She hands me a little bottle of clear liquid. I drink from it. It burns my well-worn throat.

'What is it?'

'Something small to help you,' she tells me. 'We used to use it for babies when they were teething back in the day. To shut them up. We called it Mother's Lull.'

It tastes and smells like nail-polish remover. 'Thank you?'

'You are welcome,' she says, and replaces the bottle in the glove compartment. 'Father Byrne makes his own brand too. But mine is better.'

'Who's Father Byrne?' I ask.

She snaps, 'A priest. A man of God. One of them, at any rate.'

'Everyone has secrets here. Even Brian. I wonder –'

'Madeline,' she says, 'haven't you enough to worry about, without putting names on everyone around you? And you can't just dip your toe in and out again with this sort of thing. Either I'm training you or I am not. And currently I'm not. So save your questions.' Her face is impassive, but not unkind.

'Whatever happens though, we live here now. And surely I'm entitled to some sort of explanation of what is going on around us, in the place.'

'*Entitled*. That's you, right enough.' Her tone is contemptuous. 'You can't refuse to turn around and ask someone to draw you a picture of what's behind you instead of facing it. There are things you don't know because you don't have to know them yet. Accept it. Or turn around and LOOK.'

'But Catlin –' My voice slices through the air, more whiney than I had intended.

'Look, Madeline. Your stepfather is trying,' Mamó tells me. 'And Lon won't get very far with everyone watching your sister. Reporting back. And believe me, they will be.'

'What happened with Helen Groarke? And Lon, before?'

'No one's sure of anything in this life. But if I had a daughter. Or a sister. Or a stranger. I wouldn't want them spending time with *that*.' She spits on to the dashboard. It leaves a white slick mark. An eye inside a face.

I look down at my shoes. They're wet and filthy.

'Sorry about the floor,' I say, 'and the lock.'

'Sure they're just little things,' she says. 'You'll make amends for them. It isn't complicated.'

I look down at my feet. I rub my boots, and smell my fingertips and rub again.

'Mamó?' I say.

'*What?*' she asks, and I shrink a little, but keep on going. 'There's blood on my boots, and it isn't mine. Look.' I thrust a grubby hand at her. 'It's old, I think. But it smells like . . .'

She pulls my hand to her nostrils, takes a sniff.

Our eyes meet.

She turns her face back towards the windscreen, grunts again. A different kind of grunt. Surprise, I think.

We reach the driveway. 'I'm in a hurry, so I'll leave you here,' she tells me. 'Also, I have to give you this. It was made with yourself in mind, so it's no use to me. I know enough.'

I take it. It's the small round sphere from in Bob's beak. So black it's blue and somehow also milky. I stare at it. It isn't smooth. It's pitted like a peach pit. On the surface, tufts of something cling.

'What is it for?'

'Just keep it in your pocket,' Mamó tells me. 'It's not a charm, but it is good to have.'

I step out of the car, still none the wiser, and she speeds away.

219

I stumble down the path towards my home that doesn't feel like home. The sun is pale in the sky. The air is freezing. I feel the shadow of the yew trees on my face, and carry on going, shivering and limping. Cobwebs in my hair and dirty fingers. I need to shower and I want to sleep.

I lift my hands to my nose and take a breath.

She took her eyes off the road.

This blood surprised her.

And you can't tell, from blood, where it came from. But when I smelled it, flash of recognition. Fear and fur, the forest.

And a blade.

31

Hazel

(inspiration, snakes)

I smush my face into the soft, soft pillow and ignore the beeping of my phone. They will be fine without me, I think. Yesterday, no one had even noticed I was missing, except Brian. He said he didn't want to worry Mam, that he felt really guilty that I'd gotten lost. He'd known about the door, but it hadn't been in use since his father's time.

He caught me in the hallway of the castle, pulled me into a very gangly hug.

'I told her you'd gone for a walk,' he said. 'I don't know why. I panicked, and all of a sudden, there I was, lying to my wife about her child.' Guilt doesn't suit Brian. His face looked gaunt. Shadows underneath his eyes, and what else is he hiding?

Doors inside the walls and blood on stone.

Mam swoops into the room like a raven and grips me by the shoulders. I try to burrow away, like a mole, but a girl can only be a mole for so long when her mother is removing blankets and making statements like, 'We need to talk.'

Of course she wants to know about the Catlin thing. Brian told her all about it. Mam can't bring herself to say the name Helen Groarke – she calls her 'that girl' or 'that poor girl'. The horror on her face. The weight of that. I should have told them sooner. Which is of course another thing she tells me. And I agree. Lon's big white hands. The dark bruise on Catlin's neck. Mam looks at me, her eyes reflecting my worry.

'Why did you go to Brian and not to me?' she asks, the furrows digging sideways in her brow. Two-thirds of a triangle. I don't want to have hurt her feelings. I'm just so tired.

'He's family now, Mam. And he's from here. I didn't want to worry you with nothing.' The heat is heavy, clinging to my skin. I poke a foot from under the duvet and flip my pillow. Cooler now, I shut my eyes, but only for a second.

'This Lon,' Mam asks, 'how long have they been . . . ?'

'It happened really quickly after we moved here,' I say. 'She's properly in love.'

Mam scoffs at this. 'She's sixteen years of age.'

'So am I. That doesn't mean our feelings aren't real. Catlin thinks he's her soulmate or something,' I say. 'I tried to tell her what I thought before. It didn't help.'

'She always was headstrong,' Mam says, and not like it's the good thing it once was.

She grips my hand. 'The two of you are the most important things in my life,' she says. 'It's hard to think that there's this whole side to you I don't know about. I mean, you lived in here.' She cradles her abdomen beneath her dress.

222

'Don't make me go back there,' I say, pretending to be frightened, and she laughs.

'I couldn't if I tried,' she says. 'And sometimes I think that's almost a pity.' She narrows her eyes. 'So. What's the fecker like?' Her voice is heavy, trying to be light.

'He's got this stupid, handsome face.'

'That could be anyone she's gone out with before,' Mam says. I snort.

'He calls her Catalina. And he talks over her all the time.'

'What a prick,' she says.

'I know. He's terrible, but she doesn't seem to notice. She wants to tell him that she loves him, like.' I gesture helplessly.

'Urgh,' says Mam. 'If only that were all. What can we do?'

'I don't know,' I say. 'She's properly smitten.'

'And this peacock's the one doing the smiting.' Mam is angry. She fixes her dress like she is angry with it, eroding creases out with both her hands.

'Peacock's a good word for him,' I say. 'He loves himself.'

'It is OK to love yourself, Madeline,' Mam tells me.

'Not the way he does it.'

There is a pause. So many things unsaid. I close my eyes. I open them again.

And I betray her.

'I think,' I say, 'he put his hands on her. She has these bruises.'

I feel the weight of worry and of guilt press down, press down.

She will never forgive me if I ruin this love for her. But can you even ruin a dangerous thing?

Mam sighs. She puts her two hands over her face for a

second. Like she's playing peekaboo. I see her struggle to relax her shoulders. To calm herself.

'Brian guessed as much,' she said, 'when you approached him. And I just think, *How dare he!* The cheek of him. I can't . . .' Her voice is hoarse with fear, or rage, or maybe both. 'We'll handle it, love. He won't hurt her any more,' she says, grasping my hand a little too tightly. I see cogs turning in her tidy-woman brain. Colour-coding strategies to take. Prioritising. She wants to make a list she can check off. To turn the threat into a series of small tasks. Tickable goals. But I'm not sure that Lon is even fixable. I think of his big, perfect shark smile. His shiny, even teeth. His superior chin. I'd love to slap him. Hard.

'We'll take her phone away,' Mam tells me. 'Brian can get Liam Donoghue to change his rota for a week or two, keep him away from her, he says. He knows the family.'

'Wow,' I say. Maybe this is why they all respect Brian, with his hidden talents and deep pockets.

'My husband is very protective,' Mam says, like it's a point of pride.

'It's a shame that Catlin needs protecting though,' I tell her.

'I know,' she says. 'I'm scared. And I'm honestly not sure what the best course of action is, to keep her safe.'

I nod, picturing a photograph of her and Dad together, in the back garden. They aren't smiling, but they are both kind of shining with each other. I wonder what our lives would have been like. There wouldn't have been Lon in them, for one thing. I wonder how Mam stops those kinds of thoughts from coming all the time, whenever something happens.

'Madeline?' she says, and her voice is kind and serious and low.

'Mmmm?'

'Don't do that stuff with salt and things any more. Please.' She looks at me. 'I know we've had this conversation before, but I don't want to have it again. Not with all of this Catlin stuff about to boil over. When I see that kind of thing in your room, it makes me worry. You know?'

A bubble pops. I don't say anything.

'I know the move hasn't been easy on ye. But it hasn't been easy on me either. I'm lonely here, and I need a bit of support right now. You have to try.'

There is so much that I could say to her. I feel the anger welling up inside me, the urge to yell that maybe I can't help it, and maybe if she had left the salt under Catlin's bed, maybe she would have been a little less obsessed. That I've been trying my best to be as normal as I can. I've turned down ACTUAL magic. Which exists. I can't put any more on Mam today though. I nod.

'I'll do my best,' I say. To hide it, I mean. You cannot stop the tide. This lives in me. All that I can do is work around it. But I will try my best to keep it quiet. I get a horrid feeling in my stomach. A sort of swell. I am the broken twin. The one that's not as good. The *other* daughter. My face is wet before the door clicks shut.

The foxes screaming, screaming outside.

Mourning for their friend.

The Ask.

Me and Catlin walking in the forest.

A fox is very small, somewhere between cat and dog.

So much blood in such a little case.

225

And on my boots.
And on the passage walls.
There is something that I cannot read. I need to see it.
I don't want this.
I don't want any of it.
None at all.

32

Foxglove

(slows the pulse or stops it)

We are staging an intervention for Catlin. In the library. Because Brian apparently learned his parenting skills from reality television, and Mam is going along with it for some reason. I sit on a pinstriped cream-and-white chair. It's gilded at the edges. Catlin is on the chaise longue, having a meltdown.

'I can't believe this,' she shouts. 'I can't believe you. And you. And *you*.'

She points at me, deciding I'm the one she hates the most.

'Be that as it may, Catlin . . .' says Brian in a neutral voice, holding his hands open in front of him, like a hip teacher who tries to get you to talk about your feelings because this is a safe space and, like, no judgement. '. . . we love you and we need you to trust the three of us on this. He is not a good person. You need to stop seeing him.'

'He IS a good person. He's the best person I've ever met.' The pitch of Catlin's voice is beginning to rise. I look up at the stacks and stacks of books that line the shelves. If they could talk, I think they'd probably say, *Shut up, Catlin.*

'I know it feels that way now, love –' Mam starts, and Catlin whips around to stare her down.

'You don't know HOW it feels,' she screeches like a righteous romance-harpy. 'Because if you DID know how it felt, if you even had an INKLING how it felt, how much I LOVE that boy, you would be THRILLED for me.'

'Catlin –'

'COULD YOU SHUT UP? I haven't finished speaking.'

Why are they trying to interrupt her? It's like saying excuse me to the sea.

'What I was GOING to say –' she continues, waving her extended pointer finger over us as though it were a sort of magic wand – 'before you rudely interrupted my train of thought, is that Lon and I are in LOVE. Proper LOVE. The kind you obviously know nothing about, seeing as you're not supporting me. And that makes you all PRICKS.'

She glares around the room, like twelve Mamós on speed. Her face is flushed and sweaty, like her anger is also a workout.

'Catlin,' says Mam, 'your BOYFRIEND, who you claim to LOVE, was a suspect in a murder. He hurt that girl while they were together, Brian says. That is not OK. Would you like Madeline to be with someone who is physically abusive?'

'Catlin, he tells you how to dress,' I say. I feel like Judas Iscariot.

'They're only rumours, Mam. They aren't true.' She turns to me. I know that I'm a prick. She doesn't have to say it. But she does.

'And, as for YOU, Madeline, YOU are SUPPOSED to be my SISTER. Not some gossipy sneak, going behind my BACK because you're jealous that I found love and you're a LONELY DRIED-UP LITTLE BITCH.'

I gasp. 'That isn't fair.'

'What isn't fair is that you're betraying me. That's what isn't fair. I am the fairest person in this room.'

'Love . . .' Brian's voice is calm.

'Don't call me that. You cannot use that word around me now. Love is something people like you destroy.'

Mam grasps his hand. They look at Catlin together. Drawing strength. We're used to her hissy fits, but this is something else. Her eyes are wide, her hair is ratted wild, she can't sit still. She's like a crazy person. She picks up a blue-and-white vase. It looks as if she will throw it.

'Put that down,' Mam says.

'Fine,' says Catlin, and swings it at the wall. It thunks against the paper, and plonks down on the soft maroon carpet. Not even chipped. She goes to pick it up and try again. I see the muscles in Brian's face twitch a little. He brings his index fingers to his temples. Rotates them back and forth. Twice. His voice is quiet and definite.

'*Enough.*'

'Excuse me?'

'I said, Catlin Hayes, that that is enough. Your sister and your mother and I have had enough abuse. You are forbidden from seeing this boy. He is dangerous, and can't be trusted. No matter how much you think you love him. You are not to see him. You are not to text him. You are not to email him, or message him in any way. And if you do, we will find out about it. And we will stop you.'

I utterly believe him in that moment. And so does Catlin. She sits down, still hugging the vase to her stomach.

'So I can still go to school?' she asks through gritted teeth.

'Yes. But we will drop you there and pick you up. And you need to apologise to your sister. She cares about you. Which is why she came to me.'

Brian does the hand thing again. *Did he attend a course on conflict resolution?* I wonder. *Did they teach him magic hands of trust?*

Catlin's face looks paler now, and sharp. Her mouth is set. Brian's voice drones on about 'respecting boundaries' and 'understanding that adults sometimes know things children don't'. She doesn't roll her eyes, but I feel the effort.

'Are you hearing what we're saying?' he concludes.

She meets his gaze. 'Yes, Brian. Yes, Brian. I am.' Her voice is deceptively meek. She's going to explode.

I close my eyes.

'And what you have to remember, Brian, is that while you *are* married to my mam, you are in no way my real dad. You're just Mam's husband. You do not get to tell me what to do. So you can thoroughly, utterly and completely fuck right off. I'll see Laurent if I want to. You do not get to tell me who to love.'

Brian opens his mouth and closes it again.

'And furthermore . . .' says Catlin, rising to her feet, 'I will only apologise to Maddy when she apologises to me for being a weaselly little bitch.'

'Catlin Hayes!' Mam's voice could cut through steel. 'SIT!'

230

she barks, as though Catlin were a dog. 'And let me tell you the way that things will be. There are two rules. One: you will respect your family. And Brian is that now. You need to choose what you are going to say next, Catlin. I'd think about that, and I'd shut my mouth. If I were you.'

Catlin opens her mouth.

'Sit down. Shut Up.'

Catlin sits down.

'Two: you will not see that boy again. Give me your phone.'

'I am NOT giving you my PHONE. That is an invasion of privacy.'

Mam holds out her hand. 'I don't care. Give it here.'

Catlin gets up, flounces to the door. She tries it and the door won't open.

'I hate you all,' she yells. 'I hate you all so much. It isn't fair.'

'Catlin.' I try to keep my voice calm and gentle. 'The Helen thing . . . it's scary. We don't want that for you.'

Her voice is high and sharp: 'What about what I want?' She looks me in the eye, then swings to face Brian and Mam. The one beside the other. Like a unit. 'And anyway it's LIES.'

'It isn't lies,' says Brian. 'And, unsavoury rumours aside, your sister's right. He isn't right for you. He's too controlling.'

Oh no, Brian. No, don't bring me into this, I think, and crinkle my eyelids together as tightly as they'll go.

'Controlling?' Catlin asks, addressing the imaginary jury. 'That, like you, is RICH. And not in a good way.'

Brian holds up his hand. The gesture is both tired and strangely sassy.

'I'm not doing this,' he sighs, possibly realising that he has been trying to parent too hard too soon. 'Give Sheila your phone. Then we'll let you out.'

Catlin rolls her eyes and hands it over.

'I don't care. He'll find me, with or without a phone. Our love is bigger than a phone, and you can't stop it. And, Brian – your comb-over isn't fooling anyone. You're bald. And, Mam – you are a BITCH. Thanks for ruining my life.' She pulls the door aggressively. It wasn't locked at all; she just didn't use the handle right. She swears at us again, and stamps out. I hear her muttering down the stairs. We sit until the tramp of feet fades into silence. Looking at each other.

'Well, that went well . . .' says Brian.

Mam starts to cry and he gives her a hug.

I slink away, dried-up-weasel-Judas that I am.

I hear my sister sobbing all night long. Her door is locked. She will not answer me.

33

Water Horsetail

(weak bones and heavy periods)

Drowning can be quick, but it feels slow. You cannot move, you cannot call for help. Your eyes are glassy. You may panic, hyperventilate. You try to swim, you can't control your legs; your arms are flapping but it isn't helping. In the end there's nothing you can do to cheat your death.

What I feel here, right now, is something else. It's stupid to compare it. So dramatic. But this morning there were three spots of blood upon my pillow. I think I must have coughed them in the night. When I woke, the first thing that I did was draw a breath. I drank in air like water. It tasted like new life.

Catlin is really sad, and also bitter. Lon hasn't been around in several days. To make matters worse, Brian, in another parenting move learned from blogs written by stepdads with too much Internet, has decided to bring home a kitten. Catlin is supposed to love him, and by extension Brian.

'This little scut was wandering around Jack Collins's land,' he announces, holding him up like flag of truce. Jack Collins is Charley's uncle or cousin or something. He helps Brian put up fences and things, but I had not realised he was also a kitten dealer.

The kitten looks nonplussed. Its eyes are still milky blue and its stomach is very soft and fluffy. It should not be allowed out of the castle or Bob will surely eat it. I finger the orb inside my pocket.

'I went up to talk about some things that need doing in the castle. And there she was. The only one of the litter left alive. Their mother abandoned them.'

He holds it out to Catlin, like a 99 on a sunny day. The kitten mews pitifully. Like, *What exactly am I doing here? I'm small. Put me in a box. Leave me alone.*

Brian continues talking.

'I have purchased a litter tray and a small cat bed. We can keep it in the kitchen at first until it's confident, and then transition it to other parts of the house.'

He clearly also has been learning from cat-dads with too much Internet. I resist the urge to pull up a chair and take out the popcorn. I am on Brian's side. Brian is in the right here. Team Brian.

Brian is still holding the kitten out like he's Rafiki, and we're all the cartoon animals of the African plains. Catlin reaches out and his face is all, *Yes, yes, drink the potion*, but instead she just pokes it with her finger, and scowls, and even though she's being a brat, I have never loved her more. I don't want her to stop being herself. I just want her to be safe. I let out a small, sad sigh, and she moves her scowl from the kitten to me. Fair enough. I'm bigger. I can take it. Slightly. Sort of.

Brian puts the cat down on the kitchen table, beside the sugar bowl. Mam picks it up, plonks it on the floor and wipes down the place it sat with antiseptic spray. She has pure *I wish you had told me about this, love* face. Oh, Brian. I pour myself a mug of tea. I kind of want to cuddle the kitten, but I'm worried that will look like I was in on the plan to put a fluffy bandage on a Lon-shaped wound.

'I hate cats. Which is a fact *a parent* would know.' Catlin has chosen to spend more time with us this week, so we can 'actively feel the fire' of her hatred. She glares at Brian who, I notice, has combed his hair in a slightly different way. He must have taken what she said to heart.

'I think he's cute,' I say. I touch the kitten's ear. He flinches and lets out a mewp of surprise.

'Maybe that's because you're going to be a cat lady who dies alone in an apartment that smells of cats, surrounded by cats who are secretly delighted because they always wanted to eat you all along for being awful.'

'Catlin!' Mam exclaims.

'You know I'm right, Mam. Who'd fall in love with her? She betrays people because she's jealous that they're soulmates.' There is a pause, and Catlin moves her gaze across the room. 'I'm talking about me and Lon.'

'We know,' Brian says. 'You talk of little else. And I am tired of it. I think I'll call her Bridget.'

'No,' I say, taking the little creature from Brian and plonking him on my lap. 'Look at his tiny kitten junk. His name is clearly Button, because he's tortoiseshell and shiny.'

Brian smiles at me. Puts a hand on my shoulder. 'Button,' he says. 'I like that, Maddy.'

Mam smiles too. 'It suits him.'

I feel a warm wetness bloom onto my leg. It takes a beat to work out what it is.

Catlin laughs her head off. 'Serves you right. You don't support true love, then you get pissed on. I wish I had my phone. Lon would love this.'

'Shut up,' I tell her, putting Button on the floor. 'I'm going to have a shower.'

I peel the tights off, lash them in the sink. I don't want urine in my laundry basket. I crank the shower up, and step inside. It's steamy-warm, running down my back. I wash my heavy hair. I scrub my face. I squeeze a quarter-bottle of shower gel on my poor disgusting leg. Button is cute, I think. He won't fix anything. But maybe he'll give Mam a thing to do. Train him, feed him, mind him. He's small and weak. He's such a little thing. All bones and fur, there's hardly any flesh. Just little scraps. A warm slice of ham all stuck together, purring. And maybe Catlin will like him in the end.

I already do. I mean, obviously it'll be a while before he gets lap access again. A girl's got to have a code. But Mam and Brian didn't want to see my reaction to the kitten at all. They were all focused on Catlin and her drama. I get that Lon is the worst and also dangerous. But I was being groomed by an actual witch for a bit and no one even noticed. I literally got in her van. OK, it was a car, but even so.

Everyone's concerned with Catlin's secrets. Ignoring mine. I think of the dead girls on the mountain. Their bright bones in the soft grass in the night. The parts of fox that gave beneath my feet. Catlin felt it too, the sense of dread there. Her useless prayers upon the bloody earth.

I look outside my window, at the trees. A lush, soft shape. An owl. A barn owl. I wrap the towel around me. It swishes past. I read somewhere that owls have special claws. When they grasp at you, they feel your heartbeat pulsing through them. They won't let go until they sense the stop.

There's something in the garden. I feel it wrong a while before I see it. Something's moving slowly through the shrubs. Not trying to hide. It's something tall and thin. A shadow-man. The twinkle of a phone screen. I hear a buzz begin in Catlin's room. I open the adjoining door. She's at the window, staring out and smiling. Her hand is busy, working at the latch. It doesn't budge.

'Fuck off, Madeline,' she snaps.

No chance of that.

'What are you doing?' I ask.

'The window's broken,' she sighs. I see her skin whiten and the bones push at the flesh from how hard she's working to open it.

'Let me help,' I say.

'You've done enough,' she growls, but moves aside.

My hands press at the frame. And I see Lon's form below, his head tilted up towards the window, staring. I startle, still my hands.

'Madeline, I'm all the way up here. What do you think he'll do? Stab me with a really, really, really long knife?'

The window's jammed, even with my help.

'I can't,' she mouths. 'I love you.'

He raises his hand aloft, drifts back into the dark. We watch until the forest swallows him up.

'Did Mam give you your phone back?' I ask.

'None of your business.' She pauses, and her face turns wild and bright. 'He loves me, Mad. He told me so at lunchtime. Finally. I just wanted to put it into words. To tell somebody.'

So happy now, remembering. It must have been when she went for a smoke or to the bathroom. How did I miss it? We were at school together all day long. My brain is twisting, trying to work it out. Lon worming his way into her life. Burrowing, like a parasite through flesh. How could we see him so clearly underneath the window, in the dark? He'd have to be much taller than he is for that to work. I mean, that's science.

'Catlin?'

'Yes?'

'Are you still mad at me?' My voice comes out so vulnerable. I hate it. I hate how much I need us to be friends.

'Of course I am. You're kind of dead to me,' she says.

I try not to react. It's what she wants right now, not what she needs. I look at her and think, *I'm here for you, my twin, I'm here. I'm here.*

'It was a horrible thing you did, betraying us like that. You tried to break our hearts. But it made us stronger. Did you see him looking up like that? I mean, it's like he knew what I was saying, like he heard me. Even though he couldn't. That's how in tune we are.'

Barn owls rely on noises made by prey. They search until they locate them. Soft and white and smaller than you'd think. But they will find you, razor claws and all. Pluck you up to carry, kill and eat. Catlin's brushing her hair; it ripples down her back. It's grown since we moved here. Things have happened and they've changed us both.

'Do you not worry though, Catlin?' I ask. 'That if he hurt a girl, he could hurt you? And with the Helen thing. I mean, can you see where I am coming from, at least a little?'

'With another boy, I maybe would. But, Madeline, it's *Lon*.' She says his name as though it settled everything. 'I wish that you would just let me be happy.'

'But people said –'

'What people?' Her voice is scornful. 'Was it Charley? Oona?'

'A few people,' I say. I sit on the edge of her bed. She's at her altar, rearranging candles, little Marys. There are over twenty of them now. She's obviously been raiding the castle. She holds one in her hand and strokes its hair.

'Charley hates Laurent,' Catlin tells me, 'because he turned her down and she hooks up with everyone. She *begged* him once when she was really drunk and he said no because he didn't fancy her and also it felt wrong. And then she started this rumour about him and Helen. Taking the worst thing that ever happened to him and turning it into a weapon to use against him. Lon is one of the good ones, Mad.'

I don't believe her but I really want to. Her face is all patchy, eyes filling up again. Tears splash onto the Mary. She puts her down, picks up the wizened skull. Her mascara running just a little.

'And Oona just hates men because she's gay.'

I jolt at those words out of her mouth.

'Excuse me? That is not a thing at all.' My voice is almost spluttering.

'It is a bit. Lon told me. With lesbians, they resent not being straight and often take it out on the men around them. Spreading vicious rumours and so on.' Her tone is his, but that is no excuse for what she's saying.

'That's bigoted, Catlin.' My voice is colder, stronger. How dare she parrot hateful things like this? The sister that I knew would never, ever . . .

'Sometimes bigoted things can be true. Stereotypes exist for a reason. I mean, I wouldn't say it to Oona like that. But it makes sense. I mean, when Lon explains it.' Her voice is calm. She wipes her eyes a bit. 'I can't believe he looked up at my window. It's really romantic, isn't it?'

The subject has been changed. But not for me. I think of what I'll have to tell her some day. It just got harder. I won't forget this. She hasn't noticed I'm not even listening. What does she even think of me at all? The things she said about me in the library. She fully, fully meant them at the time. I feel my hands moisten and the back of my neck tense. How could she ever, ever . . . ?

'It can't be true, Madeline.' Her voice is quieter now. It's more like hers.

'Mamó said things too though,' I say. 'And Brian. Lon hates it when you talk to other men. He watches through your window. Visits in your dreams. You sounded like him there, the things you said. They aren't what you think. It makes me worry.'

'Worry away,' she says. 'You're always worrying about stuff anyway, with your salt and your leaves and your poking into other people's business. Why can't you let me be happy? It's hard for me too. I won't always be around to protect you. I've fallen in love and eventually I'll go away. We're growing up, Madeline. Things can't always be the same forever. You need to let me have this.'

She's shifted back, her eyes bright. She's sweating, holding a little skull, fingers twisting round and round and round the yellowed cranium. Some of the jawbone is missing, I notice. It takes so little force to break a girl.

'I thought that Brian gave it to the guards?' I say.

'It might be another one . . . or something . . .' she says. 'I found it back inside the trunk again. Goodnight, Madeline.'

She wants me gone, and so I leave her there, still clutching at a part of someone's corpse. Organise things, clamber into bed. Nothing was ever proven. It's not enough for me to feel she's safe. Who says that though, about the man they love? They couldn't prove it doesn't mean it's lies. I think of Mamó feeding meat to the raven. The smooth and shining thing inside the beak. The salt. The mint. The jars in the moonlight. And the fox. I think about the fox.

Even if my life goes according to plan, if I work hard, do well, I can't fix everything. Lon's big hands on Catlin's little arms. Digging in. His face against her face. I can't just walk away from who I am, from who I choose to be. I cannot be a witch. I can't choose magic. It is over now. But in my stomach, something stirs and flutters. And it tells me that I'm wrong. Things unfinished widen and they grow. In spite of me. In shadow and untrained.

Magic feels more emotional than scientific. It's like a series of escalating inklings that end in an outcome, possibly a desired one, but sometimes a surprise. I've been wondering recently why I have to collect things at all. I always feel as if I have to keep Mam and Catlin safe. And maybe I always did. But from what? Boyfriends, husbands, colds and flus and thieves. The world's a terrifying place all by itself, without the risk of monsters, magics, Gods.

I look at my small hands, my wide and stubby fingers stretching out. The gape of bone that strains beneath the skin. So many horrors underneath the surface of a person. So many things that we can choose to be.

34

Skullcap

(expulsion of superficial evils)

Catlin smiles at me across the table. It's not a friendly smile. She looks like a predator, or a competitor. I've seen that smile before directed at other girls. People who don't matter to my sister. I am now included in their ranks, and it feels horrible. Any ground I break by listening seems to grow right back within the hour.

Catlin is smiling because she is smug about being allowed to get the bus today. It's been a week, and Mam is getting tired of giving lifts. Lon won't be waiting at the stop with coffee. Brian has made him promise. He's asked him to back off, and apparently Lon told him that he would. And Brian trusts him in the way that all stepdads should totally trust lanky older men who hang around playgrounds chatting up their brand-new teenage daughters.

It's the kitten thing all over again.

At least Button wants to be my pal, I think. He has not weed on me since the only time he weed on me, and that makes him my favourite person in the house right now. I wish all people were small, fat kittens who drink too much kitten milk and then fall asleep and their little pink mouths loll open and a bit of tongue falls out between their teeny fangs.

'Meep,' says Button, looking at his bowl.

'Shut up, Button, nobody cares about you,' Catlin says, and I actually gasp. I hope he doesn't internalise her tone. I was doing some research and it's important to be sound to your kitten. Formative soundness is key.

I think about glaring at her, like she deserves, but I just say, 'Time to go,' and grab my bag. I can tell her about how to love a kitten when she has learned how to not love an idiot. It will bring us closer together and everything will go back to normal and I won't ever have to tell anyone that I'm a lesbian witch who isn't using her powers of witchcraft or lesbianing right now because it's all far too stressful to be dealing with.

'I was thinking about refusing to go to school,' she is saying now, 'but it's the closest I can be to him.'

'Makes sense,' I say.

She's munching on a bright red apple. She usually has toast. I grab a yogurt and we leave the house. Our feet crunch on the driveway. I'm in boots and she is wearing delicate little pumps.

'I'm still angry at you, you know,' she tells me. 'You're still a bitch for doing what you did. It's just – I need someone to talk to. And you're my closest friend. Apart from Lon.'

Her smile's still forced, but it feels realer this time. I try to smile back. But Lon is more important than her family. Her blood.

'OK,' I tell her. I can't think of anything to say to that. I don't want her to only have Lon to lean on. She needs to know we're here for her as well. I've been reading up on how to support people in abusive relationships. Scrolling through the Internet for tips. Mostly it's just be there, be there, be there.

I walk in silence. Catlin is smoking a cigarette. The orange spark of it fox-bright. A burning thing. I wince. She speaks of Lon.

'He doesn't like when people bring it up. The Helen thing. It makes him feel persecuted. He comes across as confident, Madeline, but he can be quite sensitive deep down.'

She takes a long drag. We're at the bus stop. The smoke is blue-grey and it hurts my eyes. There's something strange about it. The way it curls. The air is sharp today. I feel the bite of cold and pull my coat a little tighter round.

Layla runs towards us just as the bus pulls up, her jumper inside out. She looks so tired. Everyone is weighted down today. And suddenly, like an unexpected dick pic, there Lon is, spread across the back seat of the bus, reading Bukowski. Prince Charmless. How did they even let him on? It's highly inappropriate. I glare at the bus driver, who stares blankly at me, as if I'm being unreasonable somehow. I start to say something, but Catlin, lit up with her Christmas-morning smile, pulls my arm. I find a seat, and she walks right down past me, loops her hands around him, snuggles in. I don't know whether or not to text Mam about it. *What can he do?* I think. *We're on a bus.*

The mountains roll on by, as I sit by myself, eyes out the window, panicking and wondering what to do. I wish there was a bell that you could ring in this situation. For the unsexy

245

sort of forbidden love. But suddenly it's hard to think about Catlin and Lon because Oona has returned, and is curled up on the seat beside Charley, flicking through something on her phone. I wonder what. I hope it's a YouTube tutorial on fancying me back.

I feel a sigh welling up inside me, and swallow it down. I have enough on without being visibly lovelorn on the bus.

'Welcome back, Oona,' I say.

She smiles at me. I'm glad she's reappeared, but I wish she'd chosen the seat beside me. We haven't really spoken since that night. I wonder if she feels that tension too. I open my mouth to say something, but Charley gets there first. Which is probably no bad thing, in fairness.

'Were you not well?'

'My mother needed me at home,' she says.

'For what?'

'Family things mostly. We painted the sitting room. It's blue.' She gets her phone to show us.

'Look,' says Fiachra. 'Your sister's letting Lon go under the blouse.'

'Catlin!' I say, and I have never sounded more like a middle-aged nun. I am a pleated midi-skirt and a sensible cardigan away from a bossy, lonely future, and everyone can sense it. My face flushes. But also . . . I am right. Brian and Mam would lock her in the dungeon if they knew. I should tell them. I should. I will. Just not right now. Ringing your mam because you are your sister's designated sex police is not a good way to impress a girl. I know because I am a girl and it would not impress me.

246

'Sorry, Maddy,' my twin calls, giggling. 'It's just that ours is a forbidden love.'

Lon doesn't even move his head to look at anyone. His eyes are fixed on Catlin, following her every little jolt.

School passes in a fugue.

'I thought they were supposed to be forbidden,' Layla says to me at break time. 'They don't look even a little bit forbidden.'

'It isn't really working out that well,' I tell her. 'Catlin doesn't like rules.'

'And Lon makes his own. But the rate she's going, she'll probably have a family of five before her eighteenth birthday. Brian won't like that at all. Not that I'm judging.'

She totally is judging. I am too. People always are, and we can't help it. I don't like her saying that about Catlin though. I'm kind of perturbed by the idea that everyone assumes they're at it. I mean, it hasn't been that long. Enough time to fall in love, I know. But what about falling in trust?

Oona sits with Cathal in double Irish. She looks tired. I hope that she has got a broken heart. I know you probably shouldn't wish sadness on people that you fall for. But I want her to be free to be with me. To like me back.

Catlin hops the fence at lunchtime – off to Donoghue's to look for Lon. I have a weird feeling she's going to end up pregnant out of spite. My fingers twist at loose strands of dark thread on my sleeves, and I think again about throwing Mam a quick message. Nothing alarmist. Just a quick 'So Catlin's off looking for her boyfriend the former murder suspect who was by the way on the bus this morning and I didn't contact you about it because I was worried about not seeming fun to this girl I can't stop thinking about. I am the sensible twin. Thank you bye.'

But I don't want to worry her.

Or to get in trouble.

Or be yelled at by Catlin.

I push my hair behind my ears, and plaster on a smile as though I have been paying attention to what was going on around me, instead of having a head-debate. Everything is quiet at the desks we've pushed together into a mega-desk so we can eat our sandwiches while staring at each other. I feel like I am auditioning for *Strictly Come Friending*. Say something, I think. Make it less awkward. Long car journeys. Questions in the back.

'If you could be any kind of animal, what would you be?' I ask, thinking of Button. Small, innocent Button who has also managed to annoy Catlin by just existing.

'What does that have to do with anything?' snaps Eddie. Layla, Cathal and Fiachra glare as well.

'Jesus, Madeline.' Charley rolls her eyes, like I'm the worst.

'Sorry?' I offer. It was a little random, I suppose.

Layla touches my arm, lowers her voice.

'Those kinds of questions don't go down well here, Madeline.'

'Um . . . thanks for telling me?'

'You're welcome. Do you have any pictures of Button on your phone?'

OF COURSE I do. It's fine again – we're off. Charley has some photos of Button from when he was even littler than he is now, and I have some from when he climbed into a teacup and just sat there for a while, chilling out.

'He would bring a tear to your eye,' says Cathal.

'We only have outdoor cats at ours,' says Charley. 'And they can be really mean. Like Catlin.'

'What?' I ask. 'What did she say to you?' But before I get an answer, a smooth voice rings through the classroom.

'Madeline?' I hadn't heard him creep up behind me. It is Lon. He's slouching in his battered leather jacket. I square my shoulders. 'We need to talk. Come with me, little one.'

'Don't call me that.' I feel as if he is trying to lessen me. I am small, but I am big enough to hurt him if he does anything to her that I don't like.

'It's accurate.' He grins and shrugs, like it is no big deal.

'Shut up, Lon.' I rise to my full height. 'Why are you even in school? Aren't there, like, rules about this sort of thing?'

'I play by my own rules,' he says with a little laugh, but then his voice loops into something deeper, more serious. 'Look. I wanted to –' he sighs, like the effort of talking to a girl he doesn't want to grope is a 200lb dumb-bell – 'explain some things to you. For Catlin's sake. She asked me to. So, please?'

I sigh back, like I am doing him a massive, *massive* favour, which I am, and follow him around the back of the school building. We sit on the lip of an abandoned prefab.

He smiles at me. The chasm of his mouth. His coin eyes cold.

'I wanted to apologise. If we have gotten off on the wrong foot,' he offers.

I glare at him. 'Lon. I don't care.'

'It was ages ago,' he says, 'and it didn't happen like they said. I broke her heart and she told loads of lies. Unrequited love can do things to a person's soul.'

249

He looks at me. I think of Oona's face. The moonlit lake.

'It can,' I say. 'But can you see how I would be worried for Catlin? I don't want to see her hurt.'

'Listen,' he says, and I can see the ropey muscles tensing in his neck. His long arms covered with thin black cotton fabric, fingers twining round his ribs like vines of flesh. 'Listen to me, Madeline. I love your sister. I love her. I will keep her safe. I love her.' He stares at me, as if he's willing what he's saying true. He has moved closer to me, close enough that I'm beginning to feel cornered. I square my shoulders and inhale sharply. I will not be intimidated by someone who regularly wears an ankh.

'OK, Lon.' I roll my eyes. I don't believe a word. And I don't think that he does either. He's lying to himself as well as to me, I think. I glare at him. A mouse beside a cat. He lifts his hands from off his knees and puts one on my shoulder and I jolt.

This is a dangerous thing. And not a man.

'Look . . . What do I need to do to make you believe that I am a decent human being? Nothing was proven.' His voice is angry.

'Catlin said that too. About the proof. But there are things I know that she does not. I see you, Lon Delacroix. I see you, what you are.' My voice is strange. It doesn't feel like mine. 'You should be careful. There are bigger things than you inside the woods. I've sensed them and they are hungry.'

'I don't know,' Lon says. 'I'm pretty big. Little One.' The chasm of his mouth so red and wide. What big teeth he has, I think. I swallow hard and straighten my spine.

'Don't be a prick, Lon.' He moves closer to me, his arms snaking on my shoulder. Knee. I amn't scared. I won't ask him to stop. I amn't scared. His eyes. I'm looking in his eyes. They aren't real.

'Don't hate me for no reason.' He sounds so reasoned, with his corpse's face. There is a greedy thing inside of him. It's waking. I can feel the heat bounce off me.

'There are reasons.' I tilt my face to his. I glare. I'm not afraid. I'm not afraid of Lon.

Only I am. I focus on his eyes. I put a cold hand up to the side of his face. If I could touch him, maybe I could work out who he is and what that means.

'Madeline,' he says. His breath on mine. And there is panic surging through my gut.

Getoutgetoutgetout.

Catlin rounds the corner, looks at us. Staring at each other. Touching. Flushed.

'Oh my God. You were right about her.' Her mouth is opening and closing. A fish upon the shore. 'I couldn't find you in the flat,' she says.

'I came to try to make things easier for you. For us,' he tells her. 'I know how much you care about Madeline. I wanted to explain. But she . . .' He shrugs helplessly, a victim of his own sexiness, apparently.

I want to vomit. Acid. In his face.

'Catlin . . .' I begin, and I really want to tell her that it's not what it looks like but that's exactly what I would say if it were what it looked like and my head starts going in panic circles. It's happening too fast for me to clear my head, to make it right.

'You fancy him.' She runs towards me, and her eyes are wild. 'How could you?'

'What?' I squeak.

'Don't deny it. I can see it, written on your face.' She looks at Lon. 'I love you.'

'She's your sister. I couldn't push her off. She's only small.' He looks at Catlin, all outraged and plausible. 'No matter what they say, I don't hurt women.' He doesn't glare at me; he doesn't have to.

'He's the one who put his hands on me.'

'You seemed to like it.' There's that smile again, the friendly shark.

'You need to leave,' says Catlin. 'You need to leave right now before I slap you.'

She means me, not him. He is the one whose story she believes. It isn't fair. Her face is brimming with anger, spilling over with it.

'Just go, Madelina,' says Lon. And he must have known that using that would break her. She runs at me, and scratches at my face. I hold my hands in front of my eyes. Her fingers in my hair. She's screeching, pulling. An owl with claws. She knows just where to hurt.

She is not my sister. She is someone else who's doing this to me. 'I love him,' Catlin shrieks. 'I hate you and I love him and I hate you.'

This needs to stop. She isn't making sense. I try to push her off but she wants to hurt me. I close my eyes.

'Girls, girls,' says Lon, doing nothing to help. 'Control yourselves.'

His voice is very smug. But Catlin stops.

'I didn't mean to get out of control. I'm sorry, Lon.' Her voice is humble, so apologetic.

252

'It's OK, love. You do not have to worry. You're the one I want. My little doe. Be gentle.'

She stumbles to him, his knuckles shift beneath the skin. His hand moves to wipe her face. Adjust the collar on her uniform as though she were a helpless, messy child.

'Catlin,' I say, and I can hear the piercing whine of me. She doesn't even turn. 'I didn't – I *wouldn't*. Catlin, you *know* me.'

She moves then, her back against Lon's chest.

'I thought I did. But then we came here, and you changed. And now –' her face crumples – 'I don't know who you are any more. You used to be on my side. On our side. And now it's you and them. And Lon and me.'

That stings more than her nails against my cheek. I look at them, but they have turned away. A door has closed. This is the end of something.

I look back once before I turn the corner. He is holding her to him; like yin to yang they fit beside each other. Her head on his collarbone. His chin on her head. His arms encircle her so tightly. His face is calm. I cannot see her face.

35

Self-Heal

(inflammations, swellings, boils and cuts)

Mam's angry with me. I can tell, because of the pinch of her face and her tight grip, knuckles white against the steering wheel. When she meets my eye in the rear-view mirror, her eyes have that shuttered feel to them. Like I'm only seeing what she's holding back.

I didn't tell her. About what Lon did, putting his hands on me to score points on some imaginary scoreboard he uses to control girls like my sister. I think it broke her. It's hard enough already, I think, looking at Catlin hunched over, shoulders heaving. She's sobbing. Properly sobbing. Her face and body curled against the door. As far away from me as she can manage. Everything she had been keeping in is spilling out. All of the anger, sadness. This fight between us opened up a wound, and it's infected. Something cruel has moved in, taken root.

'Love, are you OK?' asks Mam.

'You don't care,' Catlin says. 'I . . .' and then she starts again.

Tears clear as crystal, fat as ticks, crawling down her face, around her nose and into her mouth. I pass her a tissue, but she tells me to fuck off, and Mam doesn't say anything.

The drive home seems to take much longer than usual. I feel so far away from both of them. Like we are reverse getting to know each other, slipping out of bonds that held us tight. Is this what love does to people? Brian, Oona, Lon. We fall in love and then we fall apart.

The mountains in the dusk are dark and spiky, pocked with little hollows. Pools and boggy wetlands in the dips. Not for turf, but ones that suck you in and keep you there like a secret for years.

We went to see a bogman once with school. He looked like shoe leather, beaten in the vague shape of a person. Not unlike Brian's shrunken little head. I think of Catlin's warmth leaching out into the earth. Her head misshaping, warping through with time. We're only small. Easier to hide than other people. You'd hardly have to chop us up at all.

I can't say anything. I mean, I try. I start to . . .

'It wasn't . . .'

and

'I wouldn't . . .'

and

'He's lying.'

She shuts me down. I am the villain here. Mam looks at me too. I see her eyes in the mirror, all clouded with suspicion. Questioning and different to mine. Dad's eyes were green, like mine and Catlin's are. At least they were, before he burned to death. Good people suffer. I don't know if I'm good though.

I'd like to think I am. I'd like to be. But how can you be sure?

The car pulls up to the driveway. Catlin hops out, runs in. Mam stops me before I do the same.

'We need to talk. Wait upstairs in your room.'

Her voice is stern, no room for debate.

I go upstairs. The wood is dark and polished, paintings hang on chains in frames of gold. Other people's faces, staring, staring. Nobody looks happy on the walls. Or in the walls, I think.

My room is gutted, like a deer that wolves have picked clean, licked clean. All my herbs, my salt, are lined up on the windowsill. A big black bin bag sits at the edge of my bed. My eyes begin to sting. I know the drill. What Mam wants me to do. Erase that last small part of me that needed to explore my own potential.

Take the magic in my hand and clench a fist and crush it into dust.

But how can I?

I just want to feel safe.

My heart is beating faster, faster, faster. I can feel my breath catch in my throat. My eyes sting. I take my hand and make a fist and punch my forehead, hard. I haven't done that since I was a child. I used to . . . when the other children hurt my feelings sometimes. But there was always Catlin, and I stopped. I grew.

I feel alone.

Her feet are quickly coming up the stairs.

And I can hear my sister in her room, murmuring and crying to herself.

Mam opens up the door, and comes inside.

256

'Madeline, I've asked you, and I've told you.'

I stare at the wall behind her head, glaring at the stone like it was deciding not to help me. Her tone hurts my heart.

'You know what we're going through with your sister. And this nonsense – it's the last thing that I need right now.'

'Mam . . .' I say, my voice is low, ashamed.

She raises her hand to silence me.

'Stop. I have tried to be understanding, and to reason with you. But I won't do it any more. You've been leaning on this since we got here. And you can stand on your own two feet, Madeline. You do not need a crutch. All this –' she gestures around her – 'it's just a crutch. And if you go to college, you'll be living with people, and it will scare them. These strange things you do. And I don't want that.'

'I don't. I mean, I keep it . . .'

'Under the bed, I know. And in your wardrobe, and on your windowsill and in your sock drawer and in the toilet cistern . . .'

She's thorough. I'll give her that. I feel anger rising up within me. I want to say the things I do are real. I want to tell her. I am afraid to tell her. I stay silent, biting my fingernails. The little parts of me I can pare down.

'This stuff is dangerous, love,' she says. 'If you give in to these urges, your life will get smaller and smaller, until these things –' she gestures to the boxes and the jars, the little piles – 'are all you are. And you are more than that. I love you. I want you to be OK. OK?'

'OK,' I lie. I start gathering all my little pieces, bit by bit. Piling them into the black sack Mam holds open like the mouth of a dark cave. Things I've left in different places too. The little salt packets I tried to hide in her room, the ones from under Catlin's mattress.

Tears start rolling down my face. The shame for what I'd learned to be less ashamed of returns and washes over me, engulfs my face and neck in red. I'm trying very hard to hold it back.

'I know it hurts, love,' Mam tells me. 'But some things that we think we need are damaging. Look at Catlin and Lon.'

I let a bunch of dried sage, tied with twine, fall into the bag. The room is warm, it smells of bin bag, sweet, disgusting plastic. I feel like if I touched it, my fingers would emerge all soaked in tar.

This is not like that. The things I do are nothing like Lon Delacroix. I close my eyes. I think of Catlin's face. His bony fingers crawling on my skin like spiders' legs. The triumph in his smile. His stupid flaring nostrils. Like a bull. I just need to get this done. To get Mam off my back. And when she's finished doing whatever this is, asserting her control, making her point, I can decide where I will go from here.

It takes forever. When everything is packaged up, I look at her and sigh. I think of the candles and religious paraphernalia that Catlin gathers in her room. She has an actual altar, for crying out loud. Weird things are fine when they're pretty. It's when it's messy, or ugly that people get creeped out and try to stop you.

I mop the floor, dust the shelves, change the sheets. Every trace of me, of who I am, has left the room, I think.

I look at Mam. 'Are you happy now?' I ask her.

'No, Madeline,' she says, 'I'm really not.' She looks like she

258

wants to say more things, but I don't want to hear them, so I ask her if I can go. And she says that I can. I go to the garden and press my hands to the damp earth in the dark and try to breathe my way back into safety. There's something pulsing, in the pit of me, inside my blood and breath. It's at my core, and maybe it is my core. And my mother hates it. I always thought, deep down, that if I were to tell her I liked girls, that she would be supportive, that it would be OK. But – after this?

I go back inside and softly knock on the door between our bedrooms, hoping that Catlin maybe heard the thing with Mam, that she maybe feels some sympathy, some something. When I hear her in there, I reach my voice under the gap between the door and the floor. Lying on my stomach like a soldier, I try to reshape feelings with my words.

'What you saw . . . it isn't what you saw,' I say to Catlin. 'He tried to explain. To make me like him better. He put his hands on me. But not like that.'

'Shut up.'

I do. This sort of magic – normal human stuff – is far beyond me. I shut my mouth and look out at the mountains where they found them.

Amanda Shale, blonde hair attached to bone. Skull cracked almost in two, and three ribs missing.

Nora Ginn. Her father's little girl. They smashed her face to pieces like a plate.

Bridget Hora, just a few scraps left, the rest was missing.

Helen Groarke, who kept a little flesh.

I'm not a bad person. It's just I let things happen. I thought that I could stop it, but I can't.

259

I hear Catlin's voice, rising and softly falling in her room. I crack the door to look. She is asleep. And she is saying:

'Lon.

I love you.

Lon. Laurent?'

Back in my room, I lie awake. My hands still smell of dust. I think about the soft green things that grow. The hot small lives that teem under the earth and only wake when we are fast asleep. About the herbs. The garden that we used to have in Cork. Of lavender for patience. Mint for calm. The textures and the smells. Catlin's hand in mine, walking in the door of big school.

'You will be fine,' she said. 'I've got you. Always.'

It isn't true now. Something big has changed.

Soft earth. Cold wind. Wet rain.

Mountains cut the edges of the sky.

My eyes tilt shut. I flatten into sleep.

36

St John's Wort

(somatoform disorders, mild depression, bruises)

I wake up to the ringing of my phone. It's three o'clock in the morning, but also – it's Oona. I pick up, dry-throated, tongue thick with whatever grows in your mouth while you sleep. I'm glad she isn't here. I need my toothbrush.

Her voice is strange, deeper than it normally is, something in it that I can't quite place.

'Is everything all right?' I ask, as if it's perfectly normal for her to be calling me in the middle of the night.

'Are you busy?' she asks. And I say no. She asks if I can meet her in the forest. There is a little shed, halfway up the mountain, past the crossroads where Catlin and I found the fox. I've seen it on my walks, but never gone in.

This distraction is a sort of blessing. I press my hand against the windowpane and look out at the mountains and the sky. Something rustles in the wall behind me. A brittle, scratching sound. It could be rats, I think. That's all we need.

I brush my teeth and pad down to the kitchen, boots in hand. The sky is dark tonight, and I use the light of my phone to pad around, trying to keep as quiet as I can. This house is big, but Brian could be hanging out in the walls or something, because I wouldn't put it past him, what with all the secrets he's been keeping. Ugh. I'm so sick of the lot of them. Except for Button.

I pull on one of Brian's big logo fleeces. My coat is clean, but it reminds me of torture, broken foxes. I walk and walk. The forest's dark and full of night-time sounds. Ripples and clicks and my boots on the leaves marching through it. It takes me around forty minutes to get to the right place.

The wind is harder on the sloping road. It mashes grass and plants down horizontal. I zip the fleece right up. It's past my nose. My hands are in the pockets. There's a fat brass lighter there. Does Brian smoke? I wonder. What don't we know about this quiet man who's in our family?

The shed is small and stone with a corrugated iron roof that's rusted into red. Someone definitely lived there once. There is a crumbling old wall all around it. A wrought-iron gate so warped it doesn't close, just swings and flakes. A lonely place. I hope Oona's all right.

My heart. I think of the night we had that walk, of swimming in the lake. Her hand in mine, her shoulders and her smile. She let go, and maybe she was right. I don't deserve a precious thing. I'd break it. My fat hands on the handle of the door. My thick tongue in my mouth. My heart is beating hard. I breathe in deep before I venture in.

The place is nicer than I thought it would be. There's

262

electricity, for one thing. A bare light bulb swings in the middle of the wooden-plank ceiling. The floorboards bare, and grey mould on the walls, but there's a heater someone has plugged in, some cushions and a beanbag on the floor. There are some cans and old packets of crisps inside the fireplace. They must hang out here, the kids from school, without us, I think. And Oona knows about it, and we don't. And it hurts a little, being left out in another way.

I know I look a state; I run my fingers through my snarling hair and bite my lips to try to make them pinker. My cheeks are flushed. I should have made more of an effort.

Her voice says, 'Madeline.' And then I see her. Curled up on some cushions on the floor. Her face is very blotchy. Her eyes are ringed with black. Her hair is wet. Her hair is always wet.

I go to her. I put my arms around her and I say, 'Tell me what happened.'

Oona cries. I hold her and she cries. I tell her that she'll be all right. That it will change. That things always get easy in the end. I believe that when I say it to her. I stroke her hair. She snuggles in beside me, and she speaks.

'Claudine broke my heart,' she says. 'She broke my heart. It's finished.'

Then she says some other things in French. My French isn't very good and her voice is fast. I think there is another person. And they have been to the cinema. And it isn't fair. We talk and talk for ages.

'She's an idiot,' I tell her softly.

'You've never met her.' Oona sniffs a bit.

'She was mean to you,' I say. 'She had you and she lost you. She's a fool.'

'I hate him and I hate her. But mostly I just hate myself. I might as well be dead.' She starts to sob again, and curls towards my chest. My body pulses. I stroke her back awkwardly. She's crying and she needs me. I need to be a friend to her right now.

'We could go to the castle?' I suggest. 'Sneak in and watch a film? Look at cat videos? Photoshop her head onto a dinosaur?' I waggle my eyebrows, trying to seem fun. I'm rarely fun, but I could try, for her.

'I am too melancholy for such pursuits,' she says. It is the Frenchest, Frenchest sentence. 'I think that I might have to swim it off.' She sighs, and squeezes out her hair, as though it were a little burnished sponge. She's standing up.

I stand up too.

And then she looks at me.

We are facing each other and I can feel the blood rush through my skin. She doesn't move. I cannot even blink. Every part of me is waking up. I might get sick.

She looks at me again. What big eyes she has.

I can't help it. I lean in, kiss her gently. On the mouth.

Just once.

Her lips are very soft.

'She's an idiot,' I say again. Her hand snakes to my waist, she pulls me closer, and we are kissing properly. There's nothing tentative at all in this. It's fierce and warm and soft and, oh, I want her and I want her.

So many ways to make a person ache.

I always thought that when I had my first proper kiss, with

someone I felt things for, I would be worried that I was doing it wrong. I was wrong. I cannot think at all. I'm just a body. I am just a mouth. And she is Oona.

Her hands snake inside my hoodie, underneath my T-shirt to the small of my back. She traces the notches on my spine. I shiver. Everything about her is clean and soft and fresh. I breathe her in. Our skin is touching skin and we are kissing. I need her and I need this. We are touching on the cushioned floor and I am hungry. I didn't know that bodies were a thing. That they could fit like this. That there was magic.

'Madeline,' she says. I murmur something back. She sighs forever. I can feel her shoulders, tense, collapse. Her ribcage pressing in against my torso. Her soft, damp skin.

She says my name again. She moves away.

I hate the stupid world for rushing in.

'I don't think we can do this.' She looks at me. Her face is calmer now. Her hair all mussed. Her eyes are bright. I did that, with my hands, to her, I think. I made it better. Even for a while.

'Why?' I ask. But I already know.

'I think . . .' she says. Her voice trails off. She thinks. Begins again. 'I think that you could be a good friend, even a best friend, to me. And I think you're beautiful as well. I mean, I loved that. What we just did. I loved it . . . but there is another thing that must be there. I don't know what it is. But something's missing. I couldn't fall in love with you, Madeline. Whatever love grows from, it isn't there . . .' She's playing with my hair while saying this. Her hands are tender. I feel a helpless weight begin to build. Her mouth shapes words like *me* and *you* and *sorry*. There's a pause. I can't think what to say.

'So I'm beautiful. And a good friend. And you want me. And that's not enough.'

'It sounds strange when you put it like that.' She smiles. 'But something here and here –' she touches hands to stomach and to heart – 'it isn't there. And I can't make it grow.'

'Maybe it's too soon after Claudine?' I say, my hand still on her leg, tracing the soft denim up and down. I feel a panic mounting. I can't discover this and have it gone.

'That could be it. I'm not sure. Maybe it's my destiny to love people who do not love me back,' she says.

And mine as well, I think.

Because I love you.

'My mother and my father, they fight all the time,' she tells me. 'About me. It's scary. I don't like it. That was why I wasn't in school. Things were bad, with them. And with Claudine. Sometimes, when things are very bad, I find it difficult to manage in the world. I stay at home. I swim, I cry, I sleep . . .'

'I'm sorry, Oona,' I say. 'I hope you know, if things are hard, if you need someone outside your family, that I'm here. It doesn't always have to be like this. We're friends. We're still friends now. It doesn't have to go any further.'

'I wish I was a normal girl like you.' She sniffs. 'I thought it would be easier when we moved, but things are hard no matter where you are.'

'But I'm not normal,' I say. 'There are so many things that I'm not telling people. About who I want, about what I can do – Mamó . . .'

And suddenly, it all comes out of me in waves, the offer

266

that she made, the things we've seen. The warnings to be wary in the village. The thing with Lon. All of it, all at once. Oona hasn't said anything in a while, I realise. She's holding my hand, stroking the inside of my palm with her thumb.

'I'm sorry,' I finish. 'You needed to talk about your stuff, and here I am burdening you with mine.'

'It's OK,' Oona says. She looks at me. I fall into her eyes. The pull of them. I blink away. 'I want to tell you something. You have a thing – this *talent* – but you are not alone. Most of the people here in Ballyfrann have things like that – their own strange way of being in the world.'

Her face is very serious. *Grave*, I think. That's the French word for it. Like a grave. Our hands are still touching, and our heads are close – an inch apart.

'My way is that I need the water. Properly I need it. It's like the only time I'm fully calm is when I'm in there. It's part of me . . .' She looks at me. Her silver-fish eyes dance. 'I love it, but without it I would die, and that's a hard thing to explain to people. That difference. That is why we moved here. For understanding, space. My father has his people and my mother has the water – she's like me. The same as what I am.'

I don't know what to say. What do you say to something that unusual, that honest?

'What are you?' I ask.

'A lesbian,' she says, and we crack up. She curls in beside me, and looks up at my face. 'I know that's not what you meant. But it is similar, I think. I have so many parts of my identity that people do not like, that can be dangerous: how I look, who I love, and this, also. I will try . . . My father is . . . a little like the

Collinses. Sometimes, he becomes an angry thing. It was hard for him, when he met my mother. They had to struggle – both their families did not approve. And then . . . real life is not like in a story. There is more to it. After you have won, you have to live and love and keep on loving. That's where he fell down, I think, a bit.'

'And your mother?'

'She is . . . she needs the water, more than even me. Being away from it too long can really hurt her.'

'Wow,' I say. It's not the most eloquent of responses. But what do you say when confronted by a thing like this?

'I know. Even for me, it is not easy. I would like to be more typical.'

'Me too,' I say.

'It's true.' She smiles. 'Being in the world is a lot, Madeline. All of this is . . .' She sighs and flops onto her back and lies staring at the ceiling. I stare at her.

'Remember when we swam?'

I nod.

'It all seemed very clear that night. I felt that, without words, you understood me. That it didn't need to be in words . . .' She trails off, and then turns her head towards mine. Her hair is sticking up. It's really cute.

'. . . I really wished that you would kiss me then.' Her voice is low, her gaze is very soft.

I catch my breath. 'In the lake, you looked like coming home feels,' I say, and lean my head to kiss her. Knowing that I'm only second best. Her hand reaches out to stroke my waist and lingers there. She doesn't touch me like she couldn't love me.

268

I'm wrong to hope, but still. I want to hope so badly.

'Is everyone here something else as well?' I ask.

'Pretty much,' Oona says. 'The families who are here for a long time, they all have their . . .'

'Secrets?'

'It is not so much a secret, as a thing that is only for the people that you trust. A part of you that very few would understand.'

'And how do you find out, what people are?' I ask.

'The best way is to wait for them to say it,' Oona tells me. 'And it will take some time, but, Madeline, they will. They like you here. Something about you fits in to this place, I think.' I snort, but she waves her hands. 'No, no, it's true, I think – I mean, when we first met, I thought you might have something . . . I mean, the way I felt about you. There was an affinity there, a recognition . . . maybe you felt it too?'

I nod. I cannot think what else to say. Her head is on my shoulder and I feel her hair soaking through my top towards my skin. The smell of her.

Her hands scratch fabric, searching for the words.

'. . . But I get the sense that I could really hurt you, Madeline. And I don't want to do that.'

'I'll be fine,' I say. I'm used to hurting. My smile is stretching painfully on my face. I don't know what to do. This is new, so new and already it is dying.

'Maybe we could kiss again sometime?' I say to Oona. 'Not in a love way. In a friendly way. Until there's something else for me or you?'

'Would that be safe?' she asks, and I see the little crescents at the base of her fingernails as her hands smooth out imperceptible creases.

I nod, and tell a lie that serves us both. 'I think it would be.'

Her smile a happy half-moon, wide and soft. I walk her through the forest to her home. The woods are deep and dark and intricate and magical and something. There is a certainty within me now. I know a little more of who I am. Of what I can do. We live in a big world, where things can change and doors once closed can open.

Her stomach and her heart. I was bitter. Now I'm bittersweet.

I wish.

I wish.

37

Gentian

(parasitic worms, sinusitis)

I slink up the driveway through the courtyard and into the kitchen. The sky is navy blue. You wouldn't call it morning yet, but the promise of one is there. The sun is coming. Things might improve. I mean, I have managed to alienate my entire family, but on the plus side I could have a whole friends-with-benefits situation going on with Oona if I play my cards right and don't, like, accidentally get a tattoo of her name on my face or anything. And I know a little more about her now as well, and the village too. I think of Layla, Charley and them all. What secrets are they keeping? And will I ever know them well enough to get an answer?

I take my boots off at the kitchen door. They're covered in dew and leaves and mountain muck.

Mam flies at me. I'm grasped towards her in a painful hug. Her hands claw tight. Her eyes are wild and worried. 'Where were you?' Half whisper, half a scream. 'Is Catlin with you?'

'I went out for a walk.' My voice is thin. I want to pull away, want to read her face. What does it mean?

'You were supposed to be at home in bed,' she snaps, white-faced and staring. 'I went in to check on you and your bed was empty. Both your beds were empty. Oh, my heart.'

Button is under the table, batting at a little ball of dust. His eyes are big and shining in the shadow. His fur all ruffled, sticking out in different directions. I watch him with the eye that isn't smashed against Mam's breast. She smells of sweat and perfume. I push against her, squirming my way out.

'Wait,' I say. 'Mam – where's Catlin?'

'Brian has driven over to Donoghue's – in case she's with that lad,' she says. 'That Lon.' She points towards the table. There's a note. 'I thought – I thought you might have gone together – or gone after her, to bring her back. When I searched her room there was this note, stuck in the middle of her little altar.'

I pick it up. It's a page torn from a book. Thick and old and off-white, slightly textured. It's Catlin's writing, obviously. Black ink almost carving through the paper, for emphasis.

You can't keep us apart when we're the same soul inside two bodies. We've gone away until you understand.

'That's nonsense,' I exclaim. 'What is she on?' I would have gone after her if I'd heard her leave. If I hadn't been up the mountains, sexing a Frenchwoman. I am a terrible sister. What are we going to do?

'I wish I knew,' says Mam. 'Have you gotten my messages?'

'I haven't checked my phone.' I run upstairs. It's on a couch beside the secret door. I push the wall to see if it's still there. Of course it is. This castle's playing havoc with my brain. Messages from Mam, a few from Oona, one from an unfamiliar number. It's a picture of Lon and Catlin inside her bedroom. Reflections in the mirror. I only see the broad slope of his back. Her cheeky face. The collar of his shirt is askew, poking up and down. The room looks dim, the light in there a little off somehow. The Marys glow with candles on the altar. There is a caption: 'True Love Never Dies.'

She's still cross with me, I think. But she wanted to reach out. To tell me or to taunt me. It really doesn't matter. It's a clue. It's something.

I show Mam. Her face pales as we scan the screen, looking for something that would help us . . .

The ringing of her phone makes us both jump. It's Brian. I can only hear a low mumble, answering her.

'I have her here,' she says. 'Have you . . . ?' then, 'No. OK.'

'Should we call the police?' she asks, and there is a pause before his answer. It feels too normal, her voice on the phone, when something this big, this much is happening. How is the world still going on around us?

Mam hangs up after a strangled, 'Bye, love.' She takes a deep, shuddery, breath in, and turns to me. 'OK. Brian is going to contact the police. The closest station is a bit away though, so he reckons that the best thing to do would be to go up to the Collinses and organise a search party. They'll help him. They have children of their own.'

'OK,' I say. 'Should I go down and get Mamó?'

'I've tried,' Mam says. 'Her car is gone. I think she's on a

273

job. Think, Madeline – do you know where they could be, at all?' Her voice is strained from reining in panic.

'They could literally be anywhere.' I can feel the fear pooling in my gut and surging up. My eyes bulge and my feet tap. I see everything in the kitchen with such clarity. The copper bright. The wood grain. Stippled paint. Everything is begging to be noticed. I can't filter anything out. It hurts. It hurts me. Fight or flight.

Fight or flight. There is a third one someone told me once. Freeze. The way that deer or hedgehogs do with cars.

My little doe, he calls her. Writing on the walls inside the cave. In my dream I couldn't read it, but now . . . I see them, moving, clearing. Unfuzzing into such harsh familiar names.

Amanda.

Bridget.

Nora.

Helen.

Catlin.

Some of us are food.

It's looming loud. I need to act. Freezing is forbidden. So is crying. We don't have any help. It's up to us. And I think right now that us is mostly me. I take a breath. My face and hands feel cool, as though a breeze ran over me or something. I try to trace the feeling through my body.

To settle into calm before I act.

And suddenly, there is a sense of something. Adrenaline, or power. Maybe both.

I make a mental list. I get to work.

Instinct. Mainly instinct.

I can do this.

'We need to look for her, Mam. You need to get your coat.'

Mam's face is full of misery. She's sitting statue still and doesn't budge. 'Brian told me to stay here. In case she rings.'

I glare at her. 'He isn't thinking straight. You have your mobile.'

I dial the number that sent the photograph to me. Again. Straight to voicemail. Again I dial it. I leave a calm one, saying, 'Call us back. We love you. And it's OK. You and Lon. It will all be fine. Please just come home.'

I chant it through as though it were a prayer. That's one checked off. Next is . . . ?

'Do you have Mamó's number?' I ask Mam, not knowing if Mamó even has a phone.

She shakes her head. I sigh. Of course she probably only communicates by raven, or something equally witchy and useless. My shoulders tense. I let the feelings in. I stop resisting. Panic. Panic. Panic.

'You don't think she's in danger, do you, Maddy?' Mam's voice is high, pathetic.

'We need to act,' I say, 'as though she is. She is with Lon. We think Lon hurts girls. And Catlin is a girl. Horrible and simple. There it is.'

'OK,' she says, and breathes. 'OK. OK.' She stands up.

We head into the night. She holds my hand. And even though I'm almost grown, I let her. The forest waits. We venture quietly in. The trees are big tonight and almost brawny. Thick in places, sparse in others. I see lights on the mountains. Little fairy things that dot across.

'The Collinses are looking for her too,' says Mam, scrolling through her messages. 'And the Shannons. Brian has everyone.'

Lamps and phones and torches. It's almost pretty, if it wasn't grim. We have a flashlight and we have a phone. My eyes are becoming accustomed to the dark though. As my stomach tilts, my vision clears. Mam's face, half-lit, is shaded. I can almost see the skull shape poking through. When did she get so pinched and thin? I wonder. What is it about this place that eats flesh from bone?

'Do you . . . sense . . . anything at all?' asks Mam.

'No. Why? What do you mean?' I ask. I peer at her suspiciously.

'You hear about it sometimes, with twins. Psychic links, when someone is in crisis. The night your father died, you were in floods. Ye knew.'

I sigh, and keep all my replies locked in. She'll take the safety charms from under beds, thinking that I'm flawed or strange and wrong. But when she needs it, suddenly it's welcome. I save it up. I save my anger up for later on. I'll use it when it's useful. I need to find my sister. Do my job.

I pray to murdered girls like they were Gods. *Please help, Amanda Shale and Bridget Hora. Help me keep this girl from getting hurt.*

The forest stirs. I breathe the sharp night air. It smells of grass and earth and nothing else. If I were like that fox, I'd trace her scent. Predators can track their prey so well. His lanky frame that curled beneath her window. Stoats mesmerising rabbits with a dance. They move and twist until they're fascinated. And then their teeth clamp hard upon the spine.

276

Blood frenzy. Taste the blood.

My hands on edge. The hard ball in my pocket. Like a little marble. If I were Mamó's raven I could fly above and maybe see. My senses are too dull. I need them sharp. A needle in a haystack. Not even that. A needle shines bright. And it is dark and all of this is dark and I'm afraid. Mam's breathing high and strained. She's close to panic and we need to move. To keep on moving till we find our Catlin. Twin, where are you? Why did you fall in love with something wrong?

Helen and Amanda. Nora. Bridget. How long has Lon been Lon in this place? Oona telling me they never ask. They just accept each other. But certain evils need rooting out. And then the feeling hits. And it's relief.

I look at Mam. I do not ask permission. I don't need it.

'We're going back. I need things from the house.'

She replies but I don't hear, I'm running. I run towards Mamó's. My feet are harsh against the frosty path.

There'll be a price for this, and I will pay it. I see the jars I need before I'm there. Fluid. Powder. Leaves. It's just a feeling and it could go wrong. I push the door. The wound on my palm parting as I do. A little blood. It gives. She's let me in.

'Get me the salt you took from Catlin's room – the yellow packet,' I snap at Mam.

She opens her mouth. And looks at me and closes it again.

'You need to heed me if you want her back.' Apparently I sometimes speak in witch – it's like a different me behind the controls. Someone older. A me who knows the things that we should do.

I glare at her, and she complies. He cannot have her. She's

277

my sister. Mine. We grew together nestled in a womb and that means something.

Footsteps on the stairs. I focus hard.

I open up the jar of clear liquid, pour in the soft green powder. I think it once was sage. I can't be sure. One hand on the black marble in my pocket, rubbing, rubbing. I wish Mamó were here. If she would help.

Mam's footsteps, and her knock upon the door. I open it. Her face is pink and breathless. Silently she passes me the salt. She's barely here at all, I think.

I pour the whole pack in and stir it round.

Her face ashen.

'I don't want to be worried for the two of ye,' she ventures.

I look at her. A look that shuts her down. I put my right hand into the mixture. Draw a mask of it around my eyes. Pull a bright leaf from the pocket of my satchel. Spread it out on the table. Then begin.

A handful of the mixture straight against my eyeball. I feel it rough and sting and sharp and burn. The crinkle in my gut tells me I'm right. Mam gasps in horror. Keeps on gasping. Frightened rabbit breath.

'Madeline,' she says, 'Madeline,' and then she says my father's name, over and over again, just like a prayer. 'Tom. Tom. Tom. My Tom. My Tom. You promised me . . . It's happening. Oh no, no, no . . .'

'Mam!' I snap. 'There isn't time.'

She reaches for my hand. Her grip is a vice. I hope whatever's coursing through me is strong enough to bring her there as well.

'Shh,' I say. I feel a pull. A tug. I stare at the leaf. I'm blind, but something's swimming into vision. A mixture of my blood vessels and the veins on the leaves. There is a blend to it. A little map. I blink. It's burned on me. I grab the leaf. Something starts to build inside my stomach. It hurts but it's exciting.

I can do this.

Mam's voice cuts through. 'Mad, love? Are you all right? Talk to me.'

'We need to go. I know where Catlin is.'

38

Sweet Violet

(in a glass of water for quinsy)

'Come,' I tell Mam. My voice sounds strange. Authoritative. Capable. Like when I spoke to Lon at the prefab. There's a fevered focus to my actions. All I know is that I can do this.

I can find her.

We're back inside the castle, and inching our way up the stairs, towards Brian's office. I'm holding the leaf ahead of me, blinking furiously to keep the tears inside my eyes as much as possible, not streaming down my face. It's colder than it was; there is a chill. It leaches heat from me. The veins of the leaf make a road for me, and I can read them. Up the stairs, through the door. We're in.

It looks so normal. Leather office chair, and Brian's laptop. Pictures on the wall of Ballyfrann, when it was all just forest, back before. I never noticed that they were our woods until tonight. The green shade of his library lamp, the light fixture that's like a candelabra. Shelves of books, old files. There is a path that spiders from this place, that brings us somewhere I have been before. I see it on the leaf in front of me, the path to take. Once I have gotten in. I start to bang at walls, to push at them – all around where it opened up before. This has to work. It has to work.

It has to.

Mam is in the corner, tears streaming down her face. Her lips are moving but she isn't speaking. She thinks I'm breaking down. She thinks that this is it. She's lost us both. I don't have time for that. She needs to move. If we want to find Catlin, we need to look and look and keep on looking.

'Find your child,' I tell her. 'Do your job.' Shrunken head on top of the dark door frame, staring at the wall. It was a girl once, and it knew danger. I follow its dead gaze, fix on the wall. There is an extra brass flap for a light switch. I swing it up. Inside there is a cord, like the old chain flush on certain toilets. I take the little knob. I pull it out.

With a creak the wall slides away, inside the other wall. As it is swallowed up, a nook appears, a smooth black door inside it. It looks like it has always been there. No trace of wall remaining. It makes a kind of sense inside the room, an extra passage. I do not look at Mam, but I can hear the hush of muffled sobs, the wrench of tears and snot inside her throat. I can't be dealing with it. Not right now.

I jam a book to keep the door from closing and go in. I hear soft feet behind me. Going down. It should be dark, I think. But it's so bright. My stinging eyes see clearly. Cobwebs on the brickwork. Little pools.

There's moss on some of the steps and lichen on the walls, thick and lacey. The leaf against my eye still, but I hardly need it now. When I close my eyes I can see the tiny threads of blood vessels map-making on the inside of my eyelids. Helping me. They're helping me along. And how could this have always just been in me?

Something wet is trickling down my cheeks. I put my hands up. Wipe away the tears. My knuckles hot wet red. I'm crying blood. Like one of Catlin's statues. And it's a small price to pay, but I'm not sure what I'm paying for exactly.

The map is in my hand. The veins are twisting. I can see them move, like insect legs. Behind my eyes, the same shapes forming, warping. We're getting there. I can sense her closeness. I focus and unfocus, wrap my brain around the parts I need. I feel a touch. It's Mam. She holds my hand.

We turn the corner, and there is a sort of door. A slab of stone inside the wall, I push it but I cannot make it budge. Mam puts the flat of her palms on it too. We shove until it strains. Until it gives. Painfully, slowly, it moves away from us. Mam's face is red, her breathing's forcing heavy. One last effort. Both of us together, thinking of Catlin. One and two and . . . then we're in the cave. The same one from my dream, I think. But the dream cave was like a screen, there was a distance. This is very real. All my senses are screaming in this place.

'What is this?' asks Mam, taking in the stalagmites and stalactites. The piles of records. My foot brushes a scarf. It looks smaller, shabbier with my real eyes. The smell of rot and ancient mould. This place is old, older than the castle. There is a rainbow sheen to the wall like oil or petrol, pocked with strange growth, slime. My feet splash through a little water pool. It's chilly here, and dank.

'Catlin?' I call. Nobody replies.

And then I see the bed. Big enough for way more than two people. Spindly posts, intricately carved with eyes and hands and mouths and teeth. Jumbled, jutting, horrible and wrong. The sheets are rumpled. Thick fur throws and mirrors. Candles lit. It looks medieval. Arcane. I have a notion something happened here I wouldn't like. Beside me, I hear Mam's intake of breath.

'Love . . . ?' she asks. And then I see the hand. Stark white and poking out from under covers. It's small, the fingers stubby-long like mine. It isn't real. It's alabaster. Wax. It cannot be my sister. Mam ahead of me, I start to run.

39

Black Hellebore

(narcotic, poisons the heart)

Short of breath, I clamber on the bed, feeling far too small, too young for this, reaching with my arms to gain purchase. To climb. My heart thuds in my throat. A desperate knock. A door I don't want opened. I cannot look at her. I cannot look.

'Catlin.' My voice is wobbly, like a child's. I am small and lost and terribly afraid. Mam digs through sheets like a frightened rabbit. Her fingers red. There's blood on her hands. My sister's blood, I think. The black silk parts like murky river water. We see the thing that was my sister's face. It is her face, I mean. But it's been shredded. Throat in ribbons, breath coming in little gasps. Her eyes are lost. She's moving far beyond us. I think that she is trying to move her lips. They aren't there.

She's breathing though.

She's breathing.

I turn to Mam. 'She needs help.' It builds inside a screech but comes out ragged. 'You need to call someone.'

Mam's face is grey. She's staring at my sister. Half her jaw is gone and her tongue lolls out. What's left of it. A stump. I cannot let the horror of it in. No, not right now. I rummage through my bag for Mamó's jar. I bite my arm until blood spills out and then drip it through the thick and salty mixture.

I pour it on her throat. My sister screams.

Mam grabs at me. 'Stop. You'll hurt her. You will hurt her.' As though I were a toddler pulling hair. I shoot a look and watch her hands fall. I feel a rush of something to my brain. I might pass out. I bite my bottom lip hard. Almost through. I can use the parts of me to sew the bits of her. To hold her close.

'She is already hurt,' I say. 'And I can only try to help.'

My vision is still cloudy, though it sharpens on the things I need, with a quick zoom-focus. My intuition leads my brain and my body. It is driving. We were two, swimming in one womb. We grew together. There is something magic in a twin. Companion from the moment of creation. In all my life, I've never been alone. I've had a friend. And I will fight to keep her.

Something shimmers, folding slowly out. When we were little, Mam used to take us to visit aquariums on holidays. The jellyfish were kept in a dark room, the UV light shining through their soft, transparent bodies, and they would furl and unfurl underneath. Their movements looked so graceful, looked like dance, a ballerina's tutu, stacked atop a mermaid's magic hair. And we knew they could sting you, but we liked to look. To hold our hand against the glass. To wonder what would happen, if a single tentacle reached through and touched our skin. Would it sense that we were not a danger? I knew it wouldn't, but I hoped it would. The light unwrapping from around my twin is like those. It is very dim, but it is there. It ripples and it almost seems to pucker. A pale, translucent heft. It could be touched. I grab at it. If I can keep that light from going out then maybe I can keep her.

It wafts away. It's bending from my hands. There isn't time.

'ChhhhhccccchhhCCHhhhhh.'

Those sounds. Those horrid sounds. She is in pain, but she is trying, working. I put my fingers in her throat to clear an airway. There's not enough mouth left for CPR. Mam's trained, I think. She should know what to do. I look at her. She's staring and she's shaking.

'Mam. What do I do? Mam. MAM!' I yell at her. She's staring past us both.

'The wall,' she says. 'The carving on the wall.'

And then I look.

Dearbhla
Sibéal
Amanda
Laoise
Eimear
Laura
Bríd
Sorcha
Bridget
Karen
Gráinne
Julie
Roisín
Gobnait

Violet
Dymphna
Alacoque
Aoife
Fionnuala
Victoria
Elizabeth
Emer
Sinéad
Sally
Ciara
Mary-Ann
Nancy
Susan
Fiona
Delia
Maisy
Laura
Rachel
Caoimhe
Julie
Ava
Sheila
Maria
Antoinette
Cathleen
Martina
Jennifer
Carol

Nora
Lee
Colette
Ellen
Claire
Laurel
Jacinta
Mary-Bridget
Mary
Ann
Marie
Noreena
Savita
Carmel
Sarah
Aoibhe
Scarlett
Dearbhla
Katherine
Cecilia
Lisa
Lillian
Louise
Patricia
Katie
Cliodhna
Shona
Nuala
Shauna

Patricia
Monica
Meabhdh
Jean
Gillian
Elaine
Anna
Sabhdh
Sarah
Adele
Rose
Grace
Joyce
Nicola
Ruth
Frances
Naomi
Elizabeth
Sandra
Dolores
Aisling
Sharon
Lola
Chloe
Helen
Daisy
Megan
Úna
Fawn

Catlin

Oh God. Catlin.

There isn't time for fear to rise inside me. I cannot hyperventilate right now. I cannot panic. The only hurt that I'm allowed to feel must be constructive. If I let go, I'd curl into a ball. I'd shake and quiver while my sister dies.

'Call someone,' I tell her. My voice is glass-crack high.

'There isn't any signal.' She isn't moving, and it isn't helping.

'Go and find one. Send Brian our coordinates. Get help. RUN.'

You read about mothers who lift cars from on top of their children. Who move mountains. Ours is small inside the castle's gut. She nods and dashes away. I look down at my twin. And we're alone. Her face is turned to me, her eyes like saucers, rolling in her head. She's saying things. Maybe prayers. The bright around her is fading but it's there. I take a drink and see light rolling out around my body. The salt and blood disgusting in my mouth. I retch and swallow down the acrid bile.

OK. OK.

She makes another sound.

The things I can control about myself won't save her now. I'm sure she's praying.

I wish that I believed. In good. In God.

The devil, he exists. I see it now, in front of me for certain.

'I'm here,' I say. I hold my sister's hand. And she is dying. Corpsing into cold beneath my eyes.

All the bright around me almost blinding. Shining, shining, star-bright through the dim. The contrast is discouraging, I think. She's pale as pale, the day-moon next to sun. I try to grab a handful to pass over. I pull and pull but it won't budge. I can't.

Why did I tell Mamó I wouldn't? She could have taught me things. Given me more of myself to use. Maybe if I had been braver, better. Decided for myself and not for Mam. Not for this future I think I should want, because I've always wanted it. If I were qualified, as a doctor, I don't think I could save her. Not here. Not now. I would need tools, medication. Help.

I close my eyes and focus, seeking something concrete. Someone I can call on for a miracle. And there it is. I open them again. Catlin could be dead by the time I get back. I could be leaving her to die right here. And that's on me. I pull the blankets round and tuck her in.

'Catlin. I love you and I want to help you. I'm sorry for all the things I've done and haven't done. The way it's been. I have to go and ask someone for help now. I think that it might work. The only thing.'

I'm conscious that there's nothing I can say to make this right.

I kiss her forehead and I smell her blood, choke back a sound. I cannot tell if she can even hear me. My eyes are dry. I run back through the office, past Mam and down the stairs.

I don't need to tell Mam to go to Catlin. She will, and she will hold her daughter close. We've always loved each other. Our problem was we just forgot how much. I go down to the kitchen. Cram a handful of Brian's knives into a shopper.

Our father gave us this. It's in the book. The night we found the fox, Catlin remembered. And maybe that was something like a sign.

I see the text from the book roll by. As though my brain had subtitles inside it. Some things you remember in pictures, and some in words. This comes in Catlin's voice. My sister's voice.

291

If someone wants a thing – a sick child well, money, power, love – then you can ask.

The Ask, she said.

The Fox.

Twenty minutes walking to the crossroads. I plan to run. Is that too late?

A taste for blood and worship . . . You need to bring a living thing to die.

I'd cut myself again, but I can't help her if I cannot ask. I need a thing. A tender soft delicious little life.

Two eyes shine at me from under the table. I hum to him, and I stretch out my hands. Make little consonants inside my mouth. His paws approach. A gentle bat at fingers.

'Button,' I say. There's power in his name. I think he knows it. I grapple at the soft scruff of his neck. The fold that mothers bite to carry young. And he is mine. I have him.

A thing that has a taste for blood and worship.

I stuff the wriggling kitten in my bag.

Rehearse my prayers.

292

40

Feverfew

(arthritis, fever, may increase the risk of bleeding out)

I always assumed, I think, striding through the forest, that I was the gentler twin. We don't know who we are until we're tested. Here I am.

I feel the warmth of Button against my leg. The little furball, who grooms himself so hard he falls off chairs.

You'd bring it there. A dog, a goat. A baby.

And at the crossroads, you would kill the thing.

I should be more conflicted, I think. But then again, a pet is not a twin. He's not my sister. I'd rather have a sister than a kitten. So I will make the Ask so loud and clear. I'll carve him up. I'll offer up my soul.

The more pain that you cause, the louder he would hear your call.

I swallow. I am killing part of me in saving her. My eyes red raw, my bitten arm, my essence. What do souls do? What shape do they take? Will I still be able to do this when I've

293

lost mine? Will I still feel love? I run through all the things I've read about them. It isn't much. There's nothing certain there.

Just the sense that it's a thing you need.

To be a person.

I think of Catlin, stretched out like the fox. Part cut. Part bitten. The things he did to her. She cannot die. I will not let her die. I wish that I had Lon inside my bag instead. It would be easier. A pleasure almost.

My sister's voice. He took most of her tongue. I push the heels of my hands into my sockets and the pressure jars and stops the pain. I have a cat. I wear a mask of blood. That has to be worth something to the devil. I will call. I hope that he responds.

'Caw.' A raven's lurking on a branch high up. It might be Bob. It's hard to tell with ravens. Probably it only came for blood.

'Help me, Baaaaaaab,' I ask it anyway, pronouncing it the strange way Mamó does. 'I need help.'

It flaps and caws and stares. The air slicing my lungs, I keep on running.

And suddenly I'm there. I swallow. My eyes are filling up. My hands are shaking. I can do this. I can do this. A place inside the woods where two roads meet. The bright hot body of the little fox. Will Button's life be warm? I wonder. Will it have value to this old, dark thing? I need this plan to work. It's all I have now. Instinct fighting loss.

I dump my bag on the ground and it wriggles. I lay the knives out on the forest floor. The more I hurt, the louder he will hear me. I breathe in deep and choose the smallest one.

Oh, Button, I think. And then, *Oh, Catlin.*

Unzip the bag and pull him softly out. He hiss-complains at me. I stroke him and I settle him in the soft crook of my left arm. I grasp him tight and then I lift the knife. His eyes are wide. He doesn't even know what I am doing. Everyone he's ever met's a friend.

Oh.

This is the worst thing I have ever done.

His little face.

I narrow my eyes. The blade *plop-curling* in. I gouge it to the bottom of the socket. I keep my hand so tight around his neck. I never thought a cat could scream so plaintive sharp like that, like Catlin must have done. I haven't got the stomach to continue. I'll make it quick. I close my eyes.

For Catlin.

Someone grabs me tightly from behind. I scream and drop the kitten. Off he runs. I still have my knife.

'What are you at?' Mamó moves away, but just a little. She folds her arms, squinting. She looks embarrassed for me.

'Put down the knife,' she says.

'I can't,' I gasp. 'I have to try.'

'It won't work. What you're doing,' she says. 'She will be dead by the time it gets here. And what it brings back might not be your sister.'

I look at her. 'How do you know? What happened?'

Her voice is low. 'Brian found me. I am sorry, Madeline. There isn't . . . Stop that.'

My eyes are scanning the ground for Button, a rabbit, a fox, for anything that I could catch and kill.

I look Mamó directly in the eye. 'Can you help her?'

295

She inclines her head. It's not a nod.

'What do I have to do?' I ask, knowing that I'll do it.

'I'll need a soul. I'll take yours. And there'll be no more school. You'll come and work for me. For seven years. Even if she's dead when we get back to the castle. I want to train you. Do we have a deal?'

There isn't any going back from this. A beat, where I consider saying no. Walking away. Finding the kitten again, stabbing it to death. Trying my best to placate whatever comes through. She's right, I know; it wouldn't work. And Catlin would be dead and I'd be here alone.

What can I do? I swallow and I nod.

'I have your word,' she says. It's not a question, but she wants an answer.

'You have my word,' I say.

We start to walk. My mouth is dry, the sweat beads on my back are very cold. The moon is fat and yellow. The mountains dark again. They've all gone home, the people who were searching. Do they know?

'Where is she?' Mamó asks.

'In the castle,' I tell her. 'There's this big cave –'

'An old place. I know it.' Her voice is low. We get into the car, she starts the engine and we drive in silence. My sister bleeding out. I don't know what to do. I don't know what to do.

I look at my hands, stained with three bloods mixed together.

She does something with her head, a twist, a shaping, and suddenly my stomach feels like we are on a rollercoaster, going up, and up, and up. Waiting for the drop, that falling feeling.

It only takes a flash to get us home.

296

41

Betony

(to prevent dreaming)

We stride through the castle, up the stairs and in through Brian's wall – the cave, when we reach it, is leached of life, all freezing dim and dust motes, grey and beige. The black sheets hide the blood. Mam's holding Catlin on the speckled bed. I think of snow, of ash. Of fairy tales and princesses and endings. She's telling her that it will be all right. That Mammy's here. That help is on the way. That she'll be fine. Such gentle, loving lies.

Catlin's eyes are open, dull and dim. She's staring beyond Mam, gaze out to nothing. She isn't making noise. The light around her is faded next-day ash. The barest little ember clings. If I couldn't see it, I would think that she were fully dead. She's stretched out cold. Mam strokes her hair. Brian isn't back. We don't know where he is.

Nobody has come to help my family.

'Get her undressed,' Mamó says to me. I start to move. 'Sheila, have you called an ambulance?'

My mother nods. 'They said that . . . forty minutes . . . maybe longer . . .'

Mamó's glare is strong as strong can be. 'Call them back. You need to cancel. Tell them it was someone playing pranks. That everything is fine.' My mother shakes her head. Mamó blinks at her. 'You need to do this Sheila. NOW,' she barks, and Mam takes out her phone, walks towards the cave mouth. 'Come back when it is fixed,' Mamó says. She looks at me. 'We could be here all night. It will be hard.'

I'm unbuttoning my sister's dress. She moans so weak. I think I'm hurting her. Mamó opens her big doctor's bag. She takes a jar of something clear and dark. A thick, soft liquid. She takes a swig and hands it to me. I drink down some as well. And then try to give some to Catlin. Most of it just trickles on the bed. She's not responding.

Mamó lights a candle. Says some words. I feel the click of something slowing down. And everything is bright. I see the shimmer on me and on her. I did not feel it furling out of me. It has always been here, I think, invisible. I just didn't know. If I am bright, then Mamó is incandescent. It's hard to even blink at her right now.

'You started it yourself. You didn't know.' She looks at me, and nods. Then she reaches her hands towards me, grasps my light, begins to pull and tear. Pinching is the best way to describe it. She pinches fists of light and weaves them into threads towards my sister. Like a blood transfusion. Or a graft. I'm dimming as Catlin brightens, just a touch. But you can see it. I can see it. There! She pinches and she pinches and moves and moves and spins and winds and pulls. Her hands

298

are busy, lifting, dropping, smoothing, taking, helping, giving. Hurting. This is the real stuff, I think. This is the kind of thing that kills or cures.

I stagger over, look at Catlin's face. Her eyes half-open. And then, my vision pinching out of me, I'm dimming, dimming. It starts to hurt properly and I get cold. I get very cold. I lie beside my sister on the bed. My hand curls out to hers. Before I fade away I feel her take it. Just a little squeeze, but she is back. Her hand is cold. It isn't stiff though. The wax of her is warm enough to mould. Pliable. And that's a sign. I take that as a sign.

I close my eyes. When I open them again, the world is black but I can hear the movements of her hands, the little gaspy breaths that come from Catlin. Hearing's next. It's weird to moan and not to hear your voice. I know I'm making sounds but I can't hear them coming from my throat. I murmur things. I keep on saying things in case she hears me.

I love you, you're my sister. It's OK. I love you, Catlin. It will be all right.

Then
smell.
I
hardly
notice,
except relief.
The tin of blood,
the dull stone-rot of cave I do not miss.

Then there's speech,
then I can't move at all,
and lastly touch.
The soft fur of the blanket on my face,
the pinch of light,
the warmth of Catlin's hand.
I can't feel warmth or cold inside my body.
It's only blank.
It's only faded nothing.

Did it work?

42

Lavender

(for sleep and acne)

It all comes through in flashes. Sudden bursts.

Mam's face, mouth open in a tiny little O.

A squeezing of my hand, and something soft and wet against my cheek.

The taste of blood I think might be my own.

Lavender, bay leaves, sage and earth and something I can't . . . something . . . something else.

My name. My name. A voice that says my name.

And everything at once – and I wake up.

'Drink this,' Mamó says, and passes me a cup of something cold and brown. I take it, drink it in one draught.

I try to speak, her hand upon my forehead. My mother's face. My mother's face and Brian's.

'You don't understand, Brian. He did this in our house.'

'I promise you. I promise you . . .' His voice is sad and I do not hear what he promises.

'What would the police do? Sheila, he would *gut* them.'

'I know. I know.'

'I'm sorry, love.'

'I know you are. That doesn't make this fine.'

'. . . They need my care. Or they will both be dead inside a week . . .'

I make it to the door and Catlin's there. She's breathing, up and down. I see her face. Oh God. Her face.

Little flashes.

'Skin across her jaw is knitting back . . .'

Mamó is leaning in. 'She's on the mend.' She coughs into a tissue. Is that blood?

Mam rubs my face. I close my eyes and lose her.

I want my mam. My voice. 'I want my mam.'

'Ridiculous . . .'

'Look, the child agreed . . .'

'*I* didn't!'

Everyone is pale. They look so tired. Ashen grey.

Cold. My skin. My skin is very cold.

Morning. Oona at the bedside. She holds my hand but I can't see her eyes.

'. . . Call the guards on you . . .'

'And tell them what? What would you tell the guards, *Sheila*?'

'I wish that . . .' Brian's voice.

And Mam says, 'Don't.'

43

Gravel Root

(fever, stomach acids, UTIs)

I wake. Mam is beside my bed. She's sleeping in a chair. I look around. Nothing much has changed. The tapestries the same, the sheets I chose before we moved here. The wood's a little greener through the window. The sky is grey. The clouds are heavy still.

'Mam?' I say. I touch her, and she screams, and I start back.

'Oh, sorry, love,' she says, and leans in and hugs me. 'It's just a surprise. I think I was asleep. Or half asleep.'

I say that's OK. She looks at me again and I feel awkward. My hair is in a braid. They've changed my clothes.

'Catlin?' I ask. She nods at me. 'Oh, Maddy. What you did . . .'

She holds me close. My mother holds me close.

I say, 'I want to see her.'

She nods again, and helps me over to her room. The candles around the little altar quenched. The statues clean, their blank eyes staring out. It's such a bright room. Pink and gold and

303

colours. And she's so pale. My sister is so pale. A wraith. A ghost, all dappled crimson red and bluish white.

I get a head rush, walking unaided now. There is a wobble and Mam takes my arm. She looks so old. Do I look old as well? I'm still sixteen. I think. I kind of want to ask, 'What year is this?' and shake her, but I don't think she would take it very well.

Catlin lies there. She still looks like a corpse. But she's alive. A breathing corpse. Her skin resembles skin, at least the texture. Her hair is falling out. Mam collects a clump of it from the pillow. Gathers it. Puts it in her pocket.

'I have a little box,' she says, 'for it. I can't throw out the bits of her.'

'Like baby's curls,' I say.

It's almost sweet.

What grew back is starkly port-wine-stained. I wonder if it's on her torso too. I don't want to lift blankets, disturb her. She opens up her eyes. And smiles.

'Hi, Mad,' she says.

'Hey, Catlin.'

She grins at me, and closes her eyes to sleep more. Her smile is still the same. I clamber into bed beside my sister. We lie together in this horrid world.

Mam sits on the edge of the bed. I look at her. 'What's happened since that night?' I ask. 'Have you found . . . ?'

I don't want to say his name. I don't want Catlin in her dreams to hear it.

Mam shakes her head. 'Brian looked, and Mamó too – with her . . . you know.'

304

I nod at her. I do know.

'I don't know what to do,' Mam says. 'I mean – I couldn't help her. And now I can't help you.'

'You can,' I say. 'You love me. That's enough.' It isn't really. I'm just saying words. I can't change fate, but maybe I can make her feel a little bit better.

Mam takes my hand. 'You remind me so much of your father, love,' she says. 'I wanted you to have a safer life, with better things. When he died, parts of who he was died with him. There are things I can't touch, things that scare me and I don't know why . . .'

'Witchcraft things?' I ask.

She flinches. And she nods. 'I can't remember much. His plants. That book. After the fire there was . . .' I see her reaching, losing it. 'It's gone. I'm sorry . . . and I am sorry for hurting you, before. I didn't remember what he was. I'm losing it again; it's leaving me. But I knew that it was dangerous. That it killed him. I didn't want that . . . for you.'

I wait for more, but she sighs heavily and gives me the tightest, fiercest hug, before straightening up the sheets around us. She turns the light out as she leaves the room. The door-click soft. I settle down in bed beside my sister, and try my best to follow her in sleep.

44

Tansy

(joint pain, fertility)

We wake up in the dark. There's nothing. I cannot see the walls. I hear her breath.

'So, Mad, are you awake?' Her voice a whisper. Huskier than normal.

'You sound . . .'

'I know,' she says. 'I might give up the smokes. It's from the . . . throat stuff.'

I nod.

'I can't hear you when you nod.' She tugs the duvet.

'Sorry,' I say. 'Sorry.'

'Madeline, what happened in the cave?' Her voice is scared. 'Mam says you're moving downstairs in a week. When we're better.'

Oh. Right.

I nod and then she kicks me. I kick her back. And then we both go quiet. I'm the first to speak.

306

'You tell me your bit, then I'll tell you mine. Sound fair?'

I do not hear her, but I know she nods.

And she starts talking.

'Me and . . .' she says, and her voice takes a while to shape his name, '. . . Lon decided to run away. We decided it inside a dream I had. I wasn't sure. If it was really real until it was. I mean, the doors and caves. And magic. He could do things with his eyes and with his hands. Before, I mean. I didn't know. You knew,' she asks, 'that it was something?'

'Some of it,' I say. 'He showed up in my dreams once, by mistake, and weird stuff happened. But, even before – that night with the fox, the things that Mamó did, and I did too. Like, she thinks I have an instinct for it, or a talent – collecting things is part of it as well.'

'There's so much you didn't say to me. I wonder . . .'

I wait for her to finish, but her eyes glaze and she dry-swallows. I hear her move her tongue around her mouth. She sits up, takes a drink of water. Drains the glass and pours another one and drains it too.

'I get so thirsty now, Mad,' she says. 'Remember before, when I tried to make myself drink eight glasses for my skin? Now it's more like twenty. My mouth is always just so dry.'

'You came back,' I tell her. 'That can't have been easy on your body.'

'No,' she says. 'I suppose it can't. So. Me and Lon.'

The way she says his name. My eyes fill up.

'It wasn't your fault,' I tell her. 'You didn't know. And even if you had . . .'

She doesn't move, just keeps on speaking, speaking.

'We went to the cave and it was nice at first. He'd brought a picnic. Then I saw names carved in the wall. One of them was Helen. And I asked him, if he'd brought a girl here before, and he went quiet, but said that yes, he had. But it didn't mean as much as now with me. And he took a chisel. What, in retrospect, was he doing with chisels in his cave? Anyway. Hindsight.'

She takes a breath. I touch her foot with mine.

'So we started kissing and things and I'd decided this was going to be when I would lose it. Because I love . . . loved. Because I loved him so much. And also, when you run away with a boy to a sex-cave, what else is going to happen? I mean, it makes for a great story. Even if it doesn't work out well, you have the story. I remember thinking that. Which, ugh.'

She sighs. I say, 'You don't have to keep telling me this. If you don't want to . . .'

'No,' she says. 'You gave up stuff for me. And you should know. How stupid I was. God, I was so stupid. He wore an ankh, for God's sake. And that smell. You told me he was gross.'

'Well, I am a lesbian,' I say. 'So he wouldn't have been my type, even if he weren't a monster or whatever . . .'

And there it is. Unspoken things all out. The weight of words, not put down, but shared.

'What?' she rasps. 'You turned lesbian without me?' She sounds incredibly taken aback, as though there were a form I should have filled in or something.

'Catlin, this isn't about you,' I say. 'A lot of things are at the moment, but my sexuality is kind of . . . mine. It's not an adventure, or a bit of gossip. It's part of me.'

She nods almost imperceptibly.

'I get it. Fair enough. I didn't mean that you had to, like, OK it with me first or anything, but this is huge. How did you know . . . or did you . . . Oh, with Oona?' Her eyebrows widen. There are things she didn't miss, even when she was missing things.

'Yes and no. It's complicated – go on, I want to hear your story first.' I nudge her.

'But your one's got no murder and some lesbians,' she complains. 'It's probably loads better. OK, so . . .'

My sister loves to talk. She's still my sister. She takes another drink.

'You'd think I'd pee way more,' she says. 'With all that I've been drinking. Being back from the dead is honestly not great.'

'I know, right?' I say. 'I know you're more of a half ghost than me. I am only, like, ten per cent resurrected or something, but still. I get these headaches.'

'With the colours? God, they're awful. Anyway, I'll finish about Lon. There isn't very much left of the story. Basically, I cleaned up after the picnic and he kept telling me how to tidy up and I just kept doing it, like I didn't mind being given orders. Which is not like me. I mean, I really wanted to please him. I just am not sure why. And there was the wall. The wall with all the names. I asked him about it and he said it was tradition in the village, for boys to take the girls they loved to the cave. And to carve their name into the wall. That it meant that it would be forever. I asked him if he'd carve my name as well. I even said *please*.' Her voice is bitter.

'I didn't think to notice if the writing was the same. Like, that could have been a useful handy clue. You would have noticed that, I think.' Her hands rat at the sleeve of her pyjamas. I hear the thumb on fabric, *swishswishswish*. My hearing might be sharper now, or something. Prey animals do have that. Clever ears.

They know what happens while you aren't listening.

To you.

Or those you love.

Inside the gaps.

'It wasn't your fault, Catlin,' I tell her again.

'Mmm,' she says. And then there is a pause. When she starts talking again, her voice is quieter. Gravel whispers, trailing through the night.

'We started kissing, doing stuff. I really wanted him. I mean, he was my soulmate. And forbidden.'

She meets my eyes and smiles a rueful smile. Her hands are trembling.

'So . . . Lon and I did various things to each other. And then, I got a cramp in my leg. And I tried to push him off, but he wouldn't move and I looked over, saw the list of names with different eyes. Like I was another on a list. A thing to do. A thing you can cross out. I didn't like it and I tried to push him off again. And then . . .' She swallows.

'I don't think I can talk about the rest. I mean. My face and body. You can . . .' She gets out of bed, switches the bedside lamp on. Lifts up her nightdress.

Her body's more port wine than it is skin.

'The pieces that grew back,' she says, 'are the red. The bits he didn't eat are the way they always were. I'm basically a piebald. Only human.'

I hear her legs twitching against the bed-sheets. 'He comes back sometimes. Sometimes in my dreams, he's coming back.'

What can I say to that? I don't know where he is. He could be anywhere.

'I mean,' she says, 'this happened in my house. And I remember thinking, I'm at home. At home and this is happening. I mean, it's weird that our home has a secret murder cave.'

'The murder palace,' I say.

'I know,' she says. 'I called it. Mam should have listened. Should have stayed in Cork.'

I put my arms around her and I hug her.

'I love you,' I tell her.

She snuggles in.

'Me too, Mad. So much. But now you have to tell me about Oona,' she says, her voice sounds calmer now, more gossipy. 'Are you a couple now?'

And I tell her stuff. I tell her about the girl I love, and how she doesn't really feel the same, so that I don't have to tell her about the bargain I made to save her life. I don't yet know what it means, not fully. I mean, I know it's seven years. But there's the soul as well. What will that mean?

My brain is racing, full of fears and thoughts.

Catlin sleeps. I think about the feeling of the sheets and of the warmth and of the breeze that drifts inside the room. I get up, feel with my hands around the walls, looking for the place the breeze could come from. The window's raised a little. I relax. I wonder is that what we'll do here now? Always look for secret murder caves? Can we relax somewhere where it happened? Will we go back to Cork?

Oh God.

I can't.

I can't go anywhere.

For seven years.

The sooner it begins, the sooner it can finish.

A deal's a deal. It's time to settle up.

45

Persimmon

(balance)

When I arrive at Mamó's flat, I push the door. It's still not locked to me. I wait a while at the threshold, swallowing back a growing sense of dread. This is where my future is now. I can't escape it. There is no way out. I'll be a witch. My legs are still a little weak. The walk down here seemed very long and steep. I take a breath. I venture slowly in.

When we moved here from Cork, I knew exactly what we left behind. I don't know now. What I am sacrificing.

The light from lamps is dim here, almost candlelit. The shadows flicker, but the place is cosy. There's a sense of safety. Home and hearth. Cushions on the couch. She's in an armchair. And suddenly, the guilt I have been holding back ploughs through me.

There he is, little Button, nestled at her feet, his face all bandaged up. I feel sick. He's bigger now, less of a tubby bundle. He sees me, and he hisses and bolts. He knows what I became

313

that night for Catlin. That in a way I'm just as bad as Lon.

Mamó's eyes on mine. Reading all that's written on my face.

'I didn't know,' I say, 'that he came back.'

'He would have died,' she says, 'and then the sacrifice would have been made. I couldn't take the chance.'

'Did it take you long,' I ask, 'to find him?' My voice comes out all heavy. I feel as if I will cry. I don't like looking at the thing I did. I don't like what I was. Or what I am.

'A while. He tried to run, but he was very weak, and took some healing.'

'We all did.' I look around. She gestures to the sofa, and I settle. 'Mamó?'

She moves her head.

'Thank you for Catlin.'

'You know she'll never be the same again,' she says.

'She has been through a lot.' The daubs of red.

Mamó's voice is sharp through what I'm thinking.

'Not that. Oh, she'll get over what happened with that lad. In time. It's what we did to her – the coming back. It does things to a person. I've told your mam to watch for it. But she won't.' She says it like it's just the way things are.

'She's trying her best to understand.' I curl into the couch. I think of Mam's cool hands on my hot forehead. The things she said, when I was in the bed. 'She said something about my father – Tom – but she couldn't reach whatever it was . . .'

'Something was done to that woman,' Mamó says. 'Parts of her memory stolen, or locked away. Around your talent, and around your father. After everything, that became clear. I offered to help with it – but she refused.'

'What do you think they did?'

'To know that, I'd have to know who they were, or if they were . . . And without her permission to investigate, it's hard to say, exactly. It would be invasive. Her memories wouldn't be her own, but mine as well.'

'How does that work?' I ask.

'You'll learn,' she tells me, 'Madeline Hayes. Hayes is a very old name, lot of history. It wasn't from the ground you licked your talent. And she should know more about it than she does. It may have been a safeguard. For all the good it did.' Mamó's eyes are looking beyond me, as though she's searching for someone – something – else. I think of Mam chanting dad's name after mine that night.

'She did her best,' I say. 'She's a good mother. And if . . . if my dad was a witch or a wise man or whatever, would it not be worth her trying?'

'Yes,' says Mamó. 'Which is why I offered. But I don't think that she will be open to any more of my presence in her life than is absolutely necessary. She hates me now. When something terrible happens, Madeline, people look to find someone to blame. It's human nature. Also, there's the bargain that we made.' Her gaze is pale and level. Her eyes look blue again, in this half-light.

'How is it going to work?' I ask. I straighten up my shoulders. 'Can I commute?'

'We can work out details as they arise. But you will live down here with me. You'll work as needed. There will be no more school. But you can study in your free time. Homeschooling, I think they call it. You're bright enough. And you can mix

315

with some people, sometimes. I'll tell you to keep watch. On your sister. On the things that happen. Notice things before they start to start. A lot of what I do,' she tells me blandly, 'is stopping fires before they're even set. Detectiving.'

'Like Batman?' I ask.

'No,' she says, and sighs. 'I'm not like Batman. Batman isn't real.'

'But magic is.'

'Yes. Ballyfrann is a place where people who are also something else have gathered. The forests were a sacred place, before. Still are to some.'

I look at her, processing what I'm hearing. Mamó, Oona, Lon. It isn't a coincidence. A sacred place. I wonder . . .

'The fox,' I say. 'The blood. Do you think it was Lon?'

She looks at me, deciding how much I am ready for, I think. I hold her gaze and try to look as if none of this is strange and terrifying. I can take it.

'No. I don't think it was Lon.'

'Brian,' I say, and don't know why I say it, how I know.

She smiles at me. 'You're sharp. I can't be sure. But perhaps.'

'I don't think he would want to hurt us though.'

'No . . . but people can do strange things to try to keep their loved ones by their side . . .'

I think of Button, wince, as she continues.

'. . . It's not dissimilar to the kind of magic he would have been exposed to as a child. As a young man.' Her face is clouded, thinking.

'His father? Are there different kinds of magic?'

'There's a reason I live beneath the castle. I didn't always.

But after Brian senior passed, Brian asked me to move in. To keep an eye. His father taught him well, but what he taught him can be dangerous. Destructive. He was a cruel sort of man. And while he lived, this village was a different sort of place. More of a collection of isolated people than a community. Brian has been working to change that. To build. But there are always limits. And temptations.'

'Do you think he's bad?'

'I don't think any person is fully bad. Or fully good.'

'Even Lon?' I ask her quietly.

'Lon and Brian are very different fish,' she tells me. 'And one of them needs to be stopped. And one of them needs to be watched.'

'What sort of magics are there?' I ask her. 'What does Brian do?'

She sighs. 'You ask a fair amount of questions.'

'I've been through a fair amount of things.'

'With more to come.' She spits into a small bin beside her chair. 'There are three kinds of magic that can be practised, and all of them hurt. Ours, the kind that you will learn with me, is the kind that makes the most sense. You put something in, you get something out. It takes instinct and talent, but a lot of learning as well. A lot of graft.'

'OK. And the other kinds?' I ask.

'There's prayer magic, which is something like what happened with the fox. And what you tried to do with the small fella.'

'Button.'

'Terrible name. With prayer magic, a lot of people do it without knowing. It's asking someone bigger for a favour,

317

essentially. Power, money, love. A secret kept. But there's a veil between our world and theirs – the ones who'd do it – and so the help, the cost, might not be what you think. And when you open a door, and don't have the sense to lock it behind you, you might get visitors.'

'Visitors?'

'Hungry things,' she says grimly.

'Like Lon?' I ask.

'Yes, and sometimes worse. I think Lon may be what happens when something comes over, and breeds with a human. Our face on their appetites.' She scratches her chin vigorously.

'This is Brian's father's kind of magic?'

'This and the third kind.'

'Which is what?'

'When people use the second kind, it can be because of foolishness or desperation or lack of understanding. But if they use the third kind, they know what they're about. It damns your soul.' She spits into the fire. 'It's not First Day stuff.'

'OK,' I say. 'What is?'

She rises, goes to the sink, pours a massive glass of water. Brings it back and puts it in my hand. She hands me something small and round and dark. The marble from the raven. Where did she get it? I had it before. It was for me. She holds it out. I take it. Hold it in the hollow of my hand.

'Swallow this, as though it were a pill,' she says.

'What will it mean?' I ask.

'No one will hear your prayers,' Mamó tells me. 'There may be other changes as well. It's different for different people. Souls have different sizes, values, shapes. You might lose some

318

abilities, or gain them. Do terrible things without paying certain tolls.' She looks at me. 'It doesn't matter though. You gave your word.'

And so I put the small orb in my mouth. It's hard to manage, cold against my tongue and big and round. It sticks inside my throat. I need a second glass and both my hands massaging at my throat to ease it down.

Then we discuss logistics. She'll call me as I'm needed. I'll have a night a week to sleep at home. Mam wanted that for me, and Brian made her a deal.

'What sort of deal?' I ask her.

'The caves are mine to do with as I like. For a start.' That seems a lot, I think. For just one night a week. What would it take to give me up entirely?

'Do you have deals with everyone, Mamó?'

She doesn't answer. Twinkle in her eye that I don't like. My stomach starts to feel a bit peculiar. Claws at it. Sharp and big and long and gouging, gouging.

'Your soul is small,' she says. 'I used a lot. To save her. Quite a bit of mine went in as well. All I'm taking, really, is a seed.'

'You gave it to me – the marble,' I say. 'Before all of this. Why?'

'So I could track you. I needed to know where you were. In case of fire,' she says. Her voice so calm. Her voice is scary-calm and she is glaring. 'I like to keep an eye on my investments. It's good business. Get that all up now.'

She holds a bucket out in front of me and I am vomiting and vomiting and vomiting until I see the blood, the stomach lining. She holds up the little ball. It's coloured like an autumn

319

leaf, a fox fur, and something in it is moving, changing, as it passes through the light. She wipes it clean with her sleeve.

'Go back to bed,' she says.

'I'll clean it up.'

'No,' she tells me. 'I need to use some parts to make this stick.'

'That's disgusting.'

'Magic isn't mindfulness and hats, Madeline. It's work.' I hold my stomach. She says something else, I think, as well. Her mouth is moving but I cannot focus.

'What?' I ask. I'm blinking. It is bright. It's dark and bright.

'Go,' she says, and pushes me out towards the night. I stumble to the castle. I touch the door. I don't remember much.

46

Vipers' Bugloss

(in wine to comfort hearts)

Mam pours a cup of tea and looks at me across the kitchen table. Her eyes are sad.

'I don't want you to do this,' she tells me. 'To throw your life away on magic tricks.'

'Has Brian told you more about the village?' I ask. She nods. I stir in milk. 'What did he tell you?'

'Oh yes. I got the full whack. The Collinses, apparently, can shape-shift.' She throws her hands up. 'Fuck's sake.'

'You never swear,' I say. I can see why she would though. Shape-shifting is, in fairness, a bit much.

'Which is the shocking part? Madeline, how much did you know?'

'Not much. I knew that Mamó was a witch, and that I could be one too – she wanted to train me before and I said no.'

'What else?'

'Oona told me some,' I tell her, 'and I knew that Brian knew what was going on . . . That was hard. He didn't ask me not to tell you, but he said he wanted to tell you himself. In his own time.'

'To my mind,' Mam says, 'his own time should have been at least six weeks before we were married.'

'At least,' I say. And, in fairness, it should have been.

'Any marriage, and uprooting our whole lives to be with someone, is life-changing stuff. But not life-changing like your neighbours can turn into things and a witch stole your daughter. I'm furious with him. What he hid. We would never have come here.' Her hands are in her lap, her shoulders slumped down towards her stomach. She's wearing a floral shirt and jeans, her hair is in a ponytail, make-up on but she still looks exhausted.

'How would he have phrased it though?' I ask.

'"Everyone's monsters. One of them will try to murder your child. Let's stay in Cork forever"?' Mam offers. She has clearly thought about this.

'Monsters how?' I ask.

'If you look human but you aren't human, I don't know another word for what that is.'

'Am I a monster?' I ask her. 'Is Catlin?'

She sighs. 'No, love. But both of you are what this place has made you, and I don't know how to fix it. I offered to work for her. To help instead.' She pours a little hot drop in her cup. 'She wouldn't have it.'

'We made a deal,' I say, 'and Catlin's here. Alive.'

'She is,' Mam says. 'When did you get so brave?'

I shrug. 'I'm not. I just do what I can. I try. Like you.'

'Oh, love.' She sighs. 'The world is dreadful, isn't it? And

322

Brian is hardly ever home. Since ye woke up, it's been hard. He lied to me so much. To all of us.' Her eyes fill up and she starts saying sorry, and I shush her.

'It's OK, Mam. It's going to be OK. I'll be twenty-three in seven years. It's not forever.'

'Twenty-three,' she says.

'I know. So old.' I scrunch my face.

'You won't have a debs,' Mam says, like that was something that I had always dreamed of.

'I'll be a witch,' I say. 'Maybe there's a witch debs. With brooms and pointy hats.'

'Jesus, Madeline. It's not a joke.' Her voice is hard and tired. 'We're losing you. We'll miss you.'

'I'll only be downstairs.' I drink my tea.

'It's not the same.'

'I know.' And I do know. But I made a deal. And we got Catlin back. 'Look on it as paying for hospital,' I say. 'If Catlin had been saved by an operation, you would have paid the doctor. It's the same. Only I get to pay. I made the bargain and I have the talent.'

She looks at her tea but doesn't drink. 'You were going to go back to Cork, to be a doctor. And Catlin. I don't know what she can do at all. I mean. Her face.'

'She isn't dead,' I say. 'She's still your daughter.'

'I know,' Mam says. 'It's just that this is hard. All I wanted for ye. So many things. A happy, normal life . . . And that lad is still out there. I mean, they don't know where he is at all. Brian says he's trying, but it's been six weeks, and . . .' She makes a scornful sound.

She isn't wrong. I wish that Lon were dead. I wish that I were small again. A little girl. I wish that I was me before we left the world I knew. Quiet and grumpy, studying and hanging out with Catlin and our friends.

Catlin bustles in, wrapped in a kimono dressing gown. Her white skin's pale, her wine stain's very bright. Her scalp is covered up with a silk scarf.

'Hey,' she says, 'is there tea in the pot?'

Mam gets up and starts making some more. I realise she's avoiding looking at Catlin. She doesn't want to see her daughter's face now it has changed.

'Do you know Mamó found Button?' I ask Mam.

'I want him back,' she says. 'She can't have my daughter and my kitten too.' Her face is red. She pours the boiling water like she hates it. Stirs the pot as though it were a drum.

'Are you seriously going to ask the woman who saved my life for her kitten?' asks Catlin.

'Madeline saved your life,' Mam says. 'That wagon just profited from it.'

'That isn't true, Mam,' I say. 'And you need to make this easier for me, instead of harder.'

'I know,' says Mam. 'I'm trying, like.'

I roll my eyes. She isn't trying half as hard as I am. She should moan less and find out more. I wonder, again, what is there, trapped inside her brain. Memories. And maybe if she was sharing them with me and not Mamó, she'd be more open to it. I wonder how long it will take for me to learn that skill.

'Can you turn her into a frog?' asks Catlin.

'Of course not.' I smirk.

324

'You brought me back to life, Mad,' Catlin says. 'Anything is possible. Can you turn this –' she waves a coaster – 'into a crisp fifty-euro note?'

'You'd only spend it in Urban Outfitters,' I tell her.

'Excuse me. I would spend it on MAC make-up.' She straightens her back. 'To conceal my immortality blemish.'

'You're not immortal, Catlin,' I point out.

'How do you know?' she asks. She widens her eyes. 'I could totally be immortal if I wanted. You get to be a witch. Mam, tell her I'm immortal.'

'No one here is allowed to die for at least thirty years,' Mam tells us. 'Including me. Or I will bring ye back specifically to ground you, witch or no witch.'

'Fair enough,' I say.

She pulls us close. Two nestlings under wing, a mother bird. I rest my head on her shoulder and curl my arm around Catlin's back. And, for a while, this dangerous place feels safe.

It feels like home.

47

Nettle

(tumour suppression, prostatic hyperplasia)

Catlin's hair is growing in downy fuzz, like ducklings have, but white. She's fine with it – I mean, there's always dye if she gets bored – but the port-wine stains have been bothering her. Her face looks different. Less like her own face. She has been applying the concealer that make-up artists use to cover up tattoos. She orders it in bulk.

'Brian has the money,' she says. 'I asked for laser treatment, but he said it wouldn't work. Because of stupid magic.'

'Magic is stupid,' I tell her. I spent a lot of today moving things downstairs to my new room and I resent it.

'My teeth might fall out too,' she says. 'Isn't that disgusting? With fingernails and hair, it all comes back, just maybe a bit different, but if your teeth go, that's it. Dentures for life.'

I feel awkward. I don't know what to say to her. I mean, she's always been the pretty twin. But now she looks like all the things she's been through. What she is. A girl that should be dead.

And I still look like me. Only more tired. Big dark circles under my eyes from lack of sleep. From puzzling out what's happening and what might happen next.

'I don't care anyway,' she says to me, rifling through her drawers looking for something. 'I don't want to be pretty. Remember when we wanted Galway boyfriends?'

'Yeah,' I say. Her eyes fill up with tears. I go to touch her shoulder and she tenses. 'Don't touch me right now.'

I move my hand back. Put it on my lap and watch her breathe. I didn't save her. I just saved her life. My sister's broken.

'Every night,' she says, 'I see him there. I can't. I can't. I can't.'

My phone buzzes on the bedside locker.

'Who is that?' Catlin asks.

'Oona,' I say.

'You going to meet up?' she asks.

'We'll see,' I say. 'I'm basically a servant. So there's that. And also, she was kind of mean to me before. But I don't have a soul. And she is hot.'

'Not as hot as you. You're a badass witch,' she says.

'You just think I'm beautiful because I look like you,' I say.

'Not any more,' she says, with something between a laugh and a sob. I reach for her again, get pushed away.

'Mad, it's fine. I'm getting used to it, you know?'

I nod. Though I don't know. How could I know?

Catlin is opening up a drawer, and rifling through it. She pulls out a small, wooden box.

'Sit down and let me try this.'

'What?' I ask, already sitting down.

She unwraps a deck of cards from white raw silk.

'Let me read for you,' she says. 'You're not the only one who can do magic.' She wiggles her fingers and makes what I can only describe as paranormal sounds. A lot of *whoooooo*ing.

'Are you going to stop that?' I ask.

'Never,' she says. 'But look, if you're worried for the future, this might help. I've been trying to learn a bit about the cards and what they mean. I found this deck in the library, and I thought – you know – wouldn't it be nice to have a future?'

'It would,' I say, and when we look at each other our eyes begin to shine, so we look away.

'I can't get a handle on mine,' she says. 'It's all "two of swords, death, wheel of fortune". And I want to know what's *going* to happen. Not what has already.'

'It's not real though,' I say.

'It's hard to tell,' she says, 'what is and isn't real. Do you ever wonder where you got it from, Madeline? The talent, or whatever it is you have that makes that old bitch want you.'

'I tried to ask Mam, but she gave me nothing,' I say. 'There's stuff about Dad, but she can't remember properly. Or won't. Mamó told me that maybe this . . . was something I inherited . . . that Hayes was an old name . . . And I think that maybe Dad could have been something like I am.' I sigh. 'I wish I knew for sure.'

Catlin looks up from the deck, her eyes on mine. 'I have this memory, of being small, and waking up in the middle of the night. And the walls of the room were on fire. But it wasn't warm. It was just there – like a film projected on our bedroom walls. But when I reached to touch it, I could feel it.

328

And I don't remember how old I was, but I was small because we still had railings on our beds. And I don't remember any more. Just that one flash. That moment. I think that Mamó must be right. That Dad was a witch – or the male term for witch. Warlock, or whatever.' She rolls her eyes.

'Mamó calls herself a wise woman sometimes,' I say. 'But maybe there are other kinds of witches with wands and hats and things. I mean, it's possible . . . you never told me about the fire on the wall. I know you had bad dreams but . . .'

Catlin's eyes on the cards, shuffling and shuffling, her knuckles white. There is a pause, and then her voice is small, a little frightened.

'I didn't have that memory before. It came back, Mad, when I did. Things feel changed. All warped. All turned around. It's like there's more of the world to see, and all the little details bleed together. It's all these little pictures, but I have to work to make the big one out.'

'Like a mosaic.'

'Something a bit like that. And if I remember that, maybe there's more to come. And we can work on Mam. I mean, we've both been through a lot. And I, for one, am fully prepared to milk it.'

'You have a point.'

'I mean, I got murdered. Full-on murdered. And you . . . you've given so much to get me back . . .'

'Catlin,' I say, my voice low, 'I wonder – how Dad died; if he was killed. I mean, in the forest. It sounds a bit . . . like . . . what happened with the fox . . . a sacrifice or something . . .'

Her face is grim. 'I see that. Earth and fire. Jesus Christ.'

329

'I know,' I whisper.

'All we can do is keep searching, and nudging, I suppose. Now, stop terrifying me, and let me read you. Please.' Her eyes meet mine.

'OK,' I say, and watch her small hands shuffling the cards. They're bigger and thicker than playing cards, and they smell like old books and incense. The backs of them are covered in geometric patterns and stars.

'Choose three,' she says.

I do.

She turns them over.

'Death: that's probably me. It doesn't have to be an actual death. It could mean a big change. A metamorphosis.'

'That could be me as well,' I say. 'I mean. I had all of this lovely soul and now I don't know . . . Actually, Catlin – this mightn't work, what with all the soul I don't have.'

'You don't need to have a soul to have a future. I mean, look at Lon – out there, in the great wide open, looking for the next girl.' She says it like a joke. It's not a joke.

I don't know how to respond, so I turn over the next card.

It's the moon. I stare at it.

'Is that a lobster?' I ask.

'Yes, and a little dog,' Catlin says. 'He's cute. This card is about intuition. And it's upside down, which means . . .' She scrolls through the app on her phone, which is not very mystical of her, but I'll be knee deep in mystical junk soon, so it's fine.

'Insomnia. Unusual Dreams. Mysteries Unveiled. Release of Fear.'

'Yup. Yup. Nope. Nope,' I tell her.

'Well, finding out that you were a witch and that Lon was a serial killer is kind of an unveiled mystery?' she says.

'I suppose – there are too many mysteries that still have their veils on though,' I say.

'Hmmmm.'

Catlin turns the final card with a flourish.

'Oh. OK,' she says. 'This one I like.'

It's a big hand appearing in the sky with a stick.

'I get a wand!' I exclaim. 'Or Mamó is going to hit me with a stick. Definitely one or the other.'

'Shh,' she says. 'This is actually a nice one – it's about potential. It's, like, the seed of something good is there. Waiting for you.'

'Oh.' I look at the hand-stick again, green leaves growing out of it, and flowers.

'Spring is coming,' Catlin says. 'Maybe you should visit Oona, bring her a little present. Like a stick with leaves on?'

'She would love that.' My tone is wry.

'The French love sticks; it's the same shape as their bread. Facts.' Catlin says this like she has a doctorate in what French people are like.

'You're really good at sounding like you know stuff.'

'Look. Madeline. You've lost your soul. You've lost your freedom. You've lost a bit of your sister. What else could go wrong? Go get the shift.'

'Urrrgh,' I say. 'Don't call it that.'

'What's the French word? Oh, I know this. *Baiser*. Go get the *baiser*.' She grins.

'Stop being supportive.'

'Never. I am going to have a little Pride parade for you in Ballyfrann.' She cackles. 'Just me, you, Mam, Oona and maybe Brian all in rainbow colours, marching down main street.'

'I hate you and everything about you.'

'No, you don't.'

'I don't.'

'Now, go get that girl.'

She stares at me. I stare back. Neither of us blinks. I wonder for a second if I have magic unblinking snake powers now that I have no soul, but once I've thought that I immediately need to blink and Catlin does a small victory dance.

I send Oona a message, see if she's around. She replies right away. I smile, and Catlin says, 'Aww,' and I tell her where she can go with her patronising little sounds, but it doesn't come off as seriously as I meant it because I have this stupid big grin still on my face.

I get my coat and walk through the forest. I see the down of birds tangled on brambles. I see the thickets full of green and bright. Everything's awake, I think. It's lovely. Slowly I meander through the woods. I meet her halfway up the mountain path. We walk back down together, towards the castle grounds, talking about everything and nothing. School, and her dad. My headaches and the magic, and how everything has changed, will change again.

She is here, and listening to me, and I am grateful.

I want to ask her about Claudine, but I don't. I'm not strong enough to be that sort of friend to her just now. I need more distance. We walk till silence falls. I had wondered, whether I'd fancy her now. Without a soul, if there would be a lack of feeling there. I shouldn't have bothered. I still notice her eyelashes, the way they cast a shadow on her face. So long and dark. The soft look of her skin. I smell her scent.

'Madeline.' Her hand brushes my wrist. By accident. On purpose. I don't know. My stomach lurches, batting at my heart.

'I think,' I say, 'that we should just be friends.'

She looks at me. I look at her.

'Oona, I like you a lot. I mean, of course I do. You're amazing. But you don't feel the romantic stuff as deeply as I do. And that's fine.'

I'm staring at the trees ahead.

'But if we . . . well, I can see it getting harder and harder, and I would hurt, and lose you in that hurt. And I need to be careful right now, because I'm so . . . I don't have any more inside me to give.'

I feel the wobble in my voice,

'Oh, Madeline,' she says, so gently that it makes me catch my breath.

All she would have to do is reach for me, and I'd lose all resolve. Get lost inside her. But she puts her hands inside her pockets, and we walk through the grounds, beside the wells, around the physic garden. I tell her snatches of what happened. Not very much. Lon killed Catlin, I made a deal. It's hard to talk about, outside of family. But she gets it, or gets the fear of losing who you love. Her family is strange as well, compared to what people expect from people. I tell her about losing my soul, and how it hurt, like, really, really, hurt, but I don't notice that pain now; there isn't an absence. I've heard that when people have something amputated,

333

sometimes they still feel it there, a phantom limb. Maybe I have a phantom soul.

When I am twenty-three, I don't know where or who or what I'll be. And it's the same for her. I mean, I could keep hoping. If I wanted, I could keep on hoping.

But I won't.

48

Mandrake

(anaesthetic, mania, delirium and love)

I am asleep in Mamó's little box-room. My room now, I suppose. Though I still feel half guest and half employee. I'm trying to stay positive, visualising that stupid hand and stick on Catlin's cards. I mean, there's nothing to it, but at this point I'll take what hope I can. It's pretty grim here – Mamó's not big on decor. I've put pictures on the walls. Photographs of family, and friends. I've organised my textbooks on a shelf above my bed. Mam's getting me a little folding desk so I can study when Mamó doesn't need me. It's OK here at night. For one thing, it's not as warm as inside the castle. I need my blanket round me when I sleep. My dreams are softer. I can't see the moon or mountains from my window. Only the garden. There's a peace in that.

There is a tentative knock at my door. 'What?' I bark. Sometimes she gets me up to sort things out. Collecting moss or feathers. Visiting people. She makes me stay in the car most of the time. I'm only being trained. I amn't ready. I resent that almost as much as the lack of freedom.

The door creaks open. Catlin's face peeps in.

'How did you get in?' I ask, surprised.

'It was unlocked.' She's whispering, and gesturing as well.

I feel like I am in an old black-and-white film about sneaking.

'You need to come,' she says, and I say, 'What?' out loud, because Mamó clearly already knows she's here – she got in, didn't she? Nothing happens here without that woman knowing.

'Be quiet,' she whispers. 'Get your shoes. It's Laurent. I mean, Lon.'

My heart inside my throat. It beats too fast. I cannot stuff it down. I look at her. Her eyes.

She says, 'I'm scared.'

We move in silence down the garden path. I can feel the tang of her nerves in the air.

She feels it more than me, I think. I need to keep it together. To weave a world where I am calm and strong.

I follow her. Up the stairs and shut the door behind me. In the castle. Up another flight.

We're standing in front of Brian's office door and Catlin's shaking. Her voice is cracking with the weight of this.

'Brian asked me to get you. And come to the room inside the tunnel. I don't know if I can go through that door again. I . . . I don't want to see him, Maddy.'

Her voice cracks, though she doesn't say Lon's name.

'You don't have to,' I say. 'You don't have to do anything Brian says. You have had too many choices taken from you, Catlin. What matters is what do you want to do?'

336

Her face is miserable, twisted white and red. Her eyes are focused beyond me at something. Remembering, I think. She grabs the door.

'I think I want to end it.' I look at her, the blood he spilled still clinging to her skin.

Brian is in his office, next to Mam. He looks taller, I think, than I remember.

'I want to apologise,' he says. 'For not being around the past few weeks. For everything that's happened.'

The lights are bright. The yellow through the green harsh on his face. I look around for Lon, but Brian keeps talking.

'It was a shock. I never thought . . . this is my home. It's always been a safe place. For me. My father . . . he was close to Lon. They worked together for a time. I didn't think that he would hurt my family.'

'How old is Lon?' I ask, even though it isn't that important. Even though I do not really care.

'Older than he looks,' says Brian. His mouth tightens. 'Old enough to know better.'

Mam hasn't said a word. And now we move. The door sliding open again, and we walk down the passageway. Catlin grips my hand, and I can feel her shaking. We're quiet, but the mix of panting breaths carves something in the air. I hope that she will be OK. When she sees Lon. I hope she won't forgive him. Want him back.

The cave is shaped the same. The bed's gone, the stone scrubbed. You can still see some blood, pinking the grain. It's hard to get the colour out completely. I see the list of girls upon the walls. And there are so many other crumbled parts

337

that could have once been more names. So many scars through soft bright stone. Things erode here. Things just fade away.

'This was my father's place,' says Brian. 'I didn't fully know until he died. All that went on here, the cave. I tried to tell you, at least a little. Something of the truth of what he was.'

Mam snorts. 'Truth.'

Brian's voice is soft. 'Sheila. I know I've failed you. I was so afraid that you would leave, when you found out. I even tried . . .'

I think of foxes, prayers.

He carries on. '. . . but I don't have his power. Or yours, Maddy. However, there are some skills that I have learned.'

There is a steamer trunk where the bed used to be.

'He didn't get too far,' Brian says, his tone chillingly matter of fact. 'I think after a while, he knew we'd find him. John Collins . . . helped. His young lad came as well.'

He topples the box over, the lid flies open. Lon rolls, broken, out. His clothes are stained with dirt and, I think, blood. He looks a mixture of ashamed and furious. *Like a wet cat*, I think. I notice that he still has on his ankh. We stare at him, while Brian keeps on talking.

I feel like I'm in a horror film or something. When we found Catlin – there was such a panic welling up, such a lot to do to save her, that it muted things. It made them feel, if not more normal, somewhat less abnormal. There is very little more abnormal that staring down at an inhuman thing your stepdad rounded up a mob to capture, bound and gagged on the floor of his secret murder cave.

I look over at Catlin. People say it's awkward, running into your ex. She doesn't look awkward, just very, very vigilant.

Her eyes birds' ink dots focused on a cat, waiting for the flicker of a threat. He's all trussed up. I think they call it hog-tied, wrists and ankles together at his back. It isn't very dignified.

'I'm still not sure,' Brian tells Catlin, circling Lon, 'what he is. I know that we were wrong to trust him as much as we did. To allow him to spend time with people who looked his age. To believe the best and not the worst. I've made a lot of mistakes these past months, girls. Sheila, I should have told ye what Ballyfrann was, about the community we are – it can be difficult to put it into words. I was afraid that it would put you off me – and then once you were here, time and again I put it off . . . there's no excuse for that.'

I keep my eyes fixed on Lon, daring him to move, or speak, or groan.

'I broke your trust. It will take work to get that back. Those things I know. But, this lad? He's a mystery.' He pokes him with his foot and Catlin nods.

'He is,' she says. 'Hi, Lon.'

In my head, I'm wondering if two wrongs make a right. I've always felt that the death penalty was a strange one. I mean, to kill a person. Would it not kill a part of you as well, to do that? Because that's where this is going.

Brian keeps looking at Mam, as if he's given her a present. And her eyes are sad.

Lon's not a person though. He is something else. A parasite. A predator. A threat.

'Be careful,' says Brian. 'He is very strong. Even though of course he's weaker now.' The *now* speaks volumes.

339

'Where did you find him?' Catlin's voice is high. Pretending to be brave.

'We asked around. The key to Ballyfrann is knowing who to ask. And how to ask.' Brian is opening a bag. He takes out something sharp, and made of wood. A sword, I think. A long and skinny skewer with a handle. I see the edge of something like a saw inside the bag. The gleam of drill bits.

Brian holds the sword, making sure Lon sees it, before he hands it over to Mam. 'Could you hold this thing for me, Sheila, love?'

Mam nods. Her eyes are fixed on Lon and they are angry.

'He was at school with me for a bit. He goes back to education every now and then, you see. *For a refresher.* My father gave him money. He told me that he wanted to be around people who looked like he did. That the youth club was helping him control the darker parts of who he was. To empathise. It's hard to look so young and be so old.' He glares. His features harden. 'I listened to him because of Dad. Because I thought it's what he would have wanted. In retrospect, I don't think he would have cared.'

He walks towards Lon. 'He swore to me that Helen wasn't his. That it was different. I like to hope that people can change. Get better. I wasn't ever sure that I believed him.' He gives Lon a kick, he flops down on his side. 'I also wasn't sure that I didn't. Benefit of the doubt.' He kicks again. 'And then he had the temerity to interfere with my daughter. With my family.' Another vicious kick. His face is calm. His face is very calm. I don't think I have ever seen Brian like this. He's always been just a little nervous. Hands twitching at his cuffs. There's a confidence to him, a sort of horrid grace. I'm not sure if it's comforting. It's unnerving.

He closes his eyes. His voice is his again, high and uncertain. 'Forgive me, girls. Sheila. I let this happen. I'm sorry. Madeline, I've tried to reason with Mamó, to bargain, but there isn't any way . . .'

His eyes are wide. I incline my head a touch, like she does. Acknowledging.

'I know you tried. It's OK, Brian. I'm coping.'

'And coping very well, fair play to you.'

Mam walks closer to him, puts a hand on his shoulder. For better or for worse. She loves him still. I see it in her face. I'm not sure that she trusts him, but she loves him. Which is just as well. This version of Brian is definitely best kept onside. I'd hate to see that calculated rage turned against me. Every kick timed for the perfect hurt. How did our stepdad get so good at this?

Lon moans; his mouth is gagged, I think it's stuffed with rags. I'm glad, I think. I don't want him talking. Catlin's little hand inside my hand. Her fingernails have almost grown back. I stare at Lon. The thing that killed my sister. I look for my compassion. It isn't here. I used it up on Catlin, Mam and Brian. The people that he hurt with what he did.

Amanda Shale. Nora Ginn. Bridget Hora. Helen Groarke. Cold bones in rough soil. And all the other names upon the walls. Each one a girl. Each one a person's life.

Brian takes the sword from Mam. Passes it to Catlin. He strides to Lon, and cuts his feet loose from his hands. Lon is missing several fingers, I realise. They should be bleeding but the soft pink stubs seem to be forming something to replace. What is he? Is he a thing that broke through at the crossroads, in the wake of something big and old? I look at him. His copper penny eyes on mine, wide, pleading.

What did Mamó say to me that night?

Our face on their appetites.

He is a mask, a lie. He would have killed her.

'Thank you, Brian.' Catlin walks towards her crumpled ex. Mam is standing straight, but her face is hollow, caving in.

'Lon?' Catlin's hands brush the side of his face. 'Lon?'

He makes a creaking sound from his mouth, and my sister tells him, 'Shh . . .'

She looks to me. 'Maddy, can you hold him?' I venture over. Put my hands around his waist and haul.

He's very light for somebody so tall. I think of the shadow stretching through the garden. Birds have hollow bones. The swoop of claws. He makes another sound. I curl my fingers tight beneath his ribs. My sister on the bed, her face splayed wide.

'I forgive you, Lon.' Catlin's voice is jarring through my thoughts. 'I don't want you to think that I am doing this because we broke up, or out of revenge. After this is finished, I'm going to work really hard on never thinking about you ever again. On turning you into nothing. This is the first step.' She pushes the tip of the wooden sword towards his chest.

'Left a bit,' I say. 'If you want heart.'

'Thanks,' she says, and presses it into his skin. It parts like butter but he does not bleed. I put my hand down to feel where his fingers went missing. I can touch them now, the muscle and the soft nubbed baby growth that moves beneath. The blood on him, I realise, must not be his.

Catlin pushes harder, angling up between two of his ribs. I can feel him tensing and convulsing. His armpits are dry. He mustn't sweat. I wonder how he regulates his body.

Brian has looped an arm around Mam's waist. She doesn't seem to notice. She's still staring.

'You broke my heart,' Catlin says to Lon. Her voice is so, so gentle. 'You broke my heart. Because I really loved you, till you killed me. I dream about you sometimes, and I cry. Because you warped a lovely thing and turned it into something else entirely. You made me less. And then you ate my face.'

She looks at him, her eyes flashing angry.

'It is not OK for girls to be your food. We're not for eating.'

There is a pause. Her face is tense, she's putting all her weight on the sword but it isn't budging. Maybe something's stuck. Who knows where his heart is or if he even has one?

She turns to me, her face twisting against itself.

'I asked him to stop. I kept on begging, pleading with him to stop. And so he took my tongue. He tried to shut me up. But I am speaking. Mam, I need some help.'

She's crying now. I feel Lon shrink a little, slump and soften. I wonder, then, how much of her he loved. Brian's blade in Catlin's hands and inside Lon, and Catlin crying when a puppy dies on television. Me playing with my doctor dreams. I wanted to save lives, not to take them. I wanted to help people. And maybe in a weird way, this is that.

Mam starts to move towards her struggling daughter. Brian removes his hand, letting her go, stands awkward at the side. The three of us crowding around the lanky awkward half-corpse.

'It's not revenge,' she says. 'It's not for me. But it is for someone.' We all look at the wall. She starts to say their names.

'Dearbhla, Sibéal, Amanda . . .' We join in.

We say their names like prayers.

We wield the sword.

'. . . Laoise, Eimear, Laura, Bríd, Sorcha, Bridget, Karen, Gráinne, Julie, Roisín, Gobnait, Violet, Dymphna, Alacoque, Aoife, Fionnuala, Victoria, Elizabeth, Emer, Sinéad, Sally, Ciara, Mary-Ann, Nancy, Susan, Fiona, Delia, Maisy, Laura, Rachel, Caoimhe, Julie, Ava, Sheila, Maria, Antoinette, Cathleen, Martina, Jennifer, Carol, Nora, Lee, Colette, Ellen, Claire, Laurel, Jacinta, Mary-Bridget, Mary, Ann, Marie, Noreena, Savita, Carmel, Sarah, Aoibhe, Scarlett, Dearbhla, Katherine, Cecilia, Lisa, Lillian, Louise, Patricia, Katie, Cliodhna, Shona, Nuala, Shauna, Patricia, Monica, Meabhdh, Jean, Gillian, Elaine, Anna, Sabhdh, Sarah, Adele, Rose, Grace, Joyce, Nicola, Ruth, Frances, Naomi, Elizabeth, Sandra, Dolores, Aisling, Sharon, Lola, Chloe, Helen, Daisy, Megan, Úna, Fawn, Catlin.'

We move our hand and I now understand the expression 'twist the knife'. It's because of what a body does, when you curl a blade inside it. We push and worry our way deeper in. And then there is a sigh.

And he is gone.

Catlin starts to cry, and so does Mam. And I can feel a building-up behind the tops of my cheeks but there's a wall that's keeping them from flowing and I wonder if what used to push them out of me was in my soul. Maybe now I'll be a little grey cloud. Never raining. Always full of rain.

I press my face into Catlin's shoulder so hard that I feel as if when I pull back there should be the imprint of my features in her skin. Me and Mam and Catlin go to put on the kettle. Brian stays back, to safely bury Lon. He's brought cement.

Button is in the kitchen. Mamó has sewn his eye shut. He looks like a little Franken-cat. He's still small, but shaped like a cat now and not a kitten. He hisses and he starts when he sees me. He slinks away, back arched.

'He hates you now,' says Catlin, looking amused. 'I wonder why.'

I haven't told them how he lost his eye. What I was prepared to do, for her sake. I don't think there's a need to. I'm not proud.

'It's these shoes,' I say, pointing to my mucky army boots.

'On Mam's good floor. He used to love you though.'

Mam nods. 'Sure, who wouldn't love Maddy?' She kisses the top of my head and stirs the spoon round and round in the fat red teapot. Listening to the rhythm of their voices, I can't quite put away the harsh reality. I don't think Lon should be alive, but what came out of him – the stuff that was his blood but wasn't blood – the smell of it all wrong – it's on our hands. And that's the kind of thing that changes people. Button cringing out of rooms and hating me. I lost my soul, but apparently my conscience is still around to nag me. I wonder . . .

'Madeline?' Mam says. They are both looking at me, across the table. Their expressions mirroring each other. It's a little weird, I think. Aren't Catlin and I supposed to do that? Maybe that's what Mam has every day. I try to force my thoughts away from darker places and join in, but my eyes are getting heavier and heavier.

Eventually I drift off into sleep. I feel Catlin's breath against my ear. 'I'll say a prayer for you tonight, Mad. Love you.'

Mam lifting up my head, sliding a pillow gently underneath.

'Put her to bed.'

'If she gets up, she'll only go downstairs. To that . . . that *woman*.'

Feet move, lights click.

They leave me.

I'm alone.

Navelwort

(St Anthony's fire, other outward heats)

Mamó comes for me in the half-light. The moon and sun are both in the sky, two pale, one shining. We are going to find a blessed tree and cut off bits of that and then do the same thing with a cursed tree. I'm to look for acorns as well. For anything that's useful. Dying insects, feathers. Special rain. When we get back, I'm going to weed the physic garden, while she sees some clients. I might fit in some study if I'm quick.

I'm building up to helping her with people. She's easing me in slowly, so she says. My muscles ache. It doesn't feel that slow. The air is bright and cold. I kind of like this, working all the time. Being bone tired, always learning more. It kind of suits me. Weirdly.

The mountains hazy. Somewhere up there, Oona is swimming. I wonder if she's thinking about me, as she flickers through the wet. The place where she feels safe. She's been in touch. I haven't called her back. Catlin's still in bed, Button curled around her. He loves her now, as much as he hates me. Her hair and nails and eyebrows growing back, millimetre by millimetre. Piece by piece. My sister sleeps a lot. I used to sleep a lot. Before all this.

Before I worked for Mamó.

The raven flies above. Mamó is fairly sure she thinks there will be food. The raven is a she. Badb, not Bob. Mamó feeds her well. She doesn't think it's loyalty, but I amn't sure. I offered her a slice of ham yesterday. She flew it far away before she ate it.

Mamó looks behind her, making sure I'm there. I give a nod. The air's too thin for voices. She strides ahead, so my short legs can't catch up. I need to hasten. Seven years. I sigh. I don't like thinking about it. Still, I'm here. I want to do this right. I want to learn.

What we've done so far has been about herbs, and ointments. Ingredients. Mamó says the best way to learn magic is through doing. She says that I'm not ready. Says I'm weak. I have to grow a little stronger first. It almost killed me, saving Catlin's life. The shining thread.

I think about the little orange seed inside the marble sometimes. Wonder if she's using it at all. What would you need a soul for? The little missing shimmer bit of me. 'It's somewhere safe' and, if I watch and listen, maybe someday I could get it back. Be me again. Be whole.

My hands deep in my pockets, I rustle the salt packets from cafes, the rowan berries, little bits of twigs. My pockets are always full. My hands are dirty. I paint my nails to try to hide the stains.

Mamó's back is straight and proud ahead. I feel like I'm

348

alone with all my thoughts. Two thousand, five hundred and forty more days to go. A flash of something foxy through the gorse. Bright copper fur and eyes. Something ending, something else beginning.

And all of it is strange but so am I.

The morning bright, I feel like I belong.

Epilogue

Yew

(protection, poison, ghosts)

You're tired in the forest and you're running. Your breath catches in your throat. The woods around you, clean and fresh. You see the tiny oak, new growing from the earth. The soft things starting, like your baby girls. The two are there. They're coming for you now. You cannot stop them, but you try to hide. You are exhausted.

It was supposed to be a normal life. A wife. Two daughters. Clever little things, her mouth, your eyes. Catlin has her hair and Maddy yours. They're perfect. Sheila's face. There are so many good things in your world.

Checks and balances.

The steps come slower now. You try to move so silently away. Oak and ash and elm. Little flecks of bark and leaf to help. You say the words. You try to say the words. It doesn't help. You see a raven land and then another. Something's different here. There's something wrong.

You were always quiet. She liked that in you. Steady. She

350

trusted you, and almost right away. There is a sort of love that is like magic. And it grows, it draws in other people. You're kinder in your life because of her. And it will be OK. The little girls. You hope they're not like you. You hope they are.

There's goodness and there's badness in the world.

You turn. They are there. The old one and the young. There's something in his hand – the young one's hand – it's hard and heavy. Moving down towards you.

Once your legs are broken, you know what's going to happen next. It's what they do. It's what they've always done. You cannot move. When they are done with you, you cannot move. All you are is chunks of flesh on bone. The canopy of trees, the wavy oak, the fat lopsided beech. The lovely ash.

The old one takes a book out, starts to chant. The young one pours.

You close your eyes. It's warm on you and wet. Like being Christened. You can remember things. Moments of love. Eyes and little hands. Two babies in one cot, and curled together. They cannot sleep when they are kept apart. Two hands flexing around your index fingers. They grasped you right away. Such different souls, but something in them knew that you were theirs.

The young one pauses, and you see him look at your face for a long time. So long that his father stops the chant to make him carry on.

You haven't told them what they want to know. It wasn't hard; you're used to being quiet. You felt the secrets rising in your mouth sometimes with Sheila. The parts of it she didn't, couldn't, know. The weight of love from her. Those hazel eyes that look at you. That looked.

Love is hard to hide from.

You won't see her again. You know that now. He watches you on fire. Oak and ash. Elm and beech. All the living creatures. You clutch at what you can get. The earth. Blood. Bone. You spend it all. Everything you've left, one perfect coin.

You're burning and it hurts and, oh, it hurts like nothing's ever hurt. And that is something. Channel it.

On fire.

Pink flesh red and black and grey and white.

With everything. You keep the forest safe.

You do your job.

Acknowledgements

Perfectly Preventable Deaths started its life as a conversation over chips with my favourite person in the world, Diarmuid O'Brien, then ended up turning into a very busy November. I'd like to thank the Office of Letters and Light for challenging and motivating me with NaNoWriMo, and Diarmuid for loving me through many adventures, even though I can't jump up on a bale of hay.

Hot Key has been such a welcoming and supportive home for this story, and much of that has been down to the keen eye and warm heart of Georgia Murray. She put such thought, care and love into editing this book and I couldn't be more grateful to her and to Talya Baker, who copy-edited *PPD*, with such knowledge of the nuances of language in general and the twins in particular. The gorgeous cover was illustrated by the magnificent Elsa Klever, and I'm so grateful to her, and Anneka Sandher, the designer.

My agent, Clare Wallace, is insightful, supportive and brimming with kindness. I'm so grateful for her wisdom and enthusiasm. *Perfectly Preventable Deaths* would not be what it is, or where it is, today without her and the wonderful Lydia Silver.

My pal Suzanne Keaveney was a very early reader, and her love for it helped me stick with it. Claire Hennessy, whose books you should read immediately, was really kind about an early draft and then the current book, and also a lot of other things as well. I'm very grateful. Sarah Maria Griffin, Dave Rudden and Graham Tugwell are some of my favourite writers and sound people, and you should all read them too. Jacq Murphy read a version of this and was incredibly sound and supportive about it. Vanessa Fox-O'Loughlin took the time to help me out shortly after I completed this, and she does this for so many people as well as writing her own books. Juno Dawson took the time to be excited about my witch book at DeptCon and I held that support like a shiny coin. Moira-Fowley Doyle, for listening to me describe this at length back when I wasn't sure it would ever see the light of day. Celine Kiernan, for last-minute witchcraft. Melinda Salisbury, Gráinne Clear and Mary-Esther Judy for reading and loving the proof. It meant the world.

I'd like to thank Mam, Dad, Tadhg, Nana and all the Sullivans and Kings for endless support, particularly Laoise and Ciara King, who gave me such helpful advice. Cameron Taylor for positivity and book barges, 'The Pigeons' (especially Maria Griffin) and all their beautiful nestlings, Siobhán Parkinson for the most useful writing course probably ever, YA Book Club for general soundness. My students, for helping me see the world differently every day. I'm so grateful. Anyone who bought or brought me books, or worked in a place where I got my hands on them when I was a child, thank you for nourishing me. Booksellers and librarians who were kinder than they needed to be (please never change!). The Irish children's book community, and all at CBI (the beating heart of it).

And finally to Arthur Conan Doyle, the best of cats. Please never learn to read. I'm very sorry.

Deirdre Sullivan

Deirdre Sullivan is a writer from Galway. Her books include *Prim Improper*, *Improper Order* and *Primperfect*, which was the first YA novel ever to be shortlisted for the European Prize for Literature. Her 2016 novel *Needlework* was awarded a White Raven and the CBI Honour Award for fiction. Deirdre's most recent book, *Tangleweed and Brine*, a collection of dark fairy-tale retellings, won an Irish Book Award for Best Young Adult Book of the Year 2017. Deirdre loves reading, knitting, bodily autonomy and guinea-pigs.

Thank you for choosing a Hot Key book.

If you want to know more about our authors
and what we publish, you can find us online.

You can start at our website

www.hotkeybooks.com

And you can also find us on:

We hope to see you soon!